T0128889

Vamp

Maggie Holt

iUniverse, Inc.
New York   Bloomington

Vamp

Maggie Holt

iUniverse books may be ordered through booksellers or by contacting:
iUniverse
1663 Liberty Drive
Bloomington, IN 47403
www.iuniverse.com
1-800-Authors (1-800-288-4677)

ISBN: 978-1-4401-1321-5
ISBN: 978-1-4401-1322-2
Printed in the United States of America

iUniverse rev. date:1/09/2009

Chapter One

THE SUN SHONE HOTLY on that July afternoon, as Molly sat simmering in the shade of the apple tree. The sun's rays were gliding over, and whispering menacingly on her old, translucent face, which was just a little more wrinkled than the years should have shown. Life was not altogether kind to Molly through the passages of time. Molly had lead an eventful life, as she sat there, in the grounds of the Sanitarium, in the tranquility of nature's bountiful glow and cast her mind back, to almost another time, an eternity, a life beyond. She reminisced about Jordan; handsome, virile, Jordan, her beloved husband and father of her only child, Martine.

She could almost touch his face, run her fingers through his ebony hair, a cascade of curls unfurling into ringlets at the ends when he sweated, his eyes the colour of roasting chestnuts, sizzling against the whiteness of the virgin snow on the bleakest winter night. Oh, how she loved him and the memory of every precious moment they shared. She fanned herself with a dandelion, freshly uprooted from the undergrowth, on its last smile upwards to the sun, and her thoughts drifted back to Jordan. His smile enchanted her, even now just the thought of his presence in her dreams sent shivers of excitement throughout her tired, old body. She remembered in particular her unforgettable honeymoon night, on her own special paradise island in the Aegean Sea, unspoiled and untouched by the commercial side of life. She remembered the apartment, how the moon was full and awe inspiring, illuminating the sea with a dim glow which was diverted up to their private balcony, the balcony that would remain engraved in Molly's thoughts forever.

They had been out along the harbour, the walk which took them into the little town. They had danced and sipped champagne that night. They were so young, so in love; and were heady with unquenched desire for each other. Excited, and full of the pleasures of the paradise island, they walked back along the sea front to their apartment; Molly climbed the stairs to the balcony and Jordan followed. He watched her with fresh eyes, that night, marveling in her slim, well-shaped ankles; her calves, her slender thighs, and her ample buttocks which made his desire for her surge.

She ran in front of him, teasing and slipping off her tee-shirt and shorts, her panties, thrown in the air, catching on the lime tree. The air was humid, the night was wild, and tiny specks of perspiration shone like jewels on the reflection of the moon, all over her body. She stretched her arms up to the sky. She was a silhouette of loveliness, and he immediately reached for her, as she slipped her arms around his neck. He undid his pants and stepped out of them; she kissed his lips, softly at first, then more passionately and slipped a leg around his waist. She stuck her toe in his underwear and dragged his boxers to the floor, slipping slowly down his right leg. Then she gently caressed his lower back with her toe, up over his curvy bottom and around his waist, then the other leg. Jordan was ready for her; gently he slipped into her and together they enjoyed the next episode in their lives, rhythmically swaying on impulsion and flying on a cloud of desire. They were lost in their oneness for eternity; capturing the forever now, passing through timeless boundaries, and catching hold of earth again when it was time to come back to the balcony.

Molly tossed aside the dandelion, without petals and limp now, bedraggled and lucky to survive in any form after Molly's passionate day dream.

The peace and reminiscing of yesteryear was suddenly shattered, like raindrops falling on a pane of glass, by the screams and laughter of Molly's grandchildren: the twins, Sally and Sarah, coming to visit. It was almost impossible to tell them apart except that Sally's face was a little fatter than her sister's and twice as cheeky. Like granddad Jordan they too had ebony hair, but instead of granddad's eyes, they had their mother's—the deepest green, the colour of a wild, stormy sea, the whites in comparison to an angry, foaming surf as it crashed against the rocks in temperamental agony. They were truly beautiful children, just turned five years old, only six weeks ago on the 6th of June. The children disappeared about their play just as abruptly as they had entered into Molly's world of yesterday.

She was getting older now and weaker, but had lots of time to relive the days of her childhood. The sun was still shining, rays darting through the branches and leaves of the apple tree. Tranquility returned, and only the chirping of the birds broke the peaceful setting, as she leaned back, closed her eyes and drifted backwards into her own, private world with her sister Merry; her very close, beloved sister, her other half, identical too as her grandchildren, born in the same month of the year.

Molly remembered how her mother Elizabeth could only tell them apart at bath time because of the telltale birthmark on Molly's left shoulder. It was reddish purple and in the image of a dog sitting and begging. But, by the time they were two, they had developed their own characters and had very different personalities. Daddy too, who was wonderful and kind had little trouble telling them apart, probably because Merry was quiet and withdrawn and somewhat distant, even at that age. Molly was vibrant, vivacious and extremely naughty. She recollected the day, when she was only three; she stole a prized coin from daddy's wartime treasures and blamed it on Merry who was only too glad to be smacked for it to stop the shouting.

As the days and months passed, Merry was becoming more and more withdrawn even from Molly and everyone was growing intensely worried about her state of mind. Mother especially had great apprehension about Merry starting school, after the summer, as she stayed in her room staring from the attic window, most of the time not speaking to any- one much. Merry often went into a world of her own, penetrated only by Molly's chatter and play dollies. The girls loved the attic bedroom, it was so safe, a sanctuary away from the adult world, a place where little people came alive, where doll houses had wallpaper and doors which opened, and tiny little men and women going about their domestic chores in still life, only for a few seconds until the girls decided it was time to disband them and go off to another toy. Only there: did Merry come back to life. Her favourite teddy was always there for comfort, the teddy with his torn-off ear, a result of a war disaster which happened during one of the few arguments the girls had.

It rained that morning, and the girls were up early, all fresh and smart. It was a special day, the day when they started their new school.

They wore their new school uniform—purple blazer with yellow trim and a pale yellow blouse. Their hats too were purple with a band of yellow around the brim. They had the usual grey, uniform skirt, and clutching satchels they pirouetted and curtsied for the approval of their mother. Ready to go, Mother and her two offspring made for the station and the train which would take them into the next adventure in their young lives.

The rain was getting heavier now with the wind escorting it and driving it harder against the carriage windows. Molly was enjoying every minute of the journey and looking forward excitedly to the new adventures to come, whereas Merry was nervously twisting her pink handkerchief. School was an excitement for Molly as she sat there trying to remember the numbers and rhymes her mother had taught her. Everything was moving along nicely. Mother felt proud of her two girls and the journey's end was nearing, when suddenly Merry burst into tears. They crashed down her cheeks faster and more hazardously than the rain on the windows. It encouraged mother to cradle her. Merry trembled in sheer, desperate fear, thinking that the sanctuary of the attic bedroom was getting further and further away from her. She no longer felt safe, but vulnerable and alone. She wished she had brought her teddy with her. Mother comforted her with soothing words. Molly was too excited to respond or care. The train ground to a halt; and the carriage doors, were opened by dutiful guards and station waiters; who fastened each door with the leather strap attached to the inside.

The adventure was about to begin, all three of them trundled along the station and along the road to the Primrose School for Young Ladies. The school mistress, Miss Simpson, was there at the gates to greet all newcomers. Molly marched in eagerly to feast her eyes on her classroom and her desk. It was a quaint, old country school full of character, with ivy clinging all along the north facing wall. There, was a playground with a wooden swing in the corner where children were already queuing and laughing and generally getting acquainted. Most of the mothers had gone, and they were left in the capable hands of Miss Simpson, a spinster lady with thick-rimmed glasses on a necklace-type chain. Perhaps she was forgetful and had them attached to her person in case of loss. A loud ringing noise rang out, and for the very first time Molly heard her school bell.

She would learn to obey on hearing that sound. She adjusted her hat, stuck her head on a tilt, and entered her new learning place. She gazed around the room. There were desks everywhere and the biggest, blackest blackboard Molly had ever seen. She hurriedly picked her desk right at the front not to miss the rest of the class on their way to their desks. She began to chatter to the two little girls on each side of her and found out that they lived in a little town near her. Molly assured them they would all become good friends. Molly was so excited getting to know her new surroundings that she had completely forgotten about Merry. Where was she? Molly panicked a little.

There was some sort of commotion at the back of the classroom. Molly turned, open-mouthed and shocked as she saw Mother, Merry and Miss Simpson in some sort of a tussle. Merry was shouting and screaming that she did not want to be left there; her tears by now turning to great wails of painful torture. Miss Simpson had to drag Merry away from Mother who was quite distraught by the whole, unfortunate incident. Miss Simpson gestured for mother to leave, and gratefully, Mother gave a quick wave to Molly at the front. "Look after her dear." she called and was gone. Merry by this time was seated at the back, unobtrusively and reasonably secure in the thought that she was not being stared at by the other pupils.

The morning started by Miss Simpson reading the roll call; everyone was present. The girls took no time at all in getting to know one and other. The second time the bell rang, it was to summon playtime. Merry was being stubborn again and refused to leave her desk. Miss Simpson in all her wisdom let her stay where she was.

Perhaps she could not go through all that again. Molly with her two new friends; soon settled into the regime of school days. It was a very worrying time for Mother as the twins, each one at her own time, began to accept that they had a new life away from their mother.

Merry gradually started to respond in a small way with the help of Molly who was so much an extrovert even at that young age.

She appeared in the school play at Christmas as the Virgin Mary and did not fluff any of her lines. Her mother was very proud, but wondered why Merry wasn't at all like her sister or even half as confident. Merry started bed-wetting; and this continued for many years with frequent visits to the doctor who could only put it down to nerves. She was becoming very withdrawn and trance-like at times.

By the age of nine she had run away from school countless times, and inevitably her schoolwork suffered to the extent that reading simple books proved difficult for her. She was moved to a special school for backward children. It was called the Sanitarium, a huge mansion of a place, grand in its time, surrounded by grounds with flower-filled beds and large trees of every description and foliage. This was a definite step back for Merry, and she was allowed to go even more into herself and her private, lost world. She got so bad, Molly remembered, that she could only come home on weekends, and when she did come home it caused a severe strain on the rest of the family because she always made a hasty retreat to her beloved teddy and her attic sanctuary. Things got even worse, and it was beginning to effect Molly quite severely to the extent that by the age of twelve she persuaded her mother to let her move her possessions and bed to the little box room at the end of the hallway. The closeness between the sisters was severed beyond repair, but it was something Molly had to do to keep her own sanity.

Molly was growing up fast now; she was ready to begin a new course at her secondary school. It was called Hillwood Crest, and it was for more mature young ladies, the ones who were academic in their approach to life. Molly nestled in to that school and was doing well at all her subjects. She joined the netball team and the hockey team where she surpassed, all her goals and became captain of both teams. She was in demand, both at school and socially, and Molly started to take an interest in young men. She started going to the Social Club run by the school on Monday evenings, where they played records and sports, including badminton and table tennis, and just talked to boys mostly. One of the student teachers took a special interest in Molly, whose ego was soaring, and she was the envy of all the other girls.

The student teacher was Simon Warner. Even at the age of eighteen he seemed somewhat boyish with sun-bleached hair, and intense blue eyes which seemed to catch on Molly's and lock there forever. Molly was developing fast and was beginning to come into her own as a young woman. She knew boys liked her, and with the added attention of a young teacher she was much sought after at the Christmas school dance.

Molly was only fourteen, but in every way a woman; she had voluptuous breasts with the largest, brown nipples which protruded under her tee-shirt and pointed up like little mole hills pressing against the skyline. She was proud of her body and flaunted it whenever there were boys around to ogle and fancy her.

She never forgot the argument she had had with mother that fateful day when she asked for a new dress to impress Simon at the Christmas dance.

Molly wanted a dress that was tight and would show off her figure to its full potential, but Mother would have none of it. Already Molly was growing up too fast. Molly settled for a jade-green dress to match her eyes. It wasn't fitted, but it did enhance her slim figure and protruding bosoms. The night of the dance was upon them, and Molly felt good. She admired herself in the mirror from head to toe; she was every bit a woman and a beautiful woman at that. She brushed her long, black and lustrous hair; she painted some red lipstick on her luscious, kissable lips. A little touch of blusher complimented her face and her outfit—the jade dress was a good choice. She decided to meet Simon there, and she and a friend had arranged to walk down to the hall together. They had no sooner arrived when the band struck up, and sure as anything Simon was first to ask Molly to dance. He held her in a waltz, and she felt the contours of his body pressing urgently against hers. This was a new experience for Molly, but she liked it. Simon's chest was firm and hard and strong; only in the lower region could she feel a warmth and passion. Molly's sexual desire suddenly awakened; there was no stopping it now. It exploded with a million fireworks with a swelling feeling in her most private of parts. She swayed and slithered around the floor with Simon apparently unaware of the silence of the band. Her school colleagues clapped in the silence and destroyed the magic of the moment. Perhaps as well, Molly regained herself and went for a cool drink and some fresh air. It was barely 8 o'clock.

The moon on that late December night was gliding from cloud to cloud, kissing and caressing the vast expanse of sky while sliding, ducking, and only gently teasing the cotton wool clouds as they passed on their voyage to a place humans in their wildest dreams only fantasize about.

Molly gazed up at the skies; perhaps she understood; perhaps she bordered her life around fantasy. She felt warm, although the night air was cool. She pressed the glass to her cheek, the vaporized bubbles trickled down, exploding and leaving the scent of champagne on her face. She remembered the dance, so forbidden and so naughty, but extremely invigorating. The old trees from the verandah looked forlorn and almost angry as the moonlight shone on them. Molly giggled to herself; they would probably see a lot more before her time in this world was over.

The crowd from the dance floor; were lost in their excitement, laughter, music, and screams of pleasure which were audible from where Molly stood. She turned around, leaned against the ornate, pillared verandah wall, and thought how lucky she was; it surged over her like a tidal wave, she had everything going for her; she was tall, almost five feet, eight inches in her bare feet with long, thick, black hair, emerald green eyes, a beautiful figure that even a woman only ten years her senior would be envious of. Molly felt womanly tonight with a sense of deeper warmth and an inside heat which was almost a blaze of fire.

Someone had put something in her drink; perhaps Simon did, trying to loosen her up. She reached across and pulled a rose from the cascade of hanging shrubbery. Molly's dress was jade to match her eyes; the rose was the purest pale pink and stood out against the darkness of her frock. The allure she was creating around her aura was second to none. She gained an inner confidence, pinned the rose to her dress and entered through the wooden, glazed doors onto the dance floor.

Simon had been looking for her. He breathed a sigh of relief; on her return, he thought she had left for the evening. If only he had known Molly truly, he would have known Molly would never ever leave a party in full swing. Molly missed nothing, especially happiness, excitement and pleasure, pleasure of a newness she had encountered so briefly tonight. She would have a few more spoonfuls of that thank you. Simon poured Molly another drink; she hoped it would taste the same as the last one, instead of the school menu of fruit punch. It was more like champagne and already Molly was getting a taste for it. She liked champagne or whatever Simon had given her.

For the first time that evening Molly felt twinges of hunger, so much so, the smell of food was drawing her like a magnet to the table with the fruit punch as center piece. The table must have been an awesome sight for the taste glands when the first of the visitors arrived, but now it looked like a flock of vultures had had a mad hatter's tea party, several crumbs and a few bones were all that were left intact. Simon took himself off to the kitchen for any leftovers; he re-appeared feeling good about himself and the food he was bringing for his partner. Molly took one look at the plate and nibbled at the vol-au-vents and pies, enjoying them, in an instant. Simon bent down and pecked her on the cheek, but food was the most satisfying thing in Molly's mind at that particular moment in time. She took no notice of Simon, and continued with the disappearing niceties on the plate. When the plate was empty and Molly's tummy full, she dabbed her mouth with a napkin and pulled Simon gently towards her and gave him the kiss of his life.

Simon felt good, he loved Molly's presence even if it was only to talk about hockey or netball; he was all ears. But tonight was special. There was a tantalizing whiff of demon in the air, it was present all through the evening, and the exceptional situation of the school dance within the old mansion house was probably half to blame. The sheer beauty, set in the tranquility of its spacious gardens of flowers and orchards, in the melodramatic quietness of yesteryear gave everyone complete peace and a feeling of well-being. The band tiptoed into a slow, soothing melody, and Simon again asked Molly to dance. She had tasted the fruits of the dance before and swallowed some delights of the pleasures to come, but dare she take another sample? Of course, she wanted to dance, and she also wanted some fizzy drink, the one Simon had given her before.

"Its champagne Molly, I pinched it from the kitchen, it's only for the teachers."   He whispered in her ear.

"Go get some more, I like it".

Sheepishly Simon went to the kitchen and miraculously returned with another open bottle.

They both poured a glass and sipped the tickling bubbles. Simon placed the cork on top and hid it under the table for their return as they ventured onto the dance floor. They held each other gently at first, then most assertively, knowing where they were leading.

Molly suddenly saw the Headmaster's face; he was stern and very disapproving. Molly whispered to Simon who very slowly but deliberately, for the sake of his job and Molly's honour; slackened off, and regained a more teacher-pupil awareness of the situation. After the dance: Molly felt giddy as she motioned Simon to fill her glass under the table. Simon ducked down, and Molly pushed her glass under.

She nodded when it was full, the bubbling liquid spilling over and tickling her hand. Molly stared around the room at the other pupils who now looked stiff, boring, mundane and stuffy. Thank God Simon had come along; otherwise Molly would have left long ago.

Had the old Headmaster got his way, the place would have been even more morbid. He stood in one corner with a collection of teachers around him for company, and he reminded her of a wet cucumber on a frosty night. The woman who stood next to him, a Madame Butterfly type, was his wife.

They certainly did not spoil a pair. A canoe could have sailed in the crevasses of her face, and docked in her beacon-type nose. Rescued from her evil thoughts, Simon nudged her under the table, to collect her glass of champagne. She sipped it, and the warmth of the evening returned. Simon leaned across and asked if she would like to sip her drink on the verandah. It. sounded good to Molly. She nodded and told him to bring the bottle; this he did inside his jacket. Molly lead, the way remembering the previous volcanic, amorous thoughts she had suppressed on the verandah only hours before. The moon was still there, bigger than ever, almost smiling in agreement as the two young people walked on the verandah. The heavens were full of welcoming stars, alluring and pulling like static, guiding the young lovers to the flower beds at the bottom of the garden, almost another world away from the dance. Molly sat on a fallen tree. Simon brought the hidden champagne. Molly's glass was empty. He filled it up for her, and as she sipped from it, he kissed the bottom of the glass. She dropped her hand, and they kissed in oneness. They were alone at last. They placed their glasses beside the fallen tree. Tonight was for lovers, not for small talk and they knew there were different horizons for them to cross tonight...

The garden was shady, even in the face of the full moon, the fallen tree served as a sort of port in the storm, a safe place to dock, out of the way of prying eyes. The broken tree lay next to a rose bush with pale yellow roses which pricked when touched. Their radiant splendour was at its zenith in the late summer months. Now only a few roses were still in bloom, but they were even more beautiful to Molly because they had beaten all odds to remain brilliant, radiant and truly mysterious for they should have been long gone with only thorns left on the branches this late in the season.

Molly was still marveling at nature's wonderment when she felt the soft caress of lips on her bare foot, Simon took off her shoe; he ran his tongue along her toes and Molly felt a tingling. She had never experienced this before; she was trembling, she felt as if she was electrocuting. Her panties were moist. What was happening to her? Simon's caresses were moving up her leg. He slid his hands under her and undid the zip on her dress. Molly sat up and moved the dress into the rosebushes in front of her. Simon kissed her navel; then he undid her bra, the sheer weight of her bosoms causing them to bounce as the harness of the bra was removed. They plummeted down and bounced back up, her nipples erect were the darkest brown. He moved his tongue around one, then the other. He needed two hands for each bosom; they were more than a handful.

Molly rested back on her hands, enjoying every sensual moment, and let Simon explore her body. This he did to his best advantage, her bare breasts pointed towards the furthest parts of the skies. She loved her body and so did Simon. Her huge nipples were pulsating now with uninterrupted desire of the flesh. She was discovering her own body, and a feeling within her she had not imagined was taking over.

Simon pulled off his shirt, and Molly saw his hard, manly chest, his firm torso and his muscled shoulders, with blonde hairs rippling down to his navel, like a river running into a waterfall of the thickest, black hair.

He struggled a bit with his pants and underwear, hopping around on one leg, which almost spoiled the moment, but not for long. Molly had never seen a naked man before, but she liked what she saw. The experience was curious and fascinating to the extreme. Simon had a kind of hold on her—or was it just his body? He touched her breasts gently; then became more urgent with his just slain, consenting, prey. She saw and noted the look, one she would see many times in her long life, a look Molly would grow to hate. Molly's thoughts again returned to nature and the beautiful surroundings. One of the beautiful yellow roses had been trodden on by Simon's bare foot as he gripped at the world for some sort of support as he gave Molly all his passion; and vigour in the last few seconds of his love making with her body.

She picked up the rose, wiped away the mud, inter-twined it with one of the other stronger ones so it looked not so molested and again stood tall with the beauty it was meant to have. Simon, helped Molly up, and dressed, they went back towards the verandah and to the dance hall door, both checked over for any flaws as to their whereabouts, brushed off and looking as if nothing more than an amorous kissing session had taken place.

People were still there, but not so many; most had gone their separate ways to where ever their priorities took them. Molly motioned to Simon that she wanted to leave. Simon agreed and made final good-byes to their friends who were still left. Simon and Molly walked back towards Molly's house, not speaking, only knowing that on that particular night the world and its occupants seemed insane. Had the world been attacked by aliens from another planet making humans do things on command whether they liked the outcome or not. Did it happen, or was it a dream or a nightmare? Molly decided to believe the dream, for reasons only her complex mind would permit.

They neared Molly's house, the light was still on and mother sat out on the porch, probably enjoying the moonlight, the same moonlight Simon and Molly had just enjoyed. A quick peck on the cheek and Simon was gone. Molly told mother about the dance and the punch, careful not to say anything about the potency of the whole evening. Molly felt neither, good bad, nor indifferent, as she sighed and stretched in an elongated yawn in front of her mother.

Chapter Two

IT WAS NEARING CHRISTMAS and Molly was very excited. Most of the family joined in her exuberance for the festive season, not least of whom, was Merry. She was coming home on one of her few weekend visits. She no longer came every weekend as her problems had worsened, and the home and its governors decided she should be there permanently, and under no circumstances should she go home every weekend as it was no longer beneficial to Merry.

On her weekend visits she seemed to become agitated and forlorn and trance like after the first meeting with her family. She had made a friend at the home; his name was Robin, only two years older than Merry, but more seriously retarded. Mother always said that Merry enjoyed her relationship with him because for once in her life Merry was the one who gave all the comfort and felt strong and in control in his presence. The Christmas tree which Father bought was huge, fresh, and smelling strongly of pine. He was determined to make this a Christmas to remember. He was proud of his little girls; they had never grown up in their father's eyes. "Come on Merry, come on Molly let us decorate the tree." It was a truly momentous experience, and they all worked in unison, achieving the same goal.

First, the fairy was placed at the top; then the fairy lights, garlanded in a coat of tinsel. Molly and Merry placed all the presents at the bottom of the tree awaiting Santa Claus. The fire was blazing in the hearth, the logs newly chopped, ready for the next firing, lay in the brass coal basket; tinsel and mistletoe adorned the house, the velvet curtains drawn comfortingly to cut out the late December chill, the smell of turkey cooking and chestnut stuffing gave the house a feeling of safety, comfort, and luxury. Mother always cooked Christmas dinner the night before and both girls liked to help. When all the preparations were done, Mother consulted Father for the final word, but she always got her way. Father loved and cherished Mother and occasionally, in front of the girls, was known to kiss her passionately in a long embrace, especially the night before Christmas, when he was drinking brandy while the girls and Mother were preparing Christmas dinner. The girls loved their father, he was gorgeous to them; he was strong, handsome, intelligent, and they just loved him.

He disappeared into the kitchen and brought in the silver tray with four glasses of sherry on it. At last the girls were old enough to have sherry instead of lemonade, as they did at previous Christmases. They grabbed their glasses, sat together and giggled their way through the sherry. Molly was no stranger to alcohol, but she had to pretend. All four sat in front of the blazing fire, glass in hand, the Christmas tree aglow with the beautiful Christmas trimming, glinting and glistening and swaying with every wayward draft from under the front door. It was Christmas Eve the most joyous, holy, peaceful, bubbly effervescent night of the year for the whole family. It was magical, the most holy of nights, the most mystical, the night when dreams and wishes came true, when families got together, when differences were subdued, when goodwill and peace was the focus all over the world. Father and Mother sipped, their sherry, holding hands, occasionally giving each other a glance of respect, a loving gesture only they understood, or so they thought.

Molly's thoughts returned to Simon, her lover, her one-night stand, the man who took her virginity, the man uppermost in her mind, the man she had not seen from that night on at Molly's request, of course. Perhaps after Christmas she would, just perhaps, get in touch with him, who knows. He was nothing special. Molly felt confident and in charge of the situation, and she was. Simon might be much older, but Molly was in charge. She had a lot to offer men, and they were going to find out soon enough. Molly's thoughts were penetrated and shaken up by Merry accidentally knocking over her sherry. What a fool, and what a mess! Father made no fuss; he just gently wiped the mess away. The sheer look of ultimate fear and horror, showed on Merry's face and concerned Mother, as Father had got up alongside her to clear the mess, Merry had ducked as if to accept a wallop of a backhand or even worse an object of some kind. Merry jumped up and stood hard against the wall, hands spread out, shaking violently. Mother went to Merry's side and comforted her, as she had done so many times in the girls' lives. Merry was not strong; she was frightened of her own shadow most of the time. Mother asked. "What's the matter Merry? It was only a glass of sherry?" Father had wiped the mess away as soon as it happened, not bothered in the least.

Merry began to sob softly at first; then she was full of torment and emotion, her tears coming from the belly, uncontrolled, her heart breaking. Something was not right here. Mother reassured Merry that when she went back to the home she would go with her, but first Mother needed to know what, or who was frightening Merry over little accidents. Merry would not be drawn out of her fear, and she continued to sob softly. She would say nothing. Mother decided not to pursue it at this stage, but she would certainly look into the matter. It was frosty that night, the moon swam gracefully through the clouds, kissing the streets with its gleam and sparkling the pavements and roads with tiny jewels, all waiting to disintegrate into wet moisture on the return of the sun the following morning.

The village and its occupants were all asleep, only a wailing cat broke the silent serenity of the glowing, yet cold Christmas Eve. The cat quieted down and disappeared into the night, probably to feed its illegitimate brood in some dark alley, not knowing if this was Christmas or a Midsummer night.

Christmas Eve was special and because of this, Molly joined Merry in the attic bedroom. She opened the door quietly but Merry was still awake. She was quieter now, and more calm and aware of the special night. Molly sat with Merry on the window seat at the attic window; their closeness was becoming apparent once more. They gazed out at the sleeping village and the piercing cold. Molly would sleep with Merry that night, but not yet, the girls just sat together. Merry loved that room and especially the window seat. She could sit there and look out at the world, so at peace with herself and safe in the knowledge that this was her room and her sanctuary. As they sat pondering and looking at the frosty and cold world, they kept warm because the chimney from the sitting room ran right through their little room giving it a warmth and safety both girls enjoyed. They heard noises from downstairs and ran quickly to bed before they were found out.They could hear Father trying all the doors and windows before retiring. They kissed one another and jumped into Merry's single bed and drifted to sleep, both having nice thoughts and feelings about Christmas day yet to come. They thought too, of the presents neatly gift wrapped and lying under the Christmas tree.

Morning broke with a crispness only a late December day could provide. Mother was already up and was warming the turkey and chestnut stuffing; aromas were wafting all over the house. They sniffed in the nasal delights, dressed hurriedly and ran downstairs. Father was stoking the fire, piling on log after log, while Mother was singing, the melodic sounds whispered through the air bringing feelings of peace and security. Good mornings and tender kisses were exchanged.

Merry was delighted, her face beamed with pleasure and Molly too joined in the excited gestures. Father looked out from the sitting room window, and as he had forecast, it was snowing. How perfect, it would be a white Christmas after all. Merry seemed normal, she took in all the splendor of the house, the pine garlands were twisted around the open stair rail from the top, right to the bottom; there was mistletoe hung in various places, a small musical Father Christmas took pride of place on the mantel piece, Christmas cards from friends and family were all over the walls, the lights glowed on the Christmas tree and the whole setting was idyllic.

Mother called out for them to sit around the fire and get warm, she started off the carol singing, she had a beautiful voice and she sang a few cords of Hark the Herald Angels Sing and everyone joined in, they were all well and truly in the spirit of Christmas. Father brought them in a coffee and a slice of toast each. The fire was ablaze in the hearth, and the room was very warm and comforting indeed. It was nearing one o'clock and Mother had completed her chores in the kitchen, the presents were still there untouched under the tree, all begging to be opened, but that would not take place until the remaining two members of the family arrived—their grandmother and Aunty Maud, who always joined them at Christmas and birthdays. The presents were always left until everyone was there. The doorbell rang just after one o'clock, it was Aunt Maud and Grandmother as arranged, both clutching pretty little coloured parcels. Aunt Maud struggled to get through the narrow door, on entering the sitting room. The girls were quick and eager to help, giggling to each other about Aunt Maud's size, with her big hat and enormous body, she had just squeezed through, and as always she came in shouting orders to everyone else and grabbing herself a big, comfy armchair near the fire. Father asked her for her coat, which she generously offered. After a sherry or two she would warm to the occasion. Aunt Maud was full of stories of the journey she and Grandmother had just taken on the train. They were mostly about the gruesome little man who kept winking at her, everyone was sure it was in her imagination, no one could be that stupid, or could they? But one never knows. Merry gathered up all Aunt Maud's presents from the hallway table and placed them neatly under the tree. Aunt Maud, as usual, was making herself at home, taking off her shoes and wiggling her toes in front of the fire.

Mother and father sat together on the sofa obviously as excited as the girls. Grandmother had been quiet since she arrived, she was inspecting the kitchen to make sure the dinner was cooked correctly and Mother hadn't forgotten anything. Molly looked across at the presents and hoped that one of them would be some grown-up article of clothing and not some silly doll or toys. Sherries were handed all round, the girls joined in and Father was quick to remark, "Be careful with this one Merry, we don't want a repetition of last night." Merry understood and nodded. With all the family together at last and a joyous Christmas meal to follow, nothing could make them more special and content.

Merry glanced from the window and giggled. "The snow is getting deeper. "Molly shrieked with delight and they all piled to the window. Yes, indeed it was getting deeper. It was like a white blanket covering the little village, and so pretty too.

"Can we open the presents now," requested Merry who was coming out of herself once more, not all withdrawn as she was last night. They all opened their presents and thanked each other. There were socks for Father, handkerchiefs for Aunt Maud and a lovely, white apron for mother, some new silk panties for Merry and Molly, and the most special present of all, a brand new teddy to replace Merry's old one. The tears filled in Merry's eyes as she saw him; she loved him at once, and all that day would not let him out of her sight. The table was set in all its grandeur, candlesticks lit and glowing as the center piece, lovely, fresh holly made up all the place settings, and the wine glasses were sparkling. They sat down. Crackers were pulled and the usual party hats and trinkets laughed about and left to one side.

Father toasted "Merry Christmas" and they all joined in what was to be a very festive and satisfying meal. Molly loved her presents, especially the silk panties, she would have Merry's too before she went back to the home. The girls were sent into the kitchen to do the dishes and general tidying up, and this they did with pleasure. They cleared the table whilst the grown-ups satisfied themselves in Father's brandy.

Then the fire began to lose its glow, Grandmother was all set to go, but Aunt Maud had drifted off to sleep in front of the last remaining embers. Whilst they were trying to awaken Aunt Maud, the girls decided to go up to their room, but not before pinching half a bottle of sherry from the kitchen.

They sat in the window seat just as they had as little children, but now they were sipping the sherry and talking about the excited day they had had. Molly's thoughts returned to Simon, she was sure he would like her new, silk knickers. She was missing him, but she was not sure if it was him, the man, or his body and the pleasure it brought her, she comforted herself with the fact that school would soon be starting again, and she would see him then. They gazed out at the world and its splendour, Molly bit her lip, and with tongue in cheek asked Merry about her friend Robin. At first Merry was reluctant to discuss her precious friendship with him, but after some coaxing Molly got out of her that the attendants at the home were mistreating Robin. He was more than a little retarded and obviously did not respond quickly to commands, which angered the attendants and frightened Merry because she thought that when they tired of tormenting Robin they would start on her, or perhaps Molly thought, they were doing it already. Merry would not say, but sat there trembling. The girls chat was broken by the commotion downstairs, which turned out to be tipsy Aunt Maud falling off the armchair she had commandeered and almost onto the open fire. Miraculously, Father was in the way and stopped her in time. Aunt Maud dusted herself off, got up with hardly a word and staggered slightly to the door, waved a hand in acknowledgment, closed the door behind her, and made for home.

The girls listened and after the door closed, they breathed again, Aunt Maud had gone. They could hear Mother and Father discussing the events of the day, and no doubt they would be having a drink together. Molly reached for their sherry and poured two glasses. The girls sat together, chatting away happily as if they didn't have a care in the world and everything seemed normal between them again.

Molly's thoughts from time to time drifted back to the Sanitarium, and she could not help but wonder what was going on there, and was Robin maltreated or was it Merry, or both? She also made a promise to herself to find Robin and speak to him, on her next visit with Merry. She needed to find out from him, however hard it would be to communicate with him; she needed to know the truth, as Robin had no one else, and he had been disowned at birth because of his backwardness.

Goodnight kisses were exchanged between the two girls, as they had always been since childhood. Their mother called them down to say goodnight, and the girls ran to the top of the stairs and blew kisses and called goodnight from where they were. They jumped into bed. Merry quickly went to sleep, but Molly could find no sleep that night, Simon was still in her thoughts. She was missing him, and she wished at that moment that Merry was normal, and she could confide in her secrets about Simon and the verandah and the school dance. But she dare not, Merry's mind had not developed as it should have, and perhaps mentally she was only 10 years of age.

Boxing Day came and went with no particular events or thrills.

There was a shadow over the family and particularly Merry, because she had to return to the home and leave behind her favourite sanctuary, her precious bedroom attic. But as all things dreaded and hated, the inevitable day arrived, and they were all trundling to the train station and boarding the train which would take them to the Sanitarium.

On entering the train, Merry was already becoming agitated and frenzied. She was wailing, and tears rushed down her cheeks, dripping onto her coat, the same as her first day at school, Molly remembered. What was going on at that home? Was Merry just being a big baby again? Mother had to almost drag Merry from the train carriage when it stopped at the appropriate station. Merry was screaming and shouting, and a huge crowd was gathering. Finally they managed to get something coherent out of her; she had left her teddy, her new teddy on the train. Molly quickly got it from the carriage for her and peace prevailed.

Soon, they arrived at the reception desk at the Sanitarium and spoke to Miss Simpson, the Matron. Mother whispered to the matron that she was quite traumatized, and she took Merry by the hand and led her to her room. Molly felt discontent, remembering what Merry had said after a few sips of sherry and she began to wonder, was Merry making it up or was she really going through hell? Molly's conscience bothered her, and she almost said something to Mother, but pushed the thought aside. Merry could have been making the whole thing up for attention. They waved to Merry and left. On these occasions, Mother and Molly scarcely spoke on the return journey, each in their own thoughts and emotional turmoil. The frost had lifted, and the sun tried to break through the clouds which were gathering in the winter sky. Molly, on entering the house ran upstairs to the attic bedroom, and felt immediately that without Merry, the warmth had gone.

Merry was her other half, she had the same face and body and feelings as Molly, only her mind was a little slower, and the traumas Merry had, had no meaning or logic to Molly, but apart from that and the birth mark, the girls were identical.

Molly recalled that they even gave each other the same present on Christmas Day—both bought a lavender pomander with the very same words written on the card: to my beloved twin, and sister, with love, and both had written their names and signed the end with three kisses. Merry was Molly's other half, her own self, only slower. For the first time in ages Molly missed and loved her sister, perhaps because they had become close again after so long a separation.

The days passed and Molly was preparing for her return to school. She wondered if Simon remembered their passionate liaison in the verandah garden, or had he done this with the other school girls too? Molly didn't think so. She knew she was the most beautiful of the girls in every way. The day to return to school arrived quicker than Molly had imagined; she rose very early that morning, she wanted to look her best when she saw Simon for the first time after the encounter with him. She washed her hair first; then took a long, leisurely bath in her favourite lavender water; the blossom filled her nostrils and gave her the feeling of a fresh springtime flower. She put on her school uniform, and she felt clean and fresh and immaculate, ready for anything. She descended the stairs to the living room, and she must have overdone the lavender water as father got a few whiffs and commented. "Yes you are growing up fast Molly; it will be boyfriends next". Molly smiled.

The school uniform covered the body of a woman, a grown up woman. She wasn't his little girl anymore and she knew it, but did he? Father knew his daughter was becoming a young woman, he only wished the other one was there with them and normal too. Molly had no appetite that morning, a coffee would suffice, and she left the house with an air of vibrancy and expectancy waiting for the moment she would see Simon again.

Her father looked out of the window after her. He had seen the same look that had attracted him to her mother twenty years or so ago. Molly had few friends at that school, she didn't need them, she had her confidence, her twin sister and Simon, and that was more than enough to be going on with. The gates of the school which normally seemed so uninviting, were begging her to enter, but she needed no begging, she was desperate to see Simon again, but she would not make it common knowledge. She would put on an air of aloofness, fooling everyone but herself. The pupils began to gather in the playground, forming clusters of friends Molly would regard later as cliques. The bell rang, the pupils formed in lines, and for the first time in two weeks Molly saw Simon. Oh how handsome he looked, he had been working in his dad's pub over Christmas and must have met lots of girls his own age. Had he forgotten Molly, or worse still, formed a relationship with someone else?

They all filed into their prospective classrooms. The register was called, and everyone was checked off the roll call. Simon entered to take the next class. His eyes searched fervently for Molly's, it seemed an age, but when they did meet, Molly knew this was for real— they both felt the same, their eyes told the story, there was no one else for either of them, at the moment. School that day was very mundane. No one really knew what they were doing—the usual first day back feeling. Nothing was accomplished except the order of classes. It was four o' clock and now everyone was glad the first day was over. Pupils filtered through the corridors, past the Headmaster's office and out into the playground.

Molly had not seen much of Simon that day and had decided to hang on for a bit on the off chance of catching him. An hour had passed, and Molly was the only pupil left in the school grounds. She was beginning to give up hope of seeing Simon, when just as she thought it, he appeared looking rather flushed and worn out. Molly motioned with her hand for him to join her, and he came over and gave her a wink. "I'll meet you in the park, in a few minutes." he said.

Molly left knowing that they had to keep their friendship a secret because of Simon's job and her pupil standing. She slowly trudged up to the park and sat on one of the benches. The winter nights were drawing in early, and the night air had no respect for cold bodies without coats. She threw her school scarf around her neck. There was a shuffling of feet behind her, and she shot round in fear. But it was alright, it was only Simon, and he sat down beside her. He wasted no time—he kissed her passionately on the lips, the cheeks the chin, the neck, and these kisses told Molly how much he had missed her over the Christmas break. They chatted about their short vacation. Molly told him about Aunt Maud nearly setting herself on fire, and they both laughed. Simon, as yet had not met

Aunt Maud, but he would and the vivid description Molly had given of her made him laugh even more. Molly also told him of her conversation, with Merry, and her concern in case there was something not quite right going on inside that home.

It was getting quite dark, and Molly had to leave, otherwise there would be questions and concern when she arrived home. They gave each other a special kiss and vowed to meet properly the night after. Simon had promised to take Molly for a snack and a coffee somewhere quiet.

They parted, and Molly rushed home knowing only too well she would catch it for being so very, very late. She decided her excuse would be that she was helping her teacher with the books for the new winter season. She used it, and it worked. Mother had kept her supper for her.

"How did the day go Molly? Did you meet any new friends, and was the lunch nice?" Molly was only too pleased to tell her anything to stop more questions of why she had been so late.

Supper, as soon as it was presented, was tucked away. Molly changed into her casual clothes and joined mother downstairs waiting the arrival of her father. She took some of her schoolbooks with her to do some revision for the next day. This would also give her space for her thoughts to drift back to Simon and the verandah garden. It had gone on nine o'clock before they heard the key in the lock, which gave them a warning alarm of Father's arrival. He was very late tonight, and extremely tired, and therefore did not say much. Molly could not help but see the strain on his face as he hurriedly ate his supper, opened the drink's cabinet and took out the half-full bottle of brandy.

Molly could see something was troubling him; so she left both him and Mother to sort out their problems, and retired to her bedroom.

"Mother, I have more revision to do, so I'll do it in my bedroom, have a bath and an early night," and with that she took herself to bed.

Sitting alone in the attic bedroom, Molly still pondered about Merry and Robin. She was bewildered and confused. If anything was wrong then, one of the grown-ups should know and should sort it out. She dismissed the thoughts once more, as she couldn't do anything about it, herself, and returned to those of her lover. She liked that word, her lover; Simon, she thought of the date tomorrow evening, she could not go out with him in her school uniform, so she decided to take a change of blouse and shoes in her school bag.

The top would surely get scrunched up and need ironing, but as she thought the answer came to her; her last lesson tomorrow was laundry, and if she spoke nicely to the teacher, she would allow her to iron the blouse.

"Yes it was sorted." She whispered to herself. The next day went by quickly, her top was ironed in a couple of minutes, and she took it to the school bathroom and changed into it and the shoes she brought with her. She left her school bag with the teacher and borrowed a carrier bag for her jacket.

She waited in the laundry room and chatted with the teacher when Simon came in. He nodded to her, and Molly went outside and waited. She went right outside beyond the school gates. She could see Simon coming out of the main doors, and she made her way to the park and sat on the very same bench, out of the way of prying eyes. By the time she sat down, he was there by her side. They went to a coffee house several streets away. It was quiet and quaint. It sold coffee, doughnuts and all sorts of delicacies from Danish pastries to freshly baked bread, sandwiches of all kinds and at least four different types of coffee for the most discerning palate. They held hands as they sipped their coffees and munched the hot doughnuts; they did not speak much—they both knew where tonight was going to end. As soon as possible, when the last nibbled crumbs of the doughnuts had vanished from the plates, they were going to find a safe, secret place, and be alone together. That was Molly's plan for the night, but Simon had already thought of that.

"I know of an old, derelict summerhouse at the end of an overgrown, disused and disowned garden."

She smiled, "It will be our secret place". They went down a few streets and across a piece of common land, before they reached a high stone wall.

"There is a gap in the wall further along, and with a little effort we can climb over it, to the secluded summerhouse." Molly followed and sure enough, the broken wall was before them. First Simon climbed over and lent a hand to help Molly join him. The moon was high in the sky that night; it had cast only the minimum of light and silhouetted the faintest of shadows. The light was very dim allowing them to see only the contours of each other's faces. The garden was overgrown and ivy was hanging like Tarzan-type ropes in the jungle. There were rose bushes ten feet or higher, climbing the inner walls. There must have been an orchard there once, as apple and cherry trees were very large and dominant in that place. Simon had to step down on some nettles, which were in their way. He pushed some vine bushes to the side to allow him and Molly to go along what was once a pretty, stone garden path. There was a pond in the middle, and it had some ornate figures of stone looking onto it. The pond was now overgrown and full of grasses and underwater plants, only some lily leaves seemed to exist from the garden as it had been many years before.

They stepped carefully along the overgrown pathway by the summerhouse. The paint work was patchy and some of the wooden timbers were rotted, but amazingly, all the windows were intact and only one had a single crack or was broken.

Simon fiddled with the lock, a rosebush had grown all over the front door, and Simon had to break some branches, and pull off some leaves to get through the thick, wild rosebush. The ivy was also growing wild and had made its way all across the roof and along most of the sides. Simon just wanted to get the door open, to allow them some privacy. He pulled and twisted the branches and was careful of the thorns, which were like daggers ready to draw blood from his bare hands. After tussling and jerking for a few minutes, he managed to get the door handle moving, and it opened quite freely inwards.

There was an old cane seat and what was once a settee, but the legs were broken now. The floor was tiled and except for some dust and a few leaves, it was quite clean and wind and rain proof. It was ideal; the next time they came they would bring a brush and tidy the place up. It was private, and no one could see them, either from the road or the garden because of the clinging ivy.

Simon took off his coat and laid it on the floor. They both sat on it and held each other and kissed. Molly felt romantic and keen. She needed Simon so much more than she admitted to herself. Simon's hand went inside her top and she felt it slowly and gently hold her left breast, the nipple stuck out in desire. She loved being touched by him; he moved his hand to the other breast and gave a gentle moan, full of emotions to come.

Molly felt the passion rise in her, and she pushed Simon's hand aside for a moment. Things were moving too fast. He opened her legs gently, touching her, and she enjoyed the sensation. Molly felt excited and unzipped Simon's pants. She had forgotten the treasure inside. She loved being loved. She undid his belt, and his pants fell to his knees. She ran her hand across his firm tummy and lower, passion growing within her. They touched, gently and tenderly caressing, holding each other and edging closer. Then Molly took charge of the situation.

She slipped off her top and skirt, her breasts stood out against the moonlight on that winter's night, her nipples protruding from both the cold and the warm desire which filled her.

Simon glided his hand over one breast, then the other, holding them and feeling the stiff little nipples. He bent down and kissed her breasts, a little at a time, he ran his tongue over the stiff nipples and raised himself up to meet her mouth with his. Molly was excited and ecstatic at the same time, the blood was boiling within her being; she undid the rest of her clothes and pulled Simon towards her. He was waiting for this moment, and he took off his trousers and undergarments. He dropped down beside Molly and kissed her passionately all over her face.

The windows in the summerhouse were steamed up, with breathing inside; and the coldness outside, but never as hot, as the passion in the middle of the tiled floor. They stood up and saw each other for the first time completely nude against the light of the moon.

They held each other for what seemed forever, then Simon laid Molly down on his coat again, and they joined with a passion that had waited two whole weeks. They squirmed and cuddled and gyrated some more, then all passion was let loose and the two loved in a way only lovers knew.

They kissed and held each other in a clinging, satisfied, fulfilled way, each one needing the other equally. The wind was getting blustery outside the summerhouse, and leaves were blowing against the glass. The lovers got up and dressed, they jumped around to get warm while the blood started to flow back into their veins. Molly threw on her scarf and Simon put his coat around her shoulders. The night air was getting colder, or perhaps it was their ardor cooling after fulfillment, but they quickly got up and closed the summerhouse behind them, being careful to secure the door after their escapade. They climbed over the wall and Simon walked Molly home before it got too late. Molly was careful to leave Simon just before they reached her front door.

They waved to each other, and Simon stood at a safe distance watching her enter her house. Mother was anguished about the late hour her daughter had come in from school, but Molly did not care. She made up the same excuse, and Mother saw she was getting nowhere, so she let it go.

Molly would have to think of a better excuse next time, or better still get a school friend to be an alibi. Molly did not have any really close school friends, so in that case, she would have to find one who was not so much a friend, but someone who thought she was a friend whom Molly could use. Molly and Simon kept up their relationship for several months with no one finding out, and Molly by this time, had found herself a friend and alibi. Her name was Susan and she was perfect. She never asked any questions, she was quiet and just liked being a friend to Molly, who was well sought after at the school, firstly because of her extroverted ways and secondly because of her exam results.

Susan was a plain girl with glasses and insignificant in every way. No one else at school bothered with her and classed her as being somewhat odd—the perfect friend for Molly, to enable her to act out her secret meetings without raising suspicion. She simply was always at Susan's house doing homework, or chatting. Mother believed every word as she too had met Susan and realized straight away that this girl was not wayward.

Merry had been stopped from coming home since Christmas. Apparently, Robin and Merry had caused some trouble and the Matron, Miss Simpson, had stopped her visits home and had persuaded Mother that it was in Merry's best interest. It was the girls' fifteenth birthday soon, and Mother insisted that Merry come home for the weekend at least.

The day of the birthday arrived sooner rather than later than anyone had hoped. Merry had been picked up the night before from the Sanitarium. The first thing she wanted to do on entering the house was to run to the attic bedroom, but Mother would have none of that until she had greeted everyone properly and that meant a kiss and hug for all of them.

Merry obeyed and then ran for the attic bedroom where teddy waited.

No one thought this strange as it was something Merry had always done.

There was a general air of happiness and serenity around the house, the sort of contentment we all have inside, when everything is going well and everyone feels that inner peace. Mother was preparing a quiet birthday party for the twins, nothing grand, just a few close friends; Aunt Maud, and grandmother were coming. Merry made a special request for Robin to be invited, but that was out of the question.

Robin was a Downs Syndrome child and coupled with that, he had changes of moods which could be violent at times, both to himself and to others. This was backed up by the fact that there had been incidents at the home recently involving Robin; and that he was now under restraint.

Mother was puzzled and didn't know what degree of punishment that meant, but as usual took the Matron's word for everything. After all, she was the professional. Molly joined Merry in the attic, they chatted and held hands and were once again united in their closeness only identical twins understood.

Molly asked. "How's Robin?"

The reply came. "He's alright." Followed with a look Molly did not understand, but dismissed, since she did not want to spoil the day.

They both decided to dress in the same outfits but in different colours. Although Merry was away most of the time, whatever Mother bought for Molly, Merrys was there too in her room waiting for her on her occasional visits, even if she never came or got chance to wear the clothes.

Pink was Molly's colour, and Merry wore pale lilac, which suited both the girls as they were quite sallow in complexion with deep green eyes and ebony black hair. They both looked pretty and felt fresh and new.

Molly had some lavender given to her by Simon on one of their torrid nights of passion. She offered some to Merry and then they were ready. Together they came down the stairs both excited and feeling very special. The sitting room was aglow with the flames from the fire coupled with the excitements of the guests, the table was set with all the goodies, the birthday cake taking priority of place in the middle Aunt Maud had once again captured the large armchair she had at Christmas, and Grandmother had to sit on the sofa, not the proper support for the back of a lady of her years and frailty.

The girls appeared in the doorway, and everyone called out with delight saying how pretty they looked, beautiful even, and Father was the proudest man alive at that moment Aunt Maud could not understand from where all the good looks had come. Aunt Maud was far from being beautiful, the fact was she was downright ugly.

The presents were set out, every package identical, except one with a red rose on the top which was for Merry. When she saw it and recognized the writing, or perhaps scrawl was the better word, she jumped with glee, and tears welled up in her eyes, and she guessed who had sent it. Slowly, she cautiously removed the rose, pinned it in her hair, and opened the small package. It was a gold necklace with the name Merry on it in gold.

The scribbled little note inside was written in a babyish way, and read, "To my dear little Merry, and Happy Birthday, From Robin." Merry cried tears of happiness and sorrow.

She had so much wanted Robin to be with her that day. She wondered too if he was okay. Molly opened her presents then; knowing whoever opened their present first, knew what the other was getting. Although they were individuals, amazingly, both liked exactly the same things.

The prettiness and the closeness of the girls shone through on that birthday party, a closeness which should never have been interrupted. Mother pondered whether or not the institution was doing Merry much good as she seemed so normal whilst at home. Mother regained herself as she remembered some of Merry's tantrums and fits of screaming, bouts of uncontrollable temper, and the kicking and banging of her head against walls and floors. No, Merry was in the right place.

They were all seated and halfway through their meal when a knock came to the door. Father answered it and called out, "It's someone for you Molly". Molly ran to the door, perhaps it was Susan with a message for her, or even a card or present.

But no, standing there in the shadow, tall, bronzed, masculine and strong was Simon. He had dared to come to her door to wish her a happy birthday. Oh how at that moment in time she had felt deep friendship bordering on love for him, she smiled, leaned up and kissed his cheek which was burning with pleasure. She wanted to hold him in her arms but that would not be seen to be proper with her parents in the next room. He handed her a little package with a pink bow on the top. She asked him to come in and meet her family, but he declined the offer, as their relationship was so wrong in so many ways and would only spark off suspicion.

Molly being so much younger; forgot in those few moments the implications and waved good-bye to Simon. She opened the drawer in the hallway chest and placed the little package inside, to be picked up at a later time. "Who was that?" asked Aunt Maud.

"Oh, only one of my junior teachers from school who was passing and stopped to wish me happy birthday," was Molly's reply, and it sufficed.

Chapter Three

THE MEAL WAS LONG finished and all the presents opened, and everyone was full, including Aunt Maud. Father brought in some brandy and sherry glasses for the ladies. The girls being teenagers; were allowed a full glass. Molly winked to Merry, and they both smiled that knowing smile and thanked their father. A little later, Mother got up and went into the kitchen to get some coffee for her guests. Whilst she was there, she started to tidy away the dishes when suddenly there was an almighty thud and a crashing of Mother's best china.

Everyone jerked with shock, and Father ran to see what the matter was, and the girls followed. Mother was stretched out on the kitchen floor surrounded by broken crockery, I apparently she had had a black out. Father tapped her on the hand repeatedly but there was no response. He left Mother in the capable hands of Aunt Maud and rushed over to the phone to call Doctor Sommerfield, the family's general practitioner. When the doctor arrived, Mother had regained consciousness, but had a tremendous headache. She also complained that her hand was somewhat numb. The doctor examined her but found nothing wrong. This had never happened before; perhaps Mother was overdoing it. After settling her in bed, Grandmother and Aunt Maud went home, leaving father and the girls still worried over the mishap in the kitchen.

Father spent most of the evening reading to Mother in the small dimly room. The girls felt left out and quickly decided to go to bed themselves, but because it was their birthday; decided to first pinch some of Father's brandy; there was still at least four glasses left! Molly poured and the girls sipped the warming liquid, they giggled, and soon got tipsy. The fire was still blazing, and the girls exchanged gossip and small talk. Molly tried on several occasions to quiz Merry about the home and Robin, but she would not be drawn into on this matter. The water was boiling in the pipes, and Molly decided to take a bath before retiring, so as not to waste it. She turned on the taps and poured lots of Mother's lavender, some rose water, and those precious little pearls of bubble bath in the water which foamed up over the side of the bath. Molly slipped off her clothes. There was a knock at the door; it was Merry asking, "Can I come in?"

Molly unlocked the door, "What do you want Merry?"

Merry locked the door again behind her, "Look at all those bubbles," Merry started to take her clothes off.

"Hey this is my bath." Merry took no notice, she was naked just like Molly, and they looked at each other. They were exactly the same, two peas in a pod, and even they were amazed. Molly's nipples were the same colour and size as Merry's. Their hair was the same, and even their belly buttons were exactly the same, except for Molly's birth mark on her left shoulder!

"Merry this is my bath water, you'll have to wait!"

"Right then, we'll have a bath together to save arguing," Molly agreed. Molly slipped in first, then Merry. The water felt good, the lavender was beautiful, and the smells filled the bathroom.

Even father on passing the landing shouted in, "Molly, it smells like a harem in there.

I hope you haven't used all mother's toilet water."

Molly told Merry to turn round, to soap her back. Then they took it in turns to soap their fronts and legs. Both girls received enjoyment throughout the whole bath. They were giggly as the bouncing boobs and limbs slithered by each other. These two identical, beautiful young women; were enjoying each other's bodies in the raw, for the first time in their lives, since Mother had bathed them as babies. Tonight they seemed two halves of one. Had they not been parted, this would have been a normal and everyday occurrence. In this simple act the closeness between the girls was bonded with a special bond of love.

Their intimate moments were disturbed by father pounding on the door and asking where Merry was, "I'm in here having a bath with Molly." Father muttered something and left them to it. As they dried each other, their breasts were bouncing with gravity. They laughed, they were both very big girls, and they thought it very funny, in a girlish way.

Molly noticed a few scratches or marks of some kind on Merry's back. Molly questioned her sister again. "What are those marks on your back?" Merry had sunk back again into her world of secrecy, an easy way of not answering questions. After drying each other, they picked up their clothes and went back to the attic bedroom, where they got their nightdresses from the cupboard.

Merry started to speak again on entering her attic sanctuary. They're nothing really, my bath brush could have left marks; the bristles are hard and a little prickly."

Whether Molly believed her or not, she decided to let it go for now, Merry wasn't for saying anything about the Sanitarium, perhaps through fear.

They watched the sleeping village from their attic bedroom. The moon joined them, it was big, and full with a funny face on it as it glided through the heavens, touching and kissing the stars and making them sparkle and effervesce as only a long June evening could do.

The next day the whole household was up early ready for the traumatic experience yet to come when Merry had to go back to the Sanitarium. Unexpectedly, Merry was bright and cheerful. She packed her case herself, careful to take Robin's present. They were all ready, and off they set. Merry talked all the way on the bus and then all the way on the train; the conversation, no matter how everyone tried to change it, returned to Robin and her present from him.

Molly asked Merry if she had missed Robin. "Well of course, he's my special friend." She was happy now, belonging to someone. Her friendship with Robin mirrored Molly's friendship with Simon, not physical of course Molly thought, or rather hoped. Molly didn't question the marks on Merry's back again, although it worried her.

The train journey was light and relaxing, the girls chatted and Mother just sat and listened. She needed the rest after her fall the other night. Funnily enough after the fall, her hand was still feeling numb, and she got tired more easily.

They climbed the big, stone steps of the Sanitarium, and Matron, Miss Simpson was there to meet them.

"Have you been behaving yourself young lady," she said to Merry.

"Why of course," was Merry's reply. Both matron and mother lifted their eyebrows with a smile. Molly settled immediately that day.

Molly normally never spoke of Merry to Mother or ever told tales about her, but the concern had grown so deep inside Molly; that she had thought it time to share it with her mother.

"Mother," Molly said. "Have you noticed the marks on Merry's back?"

Mother looked back astonished. "What do you mean?"

"There are great long scars going down her back." Merry couldn't forget it.

Mother looked cross and promised to take it up with Matron the very next morning. Molly did not join her mother in the sitting room as normal, but decided to go to the attic bedroom and read some books or think about Simon—Simon, she remembered his birthday present to her was still in the drawer in the hallway. Molly stealthily slipped downstairs and retrieved it. Waiting for the security of the closed bedroom door, she opened the present. Inside the little box there were oodles of cotton wool, soft and full of air. She removed it and there beyond all her hopes was a tiny locket with chain in pure gold, with the initials S and M intertwined with each other, just as Simon and Molly had been the last time they made love. Molly put it round her neck, careful to wear it under her dress, so as not to arouse suspicion.

The following morning it rained and rained as if the heavens were angry with the rest of the world. Molly sat on the armchair, the one Aunt Maud nearly came to her end on, patiently waiting for her Mother, half an hour had gone by, and Mother had not come down. Molly grew impatient and went up to her room. She banged on the door, but there was no answer.

"Mother, it's me Molly, are you okay?" she banged and banged.

Father had left early again, so as not to invade Mother's privacy.

Molly banged and banged on the door, frightened to open it, but still no reply.

She had to open it no!

Shock of the unknown; shot through Molly, as she opened the bedroom door. Mother was lying on her side on the carpet, still in her night clothes. Molly grew more fearful, great shocks of adrenaline forced through her being.

"Mother, mother, I have to get you up on the bed." She called her mother's name again and again, but to no avail.

There was no reply from her mother. She lay there motionless. Molly tapped Mother on the hand, re-adjusted her nightgown carefully, untying the neckline, but still no movement from Mother. Molly was just about to leave for help when she heard a moan coming from the delicate, graceful heap on the floor. Her mother turned, groaned, wiped her forehead and tried to stand, but was too weak and dropped to the floor again.

She complained of a severe headache and a numb feeling in her right leg.

"I'll go for Aunt Maud, just stay there, I can't lift you, but Aunt Maud can." Molly was ashen faced.

She ran as fast as she could to Aunt Maud's cottage, who was the nearest of her relations. Aunt Maud dropped what she was doing and followed Molly over to Elizabeth as fast as her great bulk could carry her. She lifted Mother to the bed and sat her on the edge. Mother rubbed her right leg constantly, complaining of pins and needles shooting through it. Molly was ordered to ring Dr. Sommerfield at the hospital. Aunt Maud was good at ordering, but her heart was in the right place.

Dr. Sommerfield arrived as quickly as he could. He was worried about the condition of his patient and dear friend, especially as Elizabeth was never ill. He listened to Mother's complaints, wrote a note for some sort of relaxant pills, gave Mother a sedative and asked her to stay in bed that day. He drew the bedroom curtains and ordered Aunt Maud and Molly to leave. As he drew the bedroom door behind him, he motioned for Aunt Maud to come into the other room to talk quietly.

"Molly you wait here," Aunt Maud cautioned Molly to stay put so she was free to discuss her mother's condition openly with the doctor. Dr. Sommerfield seemed worried and sad at the same time. He had known about Mother's fainting turns for quite some time and until now had put it down to tiredness and stress. But this was different, there was a slight paralysis of Mother's right leg, and he was afraid of the outcome.

All this he explained to Elizabeth's sister. She looked worried when she came out from the other bedroom with Dr. Sommerfield.

"Thank you for coming at such short notice Doctor." She said as she saw him out of the front door and returned to her sister's bedroom. She quietly opened the door and closed it so as not to disturb her only sister Elizabeth, as she glided into a sedated sleep with no worries only dreams.

Aunt Maud stayed in Mother's room for a few hours, just sitting there and hoping for the best as the doctor's words went through her head. Elizabeth was seriously ill, and she knew it, Maud did not need Dr. Sommerfield to spell it out. Oh, how she wished she had been a better sister, and not so aggravating and ordering, but if her sister needed her she would be there on her beck and call, minding her family and visiting Merry at the home.

Molly had left Aunt Maud to see to Mother. Molly did not understand or even have any feeling that Mother was less than normal.

She went downstairs and sat in the sitting room on her own, just as she had done that morning. Aunt Maud appeared from upstairs, "I'll make you some lunch Molly, your mother is still asleep with the sedation the doctor gave her." Molly sat there wondering what was going on, and why was Mother still in her room? Mother had never stayed in her room all this time, and she was always bustling about the house at the crack of dawn.

Molly thought of Merry and of the dilemma she was in. Life was complicated and extremely tiresome, at this moment in time. Why couldn't problems happen one at a time? Molly corrected herself for the self pity, being spiteful and selfish. Aunt Maud explained to Molly that Mother was very ill, more ill than anyone thought. Molly felt guilty and disgusted with herself.

"Aunt Maud," said Molly "Mother and I were going to the home this morning to see Merry and the Matron to find out about some marks on Merry's back."

"Don't concern yourself with that. You and I, and your father, have enough to contend with at the moment," was Aunt Maud's retort. Molly could not forget Merry's scars or the sorrowful little face which lit up only at the sound of Robin's name. She was abandoned, imprisoned alone in that place. Molly felt that her world was collapsing around her; she was powerless to help Merry and did not understand Mother's condition at all. Mother always liked attention, Molly thought, and perhaps she was doing this to get all the attention she could get, as Father was hardly home anymore; and then only to sleep.

Aunt Maud cooked some light supper, Molly didn't want anything; she had to get out of the house that evening. She felt that everything was closing in around her. She donned her coat and walked along the street close to the park. The night had got so light and long now that it seemed like the middle of the afternoon. But it wasn't, it was seven o'clock and she would probably meet Father on his way home.

She passed the park, people were walking their dogs, young lovers were holding hands, and tramps, at that early hour were marking their places for the night. She passed the Inn and quickly looked in and was about to pass happily on her way, when she stopped with a jolt. She saw a face she knew. One step back, she peered through the little pane of glass on the window—it was her father with a woman. Molly's anger grew within her as the hurt, resentment, and fear completely demoralized her.

What if Mother found out, would it make her illness worse? Would it destroy her, all this on one day? Molly could handle no more; she ran hell for leather back to her home and straight up the stairs to her bedroom, the attic; the one she had moved back into with Merry. Aunt Maud called after her; but Molly was too distraught to answer, she could not think of disclosing her secret to anyone. Molly's head was splitting with the unknown knowledge—so many problems in one's head at such an early age. Was it fair? But then life wasn't fair, and she would have to cope. Molly asked herself repeatedly, Why me? She was beginning to wish she was in the security of the home with Merry and shielded from all problems!

Father arrived home directly after Molly. She heard his footsteps enter her Mother's room. She heard whispered voices, one was Aunt Maud's probably disclosing the fainting turn Mother had that morning. Father went further in towards Elizabeth's bed, and closed the door. Molly hated him at that moment. All this time, Mother had believed Father, when he said, he had been working late.

There was a click as Aunt Maud opened the front door. "I'll be back in the morning. Elizabeth has company now." Her shrill voice could be heard calling out, as she left.

Molly went downstairs, no one was in the sitting room, and she made herself comfortable on the armchair near the fire. She was just twiddling her chain from Simon, when Father came in looking rather worried. Molly found it hard to speak to him but managed some sort of mumbled conversation. She certainly was not going to share her secret of Merry's plight at the home with this deceiver.

Father poured himself a brandy, lit a cigar and just sat there motionless at the dining table near the window. He looked worried. Molly resented her father that night and cleared off to bed early so that she would not have to enter into anymore conversation with him. Molly was rudely awoken the following day by Aunt Maud's screeching voice, telling her that everyone had overslept, and Dr. Sommerfield was expected soon. Molly dressed hurriedly grabbing a quick wash in the bathroom. She sipped the coffee that Aunt Maud had prepared for her and was off to school, away from the mess.

She passed Dr. Sommerfield on his visit to Mother, and she smiled and waved. He returned the compliment, dropping his spectacles to rely on the chain they were attached to. Dr. Sommerfield arrived at the house, greeted Aunt Maud and entered Mother's room.

"So how's the patient today?" Elizabeth smiled and greeted him.

The doctor tried, but to no avail, to move Mother's leg. She had no feeling or movement in it. The doctor sighed, rested his head on his hands and took a deep breath. "We will have to wait for the results of the sample we supplied to the Pathology Lab last week Elizabeth."

Doctor Sommerfield was even more concerned than before.

"Elizabeth, my dear, I'm not going to lie this time. I think we have a problem. Things aren't too good."

Mother was waiting for this comment as she knew her leg would not move and already the strength was going from the other one. Molly by this time had arrived at the school not knowing how bad things were at home, but looking worried and distraught. She was so engrossed in her own feelings, she had not even seen Simon, or realized his presence near her.

She needed a shoulder to cry on, a strong arm around her and some love and affection. Yesterday was too much to bear or even think about. Simon whispered in her ear before Molly even realized he was there beside her.

"Meet me in the summerhouse around nine o'clock," he said. Molly nodded; she needed someone to talk to, to ask advice from, someone who would not repeat her problems, to others. Molly, at this crucial time of her life, had to grow up fast. Being seduced by Simon was only play acting next to what was happening now. School was a bore that day, every subject seemed endless, a sheer oblivion. Like the heat over a desert oasis nothing was real. How could it be?

There were too many problems, all concentrated on Molly's immediate family; involving her Mother and twin sister, her beloved Merry. How would Merry cope with Mother's illness, she could barely cope with her own, or God forbid, if she ever got to know about Father and that woman. Molly would say nothing to Merry; only try to help her with those welts on her back.

School ended and nothing very eventful happening---just as well, she had enough to cope with at home. The usual high-spirited feeling she got when meeting Simon had been taken over by this despairing, gloomy cloud of misery. Molly sat at home wondering, would she ever get back to normal or would this feeling of nothingness control her life forever? Aunt Maud was there, she had helped Mother downstairs. In fact, she had carried her. They both sat sipping tea and chatting as if nothing was happening.

Aunt Maud called Molly over, and Mother smiled, "Dr. Sommerfield is going to help me get around with my gamy legs," said Mother. "I'm getting a wheelchair in the morning." Molly stood there completely motionless, it was as if she was shot through the heart, this was a bomb shell Molly did not anticipate.

"But Mother," she said, "this is only a temporary thing. You don't need a wheelchair. We will all rally round, we will all help, we'll rub your legs, bathe you, do errands;

I will go alone to see Merry.

Father will have to give up overtime. Please don't have that wheelchair; we will get you mobile, I promise." Molly was grabbing at straws and not facing up to the truth.

"Are you ashamed of me Molly? Do you feel your mother is less than all the other mothers because she has lost the use of one of her legs? I know it's difficult to bear, I know love, I have to be the bravest of all, my pride is still there, just a little depleted because of my circumstances, but I will never stop fighting as long as I can breathe. If you don't wish to take me out in my new carriage, Father will take me." Tears were streaming down Mother's face.

How Molly loved her mother, and thought it so unkind that it had to happen to her mother, as if the family was not going through enough problems. Molly felt sick and hateful. She went to her bedroom and looked out of the attic window, on a world she had begun to hate. She felt so angry that she almost threw Merry's favourite teddy out of that window, out of deep hurt and frustration. She put her head in her hands and sobbed and sobbed. The tears were gushing out like tidal waves; her uniform was wet from them. Her dreams were shattered; all her family was disintegrating around her.

Molly lay down on the bed; and quietly drifted off to the safety of sleep.

At least sleep killed all anguish and despair and left everyone on the same footing, almost as death would, perhaps sleep was little pauses, preparing us for the final passing. There was a slam, Aunt Maud was leaving again; it must be eight o'clock. Molly rubbed her eyes, sat up and started to peel off the crumpled school uniform. She laid out a nice jumper and skirt, carefully putting Simon's chain on the top of the dresser unit, until after she washed. She felt better. Sleep had subdued the nasty things in her life and given her more zest to cope.

Molly was strong now, had to be, she had given herself to pity, that would happen no more. Molly was a woman in charge of both her life and her circumstances.

She rushed downstairs, dressed in the simple skirt and jumper, nothing special, but careful to put Simon's chain inside the jumper, calling on the way past Mother's bedroom door.

"I'm going out for a short while."

She had to get away from that house of gloom and misery, she had to live, life was going to be much harder for Molly from now on; she knew, but tonight was special; it was only there for her and Simon. God created good and bad, not always fairly balanced, but it was there to make us appreciate the good because the bad would never be far away. It was almost nine o'clock as Molly left, it was still light, children were still playing in the streets; dogs were barking, peddlers selling their wares.

Molly made her way to the summerhouse, Simon was there already; she could not see him, but she could feel his presence. As she got closer, he came out to greet her. She motioned to him with a wave and felt all her troubles disappear as she saw his face. What a lovely, manly face Simon had, a beach boy look, with strong, broad shoulders, electric blue eyes and hair bleached blond by the sun. He was precious. Molly climbed over the wall, through the fallen wooded garden past the clinging ivy and other shrubbery, dried up now from lack of water and neglect, over the broken glass, ducking and sliding over the hanging vines, that possibly in some bygone day had produced some sort of grape or berry. A small bird sat on the floor, his wing seemed to be damaged in some way.

Molly knelt by him, and Simon came to her aide. It seemed alright, only his wing feathers had got a bit bent on his landing. Molly straightened them for him, and he was up and away without a care in the world. Molly would feel that way tonight. Tomorrow, she would help out and shoulder the problems, but tonight belonged to Simon and her, no one would alter that.

Simon drew Molly up from her knees, full stretch, looked in her eyes, kissed her lovingly on the lips, embraced her, held her, then he strengthened his hold on her.

He looked into her eyes and said. "I have waited patiently to see you again Molly, you look beautiful tonight. The fire in me alights in your presence; I think I love you."

Molly needed all the caring words and tenderness which came her way that night. She liked Simon; she liked him a lot, but never loved him, or gave any indication that she ever would.

Forgetting all that tonight was special because she did need him; really needed him tonight. Gently they took hands, gave each other a smile and a peck on the cheek, and headed for the overgrown summerhouse. They sat on Simon's coat, snuggling together. Molly needed the closeness tonight; she needed the cuddles and kisses as they waited for darkness to fall in order to get the privacy they both yearned.

"Look Molly, I've brought two bottles of wine and a bottle opener!" He had of course forgotten the glasses. How typical of a man. They agreed to go to the local cafe, have a soda water and pinch the glasses.

They giggled at the thought. Simon carefully hid the two bottles of wine behind the broken chair in the summerhouse, and together they attacked the assault course in front of them, quickly making for the main road and the cafe in good time. They sipped their sodas. Luckily the cafe was full of people that night which gave them a chance to slip the glasses up their jumpers and sneak out unnoticed.

The moon was coming up and the skies were darkening, the first of the autumn leaves were only beginning to fall. Molly was no longer questioned about her whereabouts as long as she was in by eleven o'clock, so there were no problems. They encountered the wall and the broken glass, the vines and shrubbery and finally got to the summerhouse door. Simon laid down his coat, as before, they giggled remembering the last few experiences on that coat.

He leaned across and picked up the first bottle of wine, the glasses had a little drop of soda water still inside, it didn't matter, as the soda would not deflect from the taste of the wine. He poured the full-bodied red liquid into the two glasses. Molly sipped. The first sip swirled around her tongue and down her throat, my what a nice feeling, they toasted to happy days and downed a few more glasses.

Molly was beginning to feel good. She had forgotten her problems and decided to sweep them under the carpet and not spoil tonight. Tonight was for lovers, good friends and close relationships. She would confide in Simon with her troubles another night, but not tonight. There was a slight breeze, and it blew some autumn leaves into the summerhouse through the half-open door, and the two young people sat there on Simon's coat getting relaxing and enjoying each other company.

They looked up at the moon and stars, excitedly trying to spot all the different clusters. The happy glow from the wine was beginning to take effect and Simon became more amorous as he gently but deliberately took Molly's glass with his, and laid them aside.

"Are you warming up Molly?" Simon whispered in a soft tone, as he pulled her near to him, sitting on his coat on the Summerhouse floor. They held in a longed for embrace, his body felt taut and strong next to hers. His hand slowly moved inside her jumper, she gasped with excitement, as he stroked her breasts over her bra. It was too cold for undressing tonight. Unasked she wriggled out of her knickers as he dropped his pants, and they threw their undergarments aside. They were, kissing, caressing, cuddling together drawing Simon's coat around themselves.

They did not feel the breeze, now, the wine acted as thermal insulation, they touched each other's bodies, and Molly loved the excitements of Simon.

She stroked his passion from inside of his underpants, gently caressing it with her hand first, then her tongue—Simon loved these lusty moments.

"Undo my bra Simon." She said in a husky voice, just above a whisper.

He turned around to undo the harness of her bra when and his passion, large now, slithered across Molly's side. She giggled it tickled; she was longing for the excitements yet to come. He undid her bra, eventually, as she shook her large breasts, under her jumper, as you would shake long hair to give it the feeling of freedom. Her large nipples   protruded even more as the breeze caught them: her breasts were so large and firm Simon had trouble trying to hold one in his hand.

Side by side they lay across the floor, clothed except for panties and his shorts.   It did nothing to kill the passion. They held each other, kissed, ran their hands all over each other's bodies. Molly loved it when Simon kissed her toes right up her legs.

"You are beautiful tonight Molly." He meant it. Then slowly he slipped inside her, she gasped then moaned, in ecstasy, as he flooded her with his most precious gift, pleasuring both her and himself. He wanted the moment to last for ever, he couldn't she turned him on just that little too much and her gave her everything he had to give, and she loved it.

There was little time for foreplay tonight; they had waited too long for this excitement.

For fear of being found out after the event, they both pulled on their tops and sat pondering their entanglement and enjoying the lovely feelings and thoughts of well-being enveloping them.

"That was very special Simon, I think we both waited too long for that, we must make love more often, and we need the comfort of a bed, some time soon!"

Nodding, he agreed with her, "I'll have to ask friends if I can borrow their room for the evening, I know you have to be in by eleven o'clock."

Simon opened the other bottle of wine and fulfilled, and relaxed, they sat sipping the wine, enjoying the gentle breeze of the autumn night. How idyllic it was Molly thought, if only life could be so peaceful and wonderful, but tomorrow would come around again, a day full of problems and worry, Molly dismissed the thoughts until tomorrow.

Simon poured another glass of wine; Molly was getting quite tipsy; she would have to be careful. If Father found out there would be hell to play. It was nearing 10:30, and Molly would have to be getting back. They finished off the last few drops of wine, picked up their belongings and started the walk home. They passed the park and walked along the dimly lit street, smiling occasionally to each other as lovers do, making that special contact.

They didn't speak much that night, just enjoyed each other's presence and bodies.

They had just turned the corner, and there was Father standing too close for comfort with the other woman. Molly froze.

"Simon; that was what I was going to tell you tonight, he's been seeing someone else and telling mother he's been working late."

They crossed the street and Molly almost ran home, she couldn't bear the thought of Father and that woman together, especially when her mother was so ill.

"How could he do this to my Mother, and to me and Merry?" She asked Simon but he was the wrong one to ask. She gave Simon a peck on the cheek outside her gate and went inside. Aunt Maud was asleep by the fire. Molly decided not to wake her; as she was comfortable and the fire had burnt out; the embers disintegrated down the grate waiting to be emptied the next day. Molly climbed the stairs and was about to enter Mother's room when she heard an enormous bump. Molly burst in the door.

Mother had been trying to get her book, but it was just out of reach; and instead of asking, or rather banging downstairs for Aunt Maud, had tried to get it herself and consequently had fallen out of bed. Molly felt so sorry worried. She called Aunt Maud, "I'm sorry to wake you Aunty dear, I know you are tired, but Mother has fallen out of bed, and I cannot get her back in unaided."

Elizabeth apologized, to her sister and Aunt Maud scolded her, "What do you think I am here for." Molly was growing to hate her father even more now, but had she stopped to think, she was doing the same thing, herself, on a lesser scale. Mother needed her too, and she had offered her undying help. She kissed her mother and Aunt Maud and dragged herself up to the attic bedroom.

Mother's condition was worsening by the day, and Aunty was almost living at the house by now. Molly too tired to wash, got into bed and let the wine take over; she dropped immediately into a heady sleep. She was awakened the next day by a thumping noise on the window of her attic bedroom. She looked out; there had obviously been a storm that night; there were branches strewn all over, uprooted fences everywhere. Molly got up in rather a bad mood; she almost commandeered Aunt Maud into going to the home, with her, to see Merry. Already she was breaking her promise to Mother.

She said she would go alone, Aunt Maud was so tired with all the extra chores set upon her now, but she agreed to go with Molly anyway. When Molly came downstairs the breakfast table was already laid and Maud was in the kitchen alone. Molly went in to have a word with her. Aunt Maud was far too busy to talk at that moment, but promised to talk with Molly after school about whatever was bothering her.

Molly seemed reassured; she set off for school and bumped into Simon at the gate. He was dying to kiss her, but could not, so a gentle squeeze of the hand was passed between them. Molly liked Simon a hell of a lot. School went well that day. Molly was top of the class in most of her subjects, but it still seemed to drag. Molly was desperately, despairingly, trying to get some sort of help for Merry and Robin.

She was determined; she was not going to be fobbed off tonight. School finished at last, each day took longer than the one before, and she rushed home to catch her Aunty.

"After supper." was Aunt Maud's retort. She was obviously busy and Mother had been demanding that day. Aunt Maud seemed exasperated. Molly nibbled through her evening meal and helped her Aunt clear all the dishes and also collected them from Mother's room, as she no longer came downstairs. Her wheelchair was under the stairs and unused up until now. Mother was patiently waiting Dr. Sommerfield's visit as he was bringing her the final results of all the tests.

At last, Molly was alone in the kitchen with Aunt Maud. Molly sat down, head bowed forward, "I have noticed marks on Merry's back, long, bruised marks," she told Aunt Maud. She also told of Robin being maltreated or subjected to some sort of torment at the home. Aunt Maud agreed that Molly take the next day off school and as soon as she had finished with Mother and her needs, they would go to the home and start asking questions. Molly was delighted. That was what she had been waiting to hear for months now.

She went to her room that night, feeling triumphant, making peace in her head with the conflicts of reality and emotion. She sat in the attic window seat and thought of Merry, even at that distance, she could feel Merry around her, near her; she could almost sense the smell of her, the touch of her hand, the gentle, innocent smile which made

Molly glow. Her thoughts drifted to Simon and the last night they spent together. She enjoyed their lovemaking and the company. She licked her lips and savoured the red, full-bodied wine in her mind's eye, She retired that night with an easy mind and a surging love for her sister, her other self, her closest friend; her mirror image.

Next day after everything was prepared and Mother was made as comfortable as possible, they set off for the home, being careful not to make an appointment so as not to arouse suspicion. They took the usual train and were up the steps of The Sanitarium and waited in the reception for Matron before anyone knew they were there. Aunt Maud asked to speak to Merry right away. The Matron scowled, but showed them to Merry's room; the little window was so high up the wall it was barely possible to see out except if one stood on the bed. Merry's teddy with the broken ear was strategically placed on the bed alongside new teddy, Robin. The gold locket and chain were on the little dresser with her hair brush. Molly looked around, there were very few possessions. A few photographs of the two girls together, growing up at different stages added to the little treasure chest of meager possessions, offering little or no comfort.

It must have been hell for Merry here, with a loving family at home. It was no wonder that Merry ran to the safety of the attic bedroom as soon as she got home. Molly's attention was drawn to Merry sitting on the bed. Merry was looking nervous and twirling her hair sheepishly. Aunt Maud asked why she was in her room, when most of the other children were playing in the grounds. "Robin and I are confined to our rooms because we were naughty," Merry replied. "Robin was made to take a cold bath and was locked in his room all day yesterday." Merry spoke in a low, concerned voice.

Aunt Maud sat next to Merry on the bed and gave her a cuddle. She loved both girls equally; they were both her sweet nieces.

Molly sat on the other side of Merry and hugged her also. Merry took confidence and strength from that. "Your mother sends her love." Aunt Maud handed Merry a small parcel; Merry opened it and the innocent little face smiled with delight. She unraveled the brown paper and inside was the most beautiful silk ribbons, in three colours, pink, lavender, and blue, and also some white ankle socks to go with her new sandals. Merry was comforted and relaxed now, "We'll come back in a few minutes. Molly and I want to go and have a few words with Matron."

Aunt Maud questioned the reason for Merry and Robin being confined to their rooms. The answer from Matron was that they had been caught kissing in the corridor and when told to stop both started throwing tantrums and screaming. But they were doing no harm was Aunt Maud's reply. After all they were almost 17 years old now. The matron was adamant that Merry had an age of 10 years and Robin of about 7 years, and any such behaviour like that was quickly stamped out. Aunt Maud could see the reasoning but still thought it was a bit severe. They returned to Merry's room and confronted her. She agreed with the story. "After all, Molly, these children are not normal and have to be treated more strictly," Aunt Maud was satisfied with the results of the conversation with the Matron.

She like Molly, in the past, had seen many of Merry's tantrums and they were not pleasant, especially when she rolled on the floor screaming, kicking out with violent feet, not caring if anyone was in her way. Mother's ankles, on many an occasion were bruised black-and-blue by just trying to stop her screaming, but Merry would take notice of no one or any threat of any sort. After all, that was the reason she was in the home for backward children.

Next year she would be moved to a proper Sanitarium for the mentally and criminally insane. That would be when Robin and Merry would part company as boys and girls for good, and live in separate Sanitariums depending on their sex, and also in different wings, depending on the seriousness of their particular problems. Molly was still not satisfied. Why did no one believe her? Why was she too treated as mentally insane or at the least, like a child? Why was everything being brushed under the carpet? Molly could contain herself any longer; she went across to Merry, pulled up her jumper and shouted, "What do you call them?"

Aunt Maud was shell-shocked, riveted to the bedroom wall in an immobilized state, with mouth agape. She started shouting to Merry, "How did this happen, what have you been doing with that foolish boy Robin? Has he done this?" all fast and furious questions, but all at the wrong time, said in the wrong manner, to the wrong person. Merry flipped. She threw her bedclothes across the room, knocked down everything from the dressing table with one furious swoop, sending everything crashing to the floor, all photograph frames and glass objects were broken. Merry picked up her hairbrush from the floor and threw it at the mirror; she pulled curtains from the little window, she kept beating her head against the wall over and over, no one could stop her; her head was bruised and bleeding, her teeth were set, gnashed and fierce, her eyes like a cornered animal's. She frightened Molly.

The idea Aunt Maud had set in her mind was to frog march Merry to Matron's office, to pull up her jumper and ask what was going on, but under the circumstance just brought to light, she decided to get Matron over to that room now. She left Molly in charge. Molly was always weary of Merry as no one ever knew what she would do next, but Molly too was angry. Molly very seldom got angry, but on this occasion she was equally as angry as Merry and Merry knew it, there would be no trouble. Aunt Maud in her huge bulk rushed along the corridor shouting for Matron, she pushed all and sundry out of her path as she searched for Miss Simpson.

She finally caught sight of Miss Simpson with another patient, "Come Quickly Miss Simpson, we have trouble with Merry." Miss Simpson ran to Merry's room, but this time all was quiet and calm. Aunt Maud pulled up Merry's Jumper, "How do you explain that?" she said to Matron. Matron looked shocked, she promised to get to the bottom of this, as soon as possible. Merry was becoming agitated again, "She'll have to be sedated to give us time to clear up in here and replace the broken mirror and fix her photograph frames and make up the bed." Aunt Maud agreed, and Merry was sedated and taken to another room to allow the staff to clear up. Aunt Maud and Molly left, with the reassurance that Miss Simpson would do her utmost, to find out what was going on. They felt a confidence in Miss Simpson and still believed she was innocent of the goings on in that Godforsaken place.

The Matron herself was more than concerned that this sort of behaviour could go on, under her command, and she knew nothing about it. She would leave no stone unturned until she found out what was going on and bring the culprits to justice. The next day at the Sanitarium proved to be one of interrogation, suspicion and anger as one by one the staff were questioned first by Matron and them by senior members of the Hospital Authority. Matron was exhausted by the end of the day, as after all the interrogations and interviews, she still came up with nothing. No one spoke. They were either too scared to say anything or did not want to. The Matron felt powerless, she knew this would have to be taken further. She spoke to the Chief of the Governing Body of Hospitals, and they sent along some investigators.

They were there several weeks before they got a break through. Eventually one by one of the staff gave a little information, the picture was building up slowly and the investigators decided that all fingers were pointing in one direction, at two male nurses; the stories which were coming back were not just the maltreatment of Merry and Robin, but several other children too. The Hospital doctor came to the conclusion that the marks on Merry's back had been done with a thin piece of rope, there were a lot of them, and they were all in varying degrees of bruises, obviously done at separate beatings.

Merry wasn't the easiest person to deal with; everyone knew she would not take orders, and she had little trust in anyone outside her immediate family. When frightened, she shut out everyone and could not do simple commands, and would get worse and worse the more anyone shouted at her. The two nursing attendants were removed and kept under arrest in the local police station, awaiting trial. There was an outcry when it was revealed in the papers, and it didn't do the home any good. The children were all given medicals, and in some instances there were boot marks on some of their buttocks, also bite marks, and in other instances even sexual abuse took place mostly with the girls.

It was Merry's turn for her medical inspection, no one could have known the outcome, and everyone's worst fear was realized in one quick sentence. Merry was pregnant.

Matron at once blamed Robin and stood by her first admission that this was the reason the children were separated and sent to different rooms for their own protection.

Although Matron was not herself, personally to blame, she had to carry an element of the blame because it was at her Home for backward children where it had taken place; and she should have made it her business to have known everything that was going on there. Matron was very sorry, devastated by the situation which had arisen at her home, a home she had worked hard for and was proud of.

The staff was becoming more caring and relaxed now that the two bullies had gone, because as well as mistreating the children; some of the staff lived in fear of them too. Now that the threat had gone they were more open with the children and they spent more free time with them in their recreation activities and also played more sports in the grounds with them. Life at the home was returning to normal, and was a much nicer place to be kept in.

Merry's tummy was growing bigger; Merry was told she was pregnant and everyone around just hoped she knew what it meant. All the other children were excited and waiting with baited breath for the happy event. They had never had a baby born at the Sanitarium before. Merry wouldn't or couldn't say who the father was; after all she could have been sedated and would have known nothing about it. Perhaps no one would ever know until the baby was born and blood tests taken.

The dilemma of Merry was kept a close secret from her mother, and each time she asked of Merry she was told that she was doing fine. Everyone was just hoping that she wouldn't ask to see Merry before she became really ill as Merry was showing now and it was obvious to everyone she was pregnant. Even Mother with her glasses off would recognize the symptoms. Mother's illness, was taking a hold on her, and she seemed weaker each day. It was becoming difficult for her even to hold a cup; the strength was going from her hands as well as her legs now.

It certainly was black days for the whole Wentworth family with both the worry of Mother and Merry at the same time, each not knowing of the other's plight. Father was home more now and Molly thought that perhaps he had stopped seeing that woman. Molly had never said anything to anyone about the whole matter. Father spent hours in the evening reading to Mother and reminiscing about their young days. Aunt Maud was an angel; she did everything around the house, and they didn't need a maid or a nurse, which would strain the family budget even further.

Mother's wheelchair was sent back to the hospital, she had never gotten in it as her health had deteriorated so suddenly that she was too weak for it as soon as she had received it. A wheelchair was for half-disabled young people with plenty of strength in their upper body and limbs, and Mother felt that she was depriving one of them while it lay unused under the stairs. Dr. Sommerfield came around twice a week now and still the test had shown nothing that he understood or had seen before.

He put it down to some rare blood disease. Mother was deteriorating at an alarming pace and already was refusing solid food. Only a few sips of soup or tea were all she could manage. She was never told of Merry's plight and the baby which grew inside her. In fact, Mother barely stayed awake these days. She was sedated so heavily that she seldom understood when spoken to or even recognized who entered her room. Molly had to grow up fast at this sad time. She understood that all of Aunt Maud's time was already taken up by Mother.

Molly arranged to go on the usual visit to the Sanitarium by herself for the first time.

The months were moving quickly and with them, Merry's baby was kicking and moving around. Merry's time was nearing. But what was to become of it? What would become of Merry? Would she accept she had to give it up? All devastating questions, but the answers would wait for another day. Both girls would be 18years old by the time the baby was born. Would Merry be allowed to keep it? She would be moving to the Sanitarium for the Mentally Insane as she would be a young woman by then.

Molly was increasingly worried, because if Merry was not allowed to keep the baby, would she ever recover?

These thoughts emblazoned Molly's mind every day of her life. Molly asked to speak with Miss Simpson about the matter, and Matron agreed to have a word with the Governor of the Sanitarium and promised to explain the whole circumstance in full. She left feeling a little lighter in her heart. She shouted good-bye to Merry from the end of the corridor. Merry's friend Robin was by her side, they were holding hands like children of their own little lost world do. Molly promised herself on the journey home that she would visit Merry next week.

But that visit never took place because Mother had taken a bad turn during the night and gone into semi-consciousness. Dr. Sommerfield arrived and explained to the family that Mother's time on earth was very limited now, and that she was gently drifting away. Molly felt heartbroken, and she cried all that night. On waking the following morning she was almost scared to ask if Mother was still alive. The vicar arrived for a brief visit with her mother, and they whispered prayer.

Spring was almost gone now, and the view from the attic window was changing. The buds on the trees were turning into green, vibrant leaves, shiny in their newness. There was a smell of apple blossom in the air, a fresh new and alive smell. That was smell which lingered in Molly's mind always because that was the day Mother passed away. She was a young woman, beautiful in her naturalness with everything to live for.

The day of the funeral arrived. Mother had been tended to in her bedroom; she did not go to the chapel of rest, both Molly and her father wanted her to stay at home until the final day of her funeral arrived. Whilst mother lay in her coffin, the lid was placed on the top, but not screwed down so that whoever wanted a last look could do so, but not Molly. She wanted to remember Mother as she was, busy in the kitchen scolding herself, laying the Christmas dinner, helping Aunt Maud set the table; just being herself. Yes it was the day of the funeral.

Aunt Maud was there waiting with Molly and her father, and the vicar was in the middle of a prayer, then he began to read the Lord's prayer out loud, but there was a noisy commotion coming from upstairs and a great bang, bang, bang in unison coming down the stairs, almost like a light infantry charge, but eerie. It was the coffin bearers in heavy shoes carrying Mother on her last journey from her home and beloved family. The noise was deafening, it was harsh and hollow, as the great, heavy boots echoed on the cheap, thin carpet covering the stairs.

Through the noise, the vicar carried on with the prayer.

He gestured for the small congregation to follow him to the front door. Molly wore black, her head bowed; she followed her Aunt Maud to the waiting taxis. There were two only, one for immediate family, and one for Dr. Sommerfield and his wife. Neighbours were out to pay their last respects. The solemn cortege started on its way to the family church. They drove up the hill, all cars stopped at the perimeter of the church wall; the six coffin bearers got out and carried the coffin up to the church. The trees wore their Irish coat of emerald green; only a few branches poked through, demanding their garland of leaves. The last of the spring flowers were exuberant in their daffodil yellow, pansy pink and purples

The whole churchyard was aglow with life, life of a spiritual kind, life which goes on forever, and Mother was going to that life. Molly and her relatives and close friends followed the coffin up the path and into the church. The choir was there in purple and white robes, they lead the singing and the whole church echoed the songs of angels.

After paying a tribute to Mother, the vicar lead the way out with his attendants and helpers following and the six coffin bearers carrying Mother to her final resting place—a beautiful, shady little place behind the church looked over by a huge beech tree. It was angelic and beautiful, and the sun peeped in to make its presence known.

They said a prayer, and Mother was lowered to her grave. Molly, Father and Aunt Maud threw a red carnation each and a handful of soil to help mother on her way to the everlasting. The peace and tranquility, the harmony of the birds singing and the closeness and peace the event brought to all who attended, was inspiring and took away all sadness and guilt for the newly bereft. The little group made their way to the church hall where all mourners were asked to attend for light refreshments. Father stopped behind a little longer with some precious words for Mother. Head bowed and hands clasped, he looked a solitary figure.

The mourners had tea and scones and spoke in whispered voices of how very nice the funeral had been. They did not stop long; the little family group joined the taxis and were back home almost as soon as they left. Aunt Maud had prepared a light lunch for their return, but no one was hungry. Father got out his brandy and offered a glass all round. They all accepted a stiff drink was just what the doctor ordered and he did. After a few more well-deserved drinks, Aunt Maud decided to go home to her own bed that night, her help was no longer needed, and there was a vacuum in her life now. Molly went to bed herself and left Father with his brandy. She alone, knew the guilt he was carrying and that bottle of brandy would not help.

Tomorrow, Molly promised herself, she would go and see Merry and explain her mother's death.

Chapter Four

IT WAS DIFFICULT FOR Molly to find sleep that night; she tossed and turned her way through the night, finding no comfort or solace in the safety of the attic sanctuary. What Molly needed, more than anything else in the world was the feeling of Merry's body and hers entwined in their grief. Molly felt a terrible loneliness, an unbearable, desperate isolation, one which would never be fulfilled if the girls were to live apart: it would be a half life, unnatural, unfeeling, resentful—no man could fill the gap. There were so many things to be sorted out, so much growing up overnight. Molly had a creeping suspicion that Aunt Maud would come round less and less now. After all she had given up her time to see to Mother these last few months, and she too needed time to herself to rethink and recollect. Molly looked out from the attic window, and thought of all the change that had taken place from the very first time the girls were old enough to appreciate their precious attic bedroom, Merry's sanctuary. There would be a lot more change to come.

There was a general air of sadness and emptiness around the house that morning when Molly went down for breakfast. There was no one in the kitchen, the fire was not lit, no smiling faces to hurry Molly up, no one to check what she was wearing, no one to answer to—no one at all. The whole house was in desolate and empty. Molly skipped breakfast and decided to walk a little before calling round for her Aunt, then breaking the bad news to Merry. Everything outside her home remained unchanged, people were still walking their dogs; Shop keepers were selling their wares, paper boys delivering their papers, lovers holding hands.

Did no one know, or care about Molly's great loss? Life was still going on, and everyone seemed happy and cheerful. Why did this have to happen to me? She felt a furious feeling rise in, she wanted to stop the world and tell everyone to stop laughing and smiling and feel deep despair with her. But life goes on. The feeling of utter and complete bitterness coupled with hatred of the whole human race, enveloped Molly and gripped tightly to her person and would not let go, not at the moment.

How could people be so uncaring? Something which seemed so important to Molly; and brought such deep feelings of hurt inside her, seemed to have no effect on everyone else. Molly felt worse rather than better after her short walk. She hated the world for its insensitivity. She was almost at her Aunt's path. Hers was the best in garden in the neighbourhood.

She had lots and lots of roses in the garden, in hanging baskets, in flowerpots, clinging up the walls, and some were just trying to bud, the scents of the roses brought Molly quicker and closer to Aunt Maud's and a feeling of belonging gripped her. Her Aunt's house was little. It was a very charming little bungalow, but it was cozy and warm and full of old world charm. She had an open log fire and great candle sticks on the mantelpiece along with photographs of all the family and a very precious one of Molly and Merry when only two, right there, right in the middle, taking pride of place. Molly was already feeling more secure and safe. Aunt Maud greeted her and bristled past in her usual cheerful way. She too, felt hurt and sad, but had been through it all before with her husband, who died mysteriously and suddenly after only two years of married bliss.

Aunty to this day has not got over it and still has little tear attacks when she remembers him. Molly on the other hand cannot remember him at all the twins were very young when he passed away. Aunt Maud was used to grief. She had taken on the burden of all the financial and emotional problems on her shoulders from that day on. Molly took off her coat and sat, by the log fire, its glow warmed her face and seemed to warm the hurt feelings gently from her heart and allow her to mellow a little. She thought nice thoughts now. She remembered how Mother suffered in the last few months and knew she was at peace now and it was for the best. But, would Merry understand? What lasting effect would it have on her? Should she be told in her present state of pregnancy? So many questions, each question would be asked only after long discussions and decisions with Aunt Maud and Matron. Molly dared not to think of the consequences of the answers to those questions and the irreparable damage even one question could do.

Aunt Maud was a kindly person; she gave Molly a cuddle which said it all: I am here; I will go through it with you, lean on me. She sat in the armchair opposite and sipped her cocoa with Molly. They had little to say as the thoughts of yesterday were still firmly implanted in their minds. There was a knock on the door. It was the postman with a little package for Aunt Maud, who must have known what it was, because she didn't open it but left it on the mantelpiece amid the photos and trinkets and treasures.

"We'll set off now Molly" said Aunt Maud gravely. She nodded a nod of reassurance, "We'll get through it, and we'll be fine, all three of us, or should I say four, including the baby," she smiled and Molly joined in. Aunt Maud thrust her hand in Molly's and together with the strength of one another they prepared for the hardest visit they had ever had at the Sanitarium.

They boarded the train as usual, the carriage was silent, with each one lost in their own thoughts. The train hurtled its way towards the home and the occupants of the middle carriage wished for a bit more time to sort out the right words to say, but time waits for no man and there they were with Matron waiting for Merry to appear.

Matron was subdued and certainly understanding after gaining knowledge as to what the family had gone through. She knew what traumas had happened in the recent months, and she was deep in the knowledge that their journey along that path was far from ending.

Merry overheard them talking from the hall, and she ran to them with outstretched arms and cuddled both of them together. She was happy and gushing with things to say and looking so happy and content with her little world that it took the two visitors quite by surprise. This was no longer the withdrawn, sad Merry, but almost a transformation, bubbling in her approach to life and her visitors.

She took command, acted on their surprise and ushered them protesting into her little room. Merry's room seemed brighter that day; the sun was shining in through the branches of the beech trees. Merry had been taught embroidery and sewing but up until now had no interest in it at all. But to Aunt Maud and Molly's surprise and delight, she had made two colourful cushions which were proudly laid on her bed with the teddies. Apparently Matron and two of the nurses had helped her make the curtains to match and the room was looking more comfortable and lived in now than it ever had before.

Merry was also learning to knit and Molly noticed that she had started by knitting little white booties. Molly was not sure that this was a good idea, because no one at this stage knew whether or not Merry could keep her baby, especially when she was moved to the Sanitarium for the Criminally Insane. The two visitors sat and listened to Merry telling all her stories, feeling relaxed and happy, and neither one could bring herself to tell Merry of the bad news they carried. Merry's condition was one of ultimate highs and devastating lows.

They both agreed by eye contact that their news should wait until a more appropriate time. Merry asked after all the family, Father, Grandmother, she faltered a little before she asked if Mother was better and when was she was coming to see her. Molly felt vexed; Merry was like a little girl. She too loved Mother, and they both lied to Merry, something they felt neither justified in doing nor happy about, but they did lie, for her own good, for now. A few words of reassurance were all Merry needed, and she quickly switched the conversation back to Robin. Her face lit up, Robin had been doing art and was very good. Merry reached under the bed and brought out an oil painting. It had been done by Robin, and was his very first one. He had wanted Merry to have it.

It was the little church which Merry had described to him that Mother used to take them to when they were very little; it was in fact the church the girls had been christened in and the church in which Mother and Father had been married, and ultimately the church in which Mother was now lying buried. Aunt Maud questioned the flowers and the tombstones in the front of the church, but Merry was quick to respond that Robin had not seen the church and had done the painting only on Merry's mind's eye picture, and it had been such a long, long, time since Merry was home, that she too, had almost forgotten.

Aunt Maud felt saddened. She knew Merry was indirectly asking to come home for a short vacation, Aunt Maud, held Merry close to her, "I know you want to be at home love, and we want you too, but the baby is due soon and you must stay here.

We don't want anything to happen to you, and I promise, as soon as baby arrives and you are strong enough, I will come for you." Aunt Maud meant every word, she held Merry close, and Molly joined in too.

Merry bubbled with an effervescence rarely seen in her before, perhaps it was the strain and pressure being lifted forever, on the removal of the two abusive male nurses, or perhaps, and probably more so the arrival of her baby soon.

Molly was terrified to think of the consequences if Merry was not allowed to keep the baby. Still, that was a worry for another day. It was time to go. Molly felt really quite happy when leaving the home. They had gone with a heavy heart, and Merry had lifted their burden with her sparkling personality. For the first time in her life Merry was completely normal, outgoing and exuberant. How momentarily happy it had made her visitors, but with a sadness too that the vital news they brought, had gone back with them untold.

Molly knew too, as the time passed it would become harder and harder to break this heartache. But on a happier note, Merry was doing fine.

"Goodbye Merry, take care." Molly was first to kiss her.

Aunt Maud put her arms around her. "You'll be home soon, my darling, I'll come for you."

Matron too, seemed to see the difference in Merry these last few weeks. She had an inner glow and outward composure, especially stored up for heavily pregnant ladies. The train arrived and all boarded, Aunt Maud had her usual sleep and Molly watched field after field swish past, surveying everyone going about their daily chores oblivious to the passing steam horse, on its journey to wherever. Molly never did get to know the end of the line, or even wanted to.

They reached their station and Molly gave Aunt Maud a little nudge, she awoke, and collected her things, and they got off feeling mixed emotions of happiness for Merry and Robin and deep hurt of their recent bereavement. They walked together, hardly talking, Aunt Maud branched off for her own home, and Molly walked on towards hers. She opened the front door, Father was home alone; he had not gone to work that day.

"How was Merry? Is she coping with the baby and all?" He questioned Molly.

"She's happier and brighter than I've ever seen her, but we didn't mention mother to her yet." Molly answered. "Not until after the baby is born."

"Wise decision Molly, I'm glad," he put his head back in his hands.

Father looked sad and lonely, the house was quiet and creepy, the furniture was starved of attention and the dust was quickly forming, as the little bit of sunshine peeped in through the windows showing every speck. It missed Aunt Maud's maternal touch of good housekeeping. Molly had no interest in housekeeping and neither had her father, especially now.

Slowly the family which had been so happy only a few years ago was becoming less and less like a family and more like solitary individuals grasping at straws on the remnants of life. Molly decided at that moment that as soon as she reached nineteen she would move away and make a new life for herself. Father slowly dragged his feet across the room towards the brandy cabinet and took out a bottle. He placed it on the table and sat looking at it through transparent eyes filled with tears. "Just one glass," he promised Molly, but she had heard that before.

She left Father to drown his sorrows and took refuge in Mother's room.

Mother's tablets were still there on the side table, her embroidery only half done, with some petals and leaves waiting the finishing touches, lay on her bed. Towards the end Mother could not hold a needle or even see properly to finish the work, but she got a little pleasure in admiring what she had accomplished before the slow, living death took over. The room was untouched, it looked as if Mother had just gone to freshen up, or answer a phone or doorbell; the room oozed her presence. The curtains were still closed; Molly crossed the room and drew them apart letting the sunshine stream in.

She tidied Mother's bed and put the tablets in the drawer. The clock on the mantelpiece ticked so loudly it almost called out every second in unison with Big Ben.

Molly sat motionless remembering the lovely, giggling moments when she and Merry bounced in on Mother and Father in the mornings when they were small and how Mother loved to be awakened by her two lovely daughters, here on this very bed, the same bed where Mother had died only three days before. Molly was finding the death hard to deal with.

If only Merry was strong enough to carry the burden with her, how she needed Merry to comfort her at that moment. She looked around the room, Mother's silk nightdress was laid over the chair; her favourite hairbrush was on the dressing table beside identical photographs of the girls, right through their lives. There was one of Mother and Father on their wedding day, how handsome they looked and so in love. Mother's pearls lay across her jewel box; she was wearing them the day she died. Molly held them close to her breast for comfort, she pressed Mother's nightdress to her face; she could still smell the smell of her Mother on it coupled with the sweet smell of lavender, it smelled safe and comforting, as safe as when she asked Mother to tenderly care for a bruised knee or a hurt feeling.

Molly felt Mother's presence all around the room. It made her heady with the allure of everlasting safety, like being inside the womb, solitary, apart from Merry. She could see the apple blossom tree from Mother's bedroom window; the flowers were fading and being taken over by green leaves awaiting the full thrust of summer. Molly felt tranquil in that atmosphere and decided to enter the room every time she missed Mother or felt sad. It gave her the strength to carry on with the sweetness of lavender and apple blossom. She closed the door on the tranquility of sweet serenity and joined her father downstairs. He was already half way through that bottle of brandy.

"Father you have had enough for one day," was Molly's retort and with that she walked over to him, but Father did not hear or feel her presence, or wanted to. Tonight he wanted to be incoherent with his deep loss and with the bleak existence to follow. Molly realized and let him be. She sank into the big armchair and slowly returned her thoughts to Simon; it seemed so long since she had seen him. Had Simon got to know about Molly's sad loss? But surely someone would have told him. There had been no message or sympathy card from Simon which seemed very unusual. Molly again, felt lost and alone, Father had slumped over the table. Molly put an old shawl over his shoulders and left him in his grief. She decided to make her way to Aunt Maud's and pick some early roses from her garden to arrange in Mother's room and make it more pleasant; she was careful to let Aunt Maud know her intentions first and popped her head in Aunt Maud's front room to explain.

Aunt Maud nodded in agreement, "It's a nice thought Molly," she said "there are only a few buds on at the moment; it is a bit soon for roses." But Molly was determined and set to work in the garden choosing only the ones about to flower. She picked two bunches, one for Mother's room and one for Mother's grave. She would walk up the hill to the church and the graveyard tomorrow.

Aunt Maud was baking in the kitchen; keeping herself busy and her mind off the current events.

Some scones and cakes were cooling on the work tops, the smell was appetizing and mouth watering. Molly had not eaten all day; she was delirious with the enticing aromas. She was glad too of Aunt Maud's company and the two got comfort from each other. They chatted lightly and Molly helped by taking the freshly baked cakes and pies from the oven for her aunt when ready.

She got herself comfortable on the dining chair and placed herself a plate and a knife ready to sample the delicacies. "Wash your hands before you begin," called Aunt Maud in annoyance. Molly looked guilty and obeyed. Why had Aunt Maud made so many scones, cakes and pies? She was the only one there. Molly knew the reason; it was to occupy her mind to stop it drifting away in sadness. They both had tea and savoured the home made delights. Molly was full. They retired to the living room and listened to the radio for a while, both calm in their grief. Molly did not want to go home. She told Aunt Maud of Father being drunk and asleep. Aunt Maud agreed to walk back with Molly and ask if Molly could stay the night at her aunt's. They could look in on her father and make sure he was alright. By the time they reached Father's house it was evening; there was no lights on, and Molly grew concerned.

They entered apprehensively; Father's empty brandy bottle was upturned and lying on its side on the table. Molly went upstairs and heard sobbing coming from Mother's room. She peeped in and Father was laid across her bed, face down; so overfilled with grief that Molly dared not enter. She gently closed the door and motioned to Aunt Maud that they had better leave, he would probably drift off to sleep where he was, so there was no immediate worry and he could console himself in the feeling of nearness to his beloved wife.

Aunt Maud and Molly were weary with all the trundling up and down they had done today, so after a quick coffee they too both retired. Molly quickly drifted off to sleep exhausted from the jam packed day she had endured. Aunt Maud peeped in to say goodnight but Molly was already asleep. Aunt Maud smiled to herself and wished she could now look after the two girls, each with their own individual problems.

The soft scent of roses glided around the room at the breaking of dawn, the early morning mist was mingling with the first of the blossoms and creating a perfume any French Perfume House would envy.

Molly felt refreshed and happier today with an inner strength she never thought she would ever regain. Today she would visit the little church and Mother's grave. She had forgotten to put the roses in water, and they were droopy and used, so she would pick some fresh ones, and Aunt Maud would not object. After breakfast, she went out into the garden and picked her roses and set off for the church yard. As she climbed the hill she saw a figure standing in the graveyard, she could not make out the outline from where she was but on climbing several feet further on it was obvious it was Simon.

Molly felt a surge of emotion shoot through her like an electric shock. For the first time in days, apart from her joyous meeting with Merry, she felt happy, how glad she was to see Simon and to find out that he had made the journey to the graveyard on his own to wish Mother a safe and peaceful journey to the next world. He had scarcely met her mother but admired and respected her as Molly did. Molly approached the archway on the wall surrounding the church yard and graveyard.

Simon spun round, he had seen her for the first time, he ran towards her, held her in a deep caring embrace as if never to let go again. "My poor baby" he uttered, "I have been away on a course and have only found out this morning. I am deeply sorry." Molly touched his lips with shaky fingers as if to silence his sorrow and looked over his shoulder to see the fresh primroses and pansies placed on Mother's grave.

She moved closer, a little note was attached, and it read: "With my deepest sympathy and regret for not knowing you better, Simon." These few words touched Molly and for the first time since her Mother's funeral she broke down and cried. Simon held her and kept saying, "Let it out." They sat together after Molly had regained herself, just looking and pondering and feeling sadness shared; something Molly had to bear alone up until now. She told Simon of her father's grief and how she was afraid he may drink forever. Simon reassured Molly. "It's only a temporary setback, after he has got over his grief a little more he will return to normal."

He thought it was a good idea to accompany Molly to talk to her father and also that Molly should stay with Aunt Maud for a few weeks for a woman's company or at least until things settled down a bit. Father would be O.K. as soon as he got himself back to work. Molly placed her roses next to Simons. The pair left the churchyard solitary in their togetherness, still holding each other as if their very own lives depended on it. They both saw Father that evening and explained that Molly would stop with Aunt Maud for a few weeks for company as Father worked so many late nights. Father agreed reluctantly.

Molly collected a few of her things and also for extra closeness brought along Merry's teddy with the broken ear. Simon carried her few belongings and Molly carried the teddy. Aunt Maud was in the garden tending her prized flowers and shrubs, but she was pleased to see Simon with Molly and knew that he would help her through this most difficult time of her life. They greeted each other locked in the sadness and happiness too, that everyday grief would start to diminish and great fond memories would be left for everyone. Molly decided to return to school the next day.

Both Simon and Aunt Maud thought it a good idea. Aunt Maud was becoming a close friend with Simon and asked him to stop to tea. This was the first encouragement that Simon had received.

Molly was almost nineteen years old now and her twin sister was about to become a mother soon. Even throughout all the upsets Aunt Maud was in continuous contact with the home and making sure that Merry was in good hands and monitoring her progress. A month had passed and it was time to visit Merry again, Molly went on her own, she had begun to get over her bereavement a little more. Aunt Maud had helped and the two had grown closer than they had ever been. Aunt Maud was enjoying the freshness of Molly, and together they were both getting slowly back to normal. Simon too; became a frequent visitor to Aunt Maud's little home. He often helped dig in the garden and did all the heavy-duty chores which was a luxury for Aunt Maud, as she had never had a man's help before.

Molly's thoughts were interrupted by the whistling noise of the train as it rambled on its way to the station, where there were only a handful of people waiting to board.

The Station Master was putting his mail in the sack, ready for the morning pick up, and the young porter was busying himself around the office issuing tickets. Molly had never really noticed all the hustle and bustle of a busy station before.

Perhaps she was always preoccupied in anticipation of Merry's mood, which would become difficult just before a visit. Now Molly was more complacent as Merry's moods had changed dramatically, and Molly was always pleased to see more progress in her. She wasn't to be disappointed this time either. Molly had just gone through the large gates at the beginning of the driveway entrance when Merry waddled down to take her hand and greet her with a kiss on the cheek. Merry was huge now, and the girls giggled about it being twins just as they were. Merry was ecstatic in her motherhood and could not wait to drag Molly to her room to show off all the baby garments and knitting she had done. Merry certainly was picking things up at an alarming rate.

Even Molly who was always good at handicrafts could not have done any of those intricate things unaided. The girls chatted incessantly, giggling and hugging; they were closer now because of Merry's baby.

Merry had only a month to wait and she was waiting very excitedly. Molly still had not heard from the Governor of the Sanitarium whether or not Merry would be allowed to keep the baby when she was moved there soon. They spent a pleasant two hours together that afternoon.

Molly was deep in thought when Merry, kissing her on the cheek, brought her back to the present. "Oh its good-bye time already." Molly returned the kiss, said her good-byes and left for Matron's office on her way out.

"I'm sorry to trouble you, Miss Simpson, but it's about Merry's baby. Will she be allowed to keep it or not, and have you found out anything yet?" Molly waited for the reply with anxiety, The Matron had a smile on her face, "Don't look so worried, dear," she said I have been in touch with the Sanitarium, and if the mothers are capable, the babies are with them until they are 12 months old.

That will give Merry time to readjust and, who knows, if she continues to make progress as she has been doing then she may be able to leave after that time with her baby—if not to go home with you, then to go to a somewhat less strict place." Molly was reassured and left that day with a spring in her step, almost kissing everyone on the way out. It was summertime already and all of Aunt Maud's blooms were radiant and perfumed. Father had started to come over more often and had met Simon and was growing to like him as Molly did.

Aunt Maud was always busy and loved doing things like baking and preparing meals for the young people. She really had some meaning to her life now and enjoyed every minute. Father too was full of summer and gone was the gaunt death-like look. It was replaced by the smiling face of a new man, one could almost resemble it to a man in love, but Molly thought no more on those lines. He had never gone to the home to visit Merry, but he had made a fuss of her on her visits home instead—he could not bear to see her institutionalized.

He was going on the next visit with Molly, it would be in a few days and they would stay at the home in preparation for the forthcoming event, the birth of Merry's baby.

Everyone was on red alert as the day grew closer; Molly was very excited and looked forward to being an aunt. Aunt Maud hardly savoured the idea of being a great aunt, she was much too young. She smiled as she said it, and the great bulk around her person shook like jelly. Only a few months ago, this very same family was in the depths of despair. Life was good to them all at the moment, and they felt the need for some good news, and what better news than the birth of some fresh blood into the family. Molly was joyous at the sparkle in Merry's eyes and the love for the unborn child within her. Molly saddened a little remembering that after the birth

Merry would have to be told about mother. She had only occasionally asked questions about her mother but was satisfied that mother was ill, but would come to see her when she got better. That was in the future, the present was now and the delight flowed through all their veins.

School went well that day, Simon walked Molly home to Aunt Maud's, instead of leaving her at the gate as he had done so many times before when Molly lived at home, he walked in with her, but not before he picked a red rose from Aunt Maud's garden. When entering the little front room, he bowed to Aunt Maud and presented the rose to her from between his teeth, he leaned forward, clicked his heels and presented the highly perfumed flower to the old lady with the words, "the most loving lady in the area," and he bent further down and kissed Aunt Maud on the cheek. She beamed all over; she loved him being frivolous; it made her feel young and desirable. She knew of course that Simon was full of impishness and always tried to make her blush. She liked him a lot and loved to bake scones for him on his way home from the College.

Today was no exception; the kitchen table was full of all sorts of goodies, to tempt the most discerning palette. There were jam tarts, Victoria sandwiches, scones of every variety, but pride of place was Simon's favorite, chocolate cream fudge. He just loved it and took most of it for College break next day. Molly saw him out and both women laughed as he leapt over the garden gate nearly catching his trousers. "He's such a showoff," smiled Aunt Maud, "But I just love him coming over." Next day Dr. Sommerfield sent round a messenger informing the two women that Merry had started in labour, and that he was aiding in the birth.

Merry was sitting in a wheelchair waiting to be taken to an awaiting ambulance which escorted her to the new, modern wing of the Brisbank Maternity Home. Merry's pains were coming every five minutes; she was in good hands in the ambulance and Dr. Sommerfield waited for her on the hospital steps. The ambulance arrived at its destination and its precious cargo was placed into the capable protection of Dr. Sommerfield, who wheeled her up the corridor and into a small, private ward, the waiting ward the doctors called it. The pains had to be coming every three minutes before the precious delivery room was occupied, as the hospital was quite poorly equipped and lacked amenities, the main one being the scarcity of labour wards.

Some babies came sooner than ever expected and never saw the labour wards. A junior doctor came in and told her to get undressed and put on the hospital nightgown lying on the chair. Then the midwife came in and introduced herself, "It's you and me kid."

She joked with Merry and helped her undress, and change, whilst the junior doctor made his rounds of the other ladies, taking their blood pressure and blood tests, and the things junior doctors do on these occasions. The midwife timed Merry's pains, they were coming every three minutes now, and she rang the nurse bell. The young nurse appeared in seconds in the doorway, "Tell Dr. Sommerfield Merry's pains are every three minutes, and tell the auxiliaries to open the door in the labour ward, we're on our way," the nurse nodded and ran.

Dr. Sommerfield came in just as the midwife was getting Merry on to the trolley to take her to the labour ward. "Hold it a minute Nurse, I'll give her some relaxants to calm her and dull the pains." They quickly got her into the labour ward and on to the bed. Her pains were coming hard and fast now. Dr. Sommerfield held the gas and air mask to Merry's face, "Don't panic Merry just relax and breathe in deep breaths. Merry obeyed; the tears from sheer exhaustion and pain, slid down her cheeks and on to the soft pillow behind her head. "You're doing well my dear," said Dr. Sommerfield between pains. "Your baby will be born soon." It was quite a trauma for a young disturbed woman, with no experience in the outside world, but Merry was coping fine with the help of the kindly doctor.

Molly, Aunt Maud and Father arrived and were told to wait in the room provided for the anxious visitors. Father was quite neurotic and vividly remembered the night the twins had come into the world, as if it were happening now. He rung his hands continuously and paced the floor. Aunt Maud asked him to stop as she too was nervous enough to start with. The wait seemed endless, coffee was brought for the little party, and the nurses were reassuring and kindly. A few hours had passed and still nothing happened. All the nurses and doctors at the hospital bustled about their business and were quite unaware of the anxiousness surrounding the little group. But of course it was an everyday occurrence for them and nothing particularly spectacular. One of the nurses came running out of the labour ward, the one where Merry was, and ran down the corridor to the medical room. She came rushing back with an object packed in a white bag sealed at both ends. There seemed to be some sort of hysteria, pouring from the room, staff were running back and forth with all sorts of appliances and machines.

Something was seriously wrong. Then, just as it had started the commotion halted. Dr. Sommerfield emerged with a serious look on his face. Father anxiously asked, "Merry?"

"She's fine," the doctor replied. "The baby is a boy, but I'm afraid he's stillborn".

A dreadful feeling of death and despair engulfed the anxious family yet again in the space of a few months.

"And Merry, how is she now?" asked father again.

"She's sedated rather heavily; she knows nothing about the baby yet. She'll be taken to a private room upstairs and will sleep for many hours. A nurse will stay with her, and I will be at hand until she awakes to explain to Merry what has happened. The baby, of course will have to go to the hospital mortuary for a postmortem to tell us the cause of death. Merry will be asleep for about eight hours. I will appreciate it, Mr. Wentworth if you and Molly could be back here when she wakes up as the trauma might prove too much for her." Dr. Sommerfield spoke in whispers.

Father was distraught with grief for Merry, for her baby, his dearly beloved Elizabeth, and lastly for himself.

He reached for Molly's hand. They held each other and found the closeness they had lost in recent months Aunt Maud gave them both a reassuring touch on the shoulder, and with head bowed left the hospital and waited on the steps for them to follow. They walked together along the quiet corridors to the main exit. They joined Aunt Maud and silently went back to Aunt Maud's little cottage in disbelief at what they had just witnessed. It would have been bad enough if Merry was normal, but under the circumstances, no one knew or dared to think of the consequences. They arrived at the rose-clad cottage, the blooms were splendid and the perfume made the air heady. The sun had the cheek to show itself, just dawning and peeping through the clouds on its arrival on a new day. Aunt Maud made a pot of tea and offered some scones around, but no one was hungry. A knocking came to the door. Molly answered it—it was Simon with the biggest Teddy one could ever imagine.

"This is for Merry's baby, has she had it yet?" Molly dragged him in and sat him down next to father on the sofa.

"Merry's baby was born dead."

The silence was deafening and rumbled the whole room. Simon was, shocked. He laid the teddy on the floor next to his feet. Grief and sadness yet again enveloped the tiny room and its inhabitants and gripped them in complete disbelief. Aunt Maud poured the tea; they sipped it in silence, just waiting for a call to let them know Merry was coming to. They waited in silence for the next drama in the Wentworth family saga. The hours dragged and no one felt like talking. Simon too, who was always full of fun, could only sit and stare. The large grandfather clock in the hall was the only thing with voice, it chimed eleven o'clock, the day was well-aired by now, people were going about their business, and the streets near the market were full. The phone rang. It was as if a filing squad was in line and about to take aim and fire as every pair of eyes met the other.

They all got their belongings together. Simon decided to take the teddy bear for Merry as she had forgotten to take teddy Robin with her to the hospital or even the teddy with the torn ear.

They slowly made their way to Brisbank Maternity Home, a journey which was full of excitement and expectation yesterday, a journey which should have been a joyous occasion, now turned full circle with unbearable heartache. They climbed the stairs and walked along the corridor, their heels echoed the loneliness. They decided to wait for Dr. Sommerfield to join them, to give them that extra courage, and to find out if Merry knew and what her immediate response would be. The doctor was busy with some other visitors, but as soon as he spotted them, he came straight over.

"She hasn't awoken yet, I'll give her another few minutes more, and if she doesn't come round, I will give her something to arouse her." The wait of fifteen minutes seemed endless. Merry's door opened and a nurse motioned for Father and Molly only to enter, the other two sat back down.

They walked into the tiny, blank little room. It was dark; the blinds were still closed; a bedside lamp was the only light. Merry's bed was in the middle of the room, and a drip was attached to her wrist. She looked pale and child-like.

She moved a little and opened her eyes, "Father," she whispered. Father bent down and kissed her on the forehead. Molly sat on the side of the bed and held Merry's other hand, the one not tangled in wires and tubes. Merry managed a smile in response. Father asked Merry if Dr. Sommerfield had spoken to her yet. She nodded a slow, deliberate nod that showed all the feeling of hurt that no words could describe. No one spoke. The silence said it all.

Just at that moment a nurse burst in, "You have another visitor Merry, a special one." In came Robin with two male, assistants from the, home. He just waddled in as retarded children do, straight past everyone without a word and put a great, big smacker on Merry quite clumsily, but this brought a smile to Merry's eyes. She sat up and cuddled Robin—just two children close in their backwardness and their grief. It was very sad, and Molly had to fight back tears. Father could not be so strong. He constantly brushed tears from his face. Molly turned her head and blew her nose. The children just hugged forever.

Their vocabulary did not run to great words of wisdom, only their clumsy, deliberate, little actions, showed the deepest love, innocent in its ignorance. Father and Molly left them for a few minutes; the assistants too were moved and waited outside the door. Apparently everyone at the home was disappointed and were all looking forward to the baby, as very few events like that ever happened there and retarded children seemed to show a love normal people had forgotten. They especially had the knack of being gentle with babies, almost as a huge female gorilla will crush branches of shrubbery in her great jaws then gently pick up and cuddle her baby in a maternal manner, which some humans could learn from.

The small family had clustered together to relay the recent news and to plan for the future. Father said that Merry must have some incentive to get over her great loss and at that moment decided to have Merry home and tiresome as she may be, try to cope with her. Aunt Maud too, would help and of course, the best help of all would be Molly. Molly could give more support and encouragement than anyone. Robin would be allowed to visit, or if the home objected, the twins and Father would visit him. They would make these outings very special, and Merry would look her best for Robin.

They all agreed that would be the answer. Simon still clutched the large teddy bear and wanted to see Merry and offer his gift. The little group was more than enthusiastic now as they had a little lightness to offer Merry, something for which she could grow strong. Robin came out smiling with the two assistants. He shuffled along the corridor swaying from side to side as imbalanced children do, since they have no thought or concept of vanity or outward appearance but act in a way which suits them, a kind of innocence normal people would have lost in mid-childhood.

Not a word to the family, just gave a blank stare; he had done and seen what he wanted, which was to cheer up Merry, his precious friend. Dr. Sommerfield joined the family, who were all allowed in the room this time. Merry was sitting up now and seemed more at ease. They all sat round the bed.

The room was still dark and overcrowded, and they slowly spoke of their plans, careful not to upset Merry in any way. Merry was listening, but in a dazed fashion, then she spotted the huge teddy bear. She pointed to it, she stretched out her arms for it, and Simon handed it over. As he did, the teddy bear's great, big leg pushed Molly off her chair.

This broke the ice, and everyone spoke normally. Whether the tragedy had not sunk in, or Merry understood, no one knew, but she seemed to take the event and the trauma very well indeed. She called the teddy

Robbie, cuddled it frantically and said she would like to be home for her birthday—she had understood some of the conversation. Father sighed; a sigh of imprisoned relief. Dr. Sommerfield popped his head round the door, "Can I have a word with you Mr. Wentworth, please, in private," he looked more serious. The two left the room and the youngsters to talk and cheer each other in their sorrow. Dr. Sommerfield explained that the baby would have to be christened by a vicar straight away, and a funeral service would have to be sorted out in the next few days after the post mortem. The baby would have to be named.

Father grew pale, "I'm afraid to ask her for a name now, I could set her right back to her original state of nothingness and Dr. Sommerfield don't forget she still does not know about her mother's death." This was a grave situation that even the strongest person would have trouble enduring. Mr. Wentworth assured the doctor he would speak to Merry tomorrow when he felt things would be more stable. As he approached Merry's room, he heard little sweeps of giggles and felt sure the youngsters were helping each other through their troubles. He entered and donned a false smile so as not to alert the little group of the seriousness of all the legalities.

Chapter Five

THE BELL RANG FOR the visitors to leave, but the senior nurse gave Merry's family a special concession in view of the circumstances. Everyone was relieved as they did not want to leave Merry on her own now. They stopped another half hour chatting away, never bringing up the subject of the newborn child. Merry gripped her new teddy which she had named Robbie. She called the other one Robbie too, everything was Robbie to Merry, but what the heck, it was her choice anyway. She had not put the teddy down since she was given him. It seemed to fill a need in her and comfort her in a way no one else could. Perhaps she felt safe just by holding him.

The gathering was quickly broken up by the ward nurse administering Merry's sleeping tablets to her and signaling to the others to leave; and as Merry became drowsy the family left. They walked quietly from the hospital all deep in their own thoughts. Only Simon ventured to make any sort of contact by putting his arm around Molly. His gesture was gratefully accepted as she needed love and protection. She also, felt vulnerable from time to time.

They stopped outside Maud's front gate, Father waved goodnight and went off alone to his own house. The others went into Maud's and sat down in the tiny lounge. Each were exhausted in an emotional way; tea was made, and the small family unit discussed a way to have Merry home, completely forgetting how violent and obstinate Merry could be, especially after being told what to do, or not getting her own way. They all knew that Father had discussed the funeral arrangements with Dr. Sommerfield, but as Father had not volunteered to mention the discussion, it was left until the morning when the situation, after a good nights sleep, would be easier to accept.

Aunt Maud drew up her great bulk and wished the courting couple goodnight, leaving them the privacy to discuss their own plans and exchange feelings. Molly told Simon he could sleep on the sofa for the night if he wished. He thanked her and said he would. This made Molly feel much better. They just sat together on the sofa, held in their embrace, and thought about Merry.

Simon nodded off to sleep so Molly threw a blanket over him and went to bed herself. Sleep came over her right away; she was exhausted and emotionally stressed out. Aunt Maud was up early the following morning slipping across the hallway so as not to awaken Simon too early. She disappeared into the kitchen and got on with breakfast. The aroma of the smoked bacon, greeted Molly as she awoke, it reminded her of when her Mother was well and how welcoming Mother's smile had been every morning. Molly felt good until she remembered the previous day. She dressed and woke up Simon.

She was not going to school today, but, Simon having a position of responsibility had to go. He washed quickly scoffed the toast and bacon and left. Aunt Maud and Molly waited for her father, he had promised to come early in the morning, but it was past nine o clock already. Molly was growing more concerned, she could not help wondering how Merry, now out of sedation, was going to take the baby's death and also her mother's. They had to tell Merry, the baby would be buried alongside or on top of her mother, and there would be no more hiding it now.

What a cruel dilemma, Merry would not only feel sorrow for her baby and her mother, but also deceit would also come to light, mother had been dead for a while now. Father arrived sallow-faced, he made apologies for being late, and explained that he had visited Mother's grave and asked for her help in breaking the news to Merry, after placing a large bunch of mixed coloured roses in the memorial vase by her tombstone. He spoke to Aunt Maud and Molly and explained that arrangements were being made for the baby to be buried with his grandmother. They both left for the hospital, leaving Maud behind. The immediate family only, would be involved in this very sad episode.

On arriving at the hospital, they asked for Dr. Sommerfield who promised to be on hand in case sedation was needed urgently. Dr. Sommerfield came forward, the cause of death was asphyxia. The placenta was wrapped around the baby's neck twice and as he was being born, strangled him, stopping the oxygen from passing from mother to child and also, a little heart murmur may not have helped.

Father and Molly went in to Merry's tiny ward and sat by her bed; Merry was sitting up and looked less tired and drawn today. Father took her hand, "Merry we are very sorry about your baby. It is heartbreaking for all of us including Aunt Maud, but Dr. Sommerfield said it really was for the best in the end, as his heart was very weak, and he may not have lived long, and if he did, he would not be able to do all the things that the other children do." Merry understood; she was very brave; she nodded in agreement, still holding Teddy Robbie close to her. The only sign of emotion was a large, solitary tear, shining like a huge, white sapphire perfect in its shape of sorrow; which ran down her cheek, dripped from her chin, and landed on Teddy Robbie's ear.

She sat motionless as father continued, "Merry, we have to name your baby." Father was almost less than audible. Merry motioned to Teddy Robbie; she lifted it up and thrust it in Father's face. Was a tantrum about to begin? Father continued, "There is something else you must know Merry. Your mother died several months ago, we did not tell you as we were worried about your condition of pregnancy and of course, your baby." Father gave a deep sigh and awaited the reaction. Nothing:— not a glimmer of emotion. Merry just sat and rocked her teddy bear—back and forth, violently at first, then more gently, easing the pain. Then she started to chant and wail. Neither Father nor Molly knew what to do. They tried speaking to Merry but there was no reply, only this fearful wailing and moaning.

These sounds reminded them of women from developing countries, how they mourned their dead. It was very frightening and eerie. Merry would not respond in any way except for this reaction. They rang the bell, the nurse came within seconds.

"Call Dr. Sommerfield at once" was Father's direct order. Within minutes the old doctor was with them in the room. He could see that any sort of consoling would not be effective. He tried to calm Merry, but to no avail.

The doctor asked them both to leave; on the way out they explained that she now knew everything. The doctor told them to go home; he would take care of the situation. "I will sedate her again for a short while, and when she awakes I will be with her and try to talk to her again." The two left the hospital with mixed feelings.

On the one hand, they were relieved that at last their conscience was clear and Merry knew everything, but on the other, it had obviously been too much for her. But Dr. Sommerfield had told them she must know, he also said it would be better for her to deal with the double problem now rather than get over one problem and then to be told of another. Also, he felt that Merry should be there at the funeral of her baby to finalize what had happened and to enable her to deal with it in her mind. Otherwise the wise old doctor had told them she could fantasize, push it aside as if it had never happened, or worse still, if she ever got out of the home she could; turn to taking other peoples' babies.

All these alternatives had to be stamped out now. The treatment seemed ruthless but had to be done for Merry's sake. Whether Merry understood or not was another matter. Aunt Maud had seen the two from her window and was already waiting at the door for them, ringing her hands anxiously. She greeted them and maneuvered them to the kitchen table where there were hot scones and tea awaiting them.

"We broke the bad news about Mother to Merry at last; but whether it has sunk in or not; we really do not know. She seemed to take it badly, wailing and moaning," Said Father, adding, "We are calling the baby Robbie, after Merry's teddy bear, and I suppose also after Robin at the home. The baby is being buried with his grandmother in the next few days." Father sat down. "Dr. Sommerfield wants Merry to be present at the burial, but quite honestly I am against it. I will think about it tonight and perhaps have a word with the doctor in the morning."

There was no need. The phone rang early the following morning and it was Dr. Sommerfield advising Father that Merry was in no state to attend the baby's funeral. Apparently she had had a very bad tantrum during the night and scared the life out of one of the younger staff. The next couple of days seemed to drag. Merry had a constant stream of visitors to keep her mind off the event yet to take place, the event she had been excluded from.

The morning of the funeral arrived, and a car was sent for Aunt Maud. Molly would go in the first taxi with Father, Simon in the back with her aunt Because of the circumstances surrounding the baby's death and the silent plight Merry was going through; Father had decided not to push Merry for a name for the baby. He decided on her actions as she had pointed to the teddy bear Robbie when asked for a name. Molly sat in her bedroom that morning and gazed out on the world out of the attic window, wondering if the family's sorrow was coming to an end, if perhaps soon some happiness would return; a happiness which they sorely needed. Molly began to think of her mother, she felt she wanted to be close to her, so she went down to her mother's room.

It had not been slept in for weeks, and a musty dampness was present. She switched on the light, everything was as mother had left it; her nightdress still draped over the chair, her pearls on the jewelry box, only the sweet smell of Mother's lavender was missing. Molly reached in the drawer, she shook some of Mother's lavender around the room; it took away the musty smell and almost made the room come alive again. The fire was set for kindling, Molly decided to light it, and it was soon in full force. She sat on the chair and just watched the smoke from the fire rush up the chimney. She felt safe in that room.

She felt her mother's presence and the sweet feel of safety enveloped her. She sat there in the chair for what seemed like hours. The fire was calming down now and the ashes were dripping from the main log in a tired, exhausted sort of way. She almost dozed off, only the rain crashing against the window from the black, angry skies, full of temper, on their way to the ground, awoke her from near slumber.

She was interrupted by Father calling her to get ready. It was almost time to go. Molly dressed in sombre colours—grey and black. She heard a noise from downstairs; it was the funeral car bringing baby Robbie home for the first and last time. After the Funeral Director and his assistant left, Molly gripped all her courage, and went down to a sight to behold for even the hardest of beings. She could not bear it; a great ocean of the most volcanic sob surged through her body, and took all the strength away from her. She felt dizzy with grief, and utter solace took over her, as she found courage to get to the bottom of the stairs. For there at the bottom of the stairs, laid delicately on the reception table, was the smallest, white coffin Molly had ever seen or ever wanted to; it was so innocent, and it laid there in a reverent, holy way.

Only the little gold cross on the top broke up the whiteness and innocence of the little package. Molly walked to it in a daze; she leaned forward and kissed the cross. The tears were flowing from Molly as she gently ran her fingers along the line of the little box, her very first nephew, Robbie. She heard Father's footsteps as he entered the room. Molly adjusted herself and wiped away the tears. She would be strong for her father. Father beckoned to Molly to sit by him in the lounge. "I will carry the little coffin to the funeral car and then into the church. My very first grandchild, this will be the only chance I have to hold him." Father sobbed gently at first then all the bottled-up emotion flowed like a freed dam. His shoulders shook, and he was weakened by it all.

Molly poured him a brandy and one for herself too, "We will need more than this before the day is out Father," she said. Father looked tall and handsome in a distinguished way in his dark suit and black tie. They both sipped their brandies and held hands for comfort. The door opened and Aunt Maud was there. Her first sight on entering the house was the little coffin; she crossed herself, said a prayer, and kissed the little box. The funeral flowers were all around the house, but did nothing to cheer up the room or the little gathering.

"We have ten minutes to wait until the funeral directors return. Will you have a sherry Maud?"

"Yes." Was her eager reply; as he poured the sherry; and had another brandy himself. The funeral car and taxis arrived with the vicar. Molly let them in. A short prayer was said, and the little coffin was lifted by father and slowly taken to the waiting car. The neighbours were all around there to pay their last respects to a little person the world did not know or even had a chance to. Father placed the little coffin in the back, the funeral directors placed the flowers all around; there was one from Robin. It simply read; to my precious son, Daddy. The rain lashed in anger, everyone was soaked, but their grief had already soaked their souls, so no amount of water would do any damage.

As they took the bend, the little church came into view; it was misty around it, in a haunting way, darker, as the rain lashed so hard it cut holes in the pathway. The cars stopped. Father was first to get to the back of the hearse, the back hatch was opened for him, and he carefully lifted the little white coffin proudly and carried it with the gathering walking behind him, right into the church and placed it in the front where a special table was waiting. The church was full. Only the two front rows were empty waiting for the immediate family.

All sat, the vicar started the sermon. It was so sad none of the congregation were dry-eyed. As the service was ended, Father followed the vicar to the church yard carrying Robbie in his last little journey to be with his grandmother. Her grave was opened up, and the little coffin was lowered beside her. A prayer was said and a few little forget-me-nots were scattered onto Robbie, and final whispered good-byes echoed around the graveyard. Molly brought Merry's teddy with the torn ear; and placed it in the grave with the flowers, keeping Robbie safe on his final journey. It was, by this time, very muddy indeed, but no one noticed. They left the graveyard together and all got in the waiting cars. A very wet, rain-drenched figure stood by the entrance. Molly shouted to the driver to stop. It was Simon, keeping a brave distance from the gate. "Get in Simon, we could not wait any longer for you," said Molly.

"I know, there was a fire drill at the school, and I could not get away. As it is, I'm only allowed an hour, so I'll have to be getting back," was Simon's reply. They all returned to Aunt Maud's as they had done on the previous funeral. Brandies and Sherries were passed round for courage and also to warm them after the lashing they all took from the weather. Hot coffee and scones were provided in the kitchen and the family took on a lighter attitude after the sad afternoon.

Father raised his glass, "Here's to a brighter future." They all echoed his words. As the group dispersed, Father and Molly decided to go to the hospital to see Merry. They were shocked on entering her room to see that it was empty.

Molly called a nurse, "What's happened to Miss Wentworth?" questioned Molly.

"Oh, she had to be moved to another room for her own safety," was the nurse's reply.

They summoned a doctor; there was more bad news. Apparently Merry had been rocking back and forth uncontrollably, and they could not stop her, coupled with the tantrum the other night. In order to move her, she had to be heavily sedated, and she was now in the psychiatric ward for observation.

"It is a sad day for you Mr. Wentworth. We think Merry may have to be institutionalized for good. She has very severe mental tendencies." Molly and father were taken to the room, but they were only allowed to peep through the letter box size opening, on the barred door. Merry was in a bed with restraints on, in three places. She was frantically calling for Robbie. Her new teddy was on the floor, so Father asked if it could be put on the bed with her. The doctor agreed, and it was placed on the bed next to her. She immediately shut up and just laid there moaning in a very faraway fashion. Father was saddened, and Molly too could see herself on that bed. Life was so cruel. Yet again, when would the tragedies end? Deeply saddened the two left. Molly stayed with her aunt that night and invited her father to join them, but he would have none of it. He was going home. To the brandy no doubt, Molly thought.

Aunt Maud was welcoming and sweet; they sat by the fire and talked about nice things and gently helped each other over the days' events. Merry had been moved from the hospital to the Sanitarium right away; visitation was only once a month. She just sat and continually rocked backward and forward, cuddling the new teddy bear in some trance-like state, in another world. She had become aggressive and disruptive and was restrained a lot of the time and in solitary rooms. Her future looked grim, and more than ever it seemed she would be kept in this strict prison-like place for the rest of her days. She no longer recognized or acknowledged any of her family and only on certain visits showed any signs of recognizing Molly as her twin sister.

Sometimes Molly insisted Merry did recognize her. Molly said it with her eyes, and not in the words she uttered, as they were almost inaudible now, and grunts and moans were all that was left of Merry's vocabulary.

It was a sad state of affairs but none that anyone could do anything to change. The months passed and Molly saw less and less of Simon. She was growing up now, and she wanted adventure. Simon had outgrown his use. Molly had almost finished her college course, and she acquired the needed certificate to launch her on her career in the office of the local paper, the Daily Gazette—a job she had set her mind on for years. Father was proud of her, quite a young lady as she sauntered off to work that first morning.

Being the youngest, and last to start, Molly was given all the menial tasks. She didn't mind because at last she had her own money to do as she wished. She learned quite a lot from the reporters and photographers in the office. Molly spotted a young man in the office next door to the print room who took her fancy and she was sure feelings were returned. His name, she found out quite accidentally, was David. He was tall, had very dark hair, deep brown eyes and a thin black mustache, a little like Clark Gable, she smiled to herself. He was elegant and smooth. Molly liked him instantly, but gave no show of attention and waited for him to make the first move.

Aunt Maud could tell Molly had a young man in mind because of the way Molly had changed, taking more care with her appearance. She seemed more beautiful with a little glow about her which lifted her into the air.

She certainly was a beauty, with long, dark hair, flashing green eyes, and a devilment that could be awoken at the slightest gesture. Work was fine, and Molly was throwing herself into it with great enthusiasm. She liked everyone and was a popular new member of staff. Mr. Richardson her boss, was very pleased with her performance and made no bones about letting her know about his appreciation. She liked him and more so respected his position.

The months passed and the Christmas Dance was approaching. Molly had seen nothing of Simon; therefore, she could not ask him to partner her. All the others were married and were taking their husbands and wives. They all encouraged Molly to go, and one by one invited her to sit with them if she had no one to take. Molly declined all the offers; as she would rather stop at home than, be a gooseberry for someone else.

The day for the dance drew nearer. Everything was free and everyone else was excited and awaiting the event with great anticipation except Molly.

There was a general air of excitement.

The day before the dance, and everyone exchanged designs on what they were wearing. Molly felt left out; she dearly wanted to go, but not on her own. It must have been one of her vulnerable moments, when Sarah her work colleague, managed to persuade her to go at the last minute. Molly felt relieved, when at last, she was going; at least she could watch what everyone else was up to. That night she told Aunt Maud she was going, so they decided a new dress was the order of the day. Aunt Maud met Molly at lunch time the next day, and they went shopping. Molly knew what she wanted, she was nineteen now, and she could pick what she liked without being dissuaded. She decided on a green dress, her favourite colour, to match her eyes, and it had to be a sweetheart neckline, to show off her ample breasts.

It wasn't long before she found exactly what she wanted--emerald-green taffeta with a slightly shimmering effect, a tight bodice emphasizing her small waist and huge breasts, calf length, very sleek and classy. Molly was excited and felt beautiful in that dress. She gave Aunt Maud the box, kissed her on the cheek, patted her on the shoulder and was off, back to work before she was missed.

That afternoon in the office, no work was done; the excitement rose and everyone pleased to see Molly so delighted with her purchase. Everyone loved Molly with her bubbly, sparkling personality; she lifted them all and made them feel good. She chattered non stop all afternoon. It was tea time, work was finished for the day. Molly waved them all good-bye and promised to be on time as she left that night. She dashed home, greeted Aunt Maud and danced round the settee with her dress pinned to her person. "I'm going to be the belle of the ball tonight," she sang, and Aunt Maud did not doubt it.

Aunt Maud had not seen Molly so happy for such a long time, and the happiness washed off on her too. She felt young again and remembered her own first grown-up dance. Molly bathed in her mother's favourite lavender water; she wore Mother's pearls and pearl earrings. She felt fresh and sensuous. She wore no bra, as the bodice from the dress gave her enough uplift for those voluptuous breasts.

She brushed her hair and admired herself in the full length mirror. She felt wonderful. If only her mother was there to see her tonight. There was a knock on the door; it was a bit early for her lift. It was Father coming to see his precious daughter on her way to the dance. He looked on with amazement and secretly congratulated himself on producing one perfect specimen of woman-hood. Father had brought Molly a little cluster of flowers to pin to her dress—a little pink rosebud surrounded by Gibsonia; it was pretty.

She borrowed Aunt Maud's white shawl and was ready. Her friends arrived and all three got in the car and were on their way to the dance. As they neared the building, they could hear the music and loud chatter of excited voices. Molly secretly hoped that David might be there. They entered, took off their outerwear; and descended on to the main hall, where the food was laid out on the main table. The large trout taking pride of place in the centre of the table, with all the goodies presented in mouthwa-tering fashion. Molly and the others took their seats by the dance floor. Frank, Sarah's husband seemed nervous, probably because the only one member of staff he had met before was Molly. But there was no need for concern. Sarah was like a social butterfly, calling and waving to everyone who entered or passed their table.

Frank got up, made his way to the bar and got the drinks. Molly started with a little red wine to put her in good spirits and relax her. Most people had arrived by this time, and the hall was quite full. Everyone had loosened up by now and had started to really enjoy themselves, even the partners who were mostly strange when they entered, were getting into the swing of things.

Some people were already on the dance floor, and the band was in full swing. Molly could feel her feet tapping to the music. She was on her third glass of red wine and all inhibitions about herself; were fast disappearing. She dragged Frank onto the dance floor, under protest, but he went.

Everyone was pleased to see Molly, and all remarked on how lovely she looked, and so grown up too. Molly's hair was long and flowing, and she was shaking her head to the music, the black curls were unfurling and springing back in place like the bounce of a tennis ball in rhythm to the music.

By this time all had arrived except two people, Sarah commented. Molly quickly scanned the room. It was Mr. Richardson and David who had yet to come. The evening was moving along; perhaps they were not coming at all. Molly was beginning to wish that she had asked David that day if he was going to the dance or not. Then at least she would know, and not have to keep wondering, and staring at the door, Molly was enjoying herself, anyhow.

The dance finished, and Frank was glad to get off the floor. Sarah was in fits of laughter, "That's the first time I have seen Frank dance since we were married," she said. They sat back at the table and were just contemplating going up for a light snack, when David walked in. Molly's heart missed a beat. He was not alone, he had the most gorgeous looking creature with him, she was tall, slender, blonde, but worse was yet to come.

David walked across to Molly's table and said, "This is Veronica—my wife." Molly was dumbstruck, but managed to mumble some sort of greeting. The married couple made their way around the room, getting acquainted with the others.

Molly sat there in disbelief. "How could David be married," she gasped, louder than she meant to, and Frank and Sarah looked across at her. "Thought I was going to sneeze," was Molly's escape. Molly was startled and shocked. Sarah had seen the look in her eyes, and she knew Molly was sweet on David.

"There are other men here tonight Molly, single and available."

But Molly in the usual little girl spoilt voice replied, "I want him, no one else will do."

Sarah squeezed her knee, "You are young; you have plenty of time to meet Mr. Right. Now let's have a smile and enjoy ourselves. Let him see you don't care about him." Molly could not take her eyes off the beautiful pair all night; she was examining every movement of their bodies, looking for some flaw in their relationship, but either they were on their best behavior in company, or they were truly in love. Molly's instincts were usually right, and he had encouraged her at work she was sure of it, or was it her imagination?

Frank by this time; had plucked up enough courage to face the dance floor again with Molly. He could see the upset written all over her face, and Sarah did not mind.

They adorned the dance floor and slithered and swayed to the music. On every turn Molly looked to see if David was watching. He was. Molly pretended not to notice. Frank knew her game and played along with it. Sarah knew too and didn't mind her husband being used in this way. After all, thought Sarah, Molly was only a little girl. How wrong could a grown up woman be! Molly was in every sense a woman, a woman who got what she wanted no matter what it took to get it. Veronica Hilton was going to find out soon. Molly felt hungry and went up to the table with a plate. Sarah asked her to bring her something too.

Molly was choosing amongst the delights and delicacies of the fully spread table when a finger tapped her on her bare back. She looked up to the most gorgeous, dark brown eyes she had ever seen with lashes like brushes enclosing them. There was a devilment in those eyes with a sparkle that sent Molly's heart racing. This was forbidden fruit, the tastiest of all, and it could only be David with his thin mustache and flashing smile. "You look nice tonight, little office junior." Molly resented that and quickly shook off his approach with a venomous look that would have killed the deadliest viper.

She moved to the other end of the table putting this or that hurriedly on the plates, all enthusiasm drowned as an avalanche would put out a blazing fire, the fire in this case was Molly's heart. She returned to where Sarah and Frank were sitting with a frown on her face that even clown make up could not cover. Sarah realized something was said as she had seen the two together and knew Molly's feeling for David.

"Don't let that rat spoil your night; he is enjoying every minute." was Sarah's retort as Molly nodded. They were all munching, and sucking greasy fingers, when Mr. Richardson appeared at the table with his wife, a fine, homely woman who was a bit on the frumpy side but had a warm smile. Introductions were made all round and greasy fingers wiped and apologized for.

Molly was determined to enjoy herself. Sarah and Frank got up for a smooch, and she was left chewing through the last piece of chicken, when a young man she had not met before asked her to dance. He wasn't exactly Molly's type, but she was grateful to anyone who asked her to dance, the way she was feeling tonight. He was called Ronald and suited the name well. He had red hair, glasses and the biggest freckles this side of the hemisphere. On the plus side however, he was kind, courteous and entertaining, they exchanged niceties, and Sarah and Frank were pleased to see Molly with someone.

The night was coming to an end, and the band played the last waltz. Ronald danced with Molly, and she was careful not to let him get too close or give any sign or undue encouragement. She was also very careful to notice the way in which David and Veronica were conducting themselves at this late hour. Molly hated that woman; soon the roles would be reversed, Molly was sure of it. The band finished and wished everyone a safe goodnight. Slowly everyone dispersed and left for their respective sleeping places.

Ronald asked to walk Molly home and as she was about to say no, who should walk by but David and Veronica. "Yes," said Molly in a loud voice,

"You may walk me home, Ronald."

David flashed a surreptitious grin to Molly as he walked past. "See you at work tomorrow," he called with the same sickening grin. How she hated him that evening. Ronald was the perfect gentleman, they parted as they had met, strangers, alone, isolated in their own thoughts, but perhaps a little friendlier. Molly agreed to have a coffee with him some time in the future, but she was careful not to make any definite plans. Aunt Maud was waiting up for Molly, asking if she had a good night. Molly said she had, being extra careful not to say she was fancying a married man. Aunt Maud would have none of that. Molly quickly fell asleep that night, exhausted by the merriment and the wine. The next day she was up and ready for work, her hair swept back and she dressed in a very sober little dress, in a dull color that was reflecting the mood she was in.

She was first there, except for Mr. Richardson, who was always there first, and last to leave. They greeted each other after which Molly took her seat at her desk, feeling despondent. Who should place himself on the edge of that desk with that devilish flashing smile, but you know who. Molly tried not to look pleased; the truth was, she was enormously pleased, almost elated. How could someone have so much hold over her; to have the power to completely change her moods, and from the deepest despair; to exhilaration? "I think I have some explaining to do. Will you meet me at lunch, and we can have our sandwiches in the park." Molly agreed, thinking cheapskate, but it did nothing to dampen her new found feeling of happiness. "I'll meet you inside the park where it is a little more private, so as not to arouse Sarah's suspicions."

He jumped off the desk, with the same flashing smile; and twinkle in his eye; and went on his way, down the corridor to his own office. It was a nice, pleasant day, cold but sunny with a crispness which gave the feeling of a brand new day. Molly had taken her coat and scarf that morning, so she was well togged out for the open air sitting. It was lunch time sooner than she thought and without saying a word to anyone she set off for her secret rendezvous. She arrived there first and chose a bench near to the children's playground to keep herself amused whilst she sat there and waited for her clandestine co-partner.

Molly wondered what weird and wonderful excuses he had concocted for her ears. Regardless, he had already aroused her interest. She found him unorthodox in his ways and this triggered off an excitement in her. There were a few children playing on the swings and on the roundabout with their mothers. The shrieks of delight from the children gave the mothers a feeling of pride and well-being as they chatted to one and other. A dashing figure appeared through the park gates, it could only be; yes it was; flash Harry in person, only he could have that much spring in his step, tossing his scarf carelessly around his neck. "What sort of sandwiches do you have?" was his greeting.

How original, Molly thought, "Cheese and pickle," was the reply.

"I'll swap you."

"Right," replied Molly

She soon realized she had got the wrong end of the bargain; there was only jam on his. "Sorry about that, I had to make them quickly on the way out of the door this morning." How typical of the man.

"Why do you want to see me David?" Molly waited for his reply.

"Why did you come?" he was playing with her again. Molly jumped up. She liked David; she liked him a lot, but not enough to be made fun of at his every chance. She walked away leaving her sandwiches. He grabbed them and ran after her. "Don't be so childish, I am just jesting," he shouted. Molly paid no heed, she just wanted to be away from him; she had made a mistake going there that day. Sarah was right; he was better off left alone with his precious Veronica. Molly decided there and then to nickname her the Ice Lady because she resented her so much for having David. They both arrived back at the office.

David placed the sandwich box on her desk and cleared off without another word. Molly thrust the remainder in her drawer, her appetite had worn off. Thank goodness Sarah was not there, otherwise there would have been an atmosphere and dirty looks galore. Work passed off that day with no hitches. Molly remarked to Aunt Maud that evening that she felt she should go to visit Merry again as it was ages since she had gone. They both agreed to go on Saturday. It was Friday, the end of the working week for Molly, and she had just put the cover over her typewriter when the phone rang. It was for Molly; and Sarah knew by Molly's tone of voice; exactly who it was. She looked disapprovingly at Molly. To make matters worse she overheard Molly making arrangements to meet him on Sunday afternoon in the cafe in town.

Sarah shook her head as Molly replaced the receiver. "You're heading for big trouble." Molly did not answer Sarah except to say goodnight on the way out. When Molly got out of the office and on to the street she jumped with delight, she had a spring in her step and joy in her heart; the weekend was becoming much brighter already. She was looking forward to this weekend, first to see Merry on Saturday and then to see David on Sunday. Hooray!

She made herself a promise on the way home. No way would he upset her this time, no matter what he said, she would not bite. Aunt Maud could tell by Molly's face and happy, carefree air, as she rushed in the house full of smiles; that something was going right for Molly at last. It rained the next morning, the trip to the new Sanitarium was mundane and depressing; it was not the same countryside scenery as the Sanitarium, Merry had left, the journey took them through some very depressing rundown Council estates and some very deprived neighbourhoods.

Molly took some magazines with her as these journeys were so much longer than before. She also had some grapes and chocolates for Merry. She was enjoying the independence of having her own money in her purse. They arrived at the Sanitarium and were told to wait until they checked in; they were also searched for anything sharp or for drugs or anything untoward.

It was dark and dismal, and a smell of urine filled the corridors along with the occasional wet patches where inmates had relieved themselves with the lack of control or knowing. The whole place was depressing and death-like, dark with barred windows and white walls that offered no comfort.

They passed the check and were escorted to the ward where. Merry was.

Crossing their path from time to time were some inmates shuffling around aimlessly going no where, doing nothing, in a trance, like zombies, some with nightshirts still on, some in barefoot some naked, but all with that faraway look, a look that frightened the sane.

A staff nurse came over to them. "Is it Miss Wentworth you want?" They both nodded.

"She's in that room over there, solitary and restrained for her own good and for the safety of the others and the staff. She is not responding to treatment and gets into vicious rages. She is under restraint most of the time."

They were taken up to the door and asked to wait. The attendant slid back the small opening at the top of the door. It was barred and sealed with reinforced glass.

"You may look through, but there won't be any visiting this time." Molly looked through first. What she saw sickened and frightened her. Merry was there inside, restrained to a rocking chair, rocking backwards and forwards, backwards and forwards, with that same faraway look in her eyes which could only mean she was drugged or something. Her teddy was propped up on her knees as if waiting for a cuddle. Molly could look no longer.

Aunt Maud saw the shock on Molly's face, a look Aunt Maud had forgotten, as life seemed a lot kinder to Molly these days. In fact everyone was brighter, that is everyone except Merry. Aunt Maud peeped through and was shocked into silence. She took Molly by the arm, and they left that Godforsaken place, leaving Merry's gifts at the reception desk.

Still, Molly had tomorrow to look forward to and her gorgeous David. She promised herself again that she would not allow him to ruffle her feathers.

She spent a quiet day with Aunt Maud helping to bake and tidy up the house. Later on that night she bathed and had an early night. She would need all her strength for the meeting with David tomorrow. She closed her eyes dreaming of the forbidden fruits she was going to sample the next day. It had frosted during the night, and Aunt Maud was just about to light the fire as Molly went into the small sitting room pulling on her thick jumper over her jeans. She was bubbly, effervescent like a bottle of just-opened champagne bursting into the atmosphere with the vitality of a newborn lamb. Aunt Maud was cheery too, obviously none of yesterday's disappointments had lingered. Molly chattered, ate, and left.

Aunt Maud no longer questioned Molly's whereabouts or wanderings. All that concerned the elderly lady was that Molly was at last getting happiness from somewhere. Molly was off, chirpy and buoyant. She was first to arrive at the cafe. She ordered coffee for them both and looked around her. Everyone was chilled by the morning frost and was sipping hot food and drinks to warm themselves against the elements. Her gaze took her outside, towards the movement on the streets. She wiped the window with her hand, the heat from inside was causing it to steam up and made her vision blurred. Surprisingly for a Sunday there were people mulling around, pushing prams, walking dogs. She was lost in that world when the cafe door burst open and there was David flashing a mischievous grin through his upturned moustache.

David warmed Molly far quicker than any coffee could. He sat down by her, still smiling. She handed him his coffee, "Have you forgotten I only drink tea."

Molly had forgotten.

She quickly replied, "I'll drink this one too." He went to the counter and poured himself a tea leaving the correct change for the assistant. He wore a beige duffel coat which Molly thought quite bland for him, he was normally so flamboyant, but she was really pleased to see him no matter how he was dressed. Molly began to spill out what had happened at the Sanitarium yesterday and the sadness which surrounded the place. David listened and nodded in agreement but quickly changed the subject

"Hurry up Molly," he said "drink up, I mustn't be seen here with you," Molly looked startled and was still in her thoughts of Merry. But of course David had to be careful. Molly had forgotten the Ice Lady for a moment. They walked together through the park, their closeness needed no physical contact; it showed in their eyes. David apologized for teasing Molly. He realized she did not like it, and it got him nowhere except into Molly's bad books. He stopped, turned her towards him and pulled a bunch of speckled yellow and red carnations from inside his coat and presented them to her. Molly was thrilled; she had never had flowers presented in such a way before.

David grinned; he explained how he had been caught by his friend when buying them and had to pretend they were for Veronica. How he would explain the non-existence of the flowers if his friend decided to call soon was another matter. One Molly knew for sure that David would easily handle it with his silver tongue; he had a way of flattering every female who crossed his path. David pulled Molly onto the park bench almost urgently. "Molly, joking and playing around aside, I really do want to see you in a more private place then we can talk and just be ourselves without the constant fear of discovery, with people jumping to the wrong conclusions. My friend Benjamin has offered to lend me his flat one evening. If you agree, we can meet there and just be together."

Things were moving fast, and Molly had to think, but she had already made up her mind—she wanted David no matter what and that was that.

Molly knew she risked being hurt. She had a saying in her mind: "It is better to have loved and lost, than never to have loved at all." She agreed to meet him. Tuesday evening was arranged. David grinned. His usually confident face took on a look of doubt just for a moment. They kissed and parted.

Molly had a spring in her step and an arrow through her heart that day. Aunt Maud was in the garden pottering around. Molly greeted her and ran up to her room. She kicked off her shoes, threw herself on the bed, and was swarmed by warm pleasing thoughts. Next day work went well, she was grateful that although David was employed at the same place, his office was quite a distance away, and at work their paths seldom passed. She was sure she would lose her cool and show some signs of emotion, even a look would be telltale the way she felt about this man.

It was Tuesday afternoon, everyone else at work was getting on in the usual mundane fashion, but Molly's mind was reeling with excitements, apprehension, sheer joy and wickedness, she was a bitch in the making and she knew it.

She remembered her most devilish saying which shocked and sent chuckles through her friends. "There's no fun being good."

Molly was on the right path to follow her dreams. She had only one life, and she was going to live it—her way. Tuesday evening had arrived; she bathed, washed her hair and left it flowing instead of pinning it back as she did at work. She wore her new silk bra and bikini knickers—items she hoped would be removed that evening by a completely strange, devilish man. She pulled on a red dress and wore a red; vamp lipstick to mirror her mood. She hadn't had a man for so long, and she knew, if the evening went as planned that would alter tonight. She shouted good-bye to Aunt Maud and was off, careful to put the flat address in her coat pocket. She arrived on the street where the flat was.

There was a narrow, dark, mysterious alleyway between two shops. This must be the entrance, she whispered inside her head. It was forbidding, perhaps this was a precautionary warning about the whole episode. Molly would not be put off, not at this late stage. She walked along to the end of the entrance, and was just approaching some doors, not knowing which one to take, when suddenly as if by remote control, the light inside the doorway went on; lighting the whole alleyway.

There in the lit up, open doorway, was the strong masculine figure she had fantasized about for so many long days. She chose her steps more carefully now so as not to cause a disturbance and affect the privacy of her first faltering steps into David's arms, for the first time. As she came nearer to the doorway she smelled the sweet smell of joysticks burning and a lingering smell of incense was predominant. The flat was immaculately clean and uniform, surprising for a man who lived alone, or perhaps David himself had cleaned it up before her arrival.

There was a huge calendar in the hall with a large, red telephone printed on it which welcomed all visitors, the flat was plain in decor with a huge gas heater in one corner, obtrusive, ugly, incongruous, presumably to save heating bills. The kitchen was enormous and was spotlessly clean. There was something cooking in the oven which gave off a delicious aroma and tested the taste buds, swimming the whole room in flavour. David took her coat and asked her to sit in the lounge whilst he opened and brought in a glass of wine. There was some romantic music playing, and the whole atmosphere was one of complete contentment and serenity.

After pouring the wine, David joined her on the sofa. They sat and talked to each other telling of their secrecy and journey to this little nest of illicit charm. The flat was on the second floor, and the view from the front window was of the park and surrounding area. Molly felt like a bird free to love and look down from her nest, she felt safe there. David turned her round and kissed her on the forehead with such tenderness she had never before sensed, certainly not from Simon. How could she think of him at a time like this! David looked deep into her eyes, softly, admiringly, sensually, "You are something else." He said it with great feeling, and it touched Molly. Molly questioned in her mind what else, but decided not to challenge David at this time. She did not want anything to go wrong tonight, not after all the deceit and planning it took just to be there.

They listened to a few more records and sipped the wine, the night was a night for lovers; it was a dream, everything Molly wanted on that night was happening and more.

She was falling in love for the very first time with the biggest rogue and lady killer in twenty miles radius of town.

David took her by the hand, and led her into the bedroom, no words were spoken, they both knew where they were heading, and they both knew too, that whatever happened that night could not be undone. There were flowers on the bedside table and the dresser, but to Molly's disappointment there was only a single bed; she had hoped for a double. They were alone together and that was all that mattered to Molly that night. She had her new silk knickers on, the moon was shining through the little, obscure window; the town clock chimed nine o'clock as if it was the time for something special, the world knew, and Molly knew.

She slipped off her scanty clothing and slipped between the sheets. The room was dark, and David's presence was felt all around the room, his smell enveloped her. She had waited so long. His shadow came closer. Molly wanted this experience so much, she outstretched her hands to him, and he came to her like a predatory animal with all instincts on the prey he was about to claim. Molly's outstretched hand curled around his body like an octopus, but softer more sensuous. This night Molly would relive over and over again all of her life.

There was a slight gap in the ill-fitting curtains, allowing the moon to peer through and have a naughty little look on their privacy. Molly caught a glimpse of David's face, smooth, sallow with that devilish glint in his eyes. He was mischievous, he pressed his body to hers; they encircled their arms around each other pecking at each other's lips like tiny chicks on their way out of the shells. Two shells were being broken that night for the first time, and they would never be whole again without each other. They caressed, and a warm feeling of well-being and comfort filled them both. David became more demanding, and hungry. He touched her breasts, her nipples pointed in desire; she was starved for his affections.

With a gentle movement of David's groin, they were one. They moved together uncurling, rolling, swaying, engrossed only in each other, getting knotted in the bedclothes from time to time, but neither noticed. Great passion arose in both of them and they wanted this moment to last forever. It would last in Molly's mind for the rest of her days. David gave one huge; groan, and they were locked together in a dream world of ecstasy neither would ever forget. David outstretched his arms and switched on the bedside light.

They lay their sated, their desire for each other quenched.

Both were frightened to ask the other; both wanted it to be so good after all the waiting, but neither had any cause for alarm because their feelings had guided them to the ultimate emotions, and both feelings were the same.

"David where's the ladies room?" He pointed across the hallway. As Molly went into the bathroom she caught the aroma of the supper in the oven. After all the excitement and love, she relished the thought of a glass of wine and some supper.

David smacked her on the bum knowing what she was thinking. For the first time in Molly's life she felt inner happiness, the sort most people only dream about.

Dressed now, and with her light makeup touched up, she moved back into the lounge. She pulled back the curtains and stared out over the park; what a lovely evening view, the moon gliding sheepishly over the tips of the tallest trees, casting its beam on the park benches. David came in drying his hair, "Quite a nice pad old Benjamin has." Molly nodded in agreement. She poured two glasses of wine and they toasted to more evenings shared. David disappeared into the kitchen and appeared again with the much desired food. Chili-con-carne with a buttered; a baked potato.

"Yummy" was Molly's greeting. They sat down, giggled, blew kisses, caressed, sipped the wine and pecked at the chili. David explained that his dearest wish was to go to India or China to work for a while. His heart was especially devoted to going to India. Molly thought that perhaps he had family over there.

He hinted that he would like Molly to join him, but of course that was out of the question because of his commitments in other places. The night was coming to an end it was eleven o'clock already, and David had to be getting back. It was at that moment that Molly suddenly realized he was not hers and perhaps never would be; he was only on loan to her that night. She felt a chill, a shiver ran through her body, and he put his arms around her. "Never mind Molly, no one can take tonight away from us, and one never knows how situations like this can turn out." Molly smiled a half smile.

David walked her to the hallway; they kissed in the shadows and she left. It was a nice evening, and quite bright, she enjoyed the walk back; the street lights were comforting as they shone on her path home. She let herself into her aunt's. The lights were lovingly left on for her, there was still some cinders alight on the fire. She sat down, kicked off her shoes, she felt clever, satisfied, mischievous and alive. She was wicked of course, but that made her meetings with David twice as precious.

Molly remembered Aunt Maud kept some brandy for medicinal purposes in the cabinet. She unlocked it, took out the brandy and got herself a glass. She poured a generous measure and reassured herself it was only to make her inner glow more rewarding. She sipped the brandy, twiddled her toes in front of the fire feeling warmed and happy. Finally she nodded off in the chair that night thinking about her gorgeous David with the laughing eyes. Aunt Maud came bustling downstairs next morning to find Molly still in the chair with the glass still in her hand.

She shook Molly and was quite upset, "Come on my dear, some people have a living to make." Molly woke quickly, dashed upstairs and was down again at breakfast within minutes. She set off to work with an inner smile, and a secret inside her. Work went well that day; she caught a glimpse of the mischievous David in one of the corridors, but being discreet chose to ignore him. Sarah had been quiet that day and just listened to Molly's chirping. She knew something was going on but did not get involved. Perhaps she had her own worries that day.

Chapter Six

NOTHING VERY EXCITING WAS happening the week that followed, work was slipping out of one day and into another. Aunt Maud was cheerful when Father called to see them, there was only Merry to visit on Saturday morning and all was well. As the weekend neared again, Molly decided to try and catch David at work, just for a little look, and to reassure her that she wasn't forgotten. She passed Mr. Richardson's office and was just about to go down the corridor when she came in close collision with Veronica, David's wife. Sheer panic ran through Molly, but she contained herself and greeted her with a good afternoon. The greeting was returned icily. She knew nothing of David's affair. Molly was convinced of that; she just disliked Molly and the feeling was mutual. Both women passed. Molly headed for the ladies loo as it was en route to his office. She knew now that she wasn't going to see him before weekend, as it was Friday afternoon already, and the Ice Lady was with him. She probably had come to pick him up. Drat and Damn was Molly's immediate thoughts, but on recollection, it was better not to make herself too available to him. After all, he was getting the best of both worlds, and she too was free to do as she wished. Her thoughts returned to Ronald, the lad from the Christmas dance; she would use him to fill in her time around seeing David.

She left work that night with this firmly set in her mind. Her friend Sarah from schooldays also crept into her thoughts. She would call on Sarah and ask her to have a night out somewhere where Ronald went for his entertainment. She was proud of herself and thought what a good idea, so she smiled and congratulated herself. On arriving back home she was greeted by Aunt Maud who echoed her thoughts about visiting Merry; they both agreed to go on Saturday. That was that then, they would see Merry Saturday morning, then call on her school friend Sarah in the afternoon, Molly used the word school friend loosely as she could barely stand the girl, but she had her uses. Saturday morning was frosty and cold, typical of a February morning. The train of course, was late, and the pair was already frozen stiff, shuffling about to keep their feet warm. the porter came up to them to let them know of the delay and to Molly's amazement he was very attractive, tall, with dark hair, not ebony, but warm dark, with very big, blue eyes. She gave him a smile which he returned it immediately.

Aunt Maud saw the exchange, and told Molly not to tease him; they both giggled. The train arrived and Molly said good-bye, but she took a mental note for the future. She was going to get David and if making him jealous would work, then she would give it a try and also... Molly needed some amusement to get her through the long, dark nights. With the whistle from the guard, the train ground to a halt, the two bundled themselves off and wandered up to the gates of the Institution. It was cold that morning, no one was on the grounds, and even the birds were missing from the trees.

The two got to the reception desk, and a nurse greeted them and took them to Merry's room, a different one this time. She opened the door; it was a pleasant room with a big window overlooking the garden areas with a great, big oak tree taking pride of place. The room was decorated in pale lilac and the curtains matched, there was a single bed and a little dresser against the wall opposite, holding all of Merry's personal belongings. As they entered Merry looked up with a big smile on her face. She rushed to Molly and gave her a big hug. This was wonderful, she recognized them.

She kissed Aunt Maud and pulled them both inside and gestured for them to sit on her bed. "Do you like my new room?" Merry beamed with pride. She told them how she had made the curtains herself, one was a little longer than the other, but no one commented, they were just glad to see such a tremendous change in her. Teddy Robbie was sitting on the floor. Merry asked how everything was at home, she asked about Molly's job. She had evidently been taking things in from previous visits. Both Aunt Maud and Molly were so pleased with Merry. They had not seen her like this for over a couple of months and had expected Merry to be in the same transient haze, bordering on insanity.   They seemed to talk for hours, there was so much Merry wanted to know.

"How's Father why doesn't he come to see me here Molly?" Merry you know he hate's to see you here; and just wants you home again, keep getting better and that day will come soon."

Visiting time with all the exciting chatter had gone so quickly that it was time for the visitors to leave. They both hugged and kissed Merry in turn, and Molly promised to be back soon. They both left.

On their way out past reception they asked to see the Governor. She came along almost immediately. "I tried to contact you but some urgent business came up, and I was not free at the time you arrived. Well what do you think of her?" She is almost normal again, we cannot tell if this stage is temporary or if it will last, but we shall make the most of it while it is here. I'll keep you posted on her progress and don't make it too long before you come to see her again. If her progress continues, I shall consider letting her go home for the weekend soon." This pleased them both and they left with their spirits high. As Molly boarded the train she remembered her porter friend and rather hoped he would be on the station when they arrived.

Aunt Maud saw the concern on Molly's smiling face and understood. She sat back in her train seat and gave a deep sigh and with a contented look on her old face, drifted off to sleep. Today had been a good day after all. The train jolted to a halt which awakened the old lady abruptly. Molly led her aunt off, and to her delight the handsome young porter was still there, brushing up the railway station around the cafe area.

He spotted her and charmingly introduced himself as Gerrald. "My name is Molly" and with that Aunt Maud made her way home alone leaving the young people to their own affairs. Gerrald explained that he had just started work there that day, and although it wasn't his permanent job, he could not stop to talk too long. He explained he was helping out his friend on his break from university. Molly thought it a bit of a dead end job and was glad that it was not his full time one. As a career, it was rubbish.

"Look," said Gerrald "you probably think this a bit of a cheek, but will you come with me for coffee after work on Monday?"

This was Molly's chance. "Yes, meet me outside the Gazette Newspaper Office at 5.30 on Monday evening." She would teach David that she was not to be trifled with. Molly waved good-bye and made for home. No longer was she going to bother about Sarah, and her remarks about who she was dating!

Her plans had been altered for the better, and Gerrald was a better catch than that boring, ugly stupid Ronald. After all, David himself had commented on what a wimp he had been. Molly almost skipped home; evilness seemed to perk her up to no end. When she got in, Aunt Maud was already peeling the vegetables for lunch. Molly changed and helped lay the table. She would have a quiet Saturday afternoon and Sunday; then organize herself for Monday tea time.

Aunt Maud had suggested they go for a walk after lunch if Molly had nothing better to do. She agreed and off they went, all wrapped up to keep out the cold. They walked in the park; Saturday was a quiet day for the park as everyone else seemed busy with shopping and other household chores. As they passed the benches, Molly could not help stealing a glance at the flat where David and she had spent the other evening and wondered if they had left any clue as to the passion which had taken over them that evening. She warmed at the thought of him and wished he was with her, but Aunt Maud was to be her companion this afternoon. She linked arms with Aunty and felt close to her, almost as close as to her mother. As they drew nearer the other end of the park, there was a couple coming towards them talking and laughing—Molly was shocked—it was her father and that woman from last year; he was still seeing her. Aunt Maud commented, "It's your dad and Lucy. How happy they look." Molly was astonished that Aunt Maud should talk about her so readily with no bitter feelings, and should know her name and her relationship with Father.

Molly scowled, "How do you know that woman?" Aunt Maud replied if she had not been so preoccupied with her own life she would have known that her father was seeing Lucy and had been for some time now, even bringing her to Aunt Maud's house for tea on several occasions. But did Aunt Maud know that Father had been seeing Lucy when mother was still alive? Perhaps not! Molly thought again and decided to let sleeping dogs lie; after all, Father had a life too, and what little pleasure he had received lately. Father and Lucy came nearer, and were greeted by Aunt Maud, who introduced Molly, to Lucy. Molly was very polite, and managed to bear a big smile and a warm heart for her father's sake. They stood chatting for a few minutes and Molly decided she liked Lucy despite all. She was bubbly and fun and took to Molly straight off. Father looked relieved as they waved their goodbyes and made for the park gate. Aunt Maud was pleased too that their little informal meeting had taken place at last as it was upsetting for her to keep the secret from Molly; the accidental meeting had made things so much easier. The worry had gone now that Lucy may pop in to Aunt Maud's with Father, without warning when Molly was there.

The weekend, so dreaded, had turned out to be pleasing for both parties and had come and gone in a puff. Molly found herself finishing off at the office on Monday. She had seen nothing of David all day, much to her disappointment. She had wanted him to know of Gerrald's presence and the attention she was due to get. Everyone had gone home, and Molly too, was just packing her things when who should come into her office but the flashing grin and seductively mischievous David. Good Golly Miss Molly. She nonchalantly brushed her hair and refreshed her lipstick. "Going somewhere?" was David's greeting.

"As a matter of fact I am." Molly tried not to be too pompous, but that's the way it came out. David's face took on a look of concern and rejection.

He didn't ask where, because probably he could not face the answer. Molly picked up her bag and was gone. As she came out of the front door, Gerrald appeared from the next doorway where he was sheltering, from the rain. He looked handsome just as Molly had remembered him. Molly did not have an umbrella with her; so she was thankful for Gerrald's attention, and his huge golfing umbrella. She stole a glance back at the office window, and sure enough David was there with a scowl on his face. She laughed, it was working.

The new twosome called in at a local cafe and had some coffee and croissants; they were too busy getting to know each other to have time for a proper meal.

Molly soon found out that there was a lot more to Gerrald than being a railway porter. He was studying to be a doctor at a university in the neighboring town of Hampstead. His father was a doctor, and he and his mother lived in a place named Stevenage with a pet Labrador called Dizzy. Gerrald proved fun to be with. He was handsome, intelligent had good prospects and more than anything, was single. The time soon passed as they exchanged their ambitions and hopes for the future; they really did get along well together. Gerrald seemed fascinated with Molly. He was amazed at how sure she was about herself and where her place in the world would take her. It was getting on for nine o'clock, when Molly said she would have to be getting back to Aunt Maud's, as she had said she would only be an hour late.

Although Molly was nineteen years old, Aunt Maud had the tendency to treat her like a child sometimes. Gerrald understood and walked Molly to her gate. They promised to meet again, and Molly gave Gerrald her phone number at work for easy contact. Molly was amazed at how happy she felt. A meeting which was for use only, had turned out to be a very exciting occasion; and Molly would not have to share this man. She decided to let nature take its course and play along with whatever way life took her. Aunt Maud was very cross when Molly arrived almost two hours late, and soon wiped away the smile from Molly's face. Molly apologized of course, and after explaining all to Aunt Maud the situation was very quickly forgotten. Molly was looking forward to work the following day and her encounter with David. She wondered if he had slept that night. She was being overconfident.

David swept into work, dashing, smiling, completely in control and giving no evidence of concern or dissatisfaction. In fact he swept by with an allure of the all-conquering hero. Molly was angered. She hated losing in anything, especially in love. She had the equipment and intelligence of a winner and this act of sheer blaze came as a shock to her ego. A few days passed and David made himself scarce, but she had been seeing quite a bit of Gerrald and she had begun to like him a lot. However, he had no hold over her or gave any feeling of dangerous excitement and wonder, not like David did.

The weekend was nearing again; and Gerrald invited her to his parents' home. His job at the station was very temporary, sometimes he filled in for his friend; sometimes he did it Monday to Saturday. But if Molly was to decide to spend the weekend at his home, he would take Saturday off also. Molly wasn't sure whether to accept or not, she was still waiting for David to come round a bit and ask her out. But Friday afternoon came and went and there was no contact from David. She was certainly not going to make herself available to him. After all, in Molly's mind he was the one being babyish.

On Friday night Molly accepted Gerrald's offer. He was delighted and agreed to pick her up in his car, at seven o'clock that evening. Aunt Maud had reservations of Molly going to stay with a family, she didn't know, but was overwhelming swayed by Molly's enthusiasm. Gerrald arrived dead on time. Cases and immediate personal things were put in the boot of his car. With a quick peck on the cheek for Aunt Maud, they were off. Molly suddenly realized she had not introduced Aunt Maud. She turned as they drove off and said, "Aunt Maud this is Gerrald from the railway station."

Aunt Maud smiled and shook her head.

"The youth of today," she thought. Molly was happy and seemed at last to be enjoying her life. It didn't take them long to reach the country, and Gerrald was bubbling with excitement just being with Molly, whom he respected and regarded as an equal, even although Molly had not gone to university or for that matter, had any qualifications other than the usual end-of-term ones. He was chattering away telling little stories about his mother and father; they seemed a devoted and happy couple, and Gerrald seemed to be the apple of their eye, probably because he was the only son, and following in his father's footsteps in becoming a doctor.

They drove along a long, winding country lane for about two miles when they spotted the sign for Stevenage. "We're nearly there." Molly seemed excited, but tinged with a little touch of apprehension. It suddenly struck her, What if they didn't like her? She consoled herself with the fact that it was David she wanted and not Gerrald, so in any case it did not really matter. What a futile, inner conflict. What was she doing there at all? Molly frowned to herself, no black clouds; only sunshine thoughts this weekend. Two huge iron gates appeared before them as they turned the next corner. Gerrald drew the car to a halt; this couldn't be the place. Written in big letters above the gate was the word Linley, Gerrald's second name! The gates, the drive, the house, all seemed larger than life. They were entering a mansion, and the sight was breathtaking. Gerrald had not warned her of this; she had expected a little country cottage. She wasn't apprehensive any more--just shit scared. If she had known about his background, she would have taken more care with her appearance. Gerrald squeezed her knee as if reading her thoughts, "Don't worry they're very ordinary and likable you know." All of Molly's confidence seemed to slip away. As they got closer to the house, the door opened and a butler followed by an elderly couple came to the great, studded, double door.

They looked welcoming, and all smiling. Molly got out of the car almost sheepishly; this was a feeling quite new to her. Gerrald took her hand proudly. "This is Molly," he said to his parents and his pride shone through his eyes.

"You were right Gerrald, she is a beauty," answered the greying, old gentleman. Molly was later to know as Gerrald's father. Introductions now out of the way, and greetings made and accepted, they entered through the large, open studded door to the reception area. But this was not like Aunt Maud's reception area at all, this was a great, huge room filled with paintings of people of a bygone time, all resembling each other in a faint, dated way. There were swords and old pistols all over the mahogany-clad walls and antique furniture in the hall endowed with china vases and figurines. The sight was awesome.

The broad marble stairs lead to the first floor with an open balustrade in matching mahogany. All the way up the stairs there were more paintings and old pistols; there was a huge, arch-type leaded window in various colours and splendid to the extreme. Molly stood openmouthed;

she had never seen the like, not anything as grand, not even in the cinemas. Gerrald quickly took her hand and led her into one of the adjoining downstairs rooms, which was even more prestigious than the reception area, with its unspoiled elegance and sheer, unadulterated masterpieces of the art world. They moved towards the chesterfield sofa and took a much-needed seat; it was for Molly at least. Gerrald asked her if she wanted a drink.

"Yes," she said "A good, big brandy please." After sipping the drink, Molly shook Gerrald. "You didn't tell me about all this, you conniving swine," she joked almost in sheer earnest.

"It's just home to me Molly, it's what I am used to. It doesn't really mean anything to me other than a loving place I have been brought up in." My father and mother were in their middle forties when they had me and had given up hope of ever having any children, so you can imagine how much wanted and loved I was. This has done nothing but good for me as it has made me respect people and not possessions." Molly thought how easy it was to have a careless approach to material things when one had it all.

The Linleys appeared in the doorway with a couple of bottles of wine just summoned from the cellar for the occasion. They welcomed Molly with a toast to her enjoyment of the weekend. The small party, was fast becoming acquainted, all stiffness had gone. Molly was relaxed now. Her personality and charm, was spontaneous, it was captivating her Hosts, who were enjoying the moment, and embracing, her every word. Gerrald kept the wine flowing throughout the conversations. Mr. Linley, or rather Lord Linley as was his proper title took to Molly right away; he was fascinated by her bubbly, quick wit and her beauty. He was proud too that his son was so fortunate in his choice of company. The conversation got round to horses and stables and grooming and the like. Mr. Linley asked Molly if she could ride. Molly, of course could not, and in fact was not sure if she liked horses at all. To her they were huge, awesome brutes. She replied that she had only seen horses passing in the country lanes near her Aunt Maud's, but never really gave them much thought. "You'll be taking Molly for a ride tomorrow, I expect Gerrald"

Gerrald nodded in agreement, "If Molly wants to go for a ride then we'll have a trot around the grounds tomorrow." Molly said she would. Although her mouth was saying "yes," her head was debating a conflicting argument between her wishes and her inner self. They dined quietly that night, with only a light supper and a few more brandies. The old couple made their excuses and retired early leaving the young ones to spend the next two hours alone. The logs crackled in the grate, and from time to time the butler interrupted their tranquility to ask if they needed anything more, or indeed if the fire needed stoking up with logs. Molly kicked off her shoes and curled up on the rug in front of the fire. She was aglow. The wine and brandies warmed her from within as the fire was doing from the outside. Gerrald admired and respected Molly. He rubbed her shoulder and caressed her back. Molly was in the mood for love, but privacy was not theirs in the large lounge. They were contented just to sit and soak up the serenity of the old house and its warm occupants.

Molly was enjoying herself and had adapted quickly to the new routine. She felt good and knew from that moment, she, should have been born into this sort of life. She was beginning to like Gerrald more and more as the evening went on. She saw a quality in him she had never seen in any other person she had known. It was probably his breeding. The logs crackled in the open fireplace and the wine and brandy was beginning to take its toll. She yawned more than once and finally gave in and retired to bed. Gerrald showed her the room. As he opened the door, she felt the aroma of lavender which quickly reminded her of Mother—how Mother would have loved being in her place now as she was quite a lady and only Father's poorly paid job had kept them back in society.

There was a tapestry above the four-poster bed; it was of huntsmen and hounds; it was beautiful.

The drapes hung from the four posters and touched the carpet. There was a magnificent oak chest at the bottom of the bed containing more bed linen if required, there was a bay window and a window seat all around but much grander than her childhood window seat, and it was covered in the same heavy material as the four-poster bed curtains. As was usual in these large, old houses an open fire range was on the far wall of the bedroom with a portrait of an elderly gentleman on it. Gerrald explained it was his great, great granddad who was also a lord. This was another shock for Molly. She had no idea that this family had any royal connections. Molly was sleepy and excused herself. Gerrald kissed her on the cheek and retired himself. Molly pulled out her sleepwear from her weekend case, got undressed and slipped into her nightdress and welcomed the comfort of the large soft mattress, and quickly fell asleep. It was a sleep in which a little princess was awoken by her prince charming as the story books say.

The next morning this Princess was awoken by scuffling and clip-clopping below in the courtyard. She got up and went to the bay window. As she opened the window, she could see Gerrald below. He waved to her, "Come on sleepy head, I have already been for an early morning gallop to wipe away the sleep". Molly laughed, she threw him a kiss and dashed to the bathroom to freshen up, then back to her luggage and put on jeans and a sweater and some casual shoes, ready for her first lesson in horse riding. She was dashing down the grand stairway giggling and laughing with a general air of excitement about her when Mr. Lindley appeared. He smiled to himself, as he spotted her. "It's nice to have some young blood in the house as well as Gerrald". She liked him; she liked them both. She arrived at the breakfast table quickly and sat down wishing Mrs. Linley good morning and saying how excited she was.

Gerrald appeared in the doorway, "You really don't need that beauty sleep you know". Molly smiled; she felt good; she liked Gerrald and his parents, and the servants too were very welcoming, Gerard sat beside her and breakfast was served. Mrs. Linley lingered over her coffee; listening to the excited chatter of the two young people; they livened her and made her feel young again. The discussion turned to horses, and Molly got to know that she would take her first lesson with Samson later on that morning. Apparently he was the most gentle, and much older, than the rest and was too old in fact to do much jumping, which was a comfort to Molly. The conversation came to an abrupt end when Mr. Linley entered, and said the horses were waiting and ready.

"Right," said Molly. "I'll see you both later, I hope." She laughed, so did the Linleys.

Gerrald gave her a mount up. She was on a great height, much higher than she imagined, or so she seemed to be. Molly felt her first sense of apprehension. It was a long way down if she should fall off. Gerrald instructed her on how to hold the reins and put her feet in the stirrups, and slowly they trotted away. After a few hours Molly had learned the basics and had found the experience enthralling, along with her host. She thought she could be falling for Gerrald, or was it his background? Molly decided just to enjoy the weekend and think about that question at another time. She was getting the hang of the preliminaries, the trot and canter, and Gerrald thought that was enough for one day. The next obstacle was how to get off! Molly looked down, and Gerrald saw her anxiety and rushed to her aid. Off she came, and oh, how her bum hurt. She laughed, "I hope I don't get saddle sore." Gerrald smiled discreetly to himself; wait till tomorrow. Gerrald suggested a warm bath and a chance to speak with his parents again as they liked Molly so much.

The stable boys took charge of Samson and Beauty and returned them to the open field adjacent to the stables to rest. Molly looked up at Gerrald and smiled. The sun caught his hair and made it look almost chestnut. Their eyes locked and Molly found it difficult to break the trance, so she gave Gerrald a kiss and thanked him for an exciting experience and promised to do better tomorrow.

"Oh, so we're going riding again tomorrow," he grinned, because Gerrald loved riding and would go anytime the opportunity arose.

They climbed the steps and opened the large studded door leading them to the reception hall in all its grandeur. Molly noticed the floor for the first time. It was solid marble and footsteps echoed all around them. Come to think of it so did their giggles and chatter. Molly was not so nervous this time; perhaps she felt more relaxed and at home. There was a minstrel gallery at the top of the large stairway which led to the bedrooms, and all the walls there too were covered in paintings and war mementos over the decades. Mr. Linley called to them, "Before you two young ones disappear, we want to know how the novice went on this morning."

Molly giggled, "I'm going in for Horse of the Year next year." This retort pleased the old gentleman. He came over and put his arm around her and guided her to the huge room adjacent to the reception hall. On entering Molly saw Mrs. Linley on the sofa, apparently embroidering something. Molly went to her and sat down. "Mother loved embroidery too; she did a lot when she was too ill to move around the house." Mrs. Linley saw the hurt in Molly's eyes and placed her hand on her knee reassuringly. Gerrald wanted a bath and was waiting no longer for the ladies to finish their conversation, so he politely excused himself and disappeared up stairs. Mrs. Linley was glad of a chance to speak to Molly alone. She explained that Molly was the first girl that Gerrald had brought home. He had lots of girlfriends before, she told Molly but no serious ones. Molly explained to Mrs. Linley that she had only known Gerrald for a few weeks and they were just very good friends. The old lady smiled and shook her head, "This time it's different. Albert and I both noticed the difference as soon as we saw you both together."

Molly felt she had to explain that she knew nothing about Gerrald's background until they arrived at the door last night. Mrs. Linley nodded her head, "Perhaps that is the very thing Gerrald has been looking for in a girl." The embroidery Mrs. Linley was doing looked tedious to Molly who realized she would never have the patience to do it.

"I had better have a bath and change for lunch, and with that Molly went upstairs. She had an en-suite bathroom in her bedroom; the marble which was so beautiful downstairs in the hall was present all over the bathroom floor and walls and around the sinks. The taps looked gold, but perhaps they were brass. The bath was in the middle of the room with gold claw feet, the towels were all pink and there was a pink dressing gown hanging behind the bathroom door which proved handy as Molly had not brought hers. Molly ran the taps and undressed, she felt sticky with all the exertion this morning. She put on the dressing gown and sat at the window seat, feeling content and full of well-being. She gazed across the open fields, and she saw Beauty and Samson, obviously still full of energy the way they were galloping around the field, continually stopping to snuggle against each other. One was black, ebony, in fact, and the other was chestnut, the original chestnut mare.

No wonder they called her Beauty, she was that alright. Oh, the bath water; just caught it in time. Molly took off the robe and slipped in the water. She soaked her aching bones.

There was a knock on the bathroom door, "May I come in?" It was Gerrald. Molly pondered for a moment. She was no innocent with men, but she didn't want Gerrald to know she was worldly, not at the moment anyhow.

"I'm in the bath Gerrald."

"Good, he shouted, "Are all the naughty bits covered?"

"No"

"That's even better still."

Molly wrapped her arms around herself to cover the ample breasts but they were so large it was impossible. What the hell she thought, she was proud of them and he had insisted.

"Come in"

Gerrald entered, his eyes fixed on her breasts, bobbing up and down on the surface of the foaming water. He smiled a sensual smile. Molly felt sexy. She wanted to pull him in with her. Then Gerrald disappeared, and Molly was most annoyed, but she had no need, he had gone to lock the bedroom door in case of intruders. He started undressing. Molly was very excited, and she put a hand out to him. He kissed it; Gerrald was all man, right down to his feet. He was a bit hairy and muscular without being too muscled. He crouched down at the side of the bath and kissed Molly. His lips held the kiss and became more demanding. She touched his hand then pulled him nearer; he took the opportunity and slipped in the water with her. The soapy suds splashed all over the floor but neither noticed. She reached down and touched his lower body. He was aroused and swelled, waiting for her.

Her body was screaming for his, and as they tangled, the bathwater surged back and forth, making more suds as he slid down and entered her. She groaned and sighed. So did he as they kissed; and locked for ages in ecstasy before he finally succumbed to his manly desires. They held each other for a time after, just to seal their precious moments. As soon as their lovemaking was over, and they were content, they washed each others backs.

"You are amazing Molly and beautiful too, you have the most sensual body I have ever seen! And I think I'm falling in love with you!" After saying these tender words he stood up, took her hand and helped her out of the bath.

Gerrald grabbed a nearby towel and started to dry Molly tenderly, frightened to rub too hard and graze her soft skin. He made Molly feel like his special lady and she lapped it up, this was better than a cold draughty Summerhouse, lying on an old coat.

They pulled on their respective bath robes, hers pink, his navy blue and started to mop up the bathroom floor with the remaining towels. Gerrald gazed at Molly's again. "Every time I look at you I get that feeling, and want to make love to you again, and again. I love you Molly!"

Molly gasped, "But I hardly know you."

Gerrald seemed a little annoyed. "How can you say that after what we just did?"

Molly regained herself. "It was beautiful Gerrald but don't let's rush things and spoil the weekend." On a much lighter note they got dressed and raced each other to the huge lounge where they had left his mother. She was still there, embroidering away without a care in the world. They felt joined in their secret episode of passion; and Molly felt bursting with devilment, that no one, but them, knew about it.

Lunch was served in the dining room, which they all enjoyed; then they moved to the study where all but Mrs. Linley had some port. Molly liked the port it was very strong. Vintage she thought they had called it. Mr. Linley smoked a cigar and the expensive aroma encircled the study. Molly was feeling a little giddy from the four glasses of port, so she decided to excuse herself and go for a walk around the gardens of the house. She wandered around looking in at the conservatory which was full of new plants, budding and waiting to be picked for the house by Mrs. Linley. There was a very sweet smell as some of the flowers were in full bloom. Molly picked some for her bedroom. She was sure no one would mind as there were hundreds of them. She moved on round to the stables where she met one of the stable lads. He was busy mucking out some of the stables, and a little foal was following him everywhere. Molly went over to it and petted it. It was not strange, she found out later that its mother had died giving birth to it, and they had called it Bambi. It had a white flash on its forehead and was a beige color, quite a prize possession by all accounts. Mr. Linley had followed her out, still smoking his cigar, "I see you've met Bambi, she's quite something isn't she?" Molly nodded,

"How are you enjoying your stay here?" Molly felt happy that she had gotten along fine with the two elderly people and replied she loved it. Mr. Linley said she could come whenever she liked, this was very reassuring indeed. Molly looked at her watch and knew she had better get back. She picked up the flowers from the conservatory and made her way back to the house. There was a big Mercedes parked on the circular driveway that she hadn't seen before. As she entered the hall, Gerrald came to let her know his cousin and his wife had called as they were passing, and therefore it was a good time to meet some more of the family. Oh what a bore, just when everything was nice, Molly thought to herself, but she had no option. His cousin's wife was called Sylvia.

She was tall with titan hair and a freckled face which had been kissed all over by the sun, her cool blue eyes looked like the little pools the sea leaves behind, on its return to the ocean.

His cousin was called James and the name suited him. He too was tall, muscular in a gentle way with his hair greased back, dark like Gerrald and quite similar in looks, but more sure of himself and flamboyant in a crude way that Molly did not like at all. He looked her up and down and gave a low whistle, obviously in appreciation in the only way he knew how. He was what Molly would call a cad. There was no love lost between the cousins. Molly sensed it right away, Gerrald being more gentle and classy than his cousin James. They were all introduced; and Sherries were served; James did nothing but talk about himself and his conquests with horses and the hunt which had just taken place. Sylvia, on the other hand was quiet by nature, bordering on shy. Molly exchanged a few sentences with her and wondered how she put up with a self-centered bore like James.

Still, there was no accounting for taste and perhaps in his private life James was more likable. Molly had left the flowers on the hall table when she came in, and was just about to ask Gerrald where she could obtain a vase, which was not an antique or precious, but in that household the servants were there to assist in everyway they could, and before Molly could ask, Sally the kitchen maid had put them in a vase herself, and was asking where she would like them. Molly, getting quite used to the grand way of life, asked her to put them in her bedroom beside the window. Gerrald's cousins were staying for dinner that evening so Molly would get a chance to get to know them better. Molly wasn't so interested, but had no choice. Dinner was served, and they all took their places.

The Linleys apparently, loved entertaining and the more the merrier. They all chatted through dinner and as was expected, James commanded every conversation, doing everything better than everyone else. Gerrald nudged Molly under the table more than once, and Molly understood and answered with a knowing smile. They all retired to the study as on the previous night, but this time the ladies sat together and talked women-talk and left the men to discuss the hunt that morning. Mr. Linley was obviously enjoying the jovial banter by the two younger men, as every so often he let out a roar of laughter. The vintage port was handed round and Molly enjoyed the gentle conversation of the other women, each having different topics to make the conversation interesting. Molly found out that Sylvia was quite an accomplished tennis player and she promised to teach Molly. She was already learning what she had been missing out on.

She also found out that Sylvia and James spent as much time as possible skiing in the Alps and in Germany whenever they could. This was perhaps the excitement Molly had waited so long for. The evening had been very pleasant and the cousins left, telling Molly they would see her again soon. Gerrald felt pleased that she had won over another two of the family. The two old people retired and left Molly and Gerrald alone with the port. Molly was already quite tiddly but could not refuse. She kicked off her shoes and sat by the huge log fire and beckoned for Gerrald to join her. He did with hardly any encouragement, they both sat on the floor and gazed at the flames going up the chimney and sipped the port which was warming inside. They felt close at that moment together in contentment. Gerrald had planned Sunday already. He had told the servants not to disturb them too early in the morning and had requested a picnic hamper, weather permitting, with two bottles of champagne, one Dom Perignon and one Crystal.

Molly was fascinated by his forethought. She was looking forward to Sunday already. The fire was crackling and still in full swing when one of the servants knocked and came in.

"We are retiring now Sir; is there anything else?"

"Don't forget the picnic hamper for around ten o'clock tomorrow and don't prepare any lunch, we will have late dinner on our return; also check with Ralph that Samson and Beauty will be saddled up and ready for around the same time." Gerrald was used to giving commands; they flowed from him so naturally. Molly was impressed.

This life was so easy and so very pleasant Molly could certainly get used to it. She ventured to ask Gerrald about James and Sylvia and their skiing holidays. Gerrald was more than keen to impress on Molly that he too, was a very accomplished skier, and went on the slopes any chance he got.

"Would you teach me please, Gerrald?"

"My, we are keen on learning everything all at once. Yes I will, but all in good time, you haven't mastered Samson yet." It was almost one o'clock by the old grandfather clock in the corner. "Come on we've a big day in front of us tomorrow." Gerrald was sleepy. Molly was too excited about what awaited tomorrow to be sleepy.

"Just another glass of port please Gerrald."

"I'll do better than that, let's go in the kitchens and get some champagne."

"Wooee" shrieked Molly. He grabbed her hand, and led her down the steep concrete steps to the huge kitchen. It was enormous, pans and herbs were hanging from the ceiling; there was a great stove on one wall with two huge iron cupboards on either side, for baking bread, Gerrald informed her. In the middle of the floor was a massive oak table full of knife wedges and worn down in places through hard work and constant bleaching. It was all spotlessly clean, even the flag floors. The fridge was old fashioned and big, but it served their purpose for the evening. There were a dozen bottles of champagne cooling on one side.

"Pink: or white: Molly?" Gerrald waited.

"Pink please; I've never had it."

"Right, grab that." It was cold against Molly's face and little bubbles of vapor were already trickling down the neck.

"Quick it's getting warm already," said Molly. Immediately Gerrald got himself a champagne bucket, filled it with ice and put the two bottles inside. He grabbed Molly's hand and dashed up the concrete stairs, planking himself down on the rug beside the log fire. You get the glasses Molly, in that cabinet there. She needed no second telling. Excitedly she rushed back with them, and bang! It was opened, effervescent bubbles gushing into the air and flowing down the sides.

They filled their glasses, made a toast and looked into each other's eyes, while sipping. The bubbles were exploding in Molly's mouth and tickling her nose and throat. It was lovely, semi-dry and fizzy.

Molly loved the pink champagne, this would be her drink from now on; if it wasn't affordable by her partner of the time, her partner could not afford her. My, she was getting illusions of grandeur with expensive tastes. Molly felt a glow inside her; a warming serenity, a passion. She wanted Gerrald that night, and he wanted her, but it was not safe here in the drawing room. Although the servants had retired, the cook Anna, who was old often came down for a late cup of tea. They contented themselves with each other's company and sipped more of the champagne. The only thing missing from Molly's illusion of inner luxury were pink roses. She promised Gerrald she would pick some from the garden for the picnic, when she arose next morning. He smiled at her. He knew he was making her truly happy; a beam from her eyes sparkled and alighted on his. They sipped the last of the champagne and climbed the marble stairs to bed. Outside Molly's bedroom door they stopped and clinched in a passionate embrace.

"Until tomorrow: my love!" Gerrald whispered, and placed a finger kiss on Molly's lips. She closed her door, had a quick wash and retired to bed; the champagne and port had done their job. It was morning, the birds were whistling and the sun was darting through the half-closed curtains. Molly was still drowsy when a knock came to the door; it was Gerrald to wake her.

She got up, put on the pink dressing gown and asked Gerrald to run her a bath. Molly pinned up her hair so as not to get it wet.

Gerrald ran the bath and locked the bedroom door. She smiled, "You have other things on your mind beside the picnic." He took her hand and led her back to the huge, Queen Anne bed and closed the drapes. Molly felt like a Princess from a bygone age, all closed in and secure. He kissed her passionately, and threw his clothes out one by one. She peeled off the dressing gown and nightdress. They were together, alone, with no disturbances. They kissed, entangled, caressed and made love, giving everything to each other as well as their bodies. Gerrald could wait no longer and the sensual intensity of his closeness exploded with affection inside her, they lay as one for a time, just looking into one another's eyes, feeling sameness.

The moment was shattered by the dripping bath water.

"Quick", they both dashed to the bathroom just in time to see the water slurping all down the bath and onto the floor. They both laughed, "It seems we have spent the weekend moping up bath water," Gerrald said laughing.

"And a lot more besides," Molly had a twinkle in her eye. He had a quick wash and got dressed.

"See you at breakfast." was his departing whisper giving her a kiss on the forehead. She let off some of the bath water and slid inside. The water was lovely and so were her thoughts. Back into the same old casuals as yesterday and down to breakfast. Gerrald's parents had already gone out. Their day started and finished much earlier than Molly and Gerrald's, and it was just as well, she thought.

After breakfast Molly kept her promise and picked some pink roses, from the conservatory. They were in full bloom and smelled so sweet and fresh.

Gerrald was struggling with the picnic hamper, trying to get it fixed somehow to Beauty's saddle. But after a very trying time he decided the roses and the hamper would have to go on ahead. He called Ralph and told him to take it down by the river near the small waterfall and wait there until they arrived. Ralph took the jeep and was quite pleased to be in the fields for a while to give him a break from the stables and the smell of hot horse dung. They saddled up; Molly had forgotten nothing, after her riding lesson yesterday. The birds were in full song, and the sun was blazing. God had smiled on them that day as they gently trotted to what Gerrald called the most beautiful spot on the whole estate. Samson was a very well-behaved horse; it was as if he sensed Molly was a beginner.

He trotted along slowly, without a care in the world. As the ground got softer they could see the tracks left by Ralph's jeep. Gerrald changed the route somewhat, so as not to spoil the surprise. They went through some woodland for some practice for Molly, but only after careful warning from Gerrald, to mind the tree branches, as she would get a nasty blow. They were now in open fields with wild life in full splendour, a rabbit scurried across their tracks presumably back to her litter and safety, there were mole hills all over the place; someone had been busy looking for worms. There was a little brook straight ahead and Gerrald was a bit anxious as to whether Molly would make it across. He slowed down and dismounted. "Now Molly, take it easy. Don't tense up, let Samson do it, just hold on and trust him." She did, and it worked. Gerrald grinned to himself; he did all this when he was only four. Still she was getting there.

They went through some more fields and across a number of little brooks until they heard the thunder of water and a splashing noise. Molly guessed that they were near their picnic spot.

Gerrald said he wanted her to close her eyes; then he told her to dismount, because there in front of her was her surprise. They arrived at the spot and she did as she was told. He spun her round and to her delight, the most pleasing sight engulfed her. There were boulders on the other side of the river with trees growing from them; a little waterfall was crashing down the rocks into the river below. There was evidence of beavers as some of the tree branches were newly gnawed and broken. There were huge oak trees, giving shelter from the hot sun, and the softest grass, carpeting the whole landscape. This place was truly idyllic. Gerrald motioned to Ralph to leave. He did so immediately, and as soon as the noise from his engines ceased in the background, it was back to nature and wildlife with only themselves to share it. Ralph had been considerate, and as well as leaving their hamper in the shade of the huge trees, he had put the champagne in the water surrounded by small rocks to keep it upright and cool.

"Is it as nice as I portrayed?" He asked with almost bated breath. It was of course.

Molly nodded in approval, "The most beautiful place I have ever been invited to." She took the roses and placed them in the river, held fast by a nearby stone. Soon when she could obtain an empty container, she would display them on the picnic cloth, but not yet, Gerrald had other plans. He took her hand and led her around the chosen spot.

From the top of the nearest rock they could see all around the open fields and woodlands they had just ventured through. They caught a last glance of Ralph's jeep as it disappeared from sight. Molly picked some wild flowers and made chains and sat them on her head like a garland. The water was crashing down the waterfall so loud that they had to shout to one another to be heard above it. They passed down by the river again and took another route to get them closer to the waterfall. "Take off your shoes Molly, and we'll paddle under it, just as I used to do as a child; this was my hiding place, it's damp but secret." She rolled up her jeans and followed him through. It was noisy and cold and the little rocks pinched her toes a bit, but she wouldn't have missed it for the world.

Gerrald motioned to a little cave to the left. "It's quieter in there," he said. It was dark, and Molly was scared of creepy crawlies, she almost jumped out of her skin; when a sudden movement; made her scream.

Gerrald calmed her. "It's only a frog passing the time of day; out of the Sun." he assured her. Molly giggled. The rocks were slippery and covered with a green slime which made it difficult to keep upright. Gerrald told her to stay there as he was going further in; it was so dark, Molly felt so alone and vulnerable; she kept watching her feet for spiders or other beasts of the forest. Gerrald had forgotten she was a girl, and most certainly he had been there before with his friends or even his cousin James.

She called to him, almost sobbing. Please come and get me, I'm terrified." She heard his laughter; it echoed all over the place and made her feel even more eerie.

She loved nature but not at such close quarters with little insects and bugs. She need not have worried; Gerrald sensed her genuine fear, and returned to her side immediately. He guided her out of the cave; and back through the waterfall and daylight again. They opened the hamper and spread out the red-and-white checked table cloth. She set the table with all the goodies while he opened the first bottle of champagne.

"Dom Perignon this time, I think." he said to himself aloud. Molly was smacking her lips in anticipation of the tiny bubbles slipping down her throat. The kitchen maids had done them proud. Chicken legs, pate, prawns, shrimps, salad, fruit and two, long crusty, French loaves, plenty of butter and some lemonade. Molly spread it all out and placed the plates and a knife on the cloth. There were two wine glasses, and two, tall tumbler glasses.

"Good, I'll put the roses in this long glass." That she did, and called to Gerrald to bring the champagne. He poured, and they toasted the lovely summer day, and the horses and anything else which moved; they sat and sipped and kissed, and sipped and kissed some more, the food was good so fresh and wholesome, tiny birds were gathering at a safe distance for any crumbs which were left, Molly threw some towards them, and they were quickly snaffled up. They were so full, they just laid there quietly in each other's arms, feeling the tranquility of nature, and their surroundings, engulf them into another world where peace ruled.

Gerrald was first to move, "Come on, I'm going for a swim in that deep pool over there, and so are you." Molly needed no coaxing; this time he didn't need to teach her. She threw off all her clothes, in gay abandon, and as naked as the day she was born, she followed him in. The water was cold to the touch, at first, but soon became warm. They laughed and splashed each other; the champagne had made them both frisky, they swam together entwining their bodies, caressing underwater, touching each other intimately.

Gerrald was already aroused. The cold water had certainly not dampened his ardor. They kissed some more, Molly's breasts were bobbing up and down by the sway of the water. Gerrald held them with both hands spread open. They dunked together still holding each hands, she saw all his naughty bits bouncing up and down. She swam between his legs and felt his virility sensually slither down her back. Gerrald caressed her body taking her to paradise. She could wait no longer her whole body was craving for his. They swam towards the waterfall and climbed underneath; and in the intimate privacy; joined as one in the most rapturously exciting little corner of the world.

They held on with pulsating desire, Molly threw her legs around Gerrald's waist, and he took her weight as if she was floating on air. She clung on to his person as if her life depended on it, waiting for the release of all of his love. He roared with delight which echoed throughout the cave and came back like Tarzan sending a mating call to Jane. They clung together for a few minutes until Gerrald, free from all his desire, loosened his grip and kissed her. They locked in a tender embrace. The water was crashing on Molly's head and it sent tingles through her body. Gerrald appreciated the sight, of Molly's breasts poking through the fast water, nipples protruding, collecting the drops and dripping down her sides. She was awesome. They returned to the pool and washed off all their excitements. They had no towels with them so Molly twirled under the heat of the sun. Gerrald didn't mind being wet and sat down to eat the remnants of the picnic feast, "Come and help me finish the champagne, we have another bottle left."

Molly was quick to respond; she pulled on her panties and bra and sat down with him. Gerrald wasn't shy and stayed naked. Molly liked looking at his body so it suited her. Gerrald poured the champagne, Molly's favourite; pink. It gave her such a lovely feeling, like being on cloud nine, or was it ninety? It was so good. They both had a thrilling afternoon and felt close. Molly's roses were looking a bit worse for wear after the pounding they had taken on their journey there, and the beating from the hot sun. She picked one up, smelled its delicate perfume and sipped her champagne.

This was truly heaven; she would never forget it, as long as she lived, she would remember this moment, forever.

A breeze was getting up and dusk was beginning to fall. Gerrald poured the last of the champagne. Molly gave a toast. She looked at one hand, then the other, "To pink champagne and rose petal dusks." Gerrald echoed her words.

"I'll always remember those words Molly."

"Me too, and the idyllic waterfall you shared with me today."

It was starting to get dark. They got dressed; gave the horses a drink, and packed up the picnic hamper. They took the empty bottle of pink champagne with them, and Molly kept one of the pink roses. She ran to the edge of the river and tossed the others and stood and watched them float away into the horizon. She threw them a kiss and wished them a bon voyage.

They were soon mounted and on their way. It was almost dark when they returned to the house, and a chill was stirring through the evening air.

Ralph took charge of the horses, and they made their way into the house complete with picnic hamper, empty champagne bottle and one rose Molly had salvaged.

As they were leaving later that evening, they both decided to have a rest before dinner. They shouted in to Gerrald's parents that they had returned, made their excuses and promised to tell them of their wonderful day at dinner. The butler was instructed to awaken them both at eight o'clock. Molly picked up the empty champagne bottle and limp, pink rose. They disappeared into their own bedrooms after a quick peck on the cheek. Molly felt exhausted; she closed the door, and immediately ran a bath to wash off the river smells. She put some water in the champagne bottle and inserted the remnants of the once-fresh and pretty rose, and placed it on the bedside table. She undressed and slipped into the bath of foaming water. She had sprinkled some lavender. Come to think of it the lavender bottle was going down at great speed. Still no one would mind. It was a mere pittance compared with the luxury surrounding her. She just laid there soaking for about quarter of an hour. She was so exhausted she almost fell asleep and decided to dry and go to bed for a while.

She drew the curtains to shield out the remaining dusk and sunk into the soft bed and was quickly off to sleep. There was a loud knock on the door. It was the butler with their instructed call for dinner. Molly awoke out of a deep sleep feeling quite fresh. She quickly washed her face and dressed. She would wear her dusky pink suit tonight. It seemed apt after her momentous toast; even she was proud of that one. She pinned her hair up and pinned the fading rose on one side, amazingly it seemed to take life on display. A dusky pink lipstick was the mood of the evening and some pale, lilac eye shadow which fit her mood a splash of lavender cologne and she was ready. She smiled approvingly at her mirror reflection. She knew she was a beauty and loved all admiration. Mrs. Linley was in the drawing room and Molly joined her. She was a dear old lady and seemed very happy with her quiet existence on the edge of Stevenage. She asked Molly to pour them both a sherry while waiting for the men folk. Gerrald was probably having trouble getting up after his exhausting but pleasurable day. As they sipped their Sherries, Mrs.

Linley talked of when Gerrald was young, and the joy he had brought them both in middle age.

Molly had not thought about children, but imagined that growing up on that estate, must had been very lonely with only adult company. There was some laughter coming from the hall. It was Gerrald with his dad they were obviously happy about something. Molly was quick to find out what they were laughing about. It was her new-found adventures, events Molly was very proud of, and she was fast to let them know. The two men laughed away their embarrassment and reassured her, they were only joking. They joined the women in the drawing room and shared the last of the sherry. It had been such a lovely weekend, Molly did not want to go, nor did their hosts want them to leave. "The house has been so full of young laughter this weekend Molly, I do hope you'll come more often, and next time bring your Auntie." She was so sweet, Mrs. Linley. They dined and exchanged stories of the day, the two love birds were careful to keep their passion to themselves.

They didn't fool the old folk; they had forty years on them, and they had never seen Gerrald so happy. It was a sad time getting packed and going back for Molly. She wanted to say good-bye to Samson before she left, Gerrald put all the baggage into his car and spoke to his mother and father privately, while she was gone.

They all hugged and kissed, and it was back to tranquility and silence for the Linleys. Mr. Linley commented how wonderful the weekend had been, gave Ester a squeeze on the knee and said how he wished they had been able to have more children, to fill out the house. Mrs. Linley was quick to reply. "Who knows darling we may have grandchildren soon, and if those two are anything to go by, this house will have children's chatter again."

They sped off, waving good-byes. "I've had the best weekend of my life Gerrald, thank you."

He smiled, pleased with himself. "We'll do it again soon. You were a hit with my parents." They had no sooner set off, than they were back at Aunt Maud's cottage. Molly asked Gerrald in, but after leaving Molly's luggage at the door, he made apologies and left to join his flat mate. Aunt Maud was glad to see Molly and was gushing with all sorts of questions.

Molly smiled, "One at a time, after I have put down my case." The two talked for hours. Aunt Maud was pleased for Molly, she deserved some happiness.

"Oh by the way Molly, a young man called for you on Sunday. He didn't leave a name, tall dark, good-looking and a mustache."

Molly thought it must have been David from work. "Perhaps they wanted me to do some overtime at the office yesterday." This satisfied Aunt Maud for the time being.

The fire was going out, and they both retired. Aunt Maud's seemed such a little house after Gerrald's. Molly sat by the mirror in her bedroom combing her long hair and thinking about the weekend. She smiled to her reflection that was only the beginning. As she slipped into bed she wondered what David had wanted so urgently for him to come to the house uninvited. Anyway she would soon find out tomorrow at work. As she entered the office next day, Sarah was already there, bright and cheerful as usual. Molly said good morning and asked if any overtime was asked for yesterday. "No" was the reply, "Not as far as I'm aware." So it wasn't work. The day went by. Molly told Sarah all about her wonderful weekend with Gerrald, during her lunch hour.

Sarah was fascinated and looked a little envious, but only for a brief moment. She loved her husband and was happy with her life however boring it seemed next to Molly's. The day was almost over and still no sign of the dashing David with the devilish grin, Molly was mocking him, perhaps her fascination with him; was infatuation and not the real thing after all, or perhaps she had one in the bag so nothing was urgent anymore.

Spoke too soon, the lady killer swooped upon them, "Had a nice weekend with Gerrald what's his name?" he said sarcastically to Molly.

Molly drew him one of her dark looks and hissed like a venomous rattler. "It's none of your business."

Everyone else was leaving for home. Molly got up to go, "Don't go yet, I need to talk to you."

"Not here" was Molly's retort. "I'll meet you in the park after tea around seven o'clock."

"Right" was the reply.

Molly was on air, just by a little attention from David!! He could still command an audience with her when he wished. How could she let herself be putty in his hands? What was it he had that she craved so much?

Aunt Maud was out when Molly arrived home so she made herself a sandwich and freshened up for her journey to the park. She paused to wonder if Gerrald would see her, but so what, she belonged to no one, and she was going to stay like that. David was already there, pacing up and down, near the bench they had first met on that lunch time. "Right what do you want?" Molly sounded coarse, even to herself.

"I just want to talk to you. I can arrange for Benjamin's flat on a permanent basis soon, and I wondered if you would spend some time with me there?"

Molly thought for a time, "I don't know."

"You do still want to see me, don't you?" He looked sad and vulnerable for the first time. Molly felt sorry for him. She had no need; it was probably a ploy to bed her.

Molly knew this but she would be bedding him too. "Yes, alright" she said, "But we must keep these meetings quiet, at work especially." She had no need to even suggest this as David had much more to lose than she ever could. They sat together and talked small talk. David never asked her about her weekend. He was probably too scared of the answer, but the fact that she still wanted to see him, made him feel good, and proved that the weekend liaison was not serious, or wasn't at that stage. David said he would be in touch with her as soon as he had made all the arrangements. Molly nodded and left. This all seemed so cold after her loving weekend with Gerrald's family, but she had made no commitment to Gerrald. She had given her body but not her love, only little passion drops of it, and this thought gave Molly a clear conscience.

A few weeks passed. Molly had seen Gerrald several times. They had gone for walks and visited the theatre. They had talked about going riding, and Gerrald had mentioned he would like to take her home again for the weekend, but Molly had asked to wait a little longer before meeting his parents again. Gerrald had sensed something was wrong. "What is it Molly? You did like them? Or did you?"

"Why of course Gerrald, but it's a bit too soon." What she wasn't telling him was that she was still waiting for David to be in touch about the flat, and was already secretly pining for him. She had seen him briefly at the office, from time to time, but had only exchanged brief smiles of recognition, and this was not enough for Molly. She needed something substantial to live on, between her encounters with him. Perhaps it was because he was the forbidden fruit, or perhaps she needed him more than she cared to admit. She arrived at work next day to find a note hidden under her typewriter cover.

It was from David. "Come to the flat tomorrow night at eight o'clock, I'll be waiting for you. Be careful, David."

Molly's heart leaped. She quickly tucked the note in her handbag. Her heart was pounding and she felt devilishly happy with excitement. She was very cheerful that day; everyone noticed.

Sarah thought she was going on a special surprise, with Gerrald, and smiled approvingly. She would be furious with Molly had she known. That evening, and all the next day, Molly was floating on a cloud. Nothing was too much bother at work or at home.

It was time, and Molly was the first to leave. She dashed home and told Aunt Maud not to bother with any tea as she was eating out. She rushed upstairs, ran the bath, poured lavender bath salts in, and some new, foaming bath bubbles Aunt Maud had bought her, and also for extra effect, splashed some cologne. The bathroom smelled like a perfume factory.

While the bath was running, Molly was picking out her best, sexy underwear, pink satin knickers, and camisole top to match, pink suspenders and her sheer nylons. She would wear a figure-hugging dress; she flashed through her wardrobe. Nothing seemed quite right. Oh yes, the cream dress with the big shoulders. That was it. She carefully laid everything on the bed with her new shoes—the red, vamp ones. She was already in a devilish mood; David seemed to create that aura around her. Molly loved being impish, touching on sheer bitch in the making. She knew it and she loved it.

She went quickly into the bath; she wanted her body soft and silky for David. He had almost been allowed to forget her; he wouldn't be allowed to take Molly's feelings for granted again. Molly would make sure about that. After a little soak, not too much though, she caressed her body all over with the slightest touch of body lotion. Then she spun round and round drying it all off, before getting dressed. She took a look in the long mirror in the hall as she passed by.

Yes, she was still a beauty. She loved her body and knew only too well that each man she encountered loved it equally. She brushed her hair until it shone, picked her deep-red sexy lipstick for the total effect of the mood she was in, and with red shoes and red bag, she was ready. With a quick, smug smile to herself in the mirror, she was off. The evenings were becoming lighter, so she would have to be careful. It was so much easier meeting indiscreetly in the dark evenings, when everyone was wrapped up in coat and scarf, and could be mistaken for anyone.

She got to the street and the long alleyway leading to the outside of the flat, there, she took a quick, secret look, from side to side before entering.

No one was around, so she went up the stone stair to the flat. The door was open, and a figure was standing, waiting in the hall. It was the tall, masculine outline of David, probably with his flashing smile at the ready. She ran to him, he saw her and kept his ground. It was more dangerous for him than for her. He scooped her up in his arms and carried her into the hall, quickly closing the door behind him. There they were at last, in their own little nest; the rest of the world could do whatever the hell it liked. For the next three hours, this was their time to enjoy and relish the pleasure of being alone together. David went to the kitchen and brought some wine.

They sat together on the sofa, sipping the wine and asking each other what they had been up to in the weeks of their separation. Molly told him all sorts of little things she had been up to, omitting Gerrald, but of course David knew.

He just chose not to persist on those lines as he was married, and knew that both must live with the fact that they were involved with other people, so a pact was made not to mention either partner ever. They drank to that. David took her glass and put it on the coffee table. He put his arms around her and drew her back on the sofa. No words were spoken, his eyes said it all. He had missed her, much more than she realized, she could almost see love in them, but that was a word that must never be spoken, as he was not free to love her. They kissed and caressed in a gentle way, and he started undressing her. The town hall clock chimed the half hour. Already time was trying to beat them, and Molly wished someone could stop time for a whole day and night, only once. Molly's clothes were

177

strewn around the floor. She unbuckled David's belt, unzipped his trousers and pushed them to the floor.

She ran her fingers through his hairy chest, down his body, searching inside his underwear through the mass of pubic hair, touching, caressing his soft velvet skin. She almost loved him at that moment, and how she loved his body. She pulled at his scanty clothing and kissed him all over, with a passion that had been welling up inside her for weeks. She too was full of desire. He removed her satins and nylons and pulled her intimately onto the goatskin in front of the fire. He pressed his body onto hers, encircling her with his passion and kissing her all over, pausing at her ample breasts for extra arousal. She held him so tight; she was scared he would disappear as quickly as they had met. She wanted his body, and strangely, she needed his love too. He kissed her forehead. "If only we were free to love." He had said it! That was all the encouragement Molly needed. She stretched her legs and slithered them around his whole body, until their desires met, and they made love like neither of them had done before. It lasted only a short time, as they both needed each other so much, and the strain of waiting so long for Molly, had made David unable to control himself. They held each other, whispering sweet words, gently kissing until all fervor had left David's body. Molly stretched out her hand for her glass. They sat on the goatskin rug drinking the wine, looking at each other with a sparkle Molly had never experienced with Gerrald or Simon.

Had David penetrated her steel plating? Molly thought not. She put on the dressing gown behind the bathroom door. It was enormous and obviously belonged to Ben.

David put on a record, and they just relaxed in each other's arms. They said very little tonight. Their actions and feelings for each other said it all.

"Do you care for some supper?"

"It's the usual. I'm afraid it's quick and convenient to make." Molly loved chili and baked potatoes.

"Yummy, it's almost as good as you." They smiled. He set the bench table in the kitchen, and they were soon eating and sipping more wine and bubbling with laughter at the sheer joy of being alone together. Their conversation was non-existent tonight and would probably be boring to the minds of the world, but it made them feel content and happy, with that extra sparkle, that told them apart from others less fortunate. They ate and cleared up; the record had stopped. Time was not on their side. David talked of his trip to India and the months he would be away. Veronica, the Ice Lady would be going with him. Perhaps it was for the best in a way. This would give them both, time to think, and to assert the depth of their relationship. Anyhow, it wasn't for a few months yet, and David had come to some arrangement with Ben to take care of the flat in that time, as he had already left on his own trip overseas.

Molly felt good in the thought that this could be their little love nest for the next few months, and as she was given a key, she could come and go as she wished. She had already made some mental notes in her mind of what was missing from the flat; some ornaments and prints and some fresh flowers and cushions, and things which only a woman would want. Tomorrow she would start on her shopping sprees to make the flat more homely, and not so bland. But tonight was not yet over. She drew David's face to hers. "I love you David."

There, it was out, all the words which were bottled up inside her for so long. He pecked her cheek. "I love you too, Molly, but things are not going to be easy, and although we now have the flat, I still have to be careful not to arouse any suspicions for Veronica's sake."

Molly pouted. "I hate that woman!" Even the sound of her name made Molly furious. She felt no remorse or sorrow for the woman or any feelings of guilt about what she was doing. All Molly wanted was David, and she would go to all lengths to capture him and keep him, possess him, if necessary. "Can not; have!" Were words that were never allowed in Molly's vocabulary! Molly had always got what she wanted, when she wanted, and for as long as she wanted—David was the victim, and he was falling into her well-prepared trap. It was time for them to go. Molly spun round and round, she felt that this was her own little flat, and she was going to share it with David, for at least three months. It was all the time Molly needed to make David believe he could not live without her.

The night had almost ended. Time, it seemed hated them both. The town hall clock almost smiled on the eleventh chime, it was time to scurry away down the dark alleyway like a frightened rat, back to the sewer and safety—this for Molly was back to Aunt Maud's—not quite a sewer, but safety, openness, and love that was not forbidden, or shady and secret. Her aunt was already in bed and Molly went up herself. She always felt morbid and dull after leaving David. It was if her other half was paralyzed into obscurity, and this left her solitary and frightened, like the first time Merry and her had been separated.

Her thoughts returned to Merry and their attic bedroom at Father's house. She remembered their shared toys and the oneness, only twins can know. Molly was devilish and awkward almost to the extreme, sometimes as if she was living Merry's life for her too. Poor Merry, Molly went off to sleep that night with sweet thoughts of Merry.

Molly was already awake and deep in thought, when Aunt Maud called up to her, the next morning. She was thinking of the night before. She loved David and would get him if it killed her.

She set off for work the following morning, and got some weird sort of excitement passing David in the corridor, and saying a nonchalant "Good morning" as if they were strangers and friends only at work. She longed to put her arms around him, kiss him and drag him into the filing room, but all was forbidden.

Instead, she looked him in the eye and smiled. Then she flicked her hair, stuck her nose in the air, and moved away in an aristocratic, flamboyant, manner. She hoped this fooled David; it almost fooled her. Days and nights went by; Gerrald was still seeing her, and she was happy with Gerrald but only, if she knew she had a meeting David, one day that week. But David had not been in touch. She was thinking about him one evening when Gerrald came for her at work. Deep in thought, she almost passed by without acknowledging him.

Gerrald was hurt and upset. She saw the sadness in his eyes. He too loved Molly. In her wickedness she agreed to meet Gerrald that night, and in her thoughts she was going to take him to the flat—her love nest with David. She was twisting the key in her hand and almost burned her fingers with the friction, she was filled with hatred and desire for David; it was days since she had, any proper contact with him. He would burn tonight. She met Gerrald at the little cafe by the park, the one where they had first met, Gerrald thought it was romantic. Molly had other ideas. She had worn her most sensual red satin underwear that night. Her toe and finger nails were red; and her lipstick was the most seductive. She was a beauty outwardly for all to see, but in her mind, the most whorish thoughts enveloped her, turning her into a being ready to erupt, into the most bitch-ridden vampire, clawing at sanity. Evil prevailed tonight, in the clouded cloak of love, and passion, and Gerrald was at the beneficial end. All of his desires would be fulfilled tonight. Molly reassured herself David would pay for his two days lateness.

They acted like lovers on their first date. Gerrald had not been so close to Molly since their weekend at his parents, she spoke of that weekend with great tenderness. Molly had no time for it in her thoughts, tonight, but played along. She told him how she loved it, and how she had begged her girlfriend to let her have a key to her flat, so that they could share intimate moments together. Gerrald fell for it hook, line, and sinker. He was in love, and everything, except Molly, was a blur to him at that moment, and just being with her anywhere was heaven to him. They walked down towards the entrance, and the two shops on either side seemed to sneer in disapproval. Molly hated them anyway. They were forbidding and prime evil, the first time she saw them, and tonight it was her turn, the hatred was welling up inside her. She was about to do some serious damage to her relationship with David, but she did not care. Only one would survive, and it would be Molly. She smiled at Gerrald and urged him forward. "It's a bit dark, but my friend said to count the stairs; there's seven of them, remember." They both giggled. Molly was fiddling with the key when the two neighbors from the flat above came out, "Oh good," she said.

"This saves me the effort, of finding my key!""

"But are you expected?" they asked.

Molly scowled at them and shooed them off. "What business is it of yours?" The two people, now taken aback, were only too glad to disappear. Gerald unsuspecting and loving as ever, kissed Molly and rushed after her into the flat. Molly was quick to close the curtains in the event of any unsuspecting stranger looking up and wondering what was going on. She turned on the lights, and took a bottle of wine from the fridge. It was cool, white and dry, just as Molly liked it.

She was evil that night, an evil brought on by overpowering love, taken to the extreme, in the obscurity of being the other woman. Molly was the woman and would not take second place to anyone. She poured Gerrald a glass of wine; the same glasses David and she had used, promising their undying love for each other, but Molly made no reference to it. She giggled and toasted Gerrald: "To secret dark alleyways and meetings of the sinister kind."

Gerrald looked puzzled, "What happened to pink champagne and Rose petal dusks?"

Molly now angered, and beyond control said. "What the hell do you want anyway?"

Gerrald was shocked. "Molly my sweet, I want for us to be happy. Molly with her Gemini trait in full swing, changed again. After all, falling out with Gerrald would not find mission accomplished!

She sipped her wine and blew him a kiss, "Only teasing, my love." They drank some more wine and opened another bottle. Molly looked round the flat, the books were placed on the shelf all even and correct, the almanac, so precious, was left on its own on top of the cabinet. The plants were on the window ledge of life and watered; this she could see by the glowing moonlight through the light, summer curtains. The chairs were worn and obscure and hard, and David was oozing from them, his presence was all around the room. Molly felt hurt, let down and second hand; worn out like yesterday's socks. But she would go through with this charade if it killed her. She needed to do it for her self esteem and her hatred for the man she loved. She gestured to Gerrald to come to the bedroom, dropping an article of clothing at a time. He picked them up, smelled her perfume from them and laid them down where they had fallen.

She did not love Gerrald, she liked him, and liked him enough to do this. He loved her and she knew it. She went into the little bedroom. The single bed was in the corner of the room, the moon glinted through the curtains which did not quite close. The town clock was sounding its time on the hour, and its disapproval, Molly knew, but she took no notice. She slipped into the single bed throwing the covers to the floor. She had her red bask and stockings still on, the panties were thrown over the vase of silk flowers, covering them like an exquisite lampshade, shielding their eyes craving the ecstasy yet to begin. Gerrald came to her side. He kissed her tenderly in the manner he always kept for Molly.

His deep love was always there no matter what. She pulled him abruptly towards her. He was still fully clothed, and Molly was most annoyed. She undid his tie and almost ripped the last few articles of clothing from him, leaving his under pants. She wanted him in a lustful way to complete her evil feat of the night. She let her ample breasts slip from within her under garment, showing them to him; her nipples were large and forthright.

He latched on one, then the other, like a newborn lamb, frenzied for milk. She sat up and threw her arms in the air and let her breasts have their freedom. They swayed in a cumbersome manner, with a slight bounce. He was driven beyond ecstasy, his underwear pointed forward, desperate to succumb to powers beyond his. But she would not have it, not yet. She wanted to lure him on even more. She ran her fingers down her long legs, sensually, only just missing his favourite place.

Provocatively arching her back, and running her tongue over her lips, in a fashion which drives men to the end of all saving holds; she saw it in his face, and lying on her back, with her breasts pointing to the ceiling, she moaned and coaxed him nearer to his paradise.

He kissed her nipples. He got as near to her as any human being could with another, Gerrald wanted this moment to last forever. Their oneness was interrupted only, by the soft pounding movements and his gasping for as much oxygen as the air could supply, to keep him going as long as possible. But her vengeance took over, and his release became quick and unsatisfying for Molly.

Still, she did what she wanted to do. She destroyed the secret love, she and David had found in that flat. Her jealousy and hatred had destroyed something wonderful and sweet. Love had many alleyways to exit; this one was the lowest. Gerrald had enjoyed their night of love so much that she resented him also. But why spoil Gerrald's dream, he was in seventh heaven. Molly quickly got dressed. She couldn't bear to wear Ben's dressing gown, the one she wore while with David, or stay any longer. Her vengeance had only hurt herself, she felt dirty and low, and she hated mostly herself—sadness prevailed, humility and self hate, followed. She had used Gerrald, deceived David, and hurt no one but her innermost self. Anyone else she could get over, but she couldn't run away from herself. Depression took over.

Molly's thoughts returned to Merry, her other half, her dearest sister. Molly was living life at double pace, she thought. Perhaps she was trying to live Merry's too. Molly loved Merry and wished for nothing more than for Merry to be whole again in mind and in body. This was a wish Molly would carry to her grave. There was absolutely no hope, for Merry now. Molly had been left bitter and evil, but able to cope, as poor Merry had wasted away under the strain. Molly promised herself that some day soon she would visit Merry even if it upset her. Sometimes Molly got extra encouragement and strength by seeing Merry and promising her to live for each of them.

Thoughts of Merry drifted away, and Molly was left with the feelings of the venture that has just taken place. Perhaps she was better to settle for Gerrald who loved her, and could provide for her every whim. After all, lovemaking with Gerrald was very satisfying, when she gave her all to it. The love thing was something else, but surrounded by all that wealth and love, she could probably make do.

She slept that night with an underlying conflict in her mind. The next morning found Molly undecided and unsure what to do. She would have nothing to do with either man, as they both, in turn, brought her hurt and boredom. She was a free agent again and ready and willing to tackle the world as a very self-esteemed young lady. Her life was quite peaceful and uneventful for a few weeks. She had told both lovers where to go, and they had kept their distance. Molly had decided to change her job and find something more satisfying. She had heard that there was a typist needed at the factory on the other side of town, she had dismissed writing letters, and gone down there, in person, that same day. She had a meeting with an elderly man, a Mr. Morrison, who she presumed, was the owner who took to her immediately like a grandfather.

Next day there was a letter offering her the job. She was delighted, a change was as good as a rest, and a set of new faces was just what Molly needed right now. The mutual agreement was to start work the following week, and it came so suddenly, Molly had no time for leaving parties and the like. Out of sight, out of mind, was Molly's philosophy of life.

Off with the old, on with the new.

Her first day went well, and she found herself once more thinking of Merry, cooped up in that Sanitarium. She would visit her sister soon. However, soon became an empty word and the months passed, and Molly was already promoted from typist to Personal Assistant to the Managing Director. She accompanied him on his visits abroad and met the most influential people.

Molly had busied herself so much with her position at work; she had little time for, herself. She had been on her own for quite some time now. In fact, when Molly looked at the date on the calendar, she realized for the first time, that almost five months had just flown by with her hardly being involved with any man. She was beginning to feel the job was becoming too time-consuming and dull.

She had saved quite a sizable sum of money and decided to buy some property. The next day she rang in sick. Mr. Morrison the Managing Director was angry and was more than a little short with her. Molly deserved the break and took no more notice of his rather sulky mood. She picked up the local paper and looked for 'Houses for Sale'. She decided the country would be nice with all the wildlife, greenery and tranquility. There were several which took her interest, but she kept coming back to the same one. It looked idyllic in the photograph with white, stone walls and medieval windows, some of them stained-glassed. It even boasted a turret on the East side. It was a little out of her price range, but she wanted it. The appointment was made and Mrs. Locherty, the owner, sounded like a nice well-spoken lady on the phone. Molly marked in her diary 7:00 p.m. Wednesday the 13th of May—the day after next. That morning she was up and off to work early, she did not want any bad moments with Mr. Morrison, nothing was allowed to spoil her preconceptions of the prospective property.

Five o'clock came sooner than she had imagined. She stopped at the cafe on the corner of the street where she worked, grabbed a sandwich and coffee, and caught the six-thirty bus for Greenswinton Village. She asked the driver to let her know when she should get off for Thistledown Cottage. The journey was quiet and pleasant. It was a mild, early summer night and the sky was a beautiful amber and crimson—a Carmen Miranda style, fruitful bounty smiled down on her, in the form of the colourful sky. The bus dropped her at the end of a little tree-scattered lane, which ran alongside a little stream with wild roses growing to one side.

Molly trundled along with her work bag over her shoulder. It was a couple of minutes to seven as she arrived at Thistledown Cottage. It was even more beautiful and quaint than its picture had shown. There and then at the end of the path, she fell in love with it. The windows were indeed arched and also the door, the entire cottage was painted white, and the window frames and sills were matt black.

There was a little black porch over the front door sheltering visitors from the elements of the weather, whilst waiting for acceptance. The roses were growing all over the front-facing wall, parading their beauty and stretching out their branches like limbs, in a never-ending yawn.

There was movement at a down stairs window, and a little old lady with a friendly, genuine face came to the front door. Molly introduced herself and was invited in, past the two chimney pots on either side of the door, being used as planters, for the overflowing sweet peas and nasturtiums. Far too wild and too many, cramped into the tiny space, breathless and bravely smiling their greeting, on her visit.

In the entrance vestibule, stairs led to the bedrooms, remarkably still stained in their original colour. Mrs. Locherty guided her to the right, into a lounge with beamed ceilings, where copper pans and kettles, hung from hooks attached to the beams. Sunshine flooding in, through the double aspect windows, brought the room to life. It was a rather large, open lounge, with the same arched windows to the back as well as the front. There was boarding, stained mahogany on one of the walls, in a Tudor sort of fashion. Mrs. Lockerty had a cottage suite and spinning jenny in the far end of the room. A grandfather clock, made its presence known, as it loudly let them know it was Seven Fifteen already. Mrs. Locherty remarked on its excellent time keeping.

They moved out of the lounge area and into the kitchen. It was a large dining kitchen, and the units were completely fitted all the way round in antique oak, and there in the middle of the floor, was a larger than average solid, antique oak dining table, able to sit ten people quite comfortably. Mrs. Locherty had herbs of all sorts drying out and hanging from a rack on the ceiling. The aroma-scented room housed two dressers, holding blue and white porcelain plates, in the Willow pattern. The walls were spangled with pictures of fruit, milk jugs and lobster cages, and a clutter of utensils. On one of the unit tops, a long, narrow flat basket lay, with gloves and scissors carefully placed, ready for their owner's exit into the garden, at the back of the house. The windows to the kitchen, four in all, were carefully placed into the wall in regular intervals, for maximum light. Molly was amazed at just how perfect the cottage was for her own needs.

She was anxious to see the rest of the house. Without an invitation, and full of expectations, she felt herself climbing the stained, curved stairway followed by its owner. At the top of the stairs there was a minstrel gallery with three doors, spreading like fingers within the hallway. Mrs. Locherty beckoned for Molly to open the first door. It was the main bedroom, with one wall clad from top to bottom, in mahogany-carved wood, with faces and figures and court jesters and fiddlers, in gay abundance bringing the full eighteenth century to life, before their eyes. The other three walls were painted white with a small mahogany picture rail going around the room. On the far wall, there were two arched windows, both stained red-and-blue with leaded triangles cutting through the picture on them.

The wall straight ahead was courted by the most magnificent four-poster bed carved the same as the first wall; the bed was both extravagant and elaborate in its extreme, with jade coloured, green velvet curtains and bedspread, gilded with tassels and embroidery.

At the foot of this spectacular bed, was a bedding box, quilted in the same fabric as the curtains, adorning the bedroom windows! Molly felt a sense of yesteryear and peace in this room. Molly ventured open-mouthed and dazed to the next bedroom which held a shock for her. Unlike the other room with its austere and extravagant surroundings, this one was cold with bare floor boards with cobwebs falling from ceiling to floor. In the far corner next to the window was an old-fashioned crib with the lace frills all moth-eaten with wear. There were teddies and dollies from a long gone age pushed into a large wooden box. The dust had settled in this room for many years.

It was damp and cold—an uncared for oil lamp was lying on its side across a small table, the lamp was so covered in dust it was difficult to know what color the glass shade was. Even the key in the lock had been difficult to turn in its rusty state. Molly gave a shiver and turned to Mrs. Locherty who gave no explanation. They finally looked in at the bathroom. It was beautiful, all done in black-and-white tiles both on the floor and on the walls. There was a mirror from ceiling to floor on one wall. The bath still had its original feet and taps, huge brass ones with the words "Hot" and "Cold" written in blue on the small, round marble tops. The sink matched well in ceramic white, and the loo had the biggest cistern almost touching the ceiling, with a great, long, brass chain, and wooden handle.

Molly loved the house, except for unused dusty, second bedroom. But with careful decoration and a little heat, it could be made warm and inviting again. She remembered there had been an open fireplace in the room, which could be brought back to life. Molly gave her thanks to Mrs Locherty and left. As she waited at the bus stop, she could not help thinking of that second bedroom and why is had been left untouched for all those years! Perhaps had the curtains been drawn open, she may have got a better picture of the size and possibility, of how much refurbishment it required.

Molly's thoughts were drowned by the noise of the bus's engine and its brakes, as it screeched to a halt by her side. She boarded with thoughts, only of getting to be the owner of that cottage. She had been so enthralled, by the updating requirements of the second bedroom; that she had forgotten to look at the back garden. She would make another appointment and see it tomorrow.

Molly slept heavily in bed that night, tossing and turning, waking and going back into deep sleeps. Merry crept into her mind more than once, and the also the second bedroom at Thistledown cottage. She could sleep no longer, she threw open the bedroom window and gazed up at the stars. The night sky was dark; the moon only a quarter, which barely lit the heavens. The stars twinkled and shone but could not help the darkness. Still, as the air was, the cold was penetrating; Molly shivered and went back to bed, and closed her eyes.

The brightness of the morning woke her with a jolt. She bathed and dressed hurriedly, left the house and almost ran to the bus stop—work would have to miss her that day, she was so obsessed with Thistledown cottage, she made her way straight there without an appointment.

The countryside was just as pleasant the second time around and the little lane and stream just as inviting. The cottage came into view and she could see Mrs. Locherty outside in the front garden, cutting back overgrown roses and cleaning the chimney pots planters.

It was as if Mrs. Locherty had read her mind the previous day. Molly shouted to her and waved. Mrs. Locherty was surprised to see Molly so soon, but Molly knew she would be back to that cottage. They shook hands on the path, and Molly asked if she could have another look round.

"Yes." Was the reply from the friendly face; who volunteered a little more information; on her private life.

"It has become too much for me now since my husband passed away over two years ago. The garden's getting overgrown, and the walk to the village seems so much further than it did fifty years ago when we first moved in."

Molly took it all in again, and the second time she noticed much more—just how huge the stone fireplace was in the lounge, all set up with dry logs just waiting to be lit on the first notion of a chill breeze. The old lady invited Molly to look around on her own this time, taking care to let her know the second bedroom was always kept locked, and if she wanted another look, Mrs. Locherty would come upstairs and let her in. Molly nodded, but decided not to bother looking in the disused room for now.

She was careful though, to have a good look in the back garden. As she opened the back door, she saw there was a pagoda with wild roses climbing along the trellises, reaching upwards looking like Jack's bean stock! There was a patio garden right in the centre with a white ornate table and chairs, pushed aside, as if they had only minutes ago, been vacated by the lounging occupants. The garden was bizarre with flowers of all colours; shapes and sizes, smiling and beckoning the sun to shine on them alone. There was a birdhouse just next to the patio area, and it was full with blue tits, blackbirds, swallows, and magpies, all trying to get a free meal, clambering and squawking like women in the January sales at the hat stalls. The garden went a long way back, and just at the end, past the flowerbeds and birdhouse, was the most quaint, Victorian summerhouse Molly had ever had the good fortune to gaze upon. It was hexagon-shaped with leaded glass to the tops of the windows. It had not been looked after properly and some windows needed replacing, but the structure was sound. The garden furniture was made of cane, with floral antique cushions strewn around. There was also a rather large coffee table in the centre.

Molly approached the opened double doors of the Summerhouse and ventured inside. It was dry and warm with the sun beaming down. It felt safe and soothing. It gave supreme sanctuary as if in the womb. She would buy this house no matter what. Her daydreams were interrupted by Mrs. Locherty tapping on the glass. Molly smiled and greeted her. "I love the house!" She said, nodding in full appreciation of the house and all of its grandeur and secrets.

A very relaxed Molly boarded the bus for town that morning. Molly busied herself, going through the motions of the administration, but more importantly seeing solicitors and bank managers to make sure of a speedy purchase of Thistledown cottage.

Several days had passed, when, one morning she awoke with the sound of the letterbox rattling, pulled on her dressing gown and made for the bottom of the stairs.

There was a letter on the mat. She picked it up; it was from Marcus & Pickles, her solicitors, tearing the envelope open it read. "Can you make an appointment to sign the contract on Tuesday morning?" Molly was overjoyed. She was about to move away from the front door when she noticed another letter on the mat. Molly's reaction to this one was one of sudden fright.

The letter was from the Sanitarium: where Merry lived. Molly ripped back the envelope; it read. "Merry has had another setback. Please come at once." Molly telephoned to say she would be there in the morning. That morning of all mornings Molly slept late, the sudden clanging of milk bottles awoke her at 9.00 a.m. it was the milkman finishing his deliveries. She dressed and washed hurriedly and was on the train and heading for the Sanitarium in less than twenty minutes. The train journey was always tiresome for Molly as she never knew what to expect on arrival. Merry's moods could change by the minute. The train stopped, and the guard took Molly's ticket. She started the long walk up to the old mansion. It started to rain a few drops at first, then it absolutely poured down.

Molly sheltered under an old oak tree; she seemed to be there, but not there—her mind was an abyss with thoughts of Merry. What had gone wrong this time? Molly's shoes were wet and her nylons damp. The dampness and cold made Molly shiver and shudder, but that shudder was mild compared with the shudder yet to come! The rain eased, and Molly decided to brave it, up to the old mansion. She reached the wrought iron gates, which were very much in need of a coat of paint. The steps to the front door seemed steeper today, and the heavy burden Molly had in her heart made them harder still, to conquer. She was at the reception area, a bit bedraggled, but there she was. The Matron came down to greet her. She led Molly to a little room just off the main corridor. She spoke softly but firmly.

"Miss Wentworth must not be aroused in any way today Molly, as she has had to be heavily sedated and restricted for her own safety." Molly was shown to a room no bigger than eight feet by six feet, the floor was bare with only a bed and bedside table in the room. There was a cracked toilet in the corner, with no seat exposed for all to see. This was a dank, dark room indeed. Merry was laid on the bed, her hands tied down at the sides by two leather straps. Her eyes were closed, and she showed no resistance or acknowledgement. Molly spoke to her quietly. A very slight twittering of one eyelid was about all the greeting Molly received. She sat for a few more moments, just looking around. What an utterly horrible place to have to live. She tapped the door quietly for the nurse to let her out. Molly, wet and heavy-hearted, bowed her head and left that place with a promise in her mind that she would go more often and help to get Merry better.

Tomorrow would be a better day, she would be signing her contract and hoped to move house within the month. It would be her sister's birthday soon, and Molly would plan a surprise for Merry. Where had all the years gone? How the time had flown. The weather had improved on the journey back, and Molly was starting to get a little brighter about the whole situation. Next day she found herself sitting in the foyer of Marcus & Pickles. She was early and was just relaxing, when who should walk in but Gerrald Linley. Molly gasped, "My, it is nice to see you again Gerrald, what brings you here?"

"Bad news I'm afraid," was Gerrald's answer. "Dad passed away two months ago, and we have come to hear the reading of the will."

"We?" questioned Molly. Gerrald motioned to the door, and in came Mrs. Linley. She looked drawn and thin, the last few months had taken their toll. Molly went to her and put her arms around the poor old lady. Mrs.

Linley appreciated the gesture, and asked Molly to visit her again as soon as she found the time. Molly accepted the offer and promised to see her soon. The switchboard in reception buzzed, and the receptionist told Molly Mr. Pickles was ready for her now. Molly said her goodbyes and went in the direction of Mr. Pickles' office. Mr. Pickles sat behind his large desk; he was surrounded by books of all titles, but mostly law. His room was full of mahogany, the bookshelves, the desk, the windows, even half way up the walls, all smelled dusty and old Mr. Pickles, bespectacled, invited Molly to sit down on the old, worn out chesterfield chair adjoining his over-sized desk. He explained a few, minor details and got Molly to sign the contracts.

"We should be able to get you settled in Thistledown Cottage in two weeks." Molly beamed, she was delighted.

She couldn't wait to let Gerrald know on her way out, but he had already gone through with his mother, to see Mr. Marcus. Molly left it for another time. When Molly got home that evening Aunt Maud was already in. She had been baking, and the smell of freshly baked bread met Molly as she opened the door. She sat Aunt Maud down in the lounge. "I have got some news for, you Aunt Maud. At last I am about to own my own home. I did not want to let you know anything about it until I had sorted out all the details. Well, I have signed the contract today and am about to move in, in two weeks." Aunt Maud looked a bit shaken but congratulated Molly all the same. "Also I saw Merry today, she's strapped to her bed and sedated." Aunt Maud gasped. "We must go and see her as soon as possible.

"We will Aunt Maud, but I must get moved first."
Maud agreed.

Molly busied herself in the next few days hunting
around for furniture and pictures and knickknacks.
The 30th of May was the move-in date, and that suited
Molly fine. Mrs. Locherty offered to leave all carpets and
curtains, which helped Molly a lot.

The day came and the furniture van arrived, Molly
was ordering them around, being extra careful, they
didn't drop any of the new ornaments and plants. She
would not allow Aunt Maud to see Thistledown Cottage
until she had filled it with furniture. The removal men
worked hard that day, the sweat was pouring from them
when they left at 5.30 in the evening. Molly moved a few
pieces of furniture around until she had it exactly as she
wished. The floral cottage suite she had bought matched
the curtains very well; even the coffee table matched
the beamed walls and ceilings perfectly. She had some
ornaments and antique plates on stands on the picture
rail, and a really old, brass coal bucket, was placed on the
huge fire hearth, with a few dry logs placed inside. She
moved some boxes and paper into the back garden. There
was a brass kettle on stand somewhere amongst all the
debris; and she wanted it to go on the hearth adjacent to
the coal bucket as they matched like a pair.

The kitchen needed nothing extra as Mrs. Locherty
had left the huge antique oak table with all its chairs and
all the artifacts on the walls including the lobster pots
and pictures. She even left her herbs drying. Molly had
bought a huge mahogany bed for the main bedroom.
She also bought two matching bedside cabinets and a
bedding box.

The room looked softer; the four-poster bed Mrs. Locherty had was a little overbearing. Molly threw a soft peach colored bedspread over the bed. The bathroom still kept its mirror, and Molly had bought some pink towels and bath mats to soften the black and white marble. It looked expensive, and she liked it. Molly thought of the middle bedroom, she had not gone inside, and the door was still locked. She left it that way. Enough was enough for one day.

Molly went downstairs and looked around. She was pleased with what she saw. She would add more pieces, as the money came in. A bath was the order of the day; full of bubbles and oils. Molly soaked for ages; she felt good being the owner of Thistledown Cottage. She picked up the pink towel and started to dry herself. She looked at her outline in the mirror. Her voluptuous breasts and huge brown nipples were much in need of a man's hands around them.   It had been too long!

Chapter Seven

MOLLY WAS NERVOUS, AS she sat waiting for her first visitor. She had made some shepherd's pie for lunch; nothing extravagant, but wholesome. She fluffed up cushions in the lounge, moved the ornaments and adjusted the logs in the fireplace. She heard the low rumbling of the bus engine, and she ran to the end of the path. Aunt Maud's outline, could be seen coming slowly up the Lane, Molly ran to her; linking up arms, and guiding her to the front door.   Molly was full of news about the cottage.

They went up the path and past the chimney pots at the door, and entered the hallway with the stained mahogany stairs ahead. Molly gestured for Aunt Maud to go straight through; she loved the lounge, and was overwhelmed with the kitchen and bedroom. The bathroom too, got Aunt Maud's approval. "What's in there?" Aunt Maud asked and Molly replied, "At the moment, I'm using the spare room for odds and ends, and for storing things." Aunt Maud's curiosity was satisfied. The women went downstairs and had a good old chat, ending with their supper, and a glass of elderberry wine, Aunt Maud had brought with her.

Molly waited until the time was right, and mentioned to Aunt Maud about her visit to the Sanitarium, and the restrained state Merry was in.   Her Aunt was distraught. She too, would go with Molly next week on the twin's birthday, the 6th of June. In the next few days which followed, Molly busied herself tidying up in the garden and cutting back the shrubbery. Occasionally, she passed the second room and wondered how long it would take her to do it up.   Not today—it would be another day when Molly had more money and settled. The twins' birthday was nearing, only two days to go. Molly went shopping. She wanted a jumper for Merry, and she wanted it in jade, the colour of her eyes. She searched the shops and catalogues until she was almost exasperated, and out of energy. Then she came upon a little, out-of-the-way, boutique sort of shop. There in the window was a beautiful mohair jade jumper, just the style Molly had been looking for. It had sparkle and sequins done in flowers, she pictured in her mind's eye. Merry was soo beautiful, her hair cascaded in an unkempt, tempestuous way, down her back. It glowed with an unprovoked ebony shine. It was the colour of the darkest sky in the throws of fury, abandoned only moments ago, by the storm. Merry's eyes were the greenest jade, as exquisite Columbian Emeralds, Molly reflected and smiled. She had a truly beautiful sister, even if the passages of time had taken their toll.

The jumper was exactly what Molly wanted for Merry. Molly would take it up tomorrow. Nothing was planned for this birthday as nothing very eventful had happened, but secretly, Molly wanted to bring Merry home, to Molly's very own home, for their birthday. She would ask when she got to the Sanitarium. That morning she donned her favorite Sunday outfit, passed the chimney pots in the doorway, closed the little gate on Thistledown cottage and went to Aunt Maud's. The morning was warm, and the sun was just peeping behind the fluffiest of clouds as she approached Aunt Maud's door. Aunty was ready, and the two, made their way to the train station, a journey they had made together so many times before. They stood there, waiting the arrival of the locomotive, and Molly recalled this was the station where she and Gerrald had met for the first time. How times had changed. She thought of the chance meeting at the solicitor's, and of Mrs. Linley's invitation. At that moment she made up her mind she would take her up on it. Molly deserved a few days away and what better place to spend it, and in what better company than Gerrald's. The train seemed to arrive before it departed; they were on their way up the hill to the Stately Sanitarium. Each step seemed heavier than the one before, and neither party knew what was in store for them. Whichever way things turned out, there was always sadness there, and Merry was always left behind to her own devices with no one for comfort. They approached the reception area, and the Matron; welcomed them inside. They were shown towards Merry's little room. As they neared the door, it opened, and Merry stood in the door frame, excited and smiling, with a little package in her hand.

Molly ran the last few steps, and the twins embraced, twirled and giggled in excited laughter. It was difficult to tell who was who, as they both looked so happy and healthy together, Aunt Maud was delighted. The girls twirled their way into Merry's little room with its pleasant, flowered curtains and bedspread. They chatted and giggled together, they discussed their past, and they talked about Mother with deep affection, and Father. Merry even asked about Simon. Molly was so happy, Merry seemed normal at last. She would ask the Matron if Merry could come and see her new home. Molly was careful not to mention it to Merry until she had full approval of the visit. Merry pushed her little parcel into Molly's lap and gestured for her to open it. Molly kissed her sister on the cheek and gently unraveled the little package. It was two little knitted dolls, sewn together, identical. Molly knew what the gesture meant and cuddled her sister, "You and me Merry." Merry nodded, and Molly said. "We will be together one day Merry, just you and me. In the meantime I will treasure this gift and keep it always."

Merry pointed towards the window, towards two more identical dollies, sewn together, lying on her dressing table between her hair brush and her mirror. "I have mine too."

The bell rang and the three had to be separated. Merry was smiling and full of excitement; and the girls kissed and hugged. Aunt Maud remembered her present for Merry, and she left it in her hand. "Open it my dear when we have gone, you will like it, I'm sure." Molly had the same present at home waiting to be opened.

Their feet echoed in the corridors, as each footstep touched the shining, hard vinyl floor. The reception area was full of people, as they approached. Molly singled out the Matron and asked if Merry was well enough to come out for a day's visit to her new home. The Matron looked serious.

"Merry seems well enough at the moment; we are trying her on a new course of drugs, no one knows what the outcome will be. She is well today, and seems to be responding, but some days are very dark indeed, and she thinks she is someone else. Sometimes she even thinks she's you, Molly. All the little tales you tell her, she relives them in her mind, and with some courses of treatments she really sees herself as you; and you as her."

Molly bit her lip; she wanted her sister to be better, so much; time would perhaps heal all. Still, the visit to Thistledown Cottage was out of the question.

On her way home, she went into Aunt Maud's, just to talk and feel comforted by her loving Aunt. Molly asked to use Aunt Maud's phone, and she rang Gerrald.

Mrs. Linley answered. The old lady was pleased to hear Molly's voice. "Yes."

She answered. "Gerrald is staying for a couple of weeks, but he's out riding Beauty at the moment. Shall I tell him you called?"

"Please, tell him to ring me at work tomorrow, we have a lot to catch up on."

Molly felt good after the conversation and rang off.

"I'm going home now Aunty, I'll see you tomorrow!"

After saying her goodnights to Aunt Maud, she picked up her present and left for Greenswinton Village, and her beloved Thistledown Cottage.

The bus arrived almost immediately and Molly boarded, it rumbled along its merry little way, the summer nights were long and the sun enjoyed itself so much, it never wanted to go to bed. The sky was an azure and fascinating blue, with red and golden highlights. Ribbon-like clouds slid so slowly amid the heavens, sleepily drifting into aqua and then to a French smouldering blue, getting their pajamas on, and beckoning the sleep of the night. Their bedside lights, the stars, were effervescent in their multitudes.

Molly disembarked from the jolly ride and made for the lane, the night summer air was heady with wild honeysuckle and wild roses, and the warmness was apparent in its secrecy. Molly felt-good.

She opened the little gate and unlocked her door; the smell of the herbs from the kitchen made Molly a little hungry. Still, it was a little late to eat, so she made herself some hot coffee and sat in the kitchen, surrounded by her very own furniture. She loved that big antique oak table. It felt like a family should be sitting all around it, and she would have that family one day. She lit the lounge and tidied some of the dropped petals from her dried flowers. She sipped her coffee and would soon take a bath. Her thoughts returned to Gerrald and thought of the look on his face, as his mother told him Molly had rung. After all, he had been in love with her not so many months ago.

Molly went into the bathroom and ran the bath, her favourite lavender water was thrown in, and she afforded herself the luxury of the new soap she had bought herself for special occasions, along with the eau de toilette, Miss Dior. She undressed in the bedroom and donned the pink dressing gown. The mirror in the bathroom was getting steamy. Molly let the dressing gown slip to the floor. She saw her misty outline in the mirror. Tomorrow

Gerrald would service her, her huge breasts with big brown nipples had been out to pasture for too long. She had made her body wait too long.

She slept well that night, thinking of Gerrald

The morning found Molly in an effervescent mood, crunching her toast and reading the morning paper.

Gerrald was phoning today. Molly prepared herself for another weekend at the Linley mansion. The memories of her last visit filled her with uncontrollable excitement. She could almost taste the champagne bubbles tickling her nose.

At work, the office was a bustle of people, making and waiting for appointments with the senior and middle management. Molly was exhausted. The morning had gone so quickly, leaving her impatient and tense. The phones were ringing all over the place.

Molly was dashing here and dashing there. It was lunch time, and she was appreciative of the chance to put her feet up and relax for a while. "Drat, another phone call," her voice let her down. She was showing despair in her voice. The caller sounded excited and immediately Molly recognised the voice. It was Gerrald; lovely, rich Gerrald. The two chatted endlessly on the phone, both catching up with the news of the past few months. Molly expected Gerrald to ask her down to Stevenage; she was not disappointed. They arranged for it to be the weekend after next. She replaced the receiver, and smiled to herself. A little pampering would not go amiss for a change.

She had visited Merry twice in that time, each time she went, Merry seemed even better than the time before. Perhaps the new medication was working at last. Merry was filling out a little in her face, that gaunt look had gone. She was almost as healthy as Molly now. On the last visit, the girls were walking in the park, and the nurse had mistaken Molly for Merry. The two had laughed heartily at that. It was nearing the weekend when Molly would visit Mrs. Linley. Gerrald had promised that there would be other company there this time, some old acquaintances and a distant relative. Mrs. Linley had invited them all, to fill the house with young people and laughter.

The weekend at the Linley's started today, and Molly was in the middle of packing her underwear when a commotion outside Thistledown Cottage caught her attention. She needn't worry it was Gerrald peeping his horn and beckoning her down. She sat on the case tucking in the flimsy silk cameo top. Gerrald waited in the car, excited to see her again.

All packed, she ran down the stairs, and locked the Cottage door. She chucked her case into the back seat of Gerrald's open-top car. With one last look back at her beloved cottage, she was off down the lane, travelling through Greenswinton Village, and off into the open road. Gerrald guessed it would take him at least two hours in delayed traffic.

The wind was blowing Molly's hair all over the place, in her face and all around her shoulders. She grabbed the fly away hair, and twisted it round in a swivel, and knotted it on the top of her head. Gerrald commented on how lovely she looked with her hair on top. He smiled to her, and gave her a quick peck on the cheek, whilst still watching the road, ahead, and she loved it. The journey was pleasant and uneventful.

Stevenage was busy when they approached it. People were going about their business in a quiet, laid back fashion. As they approached the large iron gates, Gerrald stopped the car. "Do you remember the first time I brought you here, and just at this point; you wanted to go home!" Molly laughed. "Yes, but not today." The car sped up the long driveway, stopping only to greet Dizzy: she had come out to meet them. Mrs. Linley was standing at the top of the steps, between the two marble posts, guarding the doorway. The staff had all come out too, to welcome the couple in. Mrs. Linley explained that some of Gerrald's guests had already arrived and were freshening up after their arrival.

The butler took Gerrald's keys and moved the car to the garage at the back of the house across from the court-yard and stables.

The roses were all out in full bloom, and looked prettier than the last time. She remembered the pink petals slipping away downstream, and the toast the lovers had made. Mrs. Linley waved them into the lounge area and instructed Gerrald to pour them a sherry as a livener. Dinner would be ready soon and all the guests had been told that, at 6.30 they were expected to be sat at the table. Gerrald sipped his sherry and went upstairs to welcome the rest of his guests.

One by one, the other guests came to their door, and were introduced to Molly. Gerrald knocked a little longer on the last door in the corridor. He laughed to himself, as he knocked again and opened it. A very handsome young man came to the door, half naked, with only a towel around his loins. He had a grin on his face. "Gerrald you could have had a shock in store for this young lady. I thought it was just you at the door, and almost didn't wear the towel."

Molly smiled and wished to herself, he hadn't bothered. He was tall, a little hairy, with black, curly hair, the colour of ebony, and his eyes were like roasting chestnuts, sizzling against the whiteness of the virgin snow, on the bleakest winter night. This was Jordan De Havilland, Architect, Adonis, tennis player, heartbreaker. She shook his hand, her heart pounded, her eyes twinkled; each step back to her room was taken more nervously than the last. Gerrald left her to change and freshen up. Molly entered her bedroom and her head was full of thoughts of love. She found Jordan to be the handsomest man she had ever met.

She bathed quickly. She would wear her cobalt blue dress tonight. It seemed to give a soft glow to her face, and she felt sensuous in it. The waist of the dress clung to her, showing her nymph-like figure, to its full potential. Her breasts were heavy tonight, and so was her heart.

She wanted to impress the suave Mr. DeHavilland. She had undressed and was wearing her pink bathrobe, when a knock came to the door. Excitement filled her, could it be the Adonis? The door opened, no, it was Gerrald; he was only checking she was okay.

He kissed her on the forehead and left her to finish off.

She wanted to look good tonight from the tip of her toes to the top of her long black tresses. She picked the lacy little bra and panties, the cameo vest slipped over the top, but she felt uncomfortable and imprisoned by it, so she pulled it off and draped on the cobalt blue dress.

It clung and fitted in all the right places. Her figure was in excellent condition. She painted her lips with the dusky pink lipstick, and brushed olive green shadow on her eyelids and with a little blusher, she looked radiant. With great sweeping strokes, she brushed the moonlight in her hair, and gave the lustre of jewelled otter fur. She looked and admired herself; she was ready—ready to steal Jordon DeHaviland's heart. She heard chatter and laughter as she left her bedroom, already the group was already gathering in the huge lounge.

Gerrald was the centre of attention as usual.

She crossed the marble reception area, her heels nervously echoed on the floor, and she saw Jordan in the corner, keeping company with a tall sylph like blond. Her heart sank. Surely it was not his wife. As she entered the lounge, Gerrald moved towards her. Jordan was in sight of her, but seemed not to notice. She felt cheated and wanted his attention. She wanted it so much she excused herself from Gerrald's conversation and made a beeline for the dark Adonis in the corner. As she approached, he introduced the tall blond to her as his cousin.

Molly could come back to life now. She asked Jordan about himself, and nervously told him more about herself, than she should have, in a casual conversation. The group was noisy and getting into full swing with the sherry when Mrs. Linley gestured for them to go into the dining room. The party crossed the hall, still chattering like a clutch of chickens, fighting for the corn. The dining room was a large oval one, and the huge dining table took pride of place. The flowers were arranged in the centre, and the chandelier sparkled like a vibrant rainbow on a summer night.

The first course was served, and Molly made sure she sat straight across from Jordan. She accidentally on purpose, touched his feet with hers, throughout the meal.

The champagne was poured, and she was getting heady with desire for Jordan. He occasionally smiled towards her, but nothing more. Molly would have to work harder on this one. Gerrald called to Molly. "Do you want to go for a walk round to the stables?" Molly was about to shake her head when Jordan said. "Good idea Gerrald. I'll take her if you don't mind."

"Why, of course not." said Gerrald. He was innocent of what had been going on. Molly smiled and felt excited. Jordan smiled across once again, a devilish smile that said it all. He had noticed her and was teasing. The evening air was heady with the smell of roses and honeysuckle. There was a breeze, but it was warm and welcoming. Jordan placed an arm around Molly's waist. She liked it, and they talked idle chitchat and made their way across the courtyard towards the stables. Beauty was still standing up and nestling her nose out of the horse enclosure for any sort of petting. They stood together and stroked her. She nuzzled up to Jordan. Molly was jealous, and she gently guided him towards the bench under the oak tree. They sat together, their silhouettes etched in the moonlit sky. Molly felt good, but she wanted more.

Hardly a word was spoken, but they each in turn, knew tonight was different. They kissed, caressed, and drank in the moon. There was an owl nearby hooting menacingly and breaking the silence of the midsummer night tranquility. The couple stayed a while longer; then went back to the house.

Jordan and Molly were careful not to let anything slip. The group was by this time, congregating in the main drawing room, sipping Mr. Linley's brandy, the men smoking his cigars, had he been there, he would have joined them and thoroughly enjoyed himself. They were a jolly crowd, and each one in turn took centre stage and spun out the tales of the day.

Jordan and Molly crept in and mingled unnoticed.

The grandfather clock in the hall reminded everyone it was two o'clock; the sheer noise of its chime had already begun to disperse the revellers; each one climbing the stairs, to their own bedroom, rather the worse for wear. Gerrald took Molly by the hand, picked up the remnants of the brandy, and accompanied her up to her bedroom. The Butler, by this time, was already locking up, and one or two of the guests had already picked their sleeping places—right where they had fallen. Molly climbed the stairs with Gerrald; she only hoped that Jordan had not seen her, but there was no reason for concern as the sylph, like blond had Jordan by the arm.

Both couples disappeared into their respective bedrooms. Gerrald started to strip Molly. He was amorous already, and being quite drunk, started to struggle, to undo his jeans. Molly started to say no, but there was no point refusing his advances, tonight. Gerrald was drunk and after trying to make love to her; collapsed on the bed beside her. Molly slid out from under him and finished undressing.

Her thoughts were of Jordan; she washed and slipped contentedly into bed. Gerrald slept on top of the quilt all night, fully dressed. Molly turned out the light, cuddled her pillow and dreamt of Jordan. The only fly in the ointment was that damned blond. What was going on across the corridor? Jordan was not drunk. Her mid-morning sleep was disturbed by the maid pulling open the drapes.

Gerrald had already gone, probably woke up, in the middle of the night with cramp, and returned to his own bedroom.

"Molly." The maid called. "Jordan has saddled up Samson and Beauty if you would like to go riding." Molly smiled and thought to herself, Gerrald would have to pick one of the other horses if he was to go riding. Molly tapped on Gerrald's door still in her bathrobe, and told him where she was going, but he waved a limp hand and gestured for them to go alone; he was far too fragile to go horse riding. Molly could not believe her luck. Jordan! all to herself? Away from prying eyes! She quickly dressed in the riding habit the maid had brought in, and was downstairs in less than ten minutes.

Jordan was a handsome sight in his riding clothes astride Beauty. Molly got a lift up and was on Samson, and the pair disappeared in the direction of Sleepy Hollow Woods. The summer day was shrouded only, by one cloud in the azure blue sky.

The air was electric with excitement; both knew what the day would bring. The cantering of the two horses was both exhilarating and relaxing. The sun streamed down on the couple. The wildlife was in abundance, squirrels darting up trees, birds singing their favourite songs, little creatures scurrying through the undergrowth all going about their business of the day. Samson pulled up to a halt so suddenly, that Molly almost went somersaulting into the air, but she managed to regain her composure almost at the last minute. She dismounted and Jordan flew to her side. "Something must have scared him. Normally he is so laid back. Perhaps there is a stone in his shoe or a nail digging in." They inspected the horse's feet but could find nothing.

Whilst crouched down there together, their eyes met; he was so handsome Molly's heart leaped every time she made contact with his eyes.

He leaned forward and kissed her on the nose. She smiled, not a composed smile, but a little girl lost smile, almost innocent in its sincerity. This was different and Molly knew it. It was like being in love for the first time, being a virgin again, feeling brand new.

They stood up, gathered the horses and walked along the footpath with their two mounts following obediently. Not a word was spoken. The feeling of togetherness; was like Siamese twins joined at the hip. This was the real thing, and they would wait until the time was right to fulfill their desires. The time was certainly not right at the moment, when they had both come with different partners, guests in the same house. Their object this weekend was not to be found out, even a glance of an eye, a touch of a hand, an unprotected smile, would be certain discovery. They mounted again and rode on a little further. The horses were enjoying this morning's ride out, as much as Molly and Jordan.

There was a clearing just up in front, and they decided to let the horses rest. Molly remembered that clearing. It was the one with the waterfall, the one where she and Gerrald had had that picnic. She had enjoyed that day too, but not in the way she was enjoying this idyllic venture. They dismounted and sat on the bark of a fallen tree. The waterfall was noisy, and as the water crashed down it echoed in the cave behind. That spooky cave Molly was uncertain about. She was careful not to tell Jordan she had been there before. She had no reason to, as Jordan too had been there before and with a very different lady. Molly threw a stone in the water, and sailed some fallen leaves. She was just running her fingers through the water when Jordan pulled her to him. He held her close and strongly, she could feel his muscles on his chest against hers, and his heart was pounding with urgency. Molly succumbed and her body yielded to his. They were in an embrace neither could get out of, or wanted to.

They gently found themselves spreading across the fallen leaves and twigs kissing in an affectionate gentle way, exploring each other's emotions, touching only softly; no gyrating fast movements; they were taken away by a tidal wave of the gentlest desire. They unlocked their kisses and just stared into one and other's eyes; they knew things would never be the same again. Molly stood up and dusted the remnants of leaves, soil and grass from her riding Pants. She straightened her riding hat and got back on Samson, who by this time had a drink, and had rested. The ride back was pleasant and electric at the same time, hardly a word was spoken. As they approached the stables there seemed to be a bit of a commotion, a small crowd of workers had gathered around one of the stables.

Apparently one of the foals had collapsed and no one knew what had happened.

The vet had been called, so the all waited. Molly and Jordan went back to the house with the biggest appetites ever. As they crossed the hall, Gerrald called to them from the upper floor, "Did you have a nice ride?"

"Yes." Molly replied. "Very nice," being careful not to sound too excited. Gerrald was still in his clothes from the previous night; Jordan had taken notice and commented. He smiled a reassuring smile to Molly, who accepted with a nod. They all dined and filled themselves with the delights of the kitchen and were back in the lounge with Mrs. Linley. The group was already splitting up into couples. Mrs. Linley pointed to the drinks cabinet, "Get some wine or something Jordan."

"What does everyone want to do now?" Gerrald asked as he came down the stairs, the group was all mumbling suggestions to each other. Some of the ladies were going shopping, the men wanted to watch football on the television, Mrs. Linley would carry on her embroidering.

She decided to take herself off to the drawing room, where it was much quieter and she could watch an old film on the box. The women borrowed Ralph's jeep and went into the village. Gerrald heard it spin down the drive and on to the open road. "Good," he said. "Now chaps we can get some peace." He went to the fridge and brought in a couple of dozen beers. Jordan switched on the football, and they all had a jolly good time. Gerrald asked about the ride with Molly that morning, and Jordan passed it off as pleasant. As the others watched the football, Jordan's thoughts were focused on Molly. The football crowd was getting rather noisy, and the beer was disappearing fast. Mrs. Linley came in and just laughed. She loved people to enjoy themselves, and that house had needed some laughter for a long time. She eagerly waited for the young women's return with their wares, and tales from the shopping expedition. She didn't have to wait long.

The jeep screeched to a halt at the steps. The butler took the keys and moved it to the garage area, only after helping with the shopping. He unceremoniously dumped the packages and bags on the table in the centre of the marble reception area. The women heard all the shouting and laughing, and they quietly slipped in to see what the rumpus was. They all smiled. They couldn't leave their men folk for an hour before they were raucous. Mrs. Linley came over, and peeped in to see what the men were up to, before returning to the drawing room. The girls picked up their goods and joined Mrs. Linley in the quieter room; each in turn showed their purchases.

"It's been very pleasant having all of you here this weekend; I've missed the fun this house can provide, Ladies we'll have to do this again." Mrs. Linley hadn't enjoyed herself so much for a long while. Before taking her purchases up to her bedroom, Molly had another glimpse of Jordan, a little tipsy now and laughing with the others. He looked even more tempting, as his eyes lit up, and his face crumpled in laughter. She smiled, turned round and continued up to her bedroom. She had bought a beautiful Green dress, the colour of her eyes. It was close-fitting and showed her figure in full detail. She had bought a gold and emerald brooch to match it. It hadn't cost much, and it took her eye; it was a spider. The body was the emerald coloured stone, with gold legs; she liked it and would wear the dress and brooch tonight.

On their way back from the village, the girls decided that they would all go out dancing that night, without consulting the men folk or Mrs. Linley. But they were determined if the men wanted to come, they were invited, but first the girls were going for a meal at the little restaurant in Stevenage and then on to the local dance place. Mrs. Linley called to see if they wanted dinner at 6.30 as usual, but the reply was chorused from the top of the stairs. "No we're all going out for a meal tonight. This was the first the men had got to know about the night's plan, but they agreed also, so Mrs. Linley told cook she could have a quiet night, and just a sandwich would do for her. She was almost seventy now and life had been rather stressful for her recently.

Molly laid her dress evenly on her bed, as she ran the bath and spoiled herself with the bath oils and bubbles. She looked out of the window to see the vet still tending the foal, its mother looking on forlornly. Molly took charge of her thoughts yet again and went back to the bathroom where the bath was still running. She did not want a repetition of the last visit, when she had almost flooded the house on more than one occasion. It was very steamy; she pinned her hair on top of her head, cleansed the lipstick and foundation from her face and slipped in between the bubbles and foam. It was warming and private and the aroma of lavender filled the room.

Molly's feet were a little painful after the jaunt round town. There was a knock on the door. "Come in Gerrald," she called. He came in behind her, kneeled down by the bath and kissed the back of her neck. "It tickles," she laughed. "We have to get ready soon as we are all leaving early." But there was no reply. She looked round not to see Gerrald's face but the face of her destiny--Jordan, dressed only in a bathrobe. Molly gasped. "Jordan," did anyone see you enter my room in your bathrobe?"

"No!" Smiling he replied. I came in dressed with the bathrobe in my hand." Molly felt a little self-conscious and a little worried. What if Gerrald came up? Jordan had read her thoughts. I locked the door." Molly looked relieved.

Jordan walked around to her. He leaned over her and kissed her first on the forehead, then the nose, and then without a thought, he kissed her full on the mouth. Molly gasped in pleasure; she had waited so long for him. He stood back and dropped the bathrobe. His body was lean, his muscles taut, he was firm and hard, every inch a man. He was erect and bold and her eyes soaked him in. She stood up and stepped out of the bath; he reached for a towel, gently, caressingly her body as he dabbed her dry, she moved forward to him and her breasts swayed with their sheer size. He held her in an embrace, picked her up, and placed her on the bed. He kissed her with a deep, lingering kiss, a fulfilling wanton kiss. A demanding, menacing urgency filled his body, as he slid his leg across her and put his hands on either side of her head; she was waiting full of desire and longing, and she gasped; he moaned, he kissed and nuzzled her face, her breasts, her whole being, they rolled over and squirmed up all the bed clothes, oblivious to the world or the trouble which could erupt at any moment, rhythmically gyrating, moaning, pleasurably enjoying the oneness of each other. Joyously lasting, holding back the ultimate, in sheer ecstasy, until with the loudest roar, he let go of all his love for her. She smiled and watched his face contort with extreme pleasure, until at last, peace and relief returned, and he smiled down at her. She pecked him on the nose. Then she jumped up and got into the bath. At last sense prevailed. "What if Gerrald came in, or one of the others?" What happened was wonderful and she regretted none if it, but please don't let us be found out she thought to herself. "Quick; Jordan get dressed and go. I am terrified for someone coming in..."

He did get dressed, and left his bathrobe in one of her drawers so as not to look suspicious when crossing the corridor. He unlocked her door and was about to open his own door when Gerrald came up. "Did you get fed up with the football old boy?" Jordan smiled and nodded. He closed the door behind him. Molly was busying herself bathing. The water had got a little cold, so she was trying to reach the hot tap to run a bit more in.

She had just managed to reach the tap when a knock came at the bathroom door. "Come in." she called. "I'm under the soap suds." It was just as well it was Gerrald this time.

She was a little surprised, he was a little tipsy, and he started to unzipped his pants. This was the last thing on Molly's mind at the moment, but how could she disguise what had just happened. She reached out and took his hand, and quickly washed Jordan's love away.

Smiling Gerrald got undressed and slipped into the bath with Molly. She smiled as he brushed her lips with his. Molly, coy in her response at first, kissed him back. Not in the same way she kissed Jordan, just a kiss to get out of trouble. He slid down in the water, Molly could feel herself becoming excited again, and she moved his hand down her soft body. He touched and fondled her; with a soft caress and she loved it. She stood up so that he could see her. He enjoyed the look of her, as her breasts swayed with sheer weight. They were a huge. He wanted her, and she was turned on again and wanted him. He kneeled in front of her and gently eased his way in. A gasp first; then pleasured moans; followed: And two became one, she closed her eyes and enjoyed the ecstasy. Molly smiled that devious little smile, and told Gerrald to hurry up.

"I want to get bathed and dressed, or the others will leave me, behind." she retorted to Gerrald. He was hurt and it showed. He hurried the movements and finished, rather on a low note. He said he would meet Molly downstairs, as he picked up his clothes and got dressed in Molly's bedroom. Again, for the third time she filled up the bath. This time it was uninterrupted. She dressed in her new, Green dress and donned the brooch. She would wear brown eye shadow and cherry red lipstick tonight. Yes, it looked good. She brushed her long tresses and put on her stockings and shoes; she was ready. As she came down the stairs, Jordan was at the bottom. Love filled his eyes. Molly felt guilty but pleased. He obviously had no idea.

The party met, and they all made their way towards the main gate where two taxis were waiting to pick them up. The little village was just about to put on its nightcap and drowse off for the night when the revelling youngsters arrived to awaken it and take pleasure in the sights and enjoyments of the nightlife. The restaurant with its Christmas-type coloured lights made the place inviting. It was still light outside, but inside the little place was dark with quiet candlelight and round tables all set out in secluded places, with checked tablecloths. Each table had a red candle giving the place a warm, sensuous feeling with a secrecy hidden within the candle flame. Molly was in a quandary as to what to do and especially, who to sit with. The tables were meant for courting couples but who would make up her couple... The decision was snatched from her like the last bun on a jumble sale stall. The crowd had moved four tables into the middle of the room, all joined together so that everyone could sit around.

They ordered wine, were chattering and picking up the menus, each choosing then changing their minds, ordering this, then changing for that. The waiters were getting annoyed until Jordan took charge of the situation. "Right, I'll get all the orders and tell the waiter." A few minutes later, they ordered and the situation settled down to conversation about the men getting tipsy in the afternoon. The girls were going to make up tonight. The wine arrived, and everyone took their choice, it was warming, relaxing and nice—good company and good food. The evening went well. By around 9.30, the restaurant was full of people all a buzz with conversation and the group in the middle was laughing and talking the loudest.

The last of the coffee and mints were being finished off, but more importantly the wine was going down too well. Jordan ordered some more. One of the girls went down to the ladies room which left a seat vacant next to Molly, Jordan slid into it. Gerrald thought nothing of it. After all, Gerrald thought, he had made love to her before they all came out. He felt secure in that fact. If only he knew Molly!

Jordan put his arm around Molly. He could not seem to let her go. Molly felt uncomfortable for the first time with Jordan because Gerrald was unhappy. She whispered to Jordan. "Please play it cool here, we have our full lifetime to be close." He nodded and moved back to his original chair. Gerrald looked happier. Jordan was ill at ease, he had had a few to drink this afternoon coupled with the wine tonight, and it had put him in a loving mood, and he wanted to be with his lover. He would have to console himself with the fact that Gerrald too, wanted to be with her, but she was on her own, completely aloof from either of them. In fact when they went to the dance place, she remained on her own amid the crowd all night. Except for the time when Jordan asked her to dance a slow melancholy number. They danced too close, and showed too much of their feelings for each other. Gerrald by this time; was too drunk to stand, so did not notice. The evening was ending and everyone seemed to have enjoyed it. Gerrald had to be carried to the waiting taxis.

The weekend was nearing to a close. As they all went to bed that night; they were already planning their route home. Mrs. Linley had gone to bed earlier, and the others were too tired for any more revelry and quietly made their way upstairs, each to their own bedroom for a change. My, they must have been tired out. Molly was hoping to see Jordan for a cuddle before she closed her eyes, but the only cuddle she got that night was her pillow. There was shouting in the hall, it was the stable boy talking in a loud manner to Gerrald who was still half-asleep, dressed in his night attire. "Yes," she overheard Gerrald say, "I'll come down and look at the foal right away." Molly jumped up, grabbed her dressing gown and went out to the hallway. Gerrald was still there rubbing his eyes.

"What is the matter Gerrald?" she asked quietly so as not to disturb the others.

"Nothing, really, that was Sam, Ralph's son telling me the foal was alright, and the vet had left. I promised I'd have a look, so I might as well go now." He went back into the bedroom for his robe. Molly decided to go with him. They looked slightly odd going across the courtyard in their night clothes and gowns, but no one took any notice, or thought anything of it. They talked and laughed and spoke of last evening's events. Gerrald admitted he could hardly remember anything at all. Molly was pleased.

The group dispersed, all careful to give Mrs. Linley their regards. Molly stole a few precious moments with Jordan before he departed. They exchanged addresses and phone numbers etc. All the usual things lovers do to keep the love line ever close and open. They had all left by lunch time. Gerrald stayed on a bit longer with his mother, before driving Molly home. The three sat and discussed the weekend's events.

"Well," Mrs. Linley said. "Everyone seemed to enjoy themselves and I did too. We must do this more often." Gerrald put down his coffee cup. "Come on Molly time for us to go as well. See you next weekend Mother; hospital Rota providing."

They hugged, kissed and said their goodbyes. Out on the open road Gerrald seemed in an extra good mood. Perhaps it was the blue summer sky, the soft breeze brushing his entangled hair about his face, or the birds in sweet song, or perhaps by some odd coincidence it was the lady by his side. I think it was the latter. He pulled into a lay by, and screeched to a halt. "Molly I have something to put to you." Molly seemed surprised since all her thoughts were at that moment in time, reserved for Jordan.

Gerrald started again. "Molly I have been thinking for a long time now, we've known each other for ages and there's something I want to ask you." Molly wondered what he was going to say next, curiosity took over her. "What is it Gerrald?" He carried on. "There's only one way to say this Molly, and it's just to blurt it out!" Molly waited.

"Will you be my wife, Molly?" She gasped.

"What, your wife?" The sheer shock was printed on her face. Gerrald was very surprised indeed that she had not taken up his offer immediately.

"We have had a wonderful weekend Molly, and so have all my friends, even Jordan who normally is so reserved came out of himself more than normal. Even he; likes you."

"I like you Gerrald, but I am not 'in love' with you. In fact I like you very much indeed." Gerrald was gutted, so much so, that he never spoke all the way back to Thistledown Cottage. The evening sun had dried up the lane so much now that when the car sped along it, the dust blew in their hair and in their throats, but the dryness in their throats had nothing to do with the fact that the road was dry, and both people knew that. He got out, opened the door and placed her luggage on the doorstep of Thistledown Cottage, between the chimney pots cascading with sweet peas.

She asked him in, the gesture was fruitless. Gerrald politely said, "No," and was off down the lane so fast only a cloud of dust remained. Molly bothered herself no more about it. After all, she had Jordan's visits to look forward to. She could show him her little nest with all her personal things around her; she loved Thistledown Cottage so much.

The phone rang.

It was Aunt Maud asking about her weekend. "It was marvelous," she said, careful not to tell Aunt Maud about Jordan. Aunt Maud liked Gerrald, and she was old fashioned and would not take too kindly to Molly's deception especially in Gerrald's own home. Molly got busy at work, and the days rocketed by, faster than she thought possible.

She was beginning to think Jordan had forgotten her. She had just finished tea, cleared away the dishes and was busying herself doing some embroidery, spurred on no doubt by Mrs. Linley, when a knock came to her door. She was not used to having visitors, so her first reaction was shock, and apprehension. She put down the embroidery and went into the little hallway to answer the door. It knocked again, an urgent sort of knock. She softly lifted the latch and opened the little front door. It was Dr. Sommerfield.

"Come quickly Molly its Aunt Maud, we have her in hospital; she's had a little attack and is in intensive care." Molly's face bleached out emotion. She picked up her bag, and with the help of the dear doctor locked up and was on her way to the ill old lady. This was the last thing Molly wanted or even thought about. She had only spoken to Aunt Maud a couple of weeks ago. She felt guilt rise in her.

The orderly on duty showed her to the single, secluded ward where the old lady lay, motionless, the sweet smell of lavender pampered the rigidity of the scene; it was her mother's favourite perfume too. Stiff-like and tense Molly sat in the chair beside the bed. Tubes were coming out of Aunt Maud like spaghetti spilling from an unattended falling saucepan.

All the heavenly memories of the wondrous weekend at Gerrald's faded into oblivion; this was the real thing, no faking. She reached across the shrouded bed cover and touched the motionless, peachy softness of her aunt's tender hand. She held her in that joined pose for the whole duration of the visit. Dr. Sommerfield knocked on the window of Aunt Maud's room, without urgency this time but with great sadness. He knew only too well what Molly had gone through, and the old lady whose last hope of getting well, was fading away. "Molly, you might as well go home now, there won't be anything happening here tonight, and if anything does I will come for you straight away." Molly wanted to stay forever, but there was no point. She told Dr. Sommerfield she would rather take the bus back to Stevenage, and walk up the lane to her cottage.

It would do her good, transfixed in her own thoughts; she was remembering the heartache which had stabbed her life almost since primary school. The bus seemed to go slower that night, as if solemnly mirroring Molly's sadness. She got off the bus at the bottom of the lane; and walked slowly back to the cottage. Her head was bowed and her eyes were water pools of panic, waiting solemnly, about to pounce and spin Molly into deep despair. She lifted her head, only to look at the evening sky, draped in a French navy overcoat, waiting the coldness of the night.

Her gaze darted from the sky and fell on her own front door. A tall, square-shouldered silhouette stood there. It must be a man; it was too large for a woman. Could it be, she dared not hope, she threw her head up high and ran with outstretched arms, faster, faster, the figure came towards her; the sky turned up the collar on its overcoat and turned its back, to leave complete privacy, to the happiest couple in the universe. Not a word was spoken. They flew into each other's arms, unlocked and opened the little door, getting a sniff of the sweet-smelling flowering peas, as they rushed past. They went straight upstairs, discarding their clothes on the way, and savoured their passions whilst enclosed in the bed, as their bodies rhythmically fluffed, puffed and moaned, in the evening glow. They lay still until their bodies relaxed and returned to the world of reality. Molly climbed off the bed and drew back the curtains; she lit up the room.

Jordan had so much to tell her, his enthusiastic words did nothing to excite Molly. Finally he asked what the matter was. Molly poured out her heart to him entirely. Jordan sat back and took in all that was said. "Do you want to go back to the hospital tonight Molly?" His concern was of the utmost. Molly shook her head. They went downstairs, Molly first; she went into the kitchen and made some coffee.

She put on the lights in the house, and drew the curtains in the kitchen and the lounge. The two sat motionless; there was sadness that was out of their control. Jordan kneeled at Molly's side. "We will go in the morning to see Aunt Maud." The two were still naked; the summer air was having its effects. Jordan ran his hand along Molly's thighs. She responded by kissing his neck. They put down their coffees; Molly lay on the sofa with Jordan by her side.

He nuzzled his head in her chest, between her breasts, wishing he could wipe away the worry of Aunt Maud.

He knew he couldn't, he just wanted to take on the worry for her, he thought so much about her, and didn't want her hurting. Molly appreciated the comfort of having some one to share her sadness with, and just wanted Aunt Maud to be alright.

Chapter Eight

MOLLY WAS UP EARLY next morning and at the kitchen table, with that same cup filled with fresh coffee. Her dressing gown looked bedraggled and worn, emphasizing Molly's mood. The herbs in the morning air were heady with aroma. The sun was up already and glinting through the spaces in the curtains. She went out and stood in the doorway. The postman was on his way up the lane on his pushbike. There was a letter for Molly; she greeted him with a "Good morning."

It was a letter from the Sanitarium, Oh gosh, Molly thought. Not more bad news. She was afraid to open it and left it on the kitchen table. She could hear the gentle rumblings of Jordan awakening and a bang and very loud "Ouch!" She smiled to herself. He had probably banged his head on the bedside cabinet, or banged his toe on the bedding box at the bottom, whichever it was, it sounded painful. She decided not to investigate. A few minutes later, unshaven and tousled, he filled the gap in the kitchen door. Molly received a prickly kiss, from the lips on an unshaven face, and an enquiry for coffee. She felt warm and good again; the cottage seemed to come alive since he had arrived. Molly would not let him go in a hurry.

The morning's duties were formed around Aunt Maud with a visit to the hospital, then a trip into town to get some flowers and lemonade, and yet, another journey to the hospital. The visits were long and uneventful with Aunt Maud just lying there motionless; tubes attaching her to all sorts of equipment. Jordan played his part. He was with Molly no matter what. Perhaps the shock of Aunt Maud seeing another man in Molly's life would finish her off, but Molly took the chance. Several days had gone by and still no change. Dr. Sommerfield warned Molly not to expect too much. "Oh, by the way, I bet when you opened Merry's letter it boosted you no end." Oh my goodness, the letter!   She had forgotten about it. It had been put under the toast rack to give Molly more time to recollect her thoughts before exploring the words inside.

Molly; flushed with guilt. "I forgot to open it with all the urgency surrounding Aunt Maud."

"You are forgiven Molly." Dr. Sommerfield, smiled. "Fundamentally she is really on the mend now, and joining in on all the activities at the home, and organizing some too."

That was good news indeed for Molly. "I will go and see her as soon as Aunt Maud is out of danger."

"Meanwhile, Molly, will you send her a letter in the post, she would love it."

That good advice was noted and done the next day. Molly mentioned Jordan and promised to take him to see her on her next visit. The days slipped by, and there was no improvement in the old lady's condition. Each visit seemed more endless than the one before. Molly was becoming impatient with it all as she spent the long hours reading to Aunt Maud, which was becoming tedious; she was selfish she knew it, but she wanted to make a life with Jordan, a perfect life with no one sad or ill. The weeks were slowly becoming months, and Aunt Maud still lay there with the nurses doing everything for her.

Molly had to go and see Merry before long and she was left with the same decision as when baby Robbie died.

Should she tell Merry about Aunt Maud, or should she hide it as she hid Mother's passing. Tension and pressure were mounting up in Molly. Jordan had never moved out since that night, and each week more and more of Jordan's clothes arrived and stayed; he was gradually taking over. Still, the unused room was locked. Continuously, Jordan had asked to see inside, but Molly couldn't find the key. "That was what she told Jordan, but she knew where the key was kept. The following day, Molly told Jordan she would visit Merry. It was Saturday, and Merry liked visits on Saturday. They took the bus to the station and boarded the train. Molly remembered her first encounter with Gerrald here, her thoughts lingered on Gerrald for a while, and she wondered what he was doing and if he had gotten over her refusal. He had not been in touch, and Molly was too busy with her own life.

The whistle sound was coming closer, the guard waved the steaming machine to a halt; the doors were flung open, and all passengers embarked and disembarked.

The normally tiresome journey was very pleasant today, and they were there sooner than they thought. Jordan was excited to see Molly's sister, she had not told him they were twins—not yet; this was Molly's little surprise. The long walk up to the Mansion was peaceful and quiet today. Molly was full of the excited anticipation of Jordan's face when he saw Merry. The iron gates faced them tall and foreboding. The Mansion in all its grandeur was straight in front of them, and as they approached the main steps, the Matron greeted them. "Oh how nice Molly you have brought someone new to met Merry, she will be pleased, such a handsome young man." Jordan was flattered and smiled an egotistic smile. Molly scurried along the long corridor towards Merry's room. She knocked first; then went in, and Jordan followed her. Merry turned round, she was beautiful, her hair shone with health, her usually gaunt look had disappeared, her eyes sparkled, and she smiled at them both.

Jordan's mouth gaped. 'There are two of you Molly." The girls both laughed. "I don't think I can tell you apart. I'll close my eyes, and you two move around, to see if I know who's who."

They did and he didn't, he was astonished. Molly felt good. Merry definitely was on the mend this time. The three chatted, careful not to mention Aunt Maud. Jordan suggested a walk in the gardens, and they all went out into the garden. Jordan had an identical beautiful woman on each arm; he couldn't believe his luck.

The girls were dressed differently of course, but a man never notices what a girl is wearing anyhow. The visit lasted two hours and was very pleasant and enlightening for all three. Merry was instantly attracted to Jordan, his Latin good looks and ebony hair, coupled with his reserved attitude to life and his warm personality completely took over her. Molly was pleased they all got on, because if Merry continued to make such hasty progress, the day may come when she would be allowed out once more, and Molly could have her at the cottage.

They kissed Merry and promised to come sooner next visit. They left the matron and the nurses in a joyous mood and all of them assured Molly things were on the up.

The train and bus journey were a little longer than the trip over, but duties were done and friendships made. The only blight on the horizon was the thought that Aunt Maud might not pull through.

It was Monday. Work was as positive as the alarm clock ringing at 7 o'clock. The rain was pounding against the window panes, crashing violently with the help of an aggravated wind, with the determination of a burglar, on his last attempt to blow up the Tower of London and steal the crown jewels. The day slipped by, and the night left them, blotted out as ink, on a pasteboard pad. Aunt Maud was dying, and they both knew it. Could Molly cope? The old lady was everything to Molly. In her days of deepest distress she turned to her aunt. Jordan knew if he was to keep her love, he must be strong now, and he must support her, even if it was against her wishes. The days passed. Molly stayed at home day dreaming of herself with Merry in the attic sanctuary, together looking at the world from the open bay window. Merry's favourite place in the world and more recently Molly's too, for a while. Perhaps even the girls being apart, in different worlds made no difference; perhaps, their desires and wishes and safety came before they left the womb. Molly decided there and then to go to Merry and tell her adult to adult that Aunt Maud was dying. She would also ask her out for a couple of days. If Merry was on the mend, she must start to face up to reality. Molly needed Merry now, more than anyone else in the world, more than Jordan, who she loved dearly, but as an individual, Merry was Molly, Molly was Merry, one and the same, together, alone, night and day, light and darkness.

The continuous trips to the hospital, the lifeless face that once shone with pride and contentment at Molly had gone. The little rosy cheeks, transparent as an imitation diamond, dulled with constant dipping, in grease soaked fairy liquid, had disappeared; like bubbles down the wastepipe. The only notion of life was the bleep bleep, bleep, bleep, bleep! Molly could not stand another bleep, if her life depended on it.

Frustration, aggravation and sheer anger was the epitome of Molly's life. On top of that she would have to remain calm and collected as she made her way up to the Sanitarium Mansion and her beloved sister. This visit was unannounced, therefore, the nursing staff were unprepared, the auxiliaries were moving around the corridor with fresh bed linen and towels, the orderlies were busying themselves with the medicine cabinet, carefully ticking off which patient had what medicine. Molly waved to a familiar face, one of the nurses who had befriended Merry on her long stay, and asked if it was alright to go in. Molly told the nurse of the news she had brought Merry. The nurse said it would be better to tell matron first before seeing Merry, so as not to undo all the good work. Molly agreed and searched the corridors for Matron.

She found her trying to restrain an overexcited patient who had gone berserk and smashed some windows and thrown his chair through an open door into the corridor. "Molly" exclaimed the Matron "You should not be here in this wing." She looked at her watch, "And certainly not at this time of day." Molly had to wait outside until two male nurses strapped up the patient with the restraints, and tidied up the room. It reminded her of the time when she went with Aunt Maud to see Merry after losing baby Robbie; it was so sad. Matron finished off and the room was locked. "Now then Molly, what has brought you here looking so worried." Molly spilled out the tale. Matron was pleased that Molly had not just burst in to Merry's room, and told her. "I'll get some mild sedatives and put some in her coffee just to take the edge off it, and I'll sit in with you, just in case."

Molly approached the door, with Matron close behind and the three cups of coffee on a tray.

"Hello! Merry!" Molly was pleased to see her.

Merry too, was pleased and hugged her. "Where's that gorgeous man you brought the last time?" Matron placed the coffees down; careful to let Merry have hers first; they all sipped and exchanged small talk, when the coffee was drunk, Molly gently told her the news. Merry took it very well, "She is very old you know, Molly; and she cannot

Live forever." Molly and Matron were both shocked and pleased. They talked about old times with Aunt Maud and the little things she did for them and her funny little ways. Molly was relieved; the weight just seemed to lift from her shoulders. Merry must certainly be on the mend. "I'm feeling very well now Molly."

Molly nodded, "Yes you are. I'm so pleased for you." Molly stayed half an hour more and then left. On the way out she popped in to see Matron. "Do you think if anything happens to Aunt Maud, and Merry is still doing well, she could come out for a couple of days?"

"We'll see, Molly." Matron answered carefully. The burden was lifted, and the journey back was exhilarating. Summer was drawing to an end. Aunt Maud was still sleeping in her own world. Thistledown Cottage was getting ready for the autumn; already the leaves were slowly covering the ground. The trees took on their autumn coat, and the bountiful golden red and brown against the pale blue September sky reminded Molly of an artist's palette and the fruit stall on the market

Jordan had nestled very nicely into Molly's cottage, he seemed to come one night and stay forever; he never seemed to bring suitcases or belongings. They came so gradually Molly never noticed them until she could hardly move her things around with his drawing board and plans and instruments, in the way. His clothes were very nicely taking over Molly's wardrobe, and his slippers were always strategically placed so that Molly missed near death every time she encountered them. At the end of each working day, nothing pleased the lovers more than having a bath together, with a glass of martini, soaking the warm water and exchanging the incidents and fun of the day's experiences. It was just on one of these leisurely dips when the door knocked and the bad news came. Dr. Sommerfield's expression as Molly opened the door in her bathrobe, said it all; there was no need for words, he just nodded in answer to Molly's serious look. Dr. Sommerfield left without coming in to the house. Molly and Jordan dressed and went for Merry.

The night was dark, and the leaves were swirling in front of the bus. It wasn't a cold night but cooler than normal. The train was dull and dreary, as they looked out of the windows all they could see was their gaunt, white faces, looking back as terrestrial beings from a world above. The train was almost empty except for a rather fat lady who took up two seats. Perhaps, she only travelled at night so as not to have to stand or pay for two. The train stopped, they were there. The walk to the Mansion was taken in complete silence. The Mansion looked warm and welcoming in the evening light, there were floodlights shining up at the building, which illuminated the trees and made them look less foreboding as they shed their coats. They went to reception and asked for Merry. The Duty sister had to give her approval and sign the release form.

She did this, on the understanding, that Merry would be back promptly in three days time, and Molly would take full responsibility for her. They were warned should anything upset Merry that they must be called at once. They agreed. Merry was in bed when they called at her room; the opening of the door, and the light being switched on woke her.

She sat up and rubbed her eyes. "Is it Aunt Maud?" Molly's face confirmed. Jordan went outside as Merry got dressed. All three made their way to the hospital. The corridors were dark except for an occasional night light dotted here and there, and one on every floor on the corridor ceiling was lit.

They made their presence known to the duty nurse and she showed them to the room where Aunt Maud lay, peaceful with a little smile on her face. All tubes had been disconnected, and she looked happy in a serene way. All three kissed Aunty and said their last goodbyes. They stopped only five minutes as the nurses were eager to get the old lady downstairs for the mortuary attendants and funeral directors to go about their business and cause as little concern for the other patients as possible. On the way out they bumped into Dr. Sommerfield. "I'll make sure everything is alright for you all. I'll come and see you tomorrow and we can get things down and preparations made." The little group was ever so pleased he was taking such concern, for neither of them knew what to do.

The funeral was arranged the day after tomorrow. On the bus ride back to Thistledown Cottage, the three chatted noisily, excited that they were all together at last, away from the sanitarium. Merry looked healthy and happy. Molly had long waited this moment. Aunt Maud was on their minds too, but she was old and it was for the best, she had lain in that state of unconsciousness for months now. As the bus approached the lane they all got off, Merry was excited and could not wait to see the cottage. The September evening with its cool somber breeze and autumn sky emphasized the quaintness and warmth of the cottage. Merry stood at the end of the little path, outside the gate and sipped in the magic of its drowsing charm.

The lovers dragged behind kissing, and holding hands. Merry saw them and shouted, "Come on you two, there's plenty of time for that later. I want to look inside."

Molly laughed, "I'm coming; I'm coming." She unlocked the quaint little door and motioned Merry to enter. Molly hurriedly switched on all the lights.

"Now let's take you on the guided tour." She took Molly into the lounge first with its open log fireplace and painted white walls, passed by the dried flowers, and the log bucket, into the kitchen with its huge antique oak table, big enough for ten people to sit comfortably. The aroma of the herbs was strong in the room. Merry was impressed. She climbed up the stairs to the bathroom; with its black-and-white marble; and its great long mirror. Along the corridor, they went, past the unopened room, and into the bedroom with its mahogany poster bed.

"Where am I going to sleep?" enquired Merry. "You will sleep with me and Jordan can have the sofa."

Jordan looked shocked, "What's wrong with this room?" he pointed at the door.

Molly frowned, a frown that said "Keep quiet." He did.

"Alright ladies you two take the bed, I'll take the sofa, but be careful if any of you come down in the night, remember, I don't know you apart yet, but I will." The girls smiled. Merry never mentioned a word about the closed door in the hallway, upstairs.

Merry helped Molly cook some light supper, they all chattered away about things of the moment; then the talk got on to a more somber note. They discussed the funeral and Aunt Maud. Dr. Sommerfield was coming in the morning and they would all know what time and what was happening. Molly drew the curtains and brought down some covers for Jordan on the sofa, Merry bade them goodnight and was off upstairs.

Molly sat on the sofa with Jordan. "You don't mind do you?"

"No" came the reply. Molly told Jordan how pleased she was with Merry's progress and hoped that the funeral would do nothing to upset her. She also, told Jordan that mother and baby Robbie were both buried in that churchyard, and no doubt Aunt Maud would be taken there too as she was a parishioner of that same church. The mood became sadder, they held together and a little tear trickled from Molly's eyes. Jordan wiped it away with his kiss. The lovers kissed goodnight and Molly went up to join Merry in the bedroom.

As she entered the room she could not help but think of the sanctuary as the window in her little room reminded her of it. Merry must have been thinking the same thing as she was sitting at the window taking in the dark, oceanic sky. Molly grabbed her sister. "Are you happy?" The smile said it all; they were close again, away from the home. "We should always try to stay together Merry. After the funeral, we will all go for a day out in the village and buy some nice clothes for you to take back with you."

As dreaded things do, the funeral crept up and got them, before they were ready. Aunt Maud was leaving from the Chapel of Rest, and the funeral cars were picking up the three from Molly's front door. They all got in. The drive was slow, and silent. It went through the village and out into the country towards the little church.

The sun was shining that day, and the churchyard looked more inviting, the skeleton-like trees loomed above; the coffin was lowered from the car, and six men carried it up into the yard. They passed Mother and Robbie's grave. Merry was crying by this time. Molly felt very sad too, but for Merrys sake kept up a brave face. After about three quarters of an hour, the ceremony and burial were over, and all three were thankful. They left some flowers on Mother and Robbie's grave and got back into the waiting cars. Molly asked Dr. Sommerfield if he wanted to come back for a sandwich and some sherry, but he politely declined. The three sat huddled together not speaking. Aunt Maud had gone, and Jordan was Molly's support now. The day had come to take Merry back to the Sanitarium, but she did not want to go back. However, Molly persuaded her, "If you don't go back this time, you will never get out again." Merry understood. "But first Merry, we will go into the village as I promised and buy you some nice things."

Jordan smiled then said. "I have a surprise for both you two ladies. I'm picking them up from the jeweller's today." The girls were delighted. All sorts of thoughts went through their minds: rings, bracelets, pearls, pins. Jordan would only say. "Wait and see."

They lunched and left for the village. Molly got off the bus and made straight for the dress shop. She loved it in there. Mirianne the shop keeper; had all sorts of jumpers, blouses, coats and sweaters of every colour and design. The Autum colours, this year were red, Green and mustard. Molly loved all three, and so did Merry. Molly picked a dress and disappeared into the cubicle to try it on. Merry was still choosing.

Jordan was talking to Mirianne. Apparently they had both known Gerrald at University, but not each other. They were so engrossed in conversation that they did not see Molly come out to show her dress and shoes. Mirianne nudged Jordan. "Doesn't she, just look gorgeous!" The curtain moved and Merry came out with exactly the same dress and shoes on. They both looked at each other and laughed. "This time Merry you show me what you have picked, and I will pick something else. Merry made her choice and Molly looked and looked and found nothing that took her fancy except what Merry had picked. They both decided to buy the same things. They would be going to different places, so no one would know. This happened time and time again in the twins' life. Each would want what the other had already got and vice versa. Packages in hand, they made for the railway station; and the journey to the Sanitarium. Merry was still happy and excited, and Jordan loved her too. He occasionally gave her hand squeeze.   "Jordan why don't you have a twin too and we'd all be happy?"

Jordan replied. "There's more than enough of me: to satisfy you two ladies."

Molly was furious and kicked him on the shin. "You bastard" she shouted. Everyone on the station platform looked round. Jordan decided not to push his luck and apologized. They boarded the train and it sped off to the Sanitarium. They were in the reception and talking to Matron before they knew it. Molly and Merry were fighting for attention. They both wanted to tell the same tale to capture the matron's attention. Neither won; it was Jordan who told the stories as the girls were still bickering.

Jordan had just remembered, "I should have called at the jewellers today and you two didn't remind me." They stopped bickering and kissed him on the cheek. "I'll pick them up tomorrow and bring yours Merry on my next visit."

"I'll look, forward to that," she said. The wares were unceremoniously dumped on Merry's bed and cluttered up her little room. All three sat on the edge of the bed beside the packages and said their goodbyes. First Jordan and then Molly in turn cuddled Merry and kissed her on the cheek. They closed the door behind them and left Merry to sort out her new purchases and put them in her drawers. They were on their way back to Stevenage and Thistledown Cottage after a very pleasant and inspiring day. The nights were getting colder, and Molly decided to light the logs in the fire. It was the first time she had lit that fire since she moved in the summer. The logs were dry but it still took some lighting. Eventually Jordan got it going. There was a blue smoke haze everywhere until it got going properly. They sat on the sofa barefoot and just belonged in their solitude in Thistledown Cottage.

A couple of days passed, and Jordan decided to call at the jeweller's to pick up the girls' presents. He was getting them made up specially and felt proud that he was sure they would like them. He paid the jeweller and took the two little boxes home. He was in before Molly that night and started to peel potatoes and vegetables awaiting her return.

He put on his slippers and propped himself on the sofa with a cushion supporting his back. He reached across and picked up the newspaper, and was slowly getting engrossed in it when he heard the front door open.

He smiled, it was Molly with a face like thunder; something had upset her that day. "Come in Molly and settle yourself down here."

"That rat made me work late tonight."

Jordan put his arm around her, "Never mind, you're here now."

Jordan took her coat and produced the two little boxes from his pocket. This one is for you Molly, now open it." She did and there in front of her was a diamond brooch with the name Molly in diamonds. It was exquisite. He pinned it on for her. "I have got Merry one too, you two will never fool me again." She smiled and her bad mood passed. Molly wore her brooch all that night and couldn't wait to let Merry have hers. Jordan promised to take it to her on the next visit. Work became so oppressing for Jordan with the overtime and Saturday mornings, he never did get round to taking it, and several weeks had passed. Molly too was busying herself at work, and the two were seeing less and less of each other. There lives were becoming mundane and boring. Jordan decided that to get everything into perspective, they would both ask for the whole weekend off, just to be together.

The weekend neared, and the two were so very tired that when Saturday morning eventually got round, they just wanted to lie in bed. The next time they looked at the clock, it was four o'clock; they had almost slept the day round. Jordan gave Molly a shove, "Come on Molly its gone four o'clock." She stretched and pulled him towards her; he needed no encouragement. He kissed and fondled her, and they kissed each other. Awoken to their joint passions, they rolled over and over and fell out of the bed and on to the mat on the floor, both naked as the day they were born. He was huge and lustful. Molly too needed this pleasure. They gyrated slowly at first then jerkily moved onward until the surges were so great the rug beneath them spun across the floor and left them unnoticed and full of rapture.

The sound of a cat screeching filled the house, Molly didn't have a cat, it must have been a stray. What could it be? Jordan and Molly were both puzzled, they looked out of the window; perhaps it was some wild animal caught in a poacher's trap or a kitten looking for its mother. But no, the sounds were coming from the unopened room. Molly froze. She looked at Jordan, they went together to get the key. Gingerly, Molly turned the rusted key in the lock, it was stiff and unhelpful, but then a click and the door opened. The sun was spilling sunlight through the half-open curtains spraying it across the room in a fan-lit manner, the dust was thick and the cobwebs had become thicker. The room smelled of damp and staleness. There were no more sounds; the stillness was broken by Molly's footsteps towards the window and the crib. Right there and then she decided that Jordan would help her clear out this room, redecorate it, and do it up for Merry, ready for her next visit.

Christmas was just around the corner, so Molly decided to get some wallpaper and decorate the second bedroom in pastel colours with a feminine theme, just right for Merry. She would come home for Christmas this year. Jordan got days off from work, and Molly set off for the D.I.Y. store. She chose a pale pink wallpaper with tiny little rosebuds in pale blue dotted all over it. She bought a border to match and some pale pink paint.

Luckily she managed to get some material to match for the little window.

She left the material with the lady on the desk, with the measurements, and asked her to run up some curtains, with tiebacks and tassels in blue. The wallpaper and paint was very heavy, so Molly decided to leave it to be delivered. That would give her time to get the old furniture out of the room, and the dust and cobwebs could be shown the door. All that afternoon Molly slaved away. She was very itchy and dusty by the end of the afternoon. The room was clean and empty now. She had removed the remnants of curtains and cleaned the window. The floor too had come up very nice, at one time it had been varnished, and now that it had been cleaned, the grain showed up very well. The room looked bigger. She was just planning on where everything should go, when she heard Jordan bouncing up the stairs. He was amazed at how big the room seemed and how clean Molly had gotten it. Molly was a striver, and as soon as she had gotten anything into her head, it was done. Molly excitedly told Jordan where she was putting the single bed, what the paper was like, and how she had managed to get curtains to match, and that they were on order for running up. "I know what you're up to Molly," he smiled.

"Yes, I'm having Merry home for Christmas."

"Good," he said. Molly had not looked forward to Christmas so much since she was a child. They would visit Merry and give her the good news, but only after the room was ready so as not to disappoint her. The old crib and the dejected contents of the room were out in the back garden. They seemed to clutter the place. Molly moved them into the summerhouse until she could arrange their disposal. The wallpaper and paint was delivered around ten o'clock the next morning. Molly could not wait to get started. She donned her overalls, paste board brush and all the tools of the trade. She measured the walls and started to hang the paper. It was obvious to Molly that onceover there had been some sort of paper on these walls, as every now and then there was a little scrap gone rather brown and stiff now. Another one of these little scraps appeared right under the piece of paper, she was about to hang, and it had to be removed or it would show up as a bulge. She tore it off and threw it to the floor. The room was almost complete now, and each piece of wallpaper hung perfectly. It was impossible to see the joins. Molly was pleased.

She stepped back to take a better look. Some of the scraps from a previous age were stuck to her feet. She tried to free herself from them by kicking them off but they would not let go. She bent down and pulled one off and she almost froze —the old paper was the exact same design as what Molly had just put up. She picked up another piece and examined it closer. This piece had a small fragment of border on it too. She tore the border off and there before her eyes, the very same pale pink, right to the last detail. Molly was bewildered but strangely felt good about her choice. The room seemed to echo her mood and warmed in agreement. She took a break and made herself a sandwich and coffee.

All she had to do now was the border and the room was complete, awaiting the handmade curtains and furniture. She pondered for a moment, she would have a large scatter rug in the middle of the floor, and then the grain could be seen in its entirety. Achievement coupled with hard, work had finished the room that day. The border fit easily around the middle of the room like a giant ribbon surrounding an Easter egg. She, tidied the bulk of the paper cuttings, dried down the window bottom and cleared away the paste and work tools.

The room was finished, empty and clean, and it looked very pretty indeed. Molly ran the bath and washed away the chores of the day. She dressed in her Green dress and titivated herself up for Jordan's arrival home. She couldn't be bothered cooking that night. She had decided that they would go to the little Italian restaurant in the village.

It had gone six o'clock, and Jordan still had not appeared. She waited for him in the dimly lit room. The fire was crackling and blistering away in the hearth. She picked up a book and settled herself on the sofa. The next thing she knew was the grandfather clock striking 10.00. She looked around, still no Jordan. This was strange; he was normally home by six o'clock at the latest. What worried her most was that he had not got in touch to even let her know. She was very hungry by this time and decided to walk down to the little restaurant and get some pasta for them both. The night air was very cold, the sky darkened the wind had long since blown any clouds that may have been gathering. The lane was lit solely by the moon in its crescent shape. The trees and bushes so beautiful in the summer were skeleton-like and foreboding in their loneliness.

As she neared the restaurant she could hear the Italian music and the laughter and bustle of conversation and plates clanging and tills ringing. How she wished she could have stayed and joined in the atmosphere. As she entered, the strong aroma of parmesan cheese stole her appetite. The ground coffee was strong and enticing. She placed her order and took a seat at the bar until it was ready. Some customers were leaving just as others were arriving, and the small band played and sang all the local Italian folklore songs. The checked tablecloths and red candles set the scene. Molly was just beginning to get into the atmosphere, and the comings and goings of the restaurant guests, when her order was ready. She paid and left the premises: she was sorry to close the door on all the merriment. Where the hell could Jordan be? She made for the lane and ran the gauntlet of the stiffened trees and darkened moody sky. The lights were on in Thistledown Cottage. She was sure she had turned them off when she left. She hurried her footsteps, Jordan must be back. She rushed up the path and unlocked the front door. Standing there was not Jordan's face but Gerrald's. "What are you doing here, and where is Jordan, and how did you get in?"

"One question at a time please, Molly." Gerrald sat her down.

"Jordan rang me from work. Apparently he could not get a hold of you, he had rung several times today and was worried. He told me to pick up some keys from his office as he had to fly to Paris at a moment's notice, some Architectural Convention, and the one nominated to go came down with something at the last moment. Does that answer all your questions Molly?"

"Yes, except one. Why did my phone not ring?" She got up and picked up the receiver, the line was alright.

Perhaps she thought to herself, if the door was closed in the second bedroom, it was impossible to hear downstairs, so she brushed it aside. "Well, Gerrald now that you are here, I have just been to Ginos in town and picked up some supper, pasta, and spaghetti with garlic bread. I fancied going out tonight, but it's too late now."

"Right, get your coat." Gerrald picked up the phone and rang Ginos, "If I place my order over the phone, can we come down now?"

The waiter answered, "Why of course, we take last orders for food at 11.00 on weekdays."

Gerrald ordered over the phone. "Be there in 5 minutes." The two went scurrying down the lane. The merriment was in full swing now; they could hear it all on their approach. The little street was dark, and only the neon sign, from the restaurant; sent its glow down upon the prospective customers. Giovanni greeted them at the door, and pointed them to their table. "Can you bring us some house wine?" Gerrald enthused. The two were sat at the table sipping the wine and enjoying the delights of the evening. Molly was so pleased that Gerrald had come to her rescue. Their meals were served, Molly had built up such an appetite; she really enjoyed her meal.

The restaurant was full even into the midnight hours. They didn't have time for talking or reminiscing or any of that stuff; they were joining in the singing and laughter. Molly had not enjoyed herself so much for ages. She suddenly thought. "When is Jordan coming back?" Gerrrard twisted his glass in his hand "I'm afraid he's away for three days."

Molly looked saddened. "Oh well, it'll give me time to finish off the bedroom."

"Molly," said Gerrald in almost a whisper, "Why don't you come to Stevenage with me. I'm going up for a few days."

She thought about if for a while and turned things over in her mind. "Why not?" She answered. Gerrald was well suited with her answer and ordered more wine. The night and all its pleasures were slipping away, and they could not hold it longer than it cared to wait. They called Giovanni for the bill, said their thanks and goodbyes; and walked up the lane to Thistledown Cottage. As they approached the door, the telephone was ringing. Molly rushed in and answered it. "It's Jordan!" she said, beaming. He was a little annoyed that it had been so difficult to contact her that day. She gave him her reasons ever so humble.

"Where is Gerrald now?" he questioned.

"He's right here." Molly giggled.

"What! At two o'clock in the morning?" Molly looked at her watch—quarter to two, she hadn't realised it was that time, already. "I hope he's not staying the night!"

Jordan remarked angrily. "If he is, be sure he sleeps on the sofa, like I had to do when Merry came." With that he said his goodbye and replaced the receiver. Molly was both angry and pleased. She did not have to wait in for him, she should have told him she had just come back from the restaurant with Gerrald. Too late now!

"Right Gerrald she said, it looks like you are sleeping on the sofa, if you are staying over."

He looked at her sheepishly, "Who's going to know any different?"

"I will." Molly retorted. She put the cold takeaway meals in the fridge, put out all the lights, checked the front door, tucked her guest in and went to bed. She was awoken next morning with a knock on her bedroom door. It was Gerrald with orange juice and some hot toast. He went across the room and laid the tray on her bedside cabinet and promptly sat himself down, on the edge of her bed. He kissed her on the forehead first, then the lips, Molly liked Gerrald but she did not love or fancy him. "Now Gerrald, that's enough."

"Alright," he said. "Eat your breakfast, and we can get on the road for Stevenage." She had almost forgotten about Stevenage. They were packed and on their way in less than an hour. Gerrald's car was quite fast and the houses and trees and buildings just flew past on the blink of an eye. Molly was always relaxed in Gerrald's company. She regarded him as a very close friend, but Gerrald wanted more. Every now; and then Molly's thoughts drifted back to Jordan and Paris. How she wished she was with him. The great Stately Home appeared in the distance, the iron gates, and the huge, long drive. It was almost like Molly's home too now, she really liked Mrs. Linley. She remembered also that it was the last visit that introduced her to Jordan. She reminisced about the ride in the country, the evening meal, the whole group as they laughed and chatted. This time it would be quieter.

Mrs. Linley came out to meet them with Dizzy by her side. The butler as usual took all their bags to their rooms for them. "Come on Gerrald, pour us all some sherry. Molly, sit by me. We didn't get time to talk the last time with all activity." Molly sat down next to Mrs. Linley.

"Nothing much has happened; I have now bought my cottage. Can you remember when I saw you in the solicitor's?" She nodded in agreement and looked a little sadder, her memories of her husband were apparent. Molly changed the subject and asked about Beauty and Samson and how the poor, little foal was coming along.

"All fine now Molly." She picked up her embroidery.

"I see you are almost finished it."

"Yes." She replied. I'll finish it in time for Gerrald's and your wedding."

"Oh no!" said Molly, "Gerrald and I are only good friends, there's nothing more."

"Not according to Gerrald." Mrs. Linley smiled and patted Molly on the knee and got on with her sewing. Gerrald was in the kitchen asking about dinner. Molly joined him, Gerrald, I think you should have a word with your Mother. She thinks we are getting married."

"Well aren't we?" Gerrald grinned.

"Of course we're not," Molly was rather cross. "If you carry on in this line of affairs I'm going home."

Gerrald gave up teasing her. "Let's just enjoy our few days here. No more teasing I promise." They were friends again and could get on with things. Molly joined Mrs. Linley in the lounge again, and Gerrald went along to the stables, taking Dizzy with him. Mrs. Linley looked tranquil, enveloped in her sewing. Molly looked from outside the door and decided not to bother her again. She had a wander in the reception area looking at all the old portraits and antique ornaments. She was about to go up to her room when Gerrald came back in. "Do you want to go for a ride or a walk or anything before it goes dark?"

Molly shook her head. "I'll go for -a lie down before dinner."

The evening and dinner were uneventful, and Molly found herself missing Jordan and wishing she hadn't come to Stevenage. They sat that night quietly with hardly any conversation Gerrald got up once or twice to let Dizzy out, and apart from that nothing happened. Molly excused herself and went to bed early. She had made up her mind. She would get Gerrald to take her home in the morning. She was missing Thistledown Cottage and Jordan, and she was missing finishing off the second bedroom.

Gerrald popped his head in to say goodnight. Molly told him of her plans. Gerrald tried but could not persuade her to stay longer. Next day they kissed Mrs. Linley, and Gerrald promised to come back in the afternoon after dropping Molly off. This kept the old lady happy. Molly could not wait to get into the car and make for home. She knew that this would be the last visit to Gerrald's home, ever. It was after lunch when the car drew up outside Thistledown Cottage. She had only been away one night, but it seemed an age. As Gerrald kissed her on the cheek, he knew that Molly and he were friends, only friends, and that was all it could ever be between them. She unlocked the door and let herself in. There was a letter on the mat from Paris. It was from Jordan.

She closed the door behind her, dumped her case in the hallway, undid her coat and opened the letter. It was full of missing and undying love and treasures only two lovers would, understand and appreciate. She tucked the letter behind the candlestick in the lounge and got on with the chores of the day. A knock came to the door; it was, the delivery man with her curtains. Good, now she could finish off upstairs. She carefully ironed out the creases and took them upstairs along with the ties. Molly borrowed a chair from the other bedroom. She hung them and touched and tucked and titivated until she had got them just right. They did look good next to the wallpaper.

Chapter Nine

IN JORDAN'S LETTER HE had said that he would be home tomorrow. Molly would busy herself by getting a bed and rug for the spare room. She went down to the village to Blundell's; they never had much in the tiny shop but were very eager to order any needs customers may have. The bed was promised for the next day, the scatter rug Molly got delivered that afternoon after 3:00.

The room looked empty, but all Merry would be bothered about, would be the bed. Before Christmas, Molly would buy a bedside cabinet and a mirror for the room. Molly took the takeaway meal from the fridge and reheated it, the pasta tasted good and nourishing. She opened a glass of wine and sat in the lounge engulfed in her own thoughts. It was quiet that night and Molly swore she could hear moaning a long distance away. She went out to the back of the house to see if it was an animal, hurt, or a cat, cold. But nothing was there.

The phone rang, and it was Jordan; he said he could only spend a couple of minutes on the phone, but had just enough time to tell her he had a surprise for her. She couldn't wait for his return. All the love she had saved for him was bubbling up inside her. On the day of Jordan's return the bed was delivered and Molly asked the men to put it in the upstairs room. They were very kind and put it together for her. She had forgotten to get a lampshade for the room and a cover for the new bed. Damn, she was angry at herself, and would have to get them another day; she wasn't intending to miss Jordan's homecoming for that. She sat on the edge of the sofa listening for the sound of the bus at the end of the lane; she seemed to sit for hours. Then just as she was about to give up she heard his key in the lock. She rushed to the door and flung her arms around him; he picked her up in the air in a gush of excitement. He covered her face in kisses. When he eventually let go of her, she took his hand and dragged him upstairs to the spare room. She opened the door and told him to look inside. He was astonished and pleased, "Merry will be happy in here. It's beautiful."

"Now then, where's my surprise?"

"Alright," said Jordan. "But first let me get my coat off and shift my overnight bag."

"That's new," said Molly.

"I had to buy it there. I didn't get time to pack, and it was very cold."

He sat Molly down and presented her with a package in a tiny brown bag. She opened it; it was an engagement ring. Jordan was kneeling beside her: "Will you marry me, Molly?" She beamed all over her face.

"Yes, Yes," she said.

"Right, lets get married as soon as possible." They both agreed.

"But first." said Molly "Lets get Christmas over with."

"Talking about Christmas, we'd better go up to the Sanitarium soon and see Merry and tell her our good news." He was glad to be back, and she knew it. She also knew that she did the right thing telling Gerrald they were only friends and holding the situation at that stage.

He took the ring from the box and placed it on Molly's finger. They both knew that this was the real thing. It was love all the way. The ring had a huge diamond in the centre, with seven littler diamonds encircling it. She just gazed at it in wonderment and of what the significance of it was. It meant that Jordan was truly hers forever. The thought warmed her body and her heart. She threw her arms around him and spoke of her undying love for him. Jordan picked her up and carried her upstairs, not to the spare room this time but to their room; the mahogany bed was waiting, welcoming; sealing the commitment. He kicked the door shut behind him. Privacy was the order of the night. Molly was too excited to sleep; all night long she kept putting on the bedside light and staring at her ring, picking out bits of fluff and any smudge that may appear. The morning found Molly still gazing at the ring on her marriage finger; she could scarcely take her eyes off it in case it disappeared. Jordan woke up rubbed his eyes and questioned the light being on. "I'm just making sure my ring is still intact."

Jordan laughed to himself. "How like a woman, the ring means more to her than I do!" He smiled. He knew he had made her happy this time.

They breakfasted together. Both were off to work earlier than normal, Molly was dying to show off her ring. Jordan wanted to tell his colleagues, everything about his trip and the outcome of all the meetings with Architects and Surveyors.

Christmas was creeping up on them and nothing had yet been finalized about their joint plans for Merry, and also there were still a few items to buy for her room, they wanted to make it as comfortable as possible for her. Molly told Jordan that they must go and see her this Saturday and also must get the lampshade and the covers for her bed. "A little cabinet or dressing table would be nice." He nodded, "Saturday, we'll do it Saturday."

The rain lashed and pelted against the windows; it had been a very wild night, some branches were lying across the lane, and some tiles had blown off the roof of the cottage, Jordan promised to have a look as soon, as he got home. Saturday came sooner than either of them had hoped, and the morning rush took them on the train to the Sanitarium once again. Their life seemed to be full of the Sanitarium and train journeys. Molly was tiring of it all and just wished that Merry could stay home for good. The little room was finished and the last of the items had been bought the previous night. Everything was spick and span and awaiting its occupant.

The train sped along taking them to their destination and the Sanitarium Mansion quicker than normal. They waved to Matron on the way in and made for Merry's room. As they approached, they heard excited chatter; this was unusual because after Robin, Merry had not made any other friends at the home. They knocked and gently pushed the door open. There was Merry, large as life, sitting on the bed with another very pretty girl. Merry introduced her as Sue. She had long, blond hair bunched up in a pony tail with a huge blue ribbon.

The ribbon accentuated the colour of her electric blue eyes, almost the colour of a summer sky. She stood up and excused herself as the visitors took their places alongside Merry.

Molly called after her. "We'll pop in to say goodbye before we go." It was nice to see Merry making acquaintances again after the long illness. Merry was on top of everything today. She liked Jordan a lot and sometimes made Molly jealous. Jordan presented Merry with her surprise, the one he had forgotten about on the last visit. Merry opened it up and squealed with delight.

"It's my name in diamonds."

"No," said Jordan, "Not quite. Its not diamonds, but the thought is still there." Merry was pleased.

She pinned it on. "It's lovely, Jordan." And quick as lightning she grabbed him and gave him a big kiss, a real smacker, right on the lips. Molly had to pry them apart.

"I'm having none of that," she said annoyed. "We have some more good news for you Merry." Merry was bubbling over. "Jordan and I want you to come home for a week at Christmas."

"Oh yes, please," was Merry's answer.

"But better than that, we have decorated and furnished the spare room." Merry was ecstatic with delight, her mind was running away with her, and she was already planning to take some personal things with her.

Molly was pleased that everything was going so smoothly for a change, Merry was happier today than Molly had seen her in years: she had found herself a new friend, she was getting better, Jordan and Merry got along so well, and mostly, Merry was coming home; for Christmas, the most special time of the year for the twins. The small group chatted and laughed, and hugged and kissed. They had all become alive again, just as young people should be; their lives had been so distraught with anguish and fear for so long, all feelings and emotions erupted like the bubbles from a bottle of the finest champagne. The afternoon hours were moving on, and Matron had to remind them that visiting time was over at least half an hour ago. Not one of them minded; they were too exuberant in their happiness and closeness. The train journey back was wonderful; both Jordan and Molly were so full of happiness they thought they would explode. Molly was full of talk of Christmas day and the wonders of the excitement of it all. This really would be a Christmas to remember.

Straight away she would start buying Christmas decorations, get Jordan organised with a huge, real tree, garland all the way up the stairs and generally delight, Thistledown Cottage occupants and guests in a way that everyone would enjoy to the fullest. With all the talk of Christmas, Molly had forgotten to tell Merry about her engagement ring. She would save it for Merry's return at Christmas. The next day was taken up with thoughts feelings and excitements of Christmas. Jordan bought the tree, a huge, bushy pine, with just enough top on it for the biggest fairy.

Molly had already picked out the one she wanted, and she bought two sets of lights, all sorts of hanging ornaments in red, green and gold. The tinsel was abundant and seemed to grow on arrival on the branches of the tree.

She placed cotton wool on the branches to act as snow, but the best treat of all was when Jordan lit the lights and laughed. Molly placed the garland up the stairs and around the huge fireplace in the lounge. She had a Father Christmas on the hall table and all sorts of paraphernalia around the house. In Merry's room beside the bed, she put a light, on the newly bought bedside cabinet. It was a Christmas tree in red and green and at the push of a button it lit up the whole room into a warming, pink glow. The dressing table, which Molly had gone to great lengths to buy; stood magnificently on one wall, with a huge mirror on top, and three drawers deep enough to take all of Merry's clothes. Molly put some pictures of the girls in wooden frames, on the dressing table, and the most magnificent brush and mirror matching as one, like the twins. She stood back and admired the room, which by this time was not at all little, but big in fact, fresh, airy and alive.

She sprayed some of Mother's favourite lavender all around the room and put some lavender potpourri in all of the drawers and also in the built-in wardrobe in the alcove in the corner. As Molly opened the door to the wardrobe, a loud screech came out, and Molly shot back in fright. She had no reason to be afraid as the sound came from a rather used, tatty old doll; its mama mechanism was obviously faulty and went off at whim. That was it; that was the scary noise! Jordan and Molly had heard on various occasions, frightening them to death. Molly reassured herself but left the doll in its resting place. Merry could move it if it was annoying her. The room was pretty, feminine, sweet and comfortable. All that was needed now was for Jordan to light the little, open, fire. She called to him; he had dozed off in the lounge, with his favourite brandy almost spilling on to the carpet.

Molly shouted again and again, and she finally aroused him. "I want you to light the fire in Merry's room, just so that we can test it and know it will be alright for her." Jordan mumbled something under his breath, but did it just the same. The fire was in full swing, and the room really took to life now. They both stood in the doorway and enthused at their hard work, and felt gratified that all was done in time. They made sure the fire was safe, turned out the light and left the beautiful feminine room to itself for the night. Downstairs, Jordan picked up his half-finished brandy and took another sip.

"Do you know Molly; you're the best thing that has ever happened to me." The feeling of well-being alighted by the brandy, put him in an amorous mood.

"Not yet Jordan," she disappeared into the kitchen and picked up the brandy from the kitchen table where Jordan had left it.

She took it back into the lounge, kicked off her shoes, poured herself a large one, and snuggled up to Jordan on the sofa. "We have accomplished a lot today Molly; and we have made Merry very happy."

"I love you." they both echoed at the same time. Their talk took them through Christmas to their wedding. She wanted to be married in white with Merry as her bridesmaid. He wanted Gerrald as best man, but would Gerrald be so keen?

After all Jordan had stolen his girlfriend; and Gerrald too loved Molly. He may not have said it so many times, but his actions told her so. The night was gliding away as nights do, and the couple was getting more and more tipsy, the brandy was going down nicely and a feeling of well being overtook them, and sent tremours of ardour around the immediate vicinity.

The clock was striking two, and the lovers were almost dozing off in their togetherness and thoughts of wonderment. The weary bodies made for the stairs and immediate peace and hibernation within the mahogany bed and the privacy of their own bedroom, with curtains drawn against the elements and coarseness of the night.

Christmas was breathing over their shoulders, it was five days away. Molly took some days off work and got busy with the present shopping. She only bought for Jordan, Merry, and a little something for Gerrald and Mrs. Linley. She bought a little present between her father and Lucy, but she never seen them these days, they seemed to just drift away into their own world. She carefully packaged them all in Christmas paper with bows of every colour. The turkey she would get two days before Christmas, the chestnut stuffing she had in a recipe in the kitchen, with her herbs and spices. Potatoes and vegetables she would buy tomorrow at the market place. She would do mushroom soup to begin with, and she decided to bake her own bread from a recipe Aunt Maud had left her. For sweets she decided on strawberry sponge and custard. Molly liked baking but did not get much time for it because of the hustle and bustle of keeping up with Jordan and visiting Merry.

The house was all Christmassy and warm; Jordan had chopped some logs and placed them in the grate, both in the two bedrooms and in the lounge.

Molly had hung some mistletoe in the lounge, and she was sure to get Jordan under that on at least one occasion over Christmas. There was a small pine tree just in front of the lounge window in the garden. Molly decorated it up to look fanciful from the outside. The cottage was gleaming and welcoming with its bountiful love and warmth. Each room was welcoming and ready for its occupant. The Christmas light in Merry's bedroom cascaded a glow of warm pink and accentuated the rosebuds on her curtains. Her quilt was a pale, dewy pink and her bedclothes a pale blue. Molly had bought a teddy with a pink bow around its neck and put in on her bed. Everything was ready, and it was the day before Christmas Eve. Both Jordan and Molly had broken up from work and chose to spend the day in the kitchen. Molly had baked bread, apple pie, strawberry sponge and biscuits of all varieties. She carefully placed them in old biscuit tins for freshness; the sponge and bread she wrapped in tissue and placed in the bread bin. The kitchen was truly used that day, and Molly found out how relaxing and stimulating working in the kitchen could be. She discovered for the first time, how relaxed Aunt Maud had always seemed when she was baking.

It was Christmas Eve, time to go and get Merry. Jordan too was excited, as everyone was. Molly was careful to put the presents under the Christmas tree in the lounge, just under the front window. Jordan too placed his neatly at the foot of the tree. They put on their coats. Molly was careful to switch on the lights for a more welcoming effect for Merry, when she came down the Lane. Molly picked up her gloves from the hall table and pulled on a beret. Jordan also wrapped up well.

It wasn't snowing, but it was bitterly cold and could not daub out the warmth they felt from inside. As they walked down the lane towards the bus stop, they caught a glimpse of some carol singers belting out, Good King Wenceslas and Silent Night. Everyone was in good spirits, even on the bus; people were wishing each other Merry Christmas when it comes; and peace to the world. The train station was empty. It seemed everyone had their last minute Christmas stuff to do and were on their way home preparing the goodies for tomorrows festivities. There was a huge, Christmas tree all lit up on the station platform and inside the little cafeteria there was also one on the counter. They were told the train was running at least fifteen minutes late, so both decided to go inside for a coffee. They got their drinks, and were just about to make their way towards a table, when who should walk in but Gerrald. Apparently he was helping out tonight as porter, so that his friend could have the night off. Molly called to him. "What are you doing here tonight of all nights?" She asked curiously.

"I'm filling in as a good turn, the hospital doesn't need me, I'm not on the Rota for tonight, and what the hell; I had nothing else to do."

Molly thought quickly. "Why don't you come back to Thistledown Cottage when you get through here? My sister is coming home tonight for a week stay over at Christmas. It would be a welcome treat if you came too Gerrald." Gerrald seemed pleased.

"Yes, I will come tonight, but I will have to get up to see Mother tomorrow and Boxing- day. But I will come back, the day after, and stay for a few days to keep your sister company." They were all agreed it was a good idea.

The chatter was broken by the sound of the steam locomotive blistering the silence with its screeching whistle. "The train's here." Said Gerrald, and waved them off the station and on their way to the Sanitarium. The mansion, in its splendor, was awe inspiring, and illuminated with its Christmas lights all along the roof, and the usually bare stiff-like trees were covered in fairy lights. It was a sight to see. At every little window there was a Christmas tree or baubles of some likeness of Christmas. As they approached the reception area, there was a nativity scene with the baby Jesus taking pride of place. They had no need to seek out Merry. She was there, dressed in her bottle-green nap coat with matching hood and boots. Her hands were gloved, and she looked both beautiful and dressed for the weather. As soon as she saw them, her eyes ignited, and her face was ablaze with love.

They all cuddled, and Jordan picked up Merry's bag. The girls held each other around the shoulders, neither wanting to let go. Merry shouted goodbye and Merry Christmas to Sue as she passed her door. "Merry you will have to help me with dinner tomorrow. Jordan isn't much help in the kitchen." Merry was more than delighted to be asked. "Of course I will. I'm more domesticated than you anyway." Jordan agreed, but did not dare say anything. This time Merry was excited to get on the train, and she enjoyed every moment of the journey. Molly had been on the lookout for Gerrald on their return to introduce Merry, but he was nowhere to be found. Still, he was coming later, no need to panic. They were off the bus and walking, laughing and talking going up the lane towards Thistledown Cottage. It was a full moon; which made everything lighter with the disappearance of the clouds. Thistledown Cottage looked wonderful with its Christmas lights and tree all lit up in the garden, and the miniature tree inside the window, giving off a truly Christmas aura. Merry was delighted. "It looks lovely here tonight. I don't want it to be morning." She saw everything through childlike eyes and appreciated it all.

The first thing they did was to take Merry's case up, and show her the room. It looked pretty. They had left the Christmas light on, and the fire was just kindling down, and the whole place gave off warmth, contentment and peace. Merry started to unpack her case. She looked amazingly at the framed photographs of herself and Molly. She put her underwear in the top drawer; with jumpers, scarves and stockings in the others.

As she opened the built-in wardrobe she gave out a scream, that doll was still jammed in that awkward place and screeched at will. Merry hung up her coat and a few blouses. She lay on her bed and looked around the room. It was lovely, she could easily get used to living here. Molly was preparing supper downstairs when Gerrald came in. The two men busied themselves with past tales and men's talk, as Molly was preparing the meal. Merry had got herself organised and came down to help Molly. "I've got someone for you to meet my girl," said Molly.

She pushed Merry into the lounge first. Gerrald rushed over. "Oh Molly, you look lovelier than ever." Both Molly and Jordan laughed to themselves. Molly stepped from behind Merry. Gerrald was aghast. "There are two of you."

They did the same trick on me." Gerrald was amazed. "Still, you look identical. I cannot believe my eyes." All four, went into the lounge and got comfortable. Gerrald wanted a bath after his shift at the railway station. Merry was quick to offer to run it for him. Gerrald appreciated the gesture. She took some fresh towels up and put some bubbles in for him. Merry went up to her bedroom and waited for Gerrald to come out of the bathroom. She took him by the hand and led him into her bedroom.

Merry was excited and pleased that Molly had asked Gerrald to stay. She showed him her room, she was very proud of it. She handed Gerrald a dressing gown she had taken from Jordan's room earlier. Gerrald, to save her blushes, turned around to put it on. Merry held him by the arm and turned him round. She hadn't seen a man for a long time, and she wasn't about to miss this chance. She admired, took her fill and helped him dress.

"Merry you certainly are Molly's sister, alright." He gave her hand a squeeze. "Come on, the others will miss us." The two returned downstairs and Molly could not help but notice the flush of colour in Merry's cheeks. They nestled down on the sofa, the floor; and just about anywhere else that was available. Molly was full of talk of the dinner she was about to prepare, and Merry was getting increasingly aware of Gerrald. The evening went well, and all four enjoyed themselves so much so, that the next time Jordan looked at the brandy it was finished.

The evening came to an abrupt halt when Jordan tossed the blankets on to the sofa for Gerrald, and Merry was pointed in the direction of the stairs. It was the loveliest Christmas Eve they had ever spent, and Gerrald too, was full of enthusiasm. The next morning found the little group with all their chores laid out for them by Molly. Jordan left some strict rules also. "You two wear your brooches, so that we know who we are kissing under the mistletoe."

The girls found it very funny and thought for a moment to switch brooches but then decided against it; Molly didn't want to share Jordan, even mistakenly for a second. Christmas day lunch was appetizing and the chit chat around the table was full of adventure and travel— all four got along so well. Gerrald was supposed to be going home for Christmas lunch, but instead rang his mother and said he would call Boxing Day instead. The queen's speech over, the girls disappeared into the kitchen to tidy up. The men folk were given tasks too.

Jordan was to get the logs in, and Gerrald was to Hoover up the rugs. They did this without fault, whilst in the kitchen Molly questioned Merry about her thoughts of Gerrald.

"Mmmm very nice." was Merry's reply. Molly thought to herself better keep an eye open for these two. Merry asked.   "Gerrald, do you want to go for a walk into the village?" He was very keen to accept. They left the house and its occupants on their own for the first time for several days. Molly snuck up to Jordan and kissed him, she had plans for that hour, and Jordan was not going to disappoint her. They locked the front door and took some wine upstairs with them. Molly threw all her clothes on the floor and just stood there. Jordan leaned across the bed and pulled her to him. She was teasing and yielding at the same time. He was aroused already, and she tore at his shirt and pants like a wild animal in heat for the first time. He beckoned her to calm herself. He undid his zip in a provocative way, the way Molly liked when she was in this devilish mood. She shook her great breasts, for him. He was struggling out of his pants and shirt, ready for action with the hardest love ever, when a banging came to the front door. "Oh no," said Jordan

"Shit." Molly looked out of the window. It was Gerrald and Merry back already. She told Jordan to hold everything, literally. She threw on the pink bathrobe and went down to let them in. "Why are you back so soon?" Gerrald was the first to speak.

"I forgot to ring mother and cancel lunch for today."

Molly was furious with him, "Well, will you do it now and get on with your walk."

Merry could see what the interruption had done. "Quickly Gerrald and then let's go." He rang, and they left to reconstruct their abandoned walk. After carefully locking the door for the second time, Molly rushed upstairs. She burst into the bedroom and jumped on the bed. "It's damned hard keeping this up, Molly." Molly giggled, threw off the bathrobe and flung her arms around Jordan. They both laughed off the situation and just loved each other. Molly felt fulfilled and happy: Jordan poured the wine, and the couple talked about their plans for their Spring Wedding. Molly wanted a quiet, little wedding with only close friends, and Merry and Gerrald. They had still to ask Gerrald if he would be best man. They decided to do that this evening.

Molly got up and ran the bath. "Are you coming in with me Jordan?"

"Of course, I am." He replied. The bubbles and lavender were enhanced only, by the glass of wine Jordan had poured them. They laid and soaked and sipped the wine. Christmas Day that year was lovely indeed. Gerrald went to his mother's for Boxing Day as suggested. Merry was missing him and wished she could have gone, but Molly would not allow it as she has pledged to keep Merry safe and under her care. The days were passing with the tides of time, and Gerrald had not come back as he said he would.

Molly was a little worried in case Merry would go into deep depression, but no she just waited for his return. It was New Year's Eve, Jordan and Molly had planned to, take Merry to the little restaurant in the town.

They were all upstairs getting ready to go out when a cheerful voice called upstairs. "Hello, anyone at home?" It was Gerrald back for New Year's Eve with the biggest bunch of yellow roses he could find. Merry heard his voice and dashed downstairs to him. She flung her arms around him and kissed him all over, the way a frightened pup would slobber over its owner. Molly was pleased, and all four went to the restaurant together. They asked Gerrald to be best man and Merry to be bridesmaid. All was agreed and the date was set for 14th February, Valentine's Day.

The next day was a trial in itself. Molly was sick at the thought that Merry may not go back to the Sanitarium without a fuss, but Merry got Gerrald's phone number and address, waved him goodbye, and quietly went with Molly to the familiar route which took them to the Sanitarium. Molly put Merry's case in her room and checked that Matron knew Merry was back safe and sound. Sue was coming down the corridor, so Molly sent her into Merry to make sure she would settle back in again. There was no need for concern. She heard Merry's excited chatter telling Sue all about Gerrald and her stay. The weeks turned into months and the cold, rainy days turned into snow. The trees in the lane accepted their cotton wool coats and stiffened and shivered with every waiting wind. The arrangements had been made for the wedding, and all four were geared up and ready. They booked the church and had just a very few friends involved. Molly asked a couple from work and so did Jordan. Merry and Gerrald were looking forward to the occasion for more than one reason, it would be the first time they had been together since New Year's Day and Merry's departure for the home.

Gerrald knew that something was wrong with Merry, but after meeting her he could not see what. Only Molly had seen her at her worst. The 13th of February arrived. It caught Molly spreading her wedding dress out across the mahogany bed. It was white satin, with beaded white flowers and white sequins sewn on all around the bodice. The bodice was like an old fashioned corset with bones and stiffening down to the hips. Above the sweetheart neckline was white net with little white satin rosebuds, scattered like confetti on a windy day. Her headdress was simple, a huge, white orchid with a waist-length veil. Her shoes were white satin, and she carried a little white bible and one white orchid. Merry's dress was a beautiful peach satin in the same design as Molly's but not long to the floor like Molly's but to the knee. Jordan had hired a morning suit, and it hung in the wardrobe along with Gerrald's. She had asked Dr. Sommerfield to give her away, as her

Father and Lucy were holidaying in the Caribbean, and were not due back for another month. Dr Sommerfield's wife would come also, to join in the sacred service.

After the service they would all go back to Thistledown Cottage and the newlyweds had planned to go to Greece on their honeymoon, to a small, untouched island called Spetse, an island for lovers of peace and secrecy, a place where no one entered anyone else's space, a place to be together alone. Idyllic: Bathed in unspoiled natural beauty; which was apparent, all over the island, a place where pines trees dominated the hillsides. The local drink, Retsina; came from the island's own grown pines.

Still, that was for tomorrow, and a lot had to be done before that time.

She pulled the bag over her dress again and hung it up alongside the suits for the men and Merry's bridesmaid dress.

Merry had not seen the dress or knew what it would be like. What she did know, was that Molly had modelled it for her, and as the girls were identical, what suited Molly also suited Merry. Jordan was picking her up tonight, and both girls were leaving the cottage together tomorrow. Jordan was leaving from Gerrald's so they had quite a drive in the morning. Jordan would have to get his skates on this evening. Molly prepared the evening meal so as not to delay him.

He would go straight from work to pick up Merry, and should be back, around seven o'clock. It was 6.30 and everything was ready. The taxis were ordered, the dresses and suits were waiting. Dr. Sommerfield had rung to say he was also ready and waiting the onslaught of tomorrow's events. The flowers were arriving that night, and Molly was told to put them in the fridge for coolness. She opened the fridge door to take another look at her cake. The little man and woman on the top seemed to smile back at her as if in Toyland, it was their day too. The cake was two-tier, and the fridge was almost filled to capacity. She would have to take out the flowers from the salad drawer. The girls were only carrying a bible and one flower, Molly didn't want a bouquet or poses. Jordan and Merry arrived on time; Gerrald was on his way for Jordan, who had the suits out ready in the packages. Molly was careful to leave the flowers on the hallway table for them to collect on their way to the door. Jordan had the ring, and Molly had a secret present hidden away for Jordan in the top drawer of her dressing table.

Jordan was getting agitated he could not eat; he paced up and down like a pregnant father to be. The screech of brakes outside signalled Gerrald's arrival. He came in, gave Merry a big hug, shook Jordan's hand and kissed Molly on the cheek. "We're all together again for another pleasurable event." Gerrald joked. The men got their suits, flowers, wedding ring, kid gloves and hats. Everything was put in the back seat. The men were waved off from Thistledown Cottage, and Jordan left it for the last time as a single man. The thought was daunting.

The two girls left alone, went upstairs and tried each other's dresses on. They swapped again and tried on their own. "Let's put them away and have a few drinks to steady our nerves."

Molly opened Jordan's mature French Brandy; there was champagne and all sorts of drinks for tomorrow. "Let's have some champagne and brandy."   Merry was not used to alcohol, and it soon went to her head. They were giggly, happy, and had a deep love for each other. They talked and talked into the wee small hours, the champagne was finished, and the brandy was half-full. They were both giddy and tipsy and full of spirits in more ways than one. Molly picked up the rest of the bottle and switched off the lights and made for bed. Merry followed her up. "I better set the alarm, as Jordan usually does it, and we don't want to be late. Merry come in with me tonight, there's no point in us sleeping alone." The two staggered out of their clothes, both looking at one another's bodies, comparing—the only difference was Molly's birthmark. It was an outline of a dog begging on Molly's left shoulder. They put on their respective night attire and jumped in together.

This brought them close again, and also memories of a long time ago flooded them, and the attic window in the sanctuary focused on their conversation. The brandy took over and both snuggled and dreamt of the coming day. As Molly opened her eyes to the world the following day, her head was abuzz with thoughts and plans checking, rechecking everything over in her mind. No she had left nothing out. The caterers were coming at 12.00, whilst everyone was at the church. The cake was taken out of the fridge, awaiting their arrival. They girls bathed together that morning, they were a sight to behold, not one girl with a beautiful figure—but two; any man would give his right arm to be a fly on the Wall that morning.

They in turn scrubbed each other's backs, they rubbed moisturiser into one and other's bodies, they combed each other's hair, they helped with each dress, and makeup. The hairdresser would be arriving any minute to put the girls' hair up on the top of their heads to accommodate the head dresses. She arrived and started on Molly's first. Molly draped a towel over her dress so as not to spoil it. She was ready all made up and hair looking good. The hairdresser put on Molly's headdress and veil. Merry was next. She too looked lovely. My, they were a sight to gaze upon. The next to arrive was Dr. and Mrs. Sommerfield. She would ride in the taxi behind the bride with Merry. Everything was going according to plan. Even the sun shone on that cold, frosty morning. The first of the caterers were arriving with all the goodies. Molly said. "Just light the oven when you want or anything else you need."

The taxis arrived. Dr. Sommerfield pulled Molly's veil over her face, and they picked up the white bible, gloves and flower. "Are you ready Molly?"

"Yes, ready like I've never been before." She quickly replied. They exchanged knowing smiles. Molly turned around, "Quick Merry, my garter. I've left it in my dressing table drawer, and Merry bring Mother's pearls. They're in the jewel box on the top." Merry scurried up-stairs. She picked up the garter which was blue and frilly with a little blue bow on one side. She touched the pearls and felt Mother's presence. Quickly she went into her own bedroom and took a handkerchief from the bedside cabinet.

"Look Molly, something old: Mother's pearls, something new: your dress, something borrowed: my white handkerchief, something blue: your garter." Molly was almost moved to tears. She had completely forgotten the old superstition, but was glad to be reminded. Molly wore the pearls with pride. She gently pushed the handkerchief inside her bible and to Dr. Sommerfield's surprise lifted up her dress and put on the garter. She even asked him to help with it.

Mrs. Sommerfield laughed. "Did you not know how stuffy my husband is Molly?" Everyone ready once again, the bride and Dr.'Sommerfield took their place in the taxi at the back, and Mrs. Sommerfield and Merry followed closely behind. The sun glinted in the back of the taxi and invigorated the two people sat there. Dr. Sommerfield felt proud to have been asked to escort Molly. He had known the family for years and was devoted to them. He helped to bury them, birth them and care for them; he was an obvious choice.

The first taxi stopped and out got Mrs. Sommerfield and Merry. Mrs. Sommerfield made her way up along the path towards the little church, the organ was playing and the sound was echoing all around the churchyard.

Merry glanced over her shoulder towards the grave marked Elizabeth Wentworth and Robbie Wentworth. Her baby laid there with her mother. They should have been there today, both of them, but perhaps they were overseeing and helping in a spiritual way. Merry clutched her white bible and orchid for support. It was cold, and the dress was rather flimsy. She stamped up and down to keep warm. Then she caught sight of Molly's taxi, but it went straight past and did another route around the church and outlying streets. Merry was frozen, she was saying to herself, let's get inside. Another car drew up; it was Gerrald and Jordan, all dressed to wed. "My. Gerrald you do look smart."

"What about the bridegroom do I look smart?" Jordan teased.

"You too: dearest brother in law."

"Not yet, Merry." remarked Jordan. "I still have time to run."

"Oh: Not if I can help it!" Merry shook a finger at him. "Have you got the ring?" questioned Merry

"Yes! Yes! Don't fuss," Jordan was getting agitated. The three went up to the foyer of the church and waited for Molly. It was still cold, but at least it sheltered them from the biting wind. They didn't have to wait long. Molly arrived and as she got out of the car Jordan said. "She's like the Madonna." A tear trickled down his face. "I have never seen her so beautiful."

"We better get inside, and wait by the Alter for Molly and Dr. Sommerfield." Jordan nudged Gerrald. They walked into the church and right up the aisle, and waited at the Alter.

Dr. Sommerfield helped Molly adjust her skirts and veil; he put her arm in his and they proceeded up the Church steps. Molly turned only once. As she passed Mother's grave, she blew a gentle kiss and felt emotion welling up inside her. She couldn't help but wish that Mother was there also. Her gaze dropped a few inches and she saw baby Robbie's name, and next to that Aunt Maud's gravestone. It was a heartbreaking moment for the two girls. Molly arrived with her arm linked with Dr. Sommerfield in the foyer of the church. The signal was given and the organ struck up, here comes the bride.

Dr. Sommerfield gave Molly's arm a squeeze. "We're on." he said, and the little procession moved radiantly up the aisle. Jordan turned from the front pew and looked admiringly at Molly with all the love in the world in his eyes. As they approached the Alter, Dr. Sommerfield gave her over to Jordan, and took two steps behind. The ceremony began. It was simple and beautiful. The ring was passed over by Gerrald to Jordan who slipped it on Molly's wedding finger. They were pronounced man and wife in holy wedlock and Jordan was instructed to kiss the bride. Molly lifted her veil, he had never seen her so beautiful, never seen her eyes glow-like emeralds as much as that before; never brushed her lips with his like that before; and she had never been so much of a woman for him. He was proud and protective suddenly at once. Till his dying day he would look after her, through sickness and in health, just exactly as the reverend had said. His vows he did not take lightly; and he would fulfill them till the end of his days.

They turned and made their way back up the aisle. A few friends were wishing them good luck. These friends would be joining them at Thistledown Cottage. Gerrald took Merry back in his car. He had let the top down and her headdress had blown off. Molly and Jordan who were following them in the taxi, laughed as they overtook them with Gerrald chasing all over the road and finally retrieving it from a dead tree branch. Merry waved in delight, her hair was down now, all tangled and blowing against the wind in an upturned motion. She didn't care, she had never been so happy. On leaving the church Molly asked Dr. Sommerfield to place her orchid on Mother's grave. Just as requested Dr. Sommerfield did just that and had a few words for Mother that day. "I hope I have done a good job for you Elizabeth in your absence. You have a lot to be proud about." With that, he placed Molly's wedding orchid on the grave at the foot of the gravestone. Mrs. Sommerfield waited for him at the gates of the churchyard, and they boarded the last taxi back to Thistledown. By the time they arrived, the party was in full swing.

Molly was at the door in full bridal dress with a glass of pink champagne in her hand, waving it around and shouting at Merry who was chasing Gerrald round the garden trying to get her headdress back. They were laughing and shouting and Dr. Sommerfield would never have believed in his wildest dreams that the girls could be normal again together. The change that had taken over Merry was awe-inspiring and it was thanks to Jordan and Molly, and of course Gerrald. The atmosphere was jolly, young and extremely buoyant. The champagne was flowing; the caterers had done Molly a treat. The table was full to capacity of the most edible food, prawns marinated in exotic fruits and sparkling white wine. There was beef roasted to perfection so that it melted in the mouth like marshmallows; melons big, round and ripe sumptuous in their juice, waiting to be devoured in the most ecstatic juices of the mouth. There were salads and honey roast hams and suckling roast pigs awaiting their destruction. There were vol-au-vents filled with chicken in cream sauce and also mushrooms and asparagus. Tomatoes from every corner of the world were present. The most delicious mouthwatering tropical fruits, star fruit, mangoes; passion fruits, bananas, oranges and apples of every variety. But, right there in the middle, on a silver platter; risen up a foot from the table, was the most succulent, fresh, poached salmon, with head and tail still intact, dressed in the most colourful salad, the skin carefully peeled away to project the sheer delicacy of the fleshy meat.

To the top of the table was Molly and Jordan's wedding cake; two tier with a little man and woman in bridal dress overseeing the whole occasion, around the cake were doves of peace, satin leaves and silver bells, and most of all lucky horse shoes were abundant in their variety. A huge bladed knife was laid to the right hand side of the cake awaiting Mr. and Mrs. De Havilland's pleasure. The photographer had arrived; it was one of Gerrald's friends Grant. Molly lifted her skirts to show the garter, and toasted the cameraman with champagne. Jordan joined her in the doorway with his brandy, a little tipsy by now. The photographer clicked, clicked, clicked, some very good shots were taken.   Next he wanted a family group Merry was still trying to retrieve her headdress, Gerrald gave it to her and she planked it on ski whip, but who cares. The wedding couple, The Best Man and Bridesmaid stood for their formal pictures; then the rest of the group got roped in.

Pictures in the garden, down the lane, near Gerrald's car, kissing Dr. Sommerfield, cutting the cake, kissing the groom, kissing the best man, everyone was frenzied.

The music was playing, the guests were letting their hair down Molly and Merry, extroverts in their togetherness, exploded with an effervescence scarcely found in two sisters. Jordan was very tipsy with his bow-tie missing and his shirt front undone to his navel; some of the guests were taking advantage of his uninhibited state. Molly did not mind, he was truly hers and she trusted him, and she wanted this to be a night to remember. The corks were exploding all over the garden, the pink champagne reminded Gerrald of their picnic by the waterfall, but Molly put a finger to his lips "Not today

Gerrald." He apologised and grabbed Merry on the sofa, the two fell down taking with them Mrs. Sommerfield. The cameraman was just in the right position; Mrs. Sommerfield was showing her drawers, what a laugh. Molly wandered into the kitchen to grab a bite; it's a good job that was all she wanted, because there was scarcely a bite left, but she cared not, all the food had gone and the champagne was almost finished. The wine flowed like honey; the brandy was sharply polished off by Jordan. The day was one to remember, not just by the loving couple, but by everyone who attended.

It was winter time still, and darkness was beginning to fall; all the party goers moved inside and they listened to music, danced, some sat slumped in the corners and up the stairs. Jordan and Molly should leave soon, but it was in full swing, and Molly hated to miss a party. Jordan had gone up to the bedroom; he was gone for half an hour. Molly followed him up, she pushed open the door and there he was lying spread-eagled on the bed with a big smile on his face.

The remnants of the brandy, dredged in the bottom of the bottle, on the floor beside him. She smiled and drew the curtains, and went downstairs; they would not be going on honeymoon to Greece tonight. Bodies were slumped all over the place, empty wine bottles lay in indiscriminate profusion, ash trays well full to capacity, like fires the day after a good old spit roast. The buffet table looked like it was overcome by a crowd of locusts, everything in thistledown cottage was in disarray, but Molly was happy, her guests were happy and above all, Gerrald and Merry were happy. Out of the corner of her eye she saw them kissing in one corner, with a drunk propping himself up beside them, they didn't care, they were together alone, surrounded by people.

Molly looked in a mirror for the first time today, her hair was bedraggled, her dress was disheveled; she freshened her makeup, combed her hair and went upstairs and changed her dress into some casual trousers and top. Merry was still in her dress, Molly gestured for her to change it. They emerged from the kiss and Merry obeyed. Gerrald had a grin from ear to ear on his face and as well as being somewhat tipsy, he was extremely content. Molly started to tidy up in the kitchen; removing the dirty plates to the sink, and scrapping away the crumbs and leftovers: the salmon looked a bit forlorn, with only the head and tail still on, leaving only the clean bones, in its middle. The Bride and Groom were still standing serenely on top of the cake; forever grinning, well at least the bride, in real life was still standing. Molly smiled; Jordan had enjoyed today and was sleeping contently now. After the last guest had gone, she would undress him and get him into bed properly.

The merry making was winding down and everyone was the worse for wear. Molly asked who wanted taxis and who was staying.

She ordered the taxis and only three others besides Jordan, Molly, Merry and Gerrald were staying, one was Frank, one Emma, and Marisa: they were very drunk, and they were all slumped together. Merry offered to make coffee for them but could not wake any of them. Instead she made coffee for Merry, Gerrald and herself. Molly was becoming more serious now. "Don't forget Gerrald, Merry has to be packed and back in the Mansion by 2.00 o'clock tomorrow. I'm trusting you, Gerrald, Jordan and I are getting the first plane to Athen's airport, and that means 6:30 am."

Gerrald nodded, "I will, get her back safely,I promise."

"Where are you sleeping tonight Gerrald?" Molly was concerned.

His answer added to her concern. "I'm in Merry's room tonight."

"Oh no, you're not! You sleep down here with these three."

Merry was so angry. "Since when did you become my mother?" she shrieked, "I'm 29 years old, not a baby, and I know with whom I want to sleep."

Molly realised what she had said, and softened. "I know Merry, love, but I cannot take responsibility for any more unwanted babies."

Merry became even more furious. "Who gives you the right to speak to me like that and to tell Gerrald about my past?   Baby Robbie was wanted, desperately wanted!"

Molly readjusted herself in the chair, she felt uncomfortable. "I'm not saying the right words here Merry, I care for you; I just want you to be happy."

"In that case Molly, get off my case; I am old enough to know what I am doing." Molly apologized and bade them goodnight. She left the two of them and the late three revelers to their own devices. She approached the stairs feeling saddened by it all, today was so wondrous; why did it have to end like this? Perhaps, she thought to herself, she had taken on too much and given Merry too much leeway. On reaching the top of the stairs she went into Merry's room to make sure the fire was still alight and safe, she replaced the guard and turned on Merry's Christmas light. Perhaps it had been Molly who was too overpowering, it was a difficult situation. She went to the bathroom then joined Jordan in the bedroom; he was still out cold. What a wedding night this had turned out to be.

She started on the task of undressing her husband, she looked into his face and that same smile was still there. She loved him deeply, and he made her world seem worthwhile, he was compassionate, loving, trustworthy, completely faithful, endearing and generous. In fact she could find nothing at all about him that irritated her. I'm sure if Jordan was asked that question it would not be so favourable towards Molly. She knew what she was, but he loved her not in spite of it, but because of it. She tugged at his pants, pulled off his shoes and was undoing the remaining two buttons on his shirt when he suddenly opened his eyes and drew her towards him, "How are you? Mrs. De Havilland and what hour do you call this?"

Looking at her watch Molly became almost angry again. "Because of you, we have missed that plane and have to get up at 6.30 tomorrow." Jordan was flippant, and after the day that Molly had just had, and especially being alone for the later half of the evening, he was crucifying his luck. He knew it, and backed off. The undying love Molly had a few minutes ago for him, had gone and a sour taste presented itself in her mouth. She hurriedly undressed and got into bed with her back to his, he could bloody well finish off undressing himself, the bastard. Molly for the second time that evening could kill. Jordan quickly fell asleep again, throwing his arms and legs all over the place, Molly could not sleep; she was angry and still worrying about Merry.

She was just beginning to drift away when she heard footsteps, making first, for the bathroom and then for Merry's bedroom!   And there were two sets of them! Molly listened intently. She could hear giggling and joking and ferreting around, and someone falling out of bed. She could hear kissing and sounds of passion; she could hear lovemaking and whispering. She was dying to go next door and give them a piece of her mind, but after the row downstairs she dared not. Here she was, on her wedding night, stuffy and dry and virgin-like with Jordan lying next to her snoring, and her half mad sister, next door bonking out of eternity with her ex-lover, the man who wanted to marry her. She was furious. So much so, that when the irritating noise stopped, she went down to the kitchen for a brandy.

When she reached the fridge she opened the salad drawer, to find to her delight, a last bottle of Don Perignon. She popped it open and had a lovely bubbly glass in peace. She stretched her feet across two dining room chairs and soaked in the pleasure.

Chapter Ten

She had great thoughts of the next day's trip, or should she say; today's trip, and the mystic of the island in the sun, the one ordinary people only dream about. She hoped it was what she had imagined, she needed to get away. The last few days with Merry had been pleasurable, but an added strain for her. She felt both giddy and tired; she took the rest of the champagne and went to bed. She slipped in the covers and Jordan in his sleep placed an arm around her, kissed her on the back and said, "I love you". That compensated for Molly's bad feelings and with that she drifted off to sleep awaiting the pleasures of the next day.

It seemed the middle of the night when the alarm clock went off, ringing throughout the house, Molly was sure it had woken them all, but they were all so hung over she needn't have worried. Jordan lying right next to her, never even heard a sound; it took several pushes and shoves to waken him, but she did eventually. He awoke with a screwed-up expression on his beautiful face, and clutching at the remnants of his head, he made for the bathroom. Molly felt no pity for him; she pushed by him on the hallway and got to the bathroom first. She showered and cleaned her teeth, it was still dark out; she finished up in there and shouted to Jordan to hurry up. She dressed hurriedly; thank goodness she had already packed the cases.

As she wandered back into the bedroom she noticed the crumpled dirty wedding dress, slumped like a shrouded body, waiting its encasement of wood. Still; no time for morbid thoughts today; she took a swig of the last of the champagne. "Yuck" flat as a pancake. She jumped into her casual slacks and sweater, placed a hair band around her head to keep back her long tresses for the journey. Her slacks were white, pleated at the front, and her sweater and headband red. She brushed the reddest cherry lipstick on her lips and caressed her eyelids with a little grey eye shadow; on with the white pumps, she was ready. Makeup, hairbrush, comb and tissues, every thing she needed for the journey, passports, traveller's cheques; credit cards, all accounted for, money both British and Greek. She shouted for Jordan to hurry up once more. He was almost finished and came back into the bedroom with a towel around his middle, she had left his clothes out for him, navy slacks and white, long-sleeved cotton sweater.

He slipped into the slacks, put on his white, casual beech shoes, stopped for a second, looked in a drawer and pulled out a navy blue jumper with a V neck. He draped it around his shoulders and tied it at the front; he looked smart, in fact they looked the perfect couple. Just as they were leaving the room with the luggage Molly said. "Stop, I have something for you, and I've forgotten to get my engagement ring. I left it in my drawer yesterday before I went to church." Jordan stood expectantly, wondering what she had bought him. She handed him a small package and stood back. He opened the bag, then the little box, and there inside was the exact replica of Molly's wedding ring but a few sizes larger.

He was pleased. "Come on Molly put it on for me, I had to put yours on yesterday." She did and then replaced her engagement ring on her finger; they kissed quickly; and were on their way out of Thistledown Cottage and on their way via taxi to the airport.

When they got there, people were everywhere, the noise of conversation was electrifying; the loud speakers were constantly signaling messages and plane departures and the like. Occasionally a lost child's description came over the machine.

It was an exciting place, with people's expectations apparent on their faces and returning visitors looking tired and all the more wiser for their two weeks stay.

They quickly booked in their luggage and were making for the International lounge when a call came over the intercom system for Mr. and Mrs. De Havilland travelling to Greece. "Attention attention." it said. "Good Luck to the newly weds Mr. and Mrs. De Havilland, from friends and family." The couple was delighted. It was very early morning just gone seven o'clock, the bar was open and to their surprise was selling drinks; they decided to take the coward's way out and order coffee and croissants. They sat there enjoying the bustle of the airport and watching the planes coming and going. After about an hour, they had still not been called, so they decided to have a look around the duty-free shops. Molly treated herself to some perfume, Christian Dior, her favourite. She had worn Miss Dior for years and baked in its seductive aroma.

She'd just paid for her perfume when they were called, they quickly made their way to Gate 7 as said, produced their tickets and were escorted to the runway where the plane was waiting—a Boeing 747. They took their seats; Jordan wanted to sit by the window to take in all the view in the ascent, Molly didn't mind. Off they went and up into the air like an overfed duck.

The stewardesses came with drinks, meals, sweeties for dry throats, tissues for dirty hands, brochures for perfume and watches; in fact the flight was so eventful that Athen's airport was looming in the distance and they had only just taken off the ground. They got together their hand luggage, but were arrogantly told. "Fasten your seatbelts." The captain would have no nonsense and everyone obeyed. The plane glided down without event. They all queued up for orders to disembark, the doors were open and the steps were in place, a few passengers went before the honeymooners, then it was Molly's turn to take the great stairway in the sky to earth. She stopped for an intake of breath; the warmth was overwhelming; it cut her throat with an acute dryness.

The sun was not just shining, it was burning, she turned to Jordan, "We are going to enjoy this" and he smiled in agreement. She took to the stairs and on reaching the bottom could feel the tarmac blistering her pumps, with a hotness welcoming her to a new land. She thought of the Pope at that moment, she wondered if he got blistered lips when kissing the tarmac on such a land. It was a very long way from the air terminal, and at first they thought they would have to walk, but no, a tatty old yellow bus, that had seen its day years before, careered towards them and all were abruptly bundled in, there were no seats on this bus, but the passengers had to hang on for dear life with an umbilical cord fixed to the roof. They were thrown from side to side, but no one minded. It was refreshing and new, a different culture to the one which they belonged, it was an adventure. On reaching the terminal, the place was light and airy but with a feeling of obedience; the security and police wore hand guns strapped to their thighs. They went through various screening machines, Molly was sure no one would dare try anything, not in this airport.

Passports and other documents were checked; and the couple was free to collect their luggage, and make their way to their prospective buses and their resorts. Luckily, Molly found their transport straight away, and put the luggage in the compartment at the side of the bus, then took their seats, sitting comfortably.

Well they were, until the huge coach took to the mountain roads; the scenery was beautiful, barren, and unkempt, except for the pines conglomerating everywhere, with the odd little roadside chapels, dotted here and there. The driver was a madman; he had an antiquated form of radio contact with the other drivers, and never stopped talking, the whole trip. His concentration was more on the other drivers' conversations than the dangerous mountain roads; they were just dust tracks with no grip on them and no barriers, the mountains dropped down one side for ever—Molly estimated perhaps 200 feet. She dared not look.

Dirty, smelly, and dying for a wash and change of clothes, they reached the end of the mainland, and were now waiting for the little fishing boat to take them to Spetse. It was just going dark now, the early evening was dry and warm, except for the odd splash of water coming over the side of the little boat, it was way down in the water with the weight of all the cases; there were twelve people crossing that night, the swirl of the waves was demanding, in a discourteous way, hurrying the passengers ashore ready for the money from the next trip.

When they got to Spetse, it was worth all the travelling and the hardship of the mountain bus. The tiny cafes and bars around the harbour were all lit up, the fishing boats abandoned by their owners for the night, bobbed up and down sending themselves to sleep. The harbour was all cobblestones in various Greek designs. There were tables and chairs outside all of the restaurants with canopies to shield from sun and other elements. The night life was just beginning to get into full swing. There was a great big sign which said ROOM ONLY; in most of the Hotels, which amounted to three in number. This was the way most people enjoyed Spetse. But Jordan and Molly went self-catering, for the privacy and secrecy of being alone. There were horns and bells being honked, it drew their attention. It was their taxi service, or rather, the taxi service for the whole island.

To their amazement, it wasn't a car or coach or anything like that. It was horse-drawn carriages with tops on, they gave their luggage to the driver, and he put it in the back. The seats were leather, the driver sat in front arrogantly with a white trilby hat on and a black band around it. The two jumped in the back, and found that the bumping up and down in the carriage was exuberating. The island by dusk was beautiful, all the houses were painted white, even the sea wall; just a metre high was white. The seashore in places was pebbles with very little sand, except the private ones which were man-made, where sand was abundant. The road to their apartment was twisting but flat. The whole place was natural and untouched.

The people too were dressed in black; they did some embroidery outside their homes. The men fished for a living, and of course the restaurant workers made a living serving Greek dishes of every kind. On their route to the apartment they passed cafes and pubs, all with their customers sitting outside taking in the breathless sea views. The cart came to an abrupt halt. The driver pointed to the flat above the ironmonger's shop.

They paid and he gestured and murmured something in Greek to open that door. They did, and to their amazement the tiny little pebbled courtyard was in two different types of tiny pebbles, some grey; some darker grey in an Aztec design. The light was left on for them, the white concrete stairs led the way past a lime tree with limes, ripe, and hanging from most branches, leading the to their apartment door.   The key was in the lock, and they opened the door and switched on the lights. The floor was tiled in grey ceramic tiles, the room was bare except for two single beds and two bedside cabinets; the small wardrobe was built in.

The dust on the floor was so thick they had to brush it up before treading on it. The windows were small, and the actual window opened in and there were bars on the outside. Quite primitive Molly thought, but they were a long way up, it was more like three stories than two, perhaps it was three as the ironmonger's shop was on the bottom, and of course the owners had to have somewhere to live themselves. She left her luggage in the lounge or bedroom or whatever one would call it, and went out onto the balcony. There were ceramic terracotta tiles on the floor, the wall was smooth and white, it reminded her of igloos, she looked over the wall of the balcony, it was a long way down, and it was frightening to look. There was a patio table and two chairs, the parasol was lemon and white and it had Greek writing all over it. She sat on one of the chairs and gazed out across the old harbour to the sea.

It was tranquil and just in the distance she could hear a faint sound of Greek music probably coming from one of the cafes she had passed on her cart ride. The sky was darkening now, and the moon was large and almost disappearing off the horizon coming to one with the sea. As she looked the other way and there were small yachts with numbers on, identical except for the numbers, it must have been some sort of sailing flotilla or holiday club or the like. They filled the harbour, with the more grand yachts moored a little way off.

The evening was tranquil, and although she felt tired she wanted to sample the delights of the atmosphere in one of the little cafes. Jordan came out. "Let's go and explore," he said. She nodded; they locked up and made their way back down the white stairs. The light was still on; it was a good job, as without it, it would have been pitch black. They got on to the street, well not a street as we know it—a once paved road which had now become covered in walked-in dust, the sea was throwing its waves against the harbour wall with outstretched ferocity. Every now and then they had to dash out of the way, or be soaked to the skin. The walk was both romantic and inspiring. The first cafe with its illuminated neon sign and flashing lights was some sort of a makeshift dance area with a few people gathering outside and many more dancing inside. They decided to pass that one as tonight they were so tired they wanted to take in the pleasures of the walk and the scenery and culture around them.

They were so enthused by the walk along the outskirts of the little town that they kept on walking; they walked so far that they came back to where they had first disembarked from the little fishing boat.

They were surprised to see that even the police moved around the island and its people in little river boats with a red flashing light on the top. The locals here caught boats as we would catch buses.

Molly and Jordan sat down at a table outside one of the restaurants and a waiter came. They ordered two beers and some snacks, and what came were the freshest doughnuts ever. They stayed a bit longer, just watching the little world go by, and taking in the breath-taking views until quite late. They waved goodbye to their waiter, paid and tipped him. On their return walk towards their apartment they stopped to look at a little tour shop window, they were advertising trips around the island. They decided to go, the trip to Paraskevi included a picnic and some authentic Greek music and some fun and games in the water. They held each other on the way back and could think of nothing nicer than what they were doing right then. The tranquility was broken by some youths deciding to fight as they passed the noisy pub on their way back. They were at their apartment in no time and inside within seconds. The bed, though only basic, felt good to Molly, she quickly undressed and slipped in between the cotton sheets.

Jordan clipped in. "I'm not sleeping in separate beds on my honeymoon." So with that they decided to push them together and share sheets. They were both too tired for anything else, and Jordan promised to make it up to her, on the rest of the holiday. Molly thought to herself; already married two nights and no nookie. Still she didn't mind, she too was tired, they had had a long and pleasurable day. They slept late that morning, and when Molly got up and opened the windows and shutters, she was surprised to see all the activity going on below. There was ladies selling handkerchiefs, men carving wooden objects, ladies riding motorbikes on the back, sidesaddle, with no hands, some of them had large bags on their heads, and how they balanced, around those corners was a miracle.

They hurriedly dressed and made their way to the boat that was to take them to Paraskevi beach. They were in casual shorts and tee-shirts; and Molly on the way there stopped at a gift shop and bought herself a hat with a big brim in straw. As they arrived at the boat there was a very old gentleman, white beard open neck shirt with a red handkerchief tied around his neck, chatting up the young, single ladies and making them laugh, apparently he was 'Naughty George' and had been on that boat since the route began. They boarded and took their place on one side, the Greek music was sweet and gave an authentic thrill to the voyage; all were on board and the boat was packed, as quick as that they set sail, they went all around the island first to see the most magnificent sights, there were people lounging around in boats, there were people diving off yachts, there were already people in quiet little coves, sunbathing starker's; and only the boat with the Greek music gave any sort of intrusion into their privacy.

The sea was blue the sky was azure, with not a single cloud in sight; it was a most warming experience. Jordan looked at Molly and gave her a hug and kiss of contentment. They arrived and 'Naughty George' was first to the front of the boat to escort all the young ladies off. Molly needed no escort, she had a husband. At that thought she looked down at her hand and her wedding and engagement rings, they were new and sparkling. She had never been happier in her life. As soon as everyone was off the boat, the barbecue was lit, and the beach party began, there was beer for everyone and wine, Greek salad and baked potatoes, and the freshest of fish, just caught that morning, everyone was getting tipsy, they played at games in the water until they were exhausted. They swam and laughed and just had a jolly good time. The boat was coming back for them at four o'clock, and it was nearing that time now. They heard a loud honking sound; yes it was the boat to pick them up.

The two old ladies who came on their own had a lovely time. They sat and watched all the others and just took in the sights and fun the young ones were having. They nodded to Jordan and Molly on the way back noticing the newness of the wedding rings.

They waited in turn to get off the boat, and when safely on dry land made a beeline for the restaurant they had gone to the night before. Their waiter from before, was with them in an instant, and eagerly took their order. They sat taking in the bustle from the boats with people meandering on and off at chosen times. The little town was abuzz with activity in the harbour that day; there were new tourists arriving and parties of people leaving all queuing for hovercrafts and fishing boats; the hovercraft took them right up to Athens, whereas the fishing boats took them to the bottom tip of the mainland and a coach took them the rest of the way to Athens. The early evening air was dry and warm, Molly was glad she had taken her sun hat, the beer was cool and refreshing and going down well. The horse drawn carriages were busy now, as the new arrivals were scurrying to their living accommodations.

As the evening dusk began to settle, the police boat was making its route around the island calling in at all of the beaches for any reports of trouble.

There were no cars on the island except for the one, which belonged to some shipping magnet, who had a huge house on the top of the island. There were also two jeeps belonging to the police, and apart from that everyone made their way around on motorbikes; even the old ladies could be seen riding round all dressed in black; with huge sacks of potatoes on the handlebars. But mostly the women rode side saddle on the back.

The evening was drawing in, and the beers had gone down far too easily, and both Molly and Jordan were becoming heady and giggly.

They decided to go back to the apartment and take in the ocean drenched horizon on their walk back. It was a road used by everyone, it was romantic and calming; all along the front the bleached white houses with their terracotta roofs stood out in the evening light like half-barbecued marshmallows. Past the noisy restaurant and up towards the old harbour, that night there were different crafts in the old harbour, the fleet of around twenty had long left and a few yachts and some larger craft took their place, but quite a way further out there was the most magnificent ship. It was quite big and streamlined, the staff on board wore white and gold uniforms, and there on board was a lighter, smaller boat strung up and tied at each point ready to be lowered down to the sea at a whim if a passenger was being taken ashore.

The owner had some guests for dinner that evening and the dinner table was set in the bow of the ship in the open; they were all dressed in evening wear, the women wore diamonds with elongated dresses touching the floor, the men were in dinner suits and bow ties. The waiters were attending the table, and the wine water was just uncorking champagne. How Molly wished she was there. Still, on with their own little dream, they walked up the steep pathway towards their apartment, the street was empty tonight, the low music could be heard coming from a nearby bar, probably the one the locals used.

They opened the downstairs door into the courtyard. Molly started climbing the stairs, Jordan behind her, he stopped at the bottom stair and looked at Molly's thin curvy ankles and shapely calves taking him up to her slender thighs and ample hips, her waist, so tiny gave way to a finely proportioned back; he had seen her for the first time tonight. He followed her up to the balcony where she was already taking off her clothes. The tee-shirt was discarded in a second, off with the shorts and panties, the air was humid and tiny specks of perspiration shone like jewels on the reflection of the moon, all over her body. She stretched her arms up to the sky; she was a silhouette of loveliness. He loved her, every inch of her. He too joined her in her nakedness. He went forward to her, she slipped her arms around his neck, and a leg around his waist; now the other, Jordan was ready for her. He slipped inside her and jointly they enjoyed the next episode in their lives rhythmically swaying on impulsion and flying on a cloud of desire. They were lost in their oneness for eternity, for the forever now, passing through timeless boundaries and catching hold of the earth again when it was time to come back to the balcony.

He picked her up and carried her indoors to safety, away from prying eyes.

Their honeymoon was well and truly christened that night. Molly pulled on a long tee-shirt and went to the fridge, the cleaning lady had filled the fridge for them as she was instructed and remembered to get the champagne, which by now was chilled to perfection, Molly picked it up, and with two glasses in hand, reappeared on to the balcony. It was peaceful out there, the sea was calm tonight, and the yachts in the harbour were motionless; the dinner party was in full swing and with the tranquility, the laughter could be heard right across the bay. The ship looked even more appealing from the balcony.

Jordan came out with his shorts on. "I'll open the champagne Molly."

He toasted. "Here's to my beautiful bride!"   As he flipped the cork off the bottle, and went rocketing into the sky, almost touching the stars. The foamy bubbles ran down the side, Molly placed her hand under the bottle and caught the escaping beverage.   Jordan filled the glasses, and they sat taking in the night air, and sipping champagne.

Never were two people so happy together. The night air was warm and unquestioning; the two sat for even longer. The dinner party on the yacht had broken up, and the yacht, apart from the necessary lights was in darkness. The next few days passed, sun tanning, water sports and boat trips filled their time, except for the evenings which were spent at their favourite restaurant. The booze was going down in the fridge, so Jordan decided to hire a motorbike to get them into town quicker, and for the sheer thrill of movement. They collected their money from the bank, got back on the bike and headed for the wine shop.

Jordan parked the motorbike outside the shop, on the cobble street. Molly spotted a supermarket across the road and was just going in the door, when she heard an almighty crashing sound; she froze, spun round, and to her horror saw Jordan's hired motorbike taking its place in the window of the wine shop, surrounded by broken wine bottles in the display. Wine was running from the shop window on to the road, it was red and Molly shook with fright, she had visions of all of her holiday money going in one foul swoop, and they still had six days left to get through. The shopkeeper was aghast and was shouting and screaming in Greek. The bike had lost its standing and gone through the shop window, demolishing the display of lots of wine.

The honeymooners did not know what she was saying, but tried to reassure her they would pay; they showed her money and she stopped screaming and calmed down. The sight of the money had a wonderful effect, just as if one had used a cloth full of ether.

The joiner was called, and the bill turned out to be very little, indeed. They enjoyed the thrill so much they promised the shopkeeper, it was worth it, and could they come back and do the same thing tomorrow. She picked up her yard brush and very unceremoniously showed them off, but smiling. A few more days were spent just lazing around and enjoying the sun and beach, picnicking with champagne and dozing around.

It was Tuesday of the second week, and they decided to hire out the bike again, but this time they took no chances. They did not go near town, but to a secluded little cove at the other side of the island, overlooked by no one, in fact the only people to spot them were the people on the odd boat that passed. Jordan rested the champagne between the rocks at the edge of the sea, it wouldn't be cold but it would be cool as the water was cool to the touch. They left their salad and chicken in the hamper basket until they were ready. They undressed, naked and free; they relaxed and took in all nature, occasionally swimming, to kick off the sand, they felt that this was their dessert island. Jordan put on his flippers and sped across the horizon like a speed boat. Molly just lay there getting browner and browner.

They both had sallow skin, so burning was no object, but just to be safe, they put on some suntan oil This was one of the few coves which had sand on it, it was, fine, golden and nice to the touch. Molly picked some up and let it tipple through her fingers. The sun was beating down, and she felt that feeling of well being. She called it happiness and contentment. Jordan was still swimming in his flippers oblivious to Molly and her sunbathing, boats with Greek music blaring out, were passing nearby, but this would stop after eleven or twelve o'clock as everyone had left then, as the locals took a siesta and were up and at it again at three o'clock, picking up their revellers from the beaches. Molly turned over and felt the sun on her back, her breasts dug in the warm sand, it sent sensations all over her, she squirmed around a little, her bottom was feeling the sun; she stood up and ran into the water. Jordan saw her sink into the liquefied light blue ink, and he felt his pen ready.

Molly got into the deep just below her boobs which were buoyant now and bouncing like air wings in the ripples of the passing vessels. She slipped further in and tipped up to a swimming position, the water was cool but uplifting. She found it easy to swim in this ocean, and she swam without effort. The water was so clear she could see right down to the bottom. The sand was smooth and rippled at the same time, the pebbles were so much closer to the shore, she was now free of urchins, little black time bombs which stuck in the feet and hurt like hell. Jordan swam towards her. "At last you have ventured in; I didn't know you could swim." He kissed her; she was receptive, her hair was long and wet, her skin bronzed and healthy, she was like a mermaid, a beauty from another world, he caught her more urgently and they swam in unison: the little fish followed, their oneness was all consuming, they swam a little closer to the shore, they made love standing, but with each thrust from Jordan, the two were swept further out, the flippers were acting like an outboard motor, and before they knew it, they were almost alongside the yacht, which had decided to anchor in their secret cove.

There were prying eyes which made it difficult to leave the water, but there was no need to worry as at least six of them dived in naked too, and joined in the swimming.

Molly swam around cleansing herself and feeling fresher. She signalled to Jordan she was hungry and motioned for him to open the champagne. The other swimmers went to the other side of their yacht and carried on with the fun. Jordan and Molly were exhausted with their episode. They stepped out of the water allowing the sun's rays to dry and bronze them some more.

Jordan corked open the champagne, it wasn't ice cold, but it was cool, bubbly was just the order for a complete afternoon. They had built up an enormous appetite. The chicken and salad were magic, and the bubbles fizzed and trickled down the glass and into their mouths. After they took their fill, they just lazed and dozed and enjoyed the peace and tranquility of that cove far out along the dust track road of Spetse. This day was like the last remaining days of their holiday, enjoying the nicest things of life, being together, relaxing, away from the hustle and bustle of the town folk.

The day before they left, they took a ride into town on their well used hire bike. The sun was shining as usual;

everyone was going about their business. Their horse-drawn carriage was clip-clopping up and down taking people to their destinations. The boats too were alive with Greek music. 'Naughty George' was chatting up every single young woman in sight. Jordan and Molly were at their favourite restaurant buying postcards and presents. The postcards would have to be sent soon, so that they arrived before the two newlyweds did.

Molly removed her sunglasses. She could not believe her eyes, for there in front of her was the oddest car she had seen in her life. It was like an old Morris minor chassis in the strangest light-green colour; probably sun bleached, and there on the top was a canopy about two meters square with three-inch fringes all around; there must be two cars on the island now, Molly paused on that thought.

That night they packed all their things ready for the early departure. Molly looked in the fridge and took out the last bottle of champers. Jordan was out on the balcony reading yesterday's English paper. The sun was appealingly hot that morning. Molly uncorked the champagne and she poured two glasses of the effervescent, cold sparkling liquid and produced it on the patio table. She took a sip and disappeared into the kitchen to rustle up some omelets with the last remaining eggs. They took in the view for the last time, sipped the champagne and finished off the omelets. She had enjoyed her holiday, but she was missing her beloved Thistledown Cottage.

Both were now very brown indeed, and the holiday had done them the world of good. They shouted down a horse drawn carriage from the balcony, left a tip for the maid, and left the key in the lock as instructed. The two week episode in their lives though delightful and pleasurable was now gone forever, chased to oblivion into a tiny corner of their minds. With a little sadness the two took their luggage downstairs and boarded the carriage. The trip back was looked upon with different eyes, as by now they knew every nook and cranny of that lovely little island, its people, its culture and they found also that they could easily fit in, and perhaps one day they would, forever.

A crowd was gathering around the little fishing boat waiting to take them to the mainland where the coach was standing. As the little fishing boat pulled away from the island there was sadness in the air, everyone it seemed liked the tranquility and culture and the welcome given to tourists by the locals of that little island. The short trip across was uneventful but pleasant. People were taking their places ready to disembark, the coach was there on time, and the driver put the luggage in the compartment under the coach. Everyone had taken their seats, and they were off again around the dangerous mountain roads with the steep drops to one side. The coach trip was long and arduous, and the two honeymooners felt dirty and sticky as they produced their tickets for the air trip home. They moved into the departure lounge, Molly got some duty free vodka at a marked down price. She unscrewed the top and took a few swigs; she was still in the holiday spirit, literally. They were called and boarded, ready for their return home. Molly for some reason felt sickly, and she was amazed to see that her ankles had swollen up, something that had never happened before. The flight was over, and they were back on their way to Thistledown Cottage. The little bus dropped them at the lane, and they lugged the luggage up the dusty track. Thistledown looked even more appealing after the two week absence. Jordan opened the door and dumped the cases. Merry had left a note on the kitchen table.

Thank you my dear sister, for the most enjoyable days of my life.

Love Merry. xxx

Molly smiled to herself, yes everyone had enjoyed themselves but above all, Molly and Jordan, or rather Mr. and Mrs. De Havilland. The next few weeks were filled with work, work, work, quiet evenings in each other's arms and moments of reflection, reading, playing soft music, cuddling on the sofa with sweet thoughts of Spetse.

Molly was still feeling off so much so she visited Dr. Sommerfield. She had symptoms of a cold or some bug or other. He gave her some antibiotics, which she took dutifully too, but after the course ran out she was still the same. Back to the doctor was the only thing to do. "I will take a blood test this time Molly and a urine test, just in case something is wrong. Call me in a couple of days and I will tell you the outcome." The two days seemed like months, Molly was getting rather worried; in fact she was thinking all sorts of things; that might go wrong, she had never been ill in her life.

It was time to ring Dr. Sommerfield. She wanted to know but was afraid of the outcome. She dialed, then hesitated, then dialed again, better to know than to wonder. It rang and rang and rang. "Dr. Sommerfield is busy." Said the voice, coming from the other end. "What is it you want?"

"It's Molly Went... no, I mean De Havilland." Molly's voice came back.

"We do not have anyone registered in that name."

Molly was almost at the point of putting the phone down when Dr. Sommerfield's voice came over the phone. "Molly is that you?"

"Yes." Molly answered in a small voice.

"Don't sound so afraid Molly it's not what you think." There was a long pause, "Molly, you are pregnant, five weeks at a guess, since your last period, that makes it five weeks." Molly was shocked into silence.

"Thank you," she said and put the phone down. How was she going to tell Jordan? They had only just got married. He would want them to be on their own for a while yet, she was sure of it. She sat down and waited for him to come home that night.

She was quietly excited, even although they had not planned a family not for some time, anyhow fate had taken a hand, and there was no going back now. She waited with quiet excitements, she wondered if it was a boy or girl, would it look like Jordan or her, would it be a mixture of both.

Would she get so big she struggled, her head was abuzz with excited questions, so much so she didn't hear Jordan come in. "Hello there, why are you sitting in the dark?" he jested, Molly had not realised darkness was falling, she was too engrossed in her thoughts.

"Jordan, please sit down I have something to tell you."

His face was ashen. "You look so serious Molly what did Dr. Sommerfield say today."

Molly looked into his chestnut brown eyes. "We're pregnant."

He looked dumbstruck at first; then when the statement sank in, he picked Molly up and spun her round; they were both ecstatic with pleasure. He went into the kitchen and opened the last bottle of champagne, uncorking it as he entered the lounge. He toasted to his new offspring. Molly decided not to have any.

She had had enough on the holiday, and she did not know she was pregnant. She began to worry about the new baby.

The weeks changed to months, and Molly was keeping up with her appointments with Dr. Sommerfield; she was getting big now, and her date was nearing. She busied herself around the house, knitting baby things titivating the spare room awaiting the new arrival. Merry was a little put out as she had regarded that room as hers, but Molly promised that when it was time for Merry to leave the Sanitarium for good, the room would be ready for her, no matter what. Merry was pleased for Molly. She was waiting patiently too to hold the new baby. Molly's pregnancy was pleasant and untroubled; she just sailed through the whole thing with a bloom given to the first rose of summer. The baby was due on the 16th November that was just two weeks off. They all waited the first signs of an entrance. The room was ready. Merry's bed had been put to one side; the cot took centre place, with lace and frills in white embroidered lace hanging from the top of the cradle, all the way around the cot itself. The pillow was in satin and bows were apparent on every corner, the nappies were stacked on shelves, and talcum powder and all sorts of baby things were placed on top of drawers and on the dressing table, nappy pins were ready and every sort of accompaniment a newborn would need, its clothes were neatly re-ironed and placed in all the drawers. Merry's photographs with Molly were left in place on the bedside cabinet and on parts of the dressing table.

The baby bath was in the corner and little furry toys and musical toys of every description lay around the room.

The day came for Molly's last visit to Dr. Sommerfield. He said it was time for her to go into hospital as the baby was low, in her tummy, and all the signs were there it would be coming very soon. She packed a case, and Jordan took her in to St. Luke's next day. She was put in a single ward which suited Molly; she liked her privacy and could talk to Jordan and her family without any other interruptions. She waved Jordan off that night and got up for a walk down the corridor when the first pain started. They got heavily stronger, until the nurse rang the doctor and asked for her to go down to delivery. Jordan was notified, and he came at once, he waited outside until called, when he went in she was dressed in a white hospital gown and was clearly in pain. He kissed her on the forehead and was ushered out of the room. "We will call you when its time." the nurse told him. There was a lot of hustle and bustle going on around the wards, and babies were coming out like a production line from every door in the corridor.

Jordan got himself a coffee from the nurse in the kitchens and sat himself down for another long wait, but no. "Come quickly Mr. De Havilland, your baby's on its way". He got into the ward just in time for this curly black-haired little head popping out with eyes wide open just looking around. Molly gave a second grunt and out came Mr. De Havilland's daughter. She was beautiful. The nurse gave her a quick bath. Jordan was first to hold her, he wouldn't pass her over to Molly; wanting to hold her longer, he was almost struggling with Molly when the nurse came in. She gave Jordan a matronly look and passed the baby to Molly. They both just looked in bewilderment at the little being they had created, just perfect. Molly was quickly ushered up to the ward, unceremoniously on the trolley with baby bawling its head off; she went back into her single ward, which by this time was full of flowers of every description and colour. The next day the cards came flooding in, there was scarcely any room for anything else; in fact they had trouble getting the baby cot into the ward. Molly was blooming and very healthy, not a stitch or a problem.

The baby was sucking well, and she was putting on weight, she weighed in at 6 1bs 7 oz and already she was 7 lb and that was only after five days. Molly's stay was ending, and it was time for her to go home. They still hadn't thought of a name. The taxi arrived at St. Luke's, and the little family made their first journey home together. Thistledown Cottage was all lit up and warmed for them coming home. Molly had no mother to help her, but Mrs. Sommerfield had come along just for the first few days. She slept in Merry's bed and the doctor called every day. There was no need, everyone was beaming with vitality. They rang Merry constantly at the Sanitarium, keeping her informed of the baby's progress, they had to name her for the birth certificate, so they sat down that evening and thought of so many names, but near exhaustion they decided on Martine, simply because the very first drink after her pregnancy, Molly asked for was a Martini.

Secretly Jordan had wanted a boy and had not thought of any girl names, but he was unmovable now. Both mother and baby were doing well; they had been up to the Sanitarium twice now, and Merry had loved Martine so much, each visit she hadn't wanted them to go. The only thing which took her mind off the baby was the fact that Gerrald was becoming a regular visitor for her, they were getting pretty close, and Molly encouraged it. Christmas that year was quiet; Merry had come home again after Mrs. Sommerfield had left. Gerrald came over too, and all four spent it, not like the year before, but quieter. Merry and Gerrald had spent a lot of time in her bedroom. Talking and getting to know each other over again.

Whilst Merry was at home, Molly took the baby cot and things into the large bedroom with Jordan and herself.

Christmas that year was over; before it began the months and years were whizzing by, Merry was still in the Sanitarium, but there were definite signs that she could be discharged soon, as she had not had any of those attacks of temper and tantrums for over five years now. Little Martine was four years old and was such a good little talker. She knew all her nursery rhymes and could count to twenty without effort; she was just learning to tell the time and was getting ready for starting school. Jordan was doing well at his job and had been promoted yet again to senior management.

Years had passed without anyone noticing; Molly had long since given up her career, she was a wife and mother now, and this roll suited her at the moment. Thistledown cottage was looking pretty as all the flowers were in full bloom, the sweet peas had been cut back long since and in their place was some giant pansies and some little forget-me-nots. Dr. Sommerfield had died the year before. Mrs. Sommerfield was devastated, and so was Molly and Merry. Jordan was greying at the temples, and Molly too was getting older; she was almost forty three now, at least she would be next year. That night Jordan came in from work complaining about stomach pains, he had complained about them before and headaches as well.

Molly sent for Dr. Sommerfield's assistant a Dr. Morrow, who had taken over the running of the surgery on the old doctor's death. He was much younger than Dr. Sommerfield, and Molly had little faith in him as a person or a doctor. Anyhow he arrived and had a look at Jordan. He said that Jordan had been overdoing it, and left him some headache tablets and some stomach powders. Molly just shrugged when she closed the door behind him. "I don't think he knows what he's doing," she said to Jordan.

"Well, we have to give him the chance before we prejudge." The door opened, and it was Martine coming in from the garden.

She was the image of her mother, the same jade green eyes and long black hair, the same devilish smile and the same naughtiness about her. Jordan loved her so much. She was eleven years old and already turning into quite a young lady. She was taller than Molly had been at that age, she remembered, but everything else matched. Her Aunty Merry looked forward so much to her visits. Gerrald's visits to the Sanitarium were dwindling now, and Molly thought that perhaps he had found himself someone who was free and not incarcerated like Merry. She never had been let out, only for the odd weekend or Christmas now, and Molly was beginning to fear that perhaps it would be too late now as Merry was very much institutionalised. She never ever had to think for herself or do anything for herself. Her friend Sue was still there; and the two were very close now being in the same position. Molly always thought that there was nothing much wrong with either of them, but somebody high up in the Hospital Authority always said no, to letting them out, every time their appeals were heard.

In fact they had both stopped trying and reconciled themselves in the fact that, that was the only life available to them, as long as they lived. Molly's thoughts were always with Merry, and as they were getting older now she thought of her more and more and wondered what life could have been. Life was hard for them both being apart and part of each other. Jordan and Molly were tranquil now as the years were moving on. They lived a quieter, more sedate life; their joys were shown in Martine's eyes, as she shone, they adored her even more.

A night that sprang to mind was when Martine took the lead at the school play. She had taken to acting and drama like a fish to water, and they decided that night that if she wanted to go in that direction they would encourage it. Molly had heard in the village one day, from one of the waiters at Ginos that Gerrald had got married. Molly was glad for Gerrald, but decided not to tell Merry right away as she still spoke of him. Martine, quite a young lady and approaching her Fourteenth birthday, wanted to go with Molly to visit Aunty Merry. Molly agreed. Merry had several photographs of Martine, and they spoke on the phone, but Molly up till now was against Martine going into that place. But time was moving on at a great speed, and the women were not going to get any younger, and Merry had precious little else she could call her own. They set off and Martine thoroughly enjoyed the train trip and the walk up to the large mansion at the top of the hill.

All sorts of things clouded Molly's thoughts. She had done this journey so many times, each time never knowing what the outcome would be, whether she was helping Merry or making her worse. This time she would tell Merry about Gerrald and why his visits had almost ceased. The matron was there as usual to greet all visitors; Molly needed no directions for her sister's room. She knocked and entered. Merry did not expect Molly to bring Martine, but it made her day. She dashed across to her niece and just hugged and hugged her. Martine noticed that there were photographs all over the room of her. She was very impressed and could not believe how much her mother and Aunt Merry looked alike, identical, even the hair at the temples was greying at the same speed and colour.

"That's why your father bought us name brooches, which as you can see Aunt Merry is wearing hers and I've forgotten mine!" Martine noticed and smiled, yours is in the bedroom drawer at home, Mother, I saw it recently, when I was looking for something."

"Good, Marine, I thought I'd lost it and daren't tell your father, we've had those brooches for such a long time, since I met your father almost."

Martine had brought yet another photograph for Merry, a family group, with her father and mother. Merry commented on how content and happy they all were. She looked into Molly's eyes, this was always denied me. I do not know why I have been one of life's losers."

Molly sat down beside her. "You will always have us, and if we can get you out, we will keep trying." Merry commented that she had not seen Gerrald for several months; the opportunity was given to Molly. "I spoke to a friend of his Merry. Apparently he got married a few months ago and is living with Mrs. Linley at Stevenage." Merry froze, Molly could see the look that always came across Merry's face, when she was about to throw a tantrum. "Quickly Martine get the matron". Martine obeyed and Molly tried to reason with Merry; she tried to talk to her in a calming way. Merry threw herself at Molly, and they struggled and fell on the floor. Molly's coat got ripped in the struggle; the sleeve was almost torn out. The matron came in, and the two women were pulling lumps out of each other. Molly got up and dragged Merry up too.

She was still clawing at Molly's face and pulling her hair and uncontrollably screeching at the top of her voice. Matron sent for the male nurses. They both got an arm and escorted her to a doctor for sedation and the solitary room where Molly and Aunt Maud had once seen her rocking backwards and forward. Molly wished she hadn't gone that day. She made Martine wait outside until she had seen Merry sedated and settled. She waited half an hour or more when a male nurse sent for her. The cell door was steel.

There was a square cut out of the upper half, about one foot square with bars going vertically up it about an inch apart. Molly looked through at Merry who was laid on a bed, eyes closed and wrists restrained to either side of the bed. Molly hated seeing her sister like that. Disheartened, she left and picked up Martine on the way out. No one spoke on the return journey. Jordan was in and waiting patiently for their return. He heard the bus and went to the door awaiting his two beautiful women. Molly's face said it all.

Jordan too looked worried. "What has happened? Was it a bad day?"

Molly nodded. "I'll tell you when Martine goes to bed." They spoke long and hard that night, their decision was that Merry should stay in the Sanitarium forever; she was a danger to herself and to others. If she could do that to her own sister, then she could turn very nasty indeed.

Molly could see that Jordan was suffering very badly that night with his headaches and stomach pains. She gave him his medicines, but this time just a little more, than the stated dose to try and ease his pain. The medicines made Jordan drowsy, and he usually went to bed early on these occasions. Molly went upstairs with him, but found no time for sleep, her thoughts returning periodically to Merry and how she was. She would leave it three weeks and then return. Martine was doing some exams soon, so helping her with her homework played a big part in Molly's life for the next few weeks. Martine was already talking about what she wanted to be when she left school. After her exams she could leave and get a job or carry on and sit some more for a better qualification. Molly and Jordan wanted her to stay on, but Martine being headstrong like her mother said she was leaving school and going to the School of Dramatic Art. They wanted what was best for her, and they knew she had an aptitude for dancing and stage works. They did not stand in her way.

Chapter Eleven

THE EXAMS WERE TAKEN and the passes in all the subjects; were to be read out at the parents' meeting that month. Jordan and Molly of course, as always had to go. They were certain Martine had done well. Martine said she would meet them in the hall. Both Jordan and Molly had taken their places and were waiting for Martine to arrive, but what they saw they were not ready for. Martine came in alright; she was wearing lipstick and eye shadow and had her hair up on top of her head. She was wearing high heels and stockings with a very tight top and skirt which showed her figure, to full potential. Molly stopped herself. Who was she describing? It could have been herself a long time ago. She turned and smiled at Martine. "Come on and sit down. I have saved you a seat."

Another voice called Martine's name. There was another shock in store for Molly. "Martine, save me a seat too." This sound came from a very handsome young man pushing past people moving down the aisle. Martine looked back and waved to him, her face was beaming.

Molly looked at Jordan and said. "Is this where we came in?" They acknowledged the two youngsters without any sign of objection, and all four enjoyed the appraisals and the exam results. The two youngsters passed in all the subjects they sat, including their choice of each other, and both lots of parents' gave their approval. Jordan had a particularly bad night that night; he could not sleep for the stomach cramps. Molly mixed him a dose of the medicine. It seemed to do the work, as he was quickly sedated. It was worrying Molly, so she decided to go and see Dr. Morrow herself. She waited in his surgery the next day until it was her turn. She told him of Jordan's cramps and headaches and said they were getting worse. Dr. Morrow said that it was all brought on by stress at work, and that if Jordan wanted the pains to stop, he must give up work. Jordan was not yet fifty and Molly felt devastated for him if he was to give up work now. Dr. Morrow said if his health was suffering, he should consider at least doing part-time for a while. Whilst she was there, Molly got some more medicines for Jordan; he was going through it at an alarming rate now, just to pacify his needs.

Martine was bringing her boyfriend for tea that night, so Molly only hoped that Jordan was a bit better, otherwise he would have to go to bed soon again. Molly could keep the youngsters entertained, but it would be nice if they could all be together as Molly had gone to extremes to cook a special supper for them all.

She returned with Jordan's medicine and Dr. Morrow's advice to find Jordan already home. "My stomach was so bad I had to come out of work today Molly." Molly told him that she had been to the doctor and had got some more medicine. "But it's not working Molly, you know it isn't." Molly pondered before answering. "Yes I know Jordan." She hesitated. "Dr. Morrow thinks you should give up work, or at least go part-time instead. He thinks its all down to stress."

"Rubbish," said Jordan. "That man's a quack." Molly reminded Jordan that Martine was bringing Daniel for supper that night. With that Jordan said. "Well, I better have the medicine now, have a sleep and I'll be fine for Martine tonight. I don't want to let her down." Molly gave him double dozes, and he was upstairs and asleep in ten minutes.

Martine and Daniel were always together; in fact they had been seeing each other, every night as the months turned into years.

They were arriving at seven o'clock, tonight, for tea at Thistledown Cottage. It was only three o'clock now, so Jordan had plenty of time for a rest and a bath before they arrived. Molly busied herself cooking, and then set the table with four place settings. She picked some flowers from the garden and arranged them in the centre. She decided to get out the crystal glasses she had received many years ago as a wedding present.

The table looked lovely, and the lamb was doing nicely in the oven. The vegetables and soufflé were also coming along superbly. Molly on this occasion; baked an apple pie for sweet. It was cooling on the tray, and the custard was all ready to add to the milk when boiled. It was hot in that kitchen; she tied back her hair, wiped her brow with the back of her hand, poured herself a sherry and took a well-deserved seat in the lounge. She was there for almost half an hour. She must have dozed off herself. She shot up and looked in on the dinner. There wasn't a movement from upstairs. She would leave Jordan for another hour; then give him a shake.

Molly turned out the gas on the saucepans, and the oven as everything was now ready and only needed a little heat to bring it back to life. She went upstairs and changed. She wore her jade dress and emerald costume earrings. Molly, although almost fifty still had a very nice figure, and apart from an odd line or two, and a few greying hairs, hadn't changed at all. It was Jordan who had aged; his illness was aging him very much. The once sallow good looks had disappeared into a gaunt, lined expression of pain and weakness. Molly was considering making him give up work altogether, but making ends meet would present a problem, unless, yes, that was the answer, she would go back to work and Jordan could be at home for a change. Martine, already nineteen was indeed a young lady; and very much in control of her own life now. The clock in the lounge struck out six o'clock. It was time to waken Jordan, but just before she patted on some loose powder and a little blusher, adding to the compliment of some cherry red lipstick, she patted back her hair and climbed the stairs to Jordan's room.

As she approached his room, she could hear him singing softly to himself. Thank god, she whispered under her breath. He's up and seems to be alright; it is so important to Martine and Daniel. She knocked on his door. "Are you up darling?"

"Yes." Jordan called back. "I am not only up but I am dressed and feel champion." Molly was praying for those words. She tidied up after him and followed him downstairs, where they waited for the youngsters to arrive. They heard the bus halt at the end of the lane. Molly rushed to the door. They came along the lane in a jovial manner, hugging each other and stopping for the occasional kiss. Molly thought back to her own romance in that lane with her beloved Jordan.

They arrived at the door bursting with excitement. "Look." said Martine. "We are engaged to be married." Molly stood back in shock. She liked Daniel but wasn't quite ready for this. She took them into the lounge where Jordan was sitting.

"They have something to tell you dear." she said. Martine ran over to her father. "Look daddy, we are engaged." Jordan too was shocked into silence.

He, like Molly thought a lot of Daniel, but thought them too young to get so involved so soon. They had to accept it in the end. Martine was so headstrong—a trait she got from her mother. After the initial shocks all round, the four sat back and the parents admired the ring—two small diamonds and a large emerald in the centre.

Daniel has bought it to match my eyes." It could have been Molly saying, it about Jordan. Jordan and Molly could see the two youngsters were absolutely besotted with each other and accepted their behaviour and blessed them and wished them well. The dinner tasted exceptionally good that night. Jordan was feeling so good; he attempted his brandy, something he had not touched for months. Molly and Martine washed up and chattered away in the kitchen, as the men and the brandy disappeared into the lounge, and talked sport and current affairs. The evening went so well, so much so that the clock was signalling to them that it was almost over. Daniel heard the chimes and got himself up ready to catch the last bus back to town. Jordan and Molly said their goodbyes from the lounge and left Martine to go alone to the door with Daniel. They were there for nearly ten minutes.

Molly called to Daniel. "If you don't get a move on, you will miss that last bus." With that he rushed down the lane to the bus stop, just in time. Martine thanked her parents for such a lovely night and for being so understanding. Molly thought to herself, you can sort your own life out; perhaps you are doing the right thing. Only time will tell. Martine took herself up to bed and left her parents to do a little talking. Jordan was still feeling good, and even frivolous, something that Molly had decided to fore go, a long time ago, and not remind herself of what she was missing.

But tonight was different. "I'll join you Jordan love, I'll see if there's any booze left from Christmas, there was, and to Molly's delight a bottle of champagne was just tucked in at the back of the cabinet. She put the champagne in the ice bucket and filled it with ice cubes. Jordan's face lit up when she took it in.

"I'm glad we're celebrating Martine tonight, I may not have many more years left, so in a way, I'm glad she has decided to pick her young man while I'm still here."

Molly grew angry. "I'll have none of that talk." The frown and look was enough. Jordan cheered up and uncorked the champagne. They raised their glasses to times past and present and to the future. Molly shouted with a sneer to Jordan. "You're not leaving me on my own." He smiled, they locked in that smile, the love was still there and stronger too through their trials of life. They sat longer, and Molly checked that Martine was asleep; a brass band could not wake her. She looked so sweet lying there in that single bed. Molly tucked her in and gave her a kiss on the forehead; she was no longer a child, but a young woman, engaged already with her whole life in front of her. Molly was shaken out of her thoughts by Jordan finishing off in the bathroom. He caught sight of his wife in the bedroom looking at his daughter with such love in her eyes. He took Molly's hand and led her into their bedroom. He closed the door behind them. Molly switched on the bedside light.

Jordan was already undressed and safely in bed, watching Molly undress, Molly, my darling, you still have your girlish curves." he chuckled towards her.

She slipped off her petticoat.

"That birthmark, you have on your left shoulder, Molly, is just like a begging dog, it almost looks like a tattoo." She turned towards the mirror and tilted her left shoulder to expose the birthmark.

She put her right hand over her shoulder and over the birthmark.

"It doesn't worry me Jordan, perhaps, because I cannot see it myself."

"I think it's most endearing and makes you so individual, even from Merry, as she doesn't have one." She slipped the rest of her clothes off, dropping them to the floor. She stepped over them and joined Jordan in that mahogany bed. He bent over and kissed her, gently at first, then more demanding. She caressed his body, his skin was like silk; his manly chest was becoming grey as well as his temples. He was getting older, but he was just as handsome. He rolled over, holding her in his arms, kissing and fondling her; their love had gone from wanton lust, to deep emotional love. They locked and stayed together, kissing and touching and softly caressing each other, enjoying the other more than the self. The last kiss lingered for an eternity, carrying time through the ages and veils into the next world and back again. Molly was fulfilled; she had waited long for the caress of his body because of his lingering illness. Jordan was pleased with himself and his special longing for Molly was apparent on his face. Molly kissed his shoulder and the two cuddled in for the night.

Time was passing at an uncanny speed. Jordan was no better. Dr. Morrow assured Molly time and time again that he was fine, and perhaps the illness was in his head. Molly was becoming increasingly worried about him. His fiftieth birthday had come and gone and he had scarcely recognised the fact. Jordan always made so much of his birthdays and Molly's. Martine was almost twenty two, and Molly was worried that she and Daniel may never get married, as they had been engaged for three years now, and never mentioned marriage. Molly was constantly asking for a wedding date as Jordan was becoming weaker, and her dad wanted to be there to give her away before he became too ill.

Merry was still in that god-forsaken place, but was improving again these last few years almost to the stage where they would allow her in the grounds of the home by herself. The grounds were very pleasant with great oak trees and flower beds as far as the eye could see. There were shrubs of every description. The summer months were filled with aromas of roses and honeysuckle. It was on one of these visits that Molly told Merry that Jordan was getting worse, and Merry wanted to go home to see him as it was too much of a trial for him to visit these days. The matron was asked, but Molly was told that she was still too dangerous both for herself and others. Molly put her arms around Merry and told her she would be back to see her soon. Merry was led away by two male nurses.

When Molly got back to Thistledown Cottage that night, Jordan was sitting downstairs in the dark. She asked him what was wrong. He turned and just said. "Molly, I'm on my way out." Molly was shocked by this remark. Martine was coming downstairs and overheard the comment. She froze and rushed to comfort her father. All three sat together in silence; no words were spoken, but they all knew. Molly sat a while; then dragged herself into the kitchen to prepare the meal. She stood at the sink; the tears trickled down her face.

She called Dr.Morrow who came immediately. Again he could find nothing wrong with Jordan except for the fact that he was getting older and a little weaker. Martine was meeting Daniel that night. She phoned her mother later to tell her she may be going away for the weekend with Daniel. Molly was used to these out of the blue breaks by this time. Martine just rang at a minute's notice.

She was skiing here, flying there, this time it was Paris with Daniel. Molly's thoughts went back in time to the weekend Jordan had gone to Paris on his own, and she went to see Mrs. Linley with Gerrald, but missed Jordan too much to stay, and returned home and waited for

Jordan to arrive back with the surprise that was promised her over the phone—her engagement ring. She almost wished that she and Jordan could have gone before he became too ill. But it was not to be.

She mixed his stomach powders and headache tablets and gave him a double doze that always made him sleep, and he was always better when he woke up. Her thoughts returned to Martine. She would be winging her way to Paris by now. The house was quiet when Martine was not around, and they were getting older and a little set in their ways. Molly had taken up embroidery and was sitting peacefully sewing away when the phone rang. It was Martine she was ringing with some special news for Molly. "Mother, Daniel and I are getting married in Paris tomorrow. We have a special license, and we bought the rings today. It will be quiet. We are going to a little chapel off the Le'Arc de Triumph. Two of the choir is to be our witnesses. We have done it this way Mother as a big church ceremony would be too much for dad now. I hope you understand."

Molly muttered her good wishes, put down the phone and burst into tears. Jordan was by now asleep, so she decided not to tell him until tomorrow. The night was long, and the evening dragged. Molly was pleased that at last Martine was getting married, before anything happened to Jordan. Perhaps that was the reason she did it in such a hurry in the end, so that her father could see her settled at last. Molly was wondering where they would decide to live. She knew they had saved quite a large sum of money, with them being engaged so long, so perhaps they would buy somewhere near. Molly was considering what to buy the happy couple. That was it;

she would throw a little party for them and try to get Merry out for a couple of days to join in the fun. Jordan fidgeted and woke up. She was careful not to tell him Martine's plans until after their Wedding Ceremony the next day.

"Jordan dear would you like a glass of brandy?" Molly could do with one herself.

"Yes I would." She went in the cabinet and picked up two glasses. She sat at Jordan's feet on the mat, and they both sipped the brandy. She had her hand on his knee; he had his legs around her shoulders, giving her an occasional little squeeze.

"Feeling better now love?" Jordan assured her he was champion. They sipped some more brandy and retired to bed. The phone went again that Saturday afternoon. Molly answered; it was Martine.

Molly quickly told Martine, "I have not told your dad Martine, I have left it up to you." With that Molly called him to the phone. Martine had said they just did it on impulse, and Jordan accepted the fact, and wished them well.

Martine assured them that she and Daniel would be coming back to Thistledown Cottage for a couple of weeks until they got sorted out. Molly was pleased.

She caught a tear in Jordan's eyes, his expression said. Well she is settled now and a quiet peace was apparent inside him. Molly told Jordan of her plans to arrange a small get together for the couple on the first weekend of their return home. Jordan agreed. Molly got set to work the next day organising the little party. She made sure of the outside caterers. She ordered some wine and champagne. Molly's favourite pink. Molly loved champagne. It was by far her favourite drink. It was just becoming dusk outside.

The sky was full of crimson and pinks, and the moon was just gliding along, uninhibited in a mood similar to young lovers gliding on the threshold of life. Molly's phone was red hot, summoning up all the old friends. She had wanted to ask Gerrald, but if Merry came home and Gerrald brought his wife, it would be too upsetting for her. She gave Gerrald a miss. Merry was granted leave for two days, but Molly was warned of her behaviour and told to take no chances whatsoever.

Jordan invited his friends, mostly his university friends, the ones who came to the wedding, the ones he had barely seen since. This was going to become some reunion, in the end only two agreed to come. Molly awaited the return of the newlyweds and knew that they would bring lots of their own friends, some peculiar, some arty, some just dropouts. But for sure it would be interesting. The weekend designated to the party was arriving and all the guests were invited, and the food and drinks were on order.

It was Sunday evening, and Molly and Jordan were quietly sitting, sipping Jordan's favourite brandy, his elixir of life, when the young couple burst in. They had one overnight bag between them. Molly stood up. "How did you get married with just one piece of luggage with you?" Martine explained, I hired a wedding dress for the day, and Daniel hired a morning suit, we had a few photographs taken; my flowers were silk, and I gave them back to the vicar's wife when we were finished with them."

"Never mind all that now," said Daniel. He pulled a bottle of champagne from his coat pocket. "Let's chill this, and we'll tell you both all about it." Martine had gifts for her parents; a little Eiffel tower for Molly, and some French five-star brandy for Jordan; both were pleased with their new-found gifts. Molly placed her little tower on the mantelpiece, and Jordan got Molly to move his brandy into the drinks cabinet.

"Only for medicinal purposes." said Jordan with a smile on his face. Molly got the champagne bucket, filled it with ice, and Daniel placed the bottle inside. They left it on the coffee table, waiting for it to chill. The two youngsters were full of their trip to Paris and were keenly waiting the return of their photographs. Some had been taken up the tower, some from the little cafes below, but most importantly of all the little chapel near the L'Arc De Triumph. Molly could see that Jordan was smiling and happy for the first time in ages. The group was joyous together. Molly poured some brandy for Martine and her new husband. Jordan wished them a good, long life, and all the happiness in the world. They had lots of stories from Paris and their marvelous weekend. Molly prepared some light supper, and Daniel opened the champagne; the ice in the bucket had melted. Molly put some fresh cubes in; all glasses were tilted together in the toast to the best two people in the world, Molly and Jordan. Daniel added a little toast to his own parents.

The air was heady with chatter, laughter and family togetherness, the best feeling in the world. Molly and Jordan looked with pride at their daughter, she was happier now, than they'd ever seen her. Her green eyes flashed with excitement, her lips luscious and red, tilted up in an enchanting smile, her curvaceous body shaped to perfection—she was a true beauty, and Jordan knew it. Daniel was a handsome young fellow, with blonde hair and eyes the deepest innocent blue. He was strongly built, with square shoulders, and had simplicity about him. They were a handsome couple indeed. The champagne was going to their toes, and the night was passing by the coming up of the dawn. It was time to go to bed and start another day.

The two young ones were off for the week, so it would give them time to get themselves organised and either buy themselves a home, or rent one in the meantime. Molly went to bed only for four hours, she had a lot to do, and one of the major tasks was to let Merry know she could come home for a couple of days, and also give her the good news. As soon as Molly got to the village and the news got around, the presents started to flow in, all sorts of gifts from toasters, to dinner services to cutlery, and bedding and the most unusual ornaments. When they all sat back and looked at those presents, there was almost enough things to set up a house, with the exclusion of the furniture, which Martine and Daniel wanted to pick for themselves.

Molly was in the kitchen that morning when a knock came to the kitchen window, it was the postman, and he had a large pile of letters all addressed to Mr. and Mrs. Inglehurst. At first Molly was going to say. "Wrong address!" but then she remembered Martine's new name. She took the letters and placed them on the kitchen table amid the breakfast dishes, for collection by their owners, when they got up. The house was full of good vibrations and a feeling of laughter, and a great sense of wellbeing.

Molly sang to herself as she prepared breakfast. She would visit Merry this afternoon, and give her all the good news and make arrangements to pick her up on the Friday morning, in time for the party on Saturday night.

It was almost lunchtime when the newlyweds got up, Jordan was already in the bathroom, and Molly had heard a sound she had long since forgotten, the sound of Jordan whistling, once he used to do it all the time, then he became weaker and the house was full of silence. But today was not one of those bleak days. There was singing in the kitchen, whistling in the bathroom, idle chit chat of lovers in the bedroom. Molly left the breakfast on the table for them all, as she went, she called upstairs to let them know she would be back around teatime. Martine called down. "Give Aunty Merry my love. Oh by the way." she brought a little brown bag downstairs. "Give this to her it's the same as I bought you."

"I will love." said Molly, as she gave her daughter a hug and made off for the Sanitarium, on her thousandth journey. The sun was out in its glory that day, Molly felt its rays inside and out, it was a happy day, life at last was being kind to all of the Wentworths, or shall we say DeHavillands or Inglehursts, but it was a truly happy day. On Molly's arrival at the home, the Matron briefed her about Merry's progress. "She seems to be stabilising now, but Molly its taken three years, she must not be upset at any cost." Molly agreed. She found Merry not in her room, but enjoying the garden and the sweet smell of the flowers. Merry was sitting on the grass, and her friend Sue was with her. Molly sat with them.

Merry was very pleased to see her sister, and even more pleased with the news she had brought. She treasured her

Eiffel Tower, and promised to put it in a safe place along with her photographs of Martine. Molly explained to Merry, about Martine and Daniel's party, and that she was invited to Thistledown Cottage for it, and she was overjoyed. Merry asked Molly to get her a new dress, a red one. Molly said she would find something very nice and fitting. Merry already had some red shoes and bag and she would bring them along with her and her night clothes on Friday morning. Molly kissed her sister and left with a goodbye to Sue. When she got home there was a pleasant surprise for her, the table was set and the tea already prepared. Both Daniel and Jordan had done it and Martine was lounging on the sofa, her job was yet to come, the job of washing up. Martine didn't take too kindly to it, but she promised. After their meal Jordan got out the remaining brandy, and they sat and talked for hours.

Daniel promised his mother he would take Martine over to his parents.

Friday was looming up behind them, in fact, it was the next day, there was no panic, everything was ordered and Molly wasn't doing any cooking. The outside caterers were excellent at their job, and Molly had them so many times before she trusted them implicitly. The wine merchants were at the door with the wine and champagne. Jordan had asked the local supermarket to deliver the beer and lagers. These he stored, in the outhouse at the back of the kitchen. The summerhouse needed a tidy out, and would you believe that old crib was still there, from years gone by. The lace was old now, tattered and the iron crib was slightly rusting in old age. Jordan decided to clear out the remaining rubbish from the summerhouse; it would be nice for some of the guests to have a drink in there. Molly caught him out of the corner of her eye going up the path. "Jordan, where are you going up that path?"

"I'm going to clear out the summerhouse."

"No you're not. Daniel." she called. "Will you clear out the summerhouse for Jordan please?" He nodded and followed Jordan up the path. There was very little in the old summerhouse once the crib was removed. They just moved it into the shed for the time being. Molly took a basket work sofa and table, along with two stools, and placed them in the empty space created by the disappearance of the old crib. She washed the windows and mopped the floor. It looked quite tidy now and certainly created more space. Jordan was happier now; more at ease; he had started to take an interest in the house again. He put a dish of nuts and crisps on the table in the summerhouse and took some lagers and beers up and placed them on the floor at one side of the sofa. There were some hanging plants in the house which he thought would look nice in the old summerhouse. He got Daniel to put them up, and already it was looking good.

The sun was beaming in, and it was warm in there most of the time. The brightly coloured floral covers on the sofa; brought all the happy feeling of summertime flowing through, the hanging plants with their crimson peach and yellow added to the brightness left by the rays of sun beating through the windows. Why hadn't Jordan thought of tidying it up before? Perhaps Dr. Morrow was right, and the illness was in Jordan's head. Molly tossed the thought to one side, he was happy at present, and that was now.

Friday morning was brought in with a rainstorm quite violent in its anger on that June day. Molly was up early and preparing for her trip to pick up Merry. She had bought a red dress for her the day before and was just trying it on again. It was quite eye catching and Molly was sure that Merry would like it. As she got off the train the two figures in the station were familiar; it was that of Matron and Merry all packed up and ready to go. "Well this is a surprise Matron; you don't usually have the time to do this." Molly said with surprise. "I have to go into town myself today, so I thought I'd save you the trouble of walking all the way up to the Sanitarium. Molly was pleased, as she had a lot to do at home with the party tomorrow. She had still to collect the flowers, and a couple of last minute preparations, had to be made. The train was soon there, and all three made good conversation, finding the journey was pleasant and fulfilling. Matron had all sorts of things to talk about, and Merry was always on her best behavior when around Matron. Molly noticed that Merry was wearing her brooch which Jordan had bought her. She would have to wear hers too, or the others would keep getting them confused.

When they arrived at the Cottage, Daniel and Martine were tidying up in the front garden. Jordan had got the tidying up bug and had organised them to cut back some branches which had swayed onto the path. This they were doing with great delight. Jordan caught sight of the two sisters, arms linked, coming up the lane towards him; he waved and went out to meet them at the gate. There were kisses all round, and Martine introduced Daniel, "My, he's handsome." said Merry.

Daniel gasped in shock at how alike the women were. "You knew we were twins." said Molly.

"Yes I did," said Daniel, "But not so alike."

"Daniel the only difference between us is; that I have a birth mark on my left shoulder, and Merry has none! And that's only evident when we're undressed.

"So you see we have to wear brooches so that everyone knows who they are talking to."

"I'll go straight up and put mine on, Merry you pin yours to your dress now." She did. Molly rummaged in the drawer and found her brooch right at the back; she pinned it on her blouse and went downstairs. Merry was getting to know Daniel and had an arm around Martine. She loved her niece and the feeling was reciprocated. Merry offered to make a cup of tea. As she went to the fridge to get some milk, she noticed the champagne for tomorrow's party cooling all along the top shelf. She exclaimed to Molly. "Champagne. Oh it's been ages since I tasted it, I love it."

"Me too! I love it!" Molly beamed. "My favourite beverage, sod the tea, let's open a bottle of champers now." Merry was excited, they both called for Daniel or Jordan to open the champagne. Jordan came in,

"Molly you will have champagne coming out of your ears soon, the amount you get through, it's a good job I got a good settlement on retiring, or this would have to stop."

"Don't be so mean." She retorted. They filled their glasses and sipped the bubbles. Merry commented how they tickled and trickled down her throat making her sneeze when touching her tonsils. After a few glasses they relaxed on the sofas in the lounge.

Molly rang the florists to check that the flowers would be delivered in the morning. She wanted some gladiolas and some roses and some Gibsonia. Molly indicated to Merry that Jordan would sleep on the camp bed in the living room. Jordan heard and raised an eyebrow. "It looks like I got the short straw once again."

"You're sleeping with me tonight Merry!" Molly was quick to point out.

"Daniel and Martine will be sleeping the middle bedroom; in the single bed."

"I'm okay with that dear sister, like old times!"

The two young ones blushed away the innuendo, as the rest of the group made for the stairs and bed. Molly cleared away the remnants of the evening putting not one, but two empty champagne bottles in the kitchen bin.

Merry felt heady with a warmness, the little family she had left was all around her tonight, and Thistledown Cottage closed its eyes to the world and its problems and contained the well being of its family, keeping it safe till morning. Saturday was abuzz with excitement, and Jordan was stiff from being on the camp bed all night. The two lovers were up bright and early and so was Aunty Merry still sporting her name brooch. Molly called her to give a hand with the breakfasts as the caterers were coming at 3.00 and the kitchen was to be empty of all dishes and bodies, so that they may get on with their final preparations in Molly's kitchen. Martine switched on the radio and was dancing with Daniel as Jordan was trying to get to his feet. "Gosh I'm stiff he kept moaning, that music is too loud."

"My we are grumpy today daddy," was Martine's retort.

Jordan still stiff and rubbing his tired limbs, hobbled upstairs to the bathroom. "I don't relish many more nights on that thing." he grumbled while making his way to the bathroom. The women were in the kitchen, and the youngsters were still dancing when the phone went. It was the florist making sure there would be someone in when the flowers arrived. They would be sending them round now. Molly told Martine to get the vases from the cupboards and arrange the flowers all over the house, ready for the guests. Daniel had to make sure there was enough ice, and the two ice buckets were shinning and ready to take the champagne for the toast. This he did, and replaced the two bottles they had drunk the night before. The others were, at the side of the fridge waiting to chill. The breakfast done and eaten, the two women cleared everything up and were ready when the knock came to the front door, and the caterers came in with all the food on a long wooden tray, carrying it at shoulder level.

Molly spread her white lace table cloth over the table and closed the kitchen door and left the professionals to get on with the job at hand, along with the vol-au-vents and all the like, she had ordered, a one-tier little white wedding cake which was to be a surprise for the newlyweds. She had always kept the two little figures from her and Jordan's wedding cake, and she placed them on Martine's with great care; the groom was still smiling thirty years forward. She was sure that this party would go with a swing. Daniel had invited a load of art students and young doctors with their girlfriends. It would be a change for the house to be filled with young people, Molly stopped for a second—now she knew how Mrs. Linley had felt on her visits to Stevenage with Gerrald's friends.

Molly wondered how they were and wished she could have asked Gerrald, but it was impossible, under the circumstances. The four relaxed in the lounge and awaited the call for inspection on finishing the table. It had just gone five o'clock, and the first of the group was already making time for a bath. As there were four to be taken, they had to do it in relays. Jordan went first and decided to have a rest after his bath; these last few days were hectic to say the least, but enjoyably so.

The chef called to Molly to inspect the table and decorations. It was superb; the wedding cake was placed in the middle, with a space left, to move it to the side, for accessibility on cutting. The salmons, there were two of them, straddled the wedding cake, there were vol-au-vents of all types, there was fresh chicken, beef, honey dew roast ham, pork, salads and trifle, and sweet desserts ready to tease the strongest of wills.

The table was colourful and a silver horseshoe lay beside the wedding cake, a message inscribed on it said: "To the most beautiful newlyweds from their parents." It was signed by Molly, Jordan, Dan and Leslie, the latter two being Daniel's parents. Daniel's parents were the first to arrive and Molly was not even dressed yet. "Just sit down and Daniel will get you a drink. They had a rather large, square present with them, which they handed to Martine, who ripped it open to expose a huge crystal fruit bowl, it was beautiful, when the sun caught a glimpse of it; it changed to all the colours of the rainbow translucently.

Martine displayed it with the card in the far corner of the lounge with all the other presents. Merry was in the bath now, and Molly was trying to hurry her. "I've left your red dress on the bed Merry, will you hurry please, the guests have begun to arrive," and Merry came out of the bathroom with a huge pink towel wrapped around her. As she passed Molly, Molly could see that Merry still did not have a birthmark at all; in fact her back was perfectly clear of moles or anything else. "I've left your dress on the bed Merry, don't forget your brooch. Be ready."

Molly locked the bathroom door behind her and ran the bath. The bathroom was already filled with the aroma of lavender, but Molly tipped some more bath salts into the water with her bubbles. She undressed and slipped in. It was nice to have all of the little family there together for such a happy occasion and Jordan too seemed well and happy. "Jordan, oh no." she thought aloud. He was lying down on the bed and Merry would just drop that towel. Molly shot out of the bath and to her horror, on opening the bedroom door, there they were in an embrace, and both Merry and Jordan were naked. "Jordan." She shouted, "It's me Molly." Jordan look bewildered, Merry looked ashamed.

"Jordan, you go downstairs while Merry dresses." The situation sorted, Molly returned to the bathroom to find the door locked. She banged on the door. "Who's in there now?"

"It's me Mrs. De Havilland, I won't be long." It was Daniel's voice. "Blast" Molly would have to make do as she was. She went back to the bedroom and cleansed her face with moisturiser.

Merry apologized, "I didn't get a chance."

He just grabbed me, and you walked in, Molly," She said.

"Don't let it happen again, and wear that bloody brooch, always." Molly was furious, no bath, her sister frolicking with her husband, whatever next. Merry looked wonderful in her red dress, she put on her shoes and Molly encouraged her to wear her cherry red lipstick. This she did, and looked exquisite. "Remember that brooch Merry." She pinned it on her dress, and it dazzled with the lights in the room. Molly had not decided what to wear herself. She was drawn to her jade dress, but didn't feel in the mood for that one. She spotted a beautiful Jersey white dress with sequined shoulders fitting to the waist, and a long vent up the back of the skirt. The neckline was in the shape of a boat so Molly decided to dress it up with black beads, black shoes and her brooch which read Molly in diamonds. She heard the front door knocker go, the guests were all arriving now bearing gifts and bottles of wine. Martine was still downstairs, not dressed. "Martine," Molly screeched. "Come quickly and get dressed. You still have to have a bath yet."

Martine came running upstairs overflowing with presents, she burst into her bedroom and tossed them all on the bed and was beginning to open them up when Molly came in, "Bath, young lady! Then you can open the presents." She escorted Martine to the bathroom and got some fresh towels from the bathroom cupboard. "Bath now, everyone is here. Daniel is downstairs and you are the only one not ready." Molly was getting angry, and Martine knew all the signs, she would be ready in ten minutes. Martine asked Molly to get out the white mini dress she had bought in Paris, the one with the jagged hemline and sweetheart neckline. Molly knew which one, and wished that she, herself, was younger and could wear it. It was beautiful, white satin and boned in the middle from the bosoms to the hips. "I'll wear my hair up and some cerise pink lipstick and green eye shadow."

"Mother, will you get my shoes for me too, the high-heeled white ones." She slipped in the bath, Molly could not keep from thinking that that body could have been hers or Merry's for that matter, the full bosoms and the slim thighs and adequate hips. Martine had a beautiful body; it was certainly passed down the line of women in Molly's family. Molly did her chores for Martine, and on passing the bathroom door, gave it a knock and a shout to hurry up. Molly emerged down the stairs where she met and greeted all the guests in turn and thanked them for coming and bringing gifts for her daughter and new son in law. The room was packed with people, Molly had made sure the kitchen door was securely locked as she wanted some photographs of Martine and Daniel cutting the cake before the supper got underway.

Daniel was busying himself with the wine whilst Jordan was pouring out the champagne and sipping his brandy. Molly thought he looked a little tipsy already, but he didn't have time as yet. He told all the guests if they wanted a seat, the summerhouse had a few seats in it and also some cool lagers and beers. The men folk were quick to go up to the summerhouse where peace and tranquility ruled away from female gossip. Only the chatter of cricket, football, and manly things took place there. Martine came downstairs, she looked stunning, Daniel rushed to her side and kissed her passionately on the lips; they stood together smiling. Molly flashed the camera. Jordan was up at the summerhouse with the rest of the men. Molly sent Daniel to bring him down for the photographs and the cutting of the cake. They all came down, and the atmosphere was jovial and light-hearted. Molly opened the kitchen door and the tables were there, welcoming, mouth watering, blissful in the most delicious tasty bites imaginable.

The men had all come out from the summerhouse, everyone had a glass of champagne and Jordan gave a toast.

"Lift your glasses everyone; To the Bride and Groom!" Everyone echoed the toast and sipped their champagne. Martine and Daniel lifted the big chef s knife and cut the cake, the tiny figures on the top were still grinning through thirty years of sadness, triumph, love and ecstasy.

The revellers all scattered like ants to a secluded corner, or safe seat or indeed to be in the company of their most special person. Jordan and Molly sat together on the large sofa sipping their champagne and enjoying the activities of the young.

They were loud, outrageous and lively, their jokes were near the bone. The boys made no secret that they were finding sleeping partners for the night, their outlandishness and openness was a treat to Molly. When she was young, everything was kept a secret, but not with this fiery lot. Still they knew how to enjoy themselves and how to make everyone else laugh and give up their inhibitions. At one stage they had Merry on the table supposedly doing a strip act. Molly had to save her blushes when Merry was about to remove her panties. The party was in full swing, the table had suffered casualties, the vol-au-vents had disappeared, the fish was left with only a tail; the remnants of sandwiches were crusted and hard. The champagne was flowing like milk, the wine too was a close second, the night was a night to remember, and Molly had it all on film. She got Jordan to take a photograph of herself and Merry toasting each other in champers, the two looked so happy together. Then she got Merry to take a snap of herself with Jordan first, then with Jordan and Martine. Martine was too busy enjoying herself to bother about photographs, she was well and truly the centre of attraction, and all of Daniel's friends liked her tremendously.

Merry too was enjoying herself she was commanding the attention of a certain young man, they were dancing together and had been most of the evening. Molly and Jordan were quite happy just to survey and make sure everyone else enjoyed themselves. Jordan had had a long day and was getting tired; he made his excuses and disappeared up to bed. Molly made him up some powders and took a couple of tablets up. On opening the bedroom door Molly saw him bent over in pain, the brave facade was for Martine's sake. She helped him undress and gave him his medicine. With him safely tucked up in bed, Molly returned to her guests. It was unlikely that this party was going to end before morning. Molly caught hold of Martine and Merry and told them Jordan had gone up feeling very tired.

Martine begged Molly to stop up longer, so against Molly's better judgment she decided to stay on longer. She systematically went round to everyone to ask if anyone wanted coffee or a snack or crisps or whatever. No one wanted anything; only another top up of wine or alcoholic beverage of some description. Molly poured herself another glass of champagne and left the guests to help themselves. She was in somewhat of a dream, within the party but outside herself. She was alone in a crowd; she was losing Jordan, and she was scared. Molly and he; had been an item since the very first meeting at Gerrald's mum's. He had been her whole life and still was. Molly would sooner be next to Jordan in bed just with him, than sitting there amid the frivolities.

She had sat no longer than five minutes when this young man came over and started a conversation up, apparently he had gone to university with Daniel. Although he was ten years older than him, a mature student he had called himself, Molly saw him as a young, virile, handsome man.

He was doing something to her. She liked his company, and she felt flattered by it. He was over six foot tall. He was blonde, blue-eyed with a rugged sort of good looks. He was obviously in awe of Molly, he liked her mind, he was asking all sorts of questions, and the smile on his face followed her wherever she tossed her head, in whatever direction in the room. Time was moving on, and a few of the guests were starting to leave. Molly followed them to the front door and waved them off and thanked them for coming. Some left in taxis, some took their own transport, and some just walked.

She was just saying goodbye to some friends of Daniel's parents and was just closing the door in the hallway, when this good looking young man moved up behind her and kissed her on the back of her neck. She spun round to see her young companion of half an hour ago. She didn't know his name even, but she liked the tingle of his kiss on her bare neck. She smiled and pushed him gently to one side.

There were only a few people left by now. Daniel was just saying goodbye to his parents, and Martine was chatting to two girls in the corner of the room beside her present display. They too were getting ready to leave. Molly put on the kettle when they had gone. Well, they had all gone except the good looking young stranger whom everyone called Christopher. Molly asked him if he was staying the night. A broad grin came to his face; there was a devilishness there that Molly once saw in the dashing David, many years ago. "No," said Molly. "I am asking you in general, not personally, if you want to stay the night. You'll have to sleep on the floor. Martine will get you some blankets." Martine went up stairs and dumped a few bed covers on the lounge floor. "Chris, that's all we have, and you'll have to share with, oh no, you can't, he's asleep in the main bedroom." Molly had forgotten about that, Jordan was in bed, in a deep sleep. Well the only thing for it was that Merry and Martine would sleep in the spare, and Daniel would have to sleep on the floor with Chris. Martine' broke the good news to Daniel

"Some marriage this has turned out to be." He said it, not in malice, but in jest.

Chris chirped, in. "Don't get any wedding night ideas with me." They all laughed. The five sat on a bit longer, discussing the events of the evening, and all were agreed that it was very good fun. Chris was good company and was very courteous towards the ladies. He brought them tea and biscuits and helped tidy up the downstairs rooms.

Molly kicked off her shoes and let her hair fall to her shoulders. "I'm glad it went well for everyone concerned." she said. "The only blight on the horizon is the fact that your dad isn't very well tonight, Martine. That's why he went to bed." Martine sat on Daniel's knee, and devilishly Chris asked Molly to do the same. She gave him a motherly tap on the hand and jokingly reprimanded him. "Well everyone off to bed. Those who are going, get to sleep, those who are camping, downstairs. Sleep where you are, Good night!" With that Molly and the women ascended the stairs, each taking their turn in the bathroom.

Jordan was deep in sleep when Molly retired, and she kissed him on the forehead and dozed off herself.

There was little washing up or tidying left to do the next morning as the young men had done most of it before getting their floor places ready. Molly, still dressed in her bathrobe, knocked on the lounge door. A few groans were the reply. "Are you decent?" With that she opened the door. The two men were still fast asleep. She opened the curtains and picked up their jackets and jumpers, neatly piled the shoes to one side, and generally moved the odds and ends from the previous night. Just as she was passing Chris, he grabbed her by the ankle, and he boyishly blew her a kiss. Molly liked him and treated him as a young brother. "Come on lazy bones; let's be having you two up." She gave Daniel a shove. "Merry is in the bathroom and about to come downstairs. You can go up to your wife now if you wish." Daniel needed no coaxing and went up to Martine. Molly started breakfast. Chris went upstairs to freshen up and passed Merry coming down the stairs, with the same dressing gown as Molly. Chris stopped.

He looked again and said. "I'm sure I just left you in the kitchen."

Merry smiled down at him. "You know perfectly well, that was Molly, and I'm Merry."

"I know." replied Chris, "But you two look so alike, you even have the same voice." He carried on up the stairs. Merry joined Molly in the kitchen. She was looking in the cupboard for something to ease the bad headache she was left with. Molly pointed to the cupboard on the far left. Merry was astonished when she opened that cupboard. It was full of pills and potions of every size and shape, almost like a chemist shop.

Molly noticed her astonishment. "Don't worry; its Jordan's medicine. I like to keep plenty on hand."

"You know you have to go back today Merry.

"Merry sulked, "I don't want to go back ever again!" Molly thought to leave her in the mood.

Once she got accustomed to the fact she had to go back, there would not be a problem, "Come on Merry, help me set the table and prepare breakfast, there are six of us this morning." Merry set the table without a word. After she took herself into the lounge, Chris sat there on his own looking at the morning papers. She went in and sat down, her head in her hands, looking exceedingly gloomy.

"What's the matter Molly," he asked.

"I'm not bloody Molly!"

"What's going on in here?" exclaimed Molly. She took Chris to the side. "Please don't upset her; it will be difficult enough getting her back to the Mansion." Molly looked concerned. Chris looked bewildered, he obviously did not know about Merry and her past. "Please Chris, when you have had your breakfast, it would be better if you go, things are going to become difficult here."

He saw the look on Molly's face. "I'll have a coffee and be off then," he looked dejected. Molly felt sorry, but this was not the time to explain, maybe another day or place. She took a coffee into the lounge for him; he got the message and drank it swiftly and left, calling goodbye to the others. Molly set the breakfast out and called Martine and Daniel. She went upstairs for Jordan, who was awake by this time and fumbling for his pills. She got them out for him and mixed up a powder. "Come on dear, breakfast is ready." she helped him out of bed and into the bathroom, whilst giving a knock on the honeymooner's door.

"We'll be down in a few minutes came the reply." Molly decided to leave them a little longer. She put their breakfast into the oven to keep warm. Jordan just picked at his toast and eggs. Merry sat at the table with a face so long it could have made a new motorway to John O Groats. Molly mimicked to Jordan that she had become difficult again. Jordan made himself scarce into the front room. He picked up the half-crumpled newspapers and disappeared into the world of today's news.

It was almost time for Molly to take Merry back. She went upstairs to dress. Molly felt saddened by it all. Of course she would like Merry to stop for good, especially now since Martine was obviously going to find her own place, and the room would once again be free. But it was not possible, Merry needed care, and Molly was quite frightened when Merry became obstinate. Dressed and gearing herself up for an uproar, Molly descended the stairs. Merry was in the kitchen still sitting at the table refusing to budge. Molly went in to her.

"Right Merry, get dressed you're going back now, whether you like it or not, I have given my word to Matron." Merry did not move but froze and became trance-like, in a vegetative state. Molly became more furious. She pushed Merry to unlock her from this hypnotic coma. No response, so she shouted to Daniel to come down. There was sharpness in Molly's voice that Daniel did not recognise. He rushed downstairs. Molly ordered him to pick Merry up and take her upstairs. Martine was coming down to see what the commotion was. "Martine, you must stay here with your father, no matter what happens, unless I call you." Molly followed Daniel and Merry upstairs. "Put her on that bed, while I get her dressed." Molly was authoritative when she liked. Daniel was more than a little scared of what was to come next. He joined his wife and Jordan downstairs.

"Let your mother handle this alone, she has a lifetimes experience to deal with the matter, only she can do it." They heard raised voices and thumping and banging about. Molly's voice was the most clear and commanding, the doors upstairs were slamming, and footsteps were thudding on the floor above. Then suddenly without notice or further event, the noises silenced, there was quietness for over ten minutes, all downstairs were concerned for Molly's safety, but they needn't have worried, for shortly after, Molly and Aunt Merry came very quietly downstairs, all packed up and ready for the journey. Merry still would not speak. She just froze into stone, at any attempt to awaken her from, this trancelike state. Molly left her instructions and time of return and reassured everyone that she had taken hand of the situation and everything would now go smoothly.

The journey seemed to drag on and on and the tension between the two women was stressful and silent, shrouded in a death-like ending. Molly was relieved when the station appeared in the distance. She picked up Merry's luggage and made the climb to the big mansion. She had instructed Jordan to ring forward to let Matron know that Merry was in a transfixed state of relapse. As they walked up the path towards the mansion, Matron was there flanked by two huge male nurses, just in case of trouble, she had a syringe in her hand already filled up; again a precautionary measure, but funnily enough Merry seemed calm and unaffected by all the fuss. Matron left the two women to go along to Merry's room. Molly had her by the right arm, and was holding her own handbag in her other free hand. They approached the door, the nurses and Matron following at a safe pace behind. Molly turned the handle and opened the door. As soon as Merry saw all her things, the tenseness went from her face and body. Molly knew the scare was over, and she signaled to Matron she would be all right.

Matron left one of the male nurses outside the door just in case. Molly took off her coat and threw it on the bed with her handbag. Merry hung her coat up on the hook, on the wall, and shifted her things. They were chatting whilst Merry was placing her new photographs of the family on top of the dressing table and carefully placing her brooch in the drawer at the top of the unit, Molly's brooch was still fastened to her coat, on the bed.

Everything was back to normal, and the little room looked brighter.

Merry asked when she could go back to Thistledown Cottage. Molly, trying not to upset her again, told her quietly. "It will be a long time before you can go back there Merry, today was the worst I have seen you since you were five years old."

Merry threw herself at Molly; they tugged and pulled and fell on the floor together. The furniture was being knocked over, the things on the dressing table fell to the floor; the room was fast becoming a shambles. Then the door sprung open, and the male nurse came pounding in. Molly grabbed her coat from the bed, then her handbag, and dashed for the door. The male nurse restrained Merry; he rang the alarm for more assistance. Merry was protesting and shouting "I'm Molly I'm Molly!" The male nurse; answered, trying to calm her down. "Now Merry, don't start all that again, Molly is outside!" Molly stood outside shaking and very frightened. The other male nurse arrived, and the two between them held Merry down and Matron injected her with some sort of sedative. They took her in a wheelchair to the solitary room, the one with the steel door, with only a space the size of a letterbox in it. The bed was in the comer, and they gently laid Merry on it and restrained her wrists to either side. The door shut loudly with a clunk behind them as they left. Matron turned the huge steel key in the door.

Molly was still, shaken, and could not control the tremors going through her body. "A nice cup of tea Mrs. De Havilland will calm you down." and with that they went up to Matron's office. Matron told Molly not to come to see Merry for several weeks or until Matron sent for her. "Seeing you or any member of the family will only send her further back at this stage. I think Molly, that Merry will never leave this place as long as she lives, she's had all the chances and each time something goes miserably wrong." Molly left with these final words embedded in her mind forever.

By the time Molly returned, the rest of her family was settled and anticipating the journey and any events that may have happened. Molly was distraught and upset. She gave a brief description of what had happened, but it had clearly affected her deeper than anyone knew. She excused herself and went to lie down for a while. She hung up her coat, with her name brooch still attached, and slid into the bed. She must have dozed for two hours or more.

It was dark when she awoke, the bedroom curtains were open, and the moon was smiling in. She felt tranquil, and her headache had gone. She splashed her face in the bathroom to freshen herself, tidied up her hair, put fresh lipstick on and went downstairs to join the others, but when she got down there, Martine and Daniel had gone. Jordan said they had gone house hunting.

Molly just nodded and sat there gazing at her hands. She was subdued from the afternoon and the two fights she had had with Merry, and the words the Matron had emblazoned on her mind. Jordan understood. A few weeks had passed and nothing very much had happened. Martine and Daniel had found themselves a house. It was on the other side of the village, and they seemed very happy about it, and at that present time were buying furniture and curtains and the like, setting up their own little love nest, quite uninterested in the change in Molly, since that dreadful day at the home. She had become more subdued and the sparkle had gone. Jordan had noticed, too, that she had become more fidgety and shaky, but put it down to the pressure of his illness and the worry over Merry.

The summer had long gone and the winter chills were taking their place in the weather world, the trees in the lane were stiffening and tense-like awaiting the snow. Thistledown Cottage was as comfortable as ever with the log fires blazing away. Jordan had taken to smoking a pipe, and Molly had teased him about being a pipe and slippers man. This was the first sign Jordan had had from Molly that she was coming back to herself, their love life was non-existent; again this was put down to stress and worry.

Molly sat on the floor between Jordan's feet while he smoked his pipe, another good sign that things were on the up. Jordan was feeling good now for several months, he was not taking so many powders and pills, and the headaches were going; his stomach too was giving less pain.   Molly, suddenly, started to make different meals; for him as well as her; giving him more salads; and fresh foods from the market.

Daniel and Martine were well and truly settled in their home and were very comfortable indeed. They had invited Jordan and Molly over for tea, and the parents were delighted, Jordan took some wine with him. They were met at the door by Martine who was getting a little fatter, her father commented. Molly said it was good living. Martine warned them, "I've got something to tell you two after." Daniel came in from the kitchen to greet them. He made them welcome and settled them down on the settee. "Brandy, Jordan?" he asked. No one ever knew of a refusal from Jordan for that.

"Yes," he said.

Molly chirped in. "No need to ask him."

"What have you got to tell me?" Molly was inquisitive. Martine wanted to wait till later. She poured her mother a glass of wine. Molly had not had any wine for almost six months, not since that fateful day at the Sanitarium.

Martine saw the expression on her mother's face and asked how Aunt Merry was. "You know I haven't been up to see her since the day I took her back, on the matron's instructions, but I have rung up constantly. Apparently, she is no better, shouting to be let out, being confused saying she is not Merry, and generally being very disruptive and none co-operative with the staff, calling them all lunatics"

Martine changed the subject to a happier one. "I'll tell you what the secret is. I'm three months pregnant, and the doctors think its twins." Martine was obviously very pleased, "That is the reason we asked you both over tonight." The grandparents to be were very pleased indeed. Jordan raised his glass and sipped the brandy. Molly polished off the wine. There were all sorts of questions, what will you call them, do you want one of each or two boys, two girls, the questions were endless and the talk of babies controlled the whole conversation for the rest of the night. Martine had prepared a lovely meal which went down nicely and the brandy and wine added to the atmosphere and comfort of the occasion, especially for Daniel, with his first in-law visit. They said their farewells and caught the last bus home. Jordan commented. "Grandparents, now, we are getting old." Neither minded and felt quite accomplished within their family circle.

Jordan felt his stomach ache for the first time in months. Perhaps it was the rich food which Martine had prepared. It was the sort of food that Molly used to make, but changed to enable Jordan to have a less fat diet. She reached for the cupboard, picked up a glass and mixed his usual, but instead, put a triple doze of medicine, in the glass and added several pills!!

"I'm going up now Molly, I'll soon be asleep as you've given me my usual doze of medicine, tonight the pain is excruciating. She nodded. "I'll be up in a minute." She let him get a heads start to enable him to be asleep before she got up. She took her time and closed the curtains on the world, poked the fire, to let the settling embers drop into the grate below. She switched off the lights and climbed the stairs. As she went into the bathroom, she could hear Jordan still moving around in the bedroom. She finished in the bathroom and entered the bedroom.

Jordan was sitting up in bed. "It's worse if I lay down." he said. Molly went across to the dressing table; she removed her blouse, sat on the stool facing the mirror, with her back to him, and combed her long tresses. She slipped her cameo top off her left shoulder! Jordan called to her. "Molly, your shoulder, your birth mark has gone!" His mouth was open, and he was pointing towards her shoulder. She looked around smiling, wickedly, and deviously said. "I'm not Molly!!!"

She put on her night dress and was about to get into bed, when Jordan's head fell sideways; and his glass dropped under the bed. She shot over to the bed and felt his forehead; he didn't move, she felt for a pulse, there was none. Frantic, she called for Dr. Morrow. The doctor arrived within ten minutes. She was downstairs, having a sip of Jordan's brandy. She was shaking and frightened. The doctor went upstairs, her worst fear was confirmed. "Yes, Molly, he's gone." The doctor called the funeral directors, but because of Jordan's age and the fact it had happened suddenly, the doctor called for a post mortem. This was kept from the family to avoid upset. Within the hour the funeral directors came and took Jordan away.

'His wife' wasn't sure where to, she was disorientated, child-like, vague, uncannily shocked into silence. Dr. Morrow sent for Martine and Daniel to comfort her. They were there within minutes.

The funeral directors arrived. She stayed in the lounge, with Martine and Daniel and the doctor, until all was taken care of. Martine went up into the bedroom and took off the bedclothes. She remade the bed, sprayed some air freshener and opened the windows. She removed her father's pipe and ashtray with his tobacco. She put his slippers and personal possessions away for her mother to take care of properly, when she felt able. Martine went into the middle bedroom and titivated it.

She sprayed some of her mother's perfume, the Miss Dior she loved, in and around the room and on the pillows. Daniel and Martine would stay with her mother for as long as she needed them. She seemed calmer now, living in her own world of thoughts and grief, stunned into quietness and disbelief of what was happening to her life. Jordan lately was feeling much healthier and energetic, Martine thought it strange.

This had all come at the wrong time for her mother, her lover and her friend, had gone for good. Her mother was quiet and subdued, just when she was coming back to normal. She left Martine and Daniel in the lounge. "I'm going to take a bath; I can't sleep tonight, not in that bedroom." The children understood. They decided to sleep downstairs as it was eerie in the main bedroom, and like their mother, they felt shaken and a little apprehensive. 'Molly' closed the bathroom door behind her, and ran a bath. She poured in lashes of lavender and lots of bubbles, she was feeling better already. She dropped the toweling pink bathrobe to the floor. The huge mirror was all steamed up, she wiped the mirror clear with a guest towel taken from the vanity unit, and she admired her reflection in it. She turned around and looked at her flawless, perfect skin; she reached her right hand across and touched her flawless silky skinned left shoulder. She looked up into the mirror with a devilish grin, at the same time, a pair of tormented innocent, jade-green eyes, despairingly stared out of the solitary imprisonment, through the slotted letter box hole; out into the corridor of the mental home for the psychologically insane.

Thistledown Cottage was quiet with a death-like tranquility, the bathroom was steaming over again, the lavender aroma gave Mrs. De Havilland a feeling of well being, she was baking in a sense of serenity; untouchable, supreme power, second to none.

She had pulled off the final ultimate dominance against a sister she had envied all her life, a sister who had everything as she had nothing, until now. She looked at herself again in the mirror. She liked what she saw, and she oozed the sheer delight of being in control.

Suddenly; a few weeks later, her inner thoughts of satisfaction; were crushed to the ground, like a trodden beetle, when the sound of the front door bursting open, with a police officer asking for Mrs. De. Havilland! Grasping a white paper in his hand! What was happening? A group of men passed her and entered the room where Jordan died. She was later to find out they were forensic experts. They did their job perfectly, finding the glass which had rolled under the bed, the glass with her fingerprints on it, the one which had held Jordan's last triple doze and the other pills, she had administered. Some of his medicine was still settled on the bottom. She stood motionless but found the courage to speak. "I'm Mrs. De Havilland." The officer grasping the paper looked up.

"I have a warrant here for your arrest, you are charged with the poisoning and the murdering of your husband Jordan De Havilland. Anything you say may be taken down and used against you in a court of law." She slumped to the floor and cowered in the corner like a frightened animal, locked in a frozen hypnotic state.

Meanwhile, years later, back at the home for the psychologically insane, Miss Wentworth was escorted by her nurses out into the grounds, surrounded by trees and gardens. She took her place beneath the old apple tree, the old apple tree where she had sat for many an afternoon awaiting her visitors. This afternoon it was to be her grandchildren, Sally and Sarah coming to visit. It was almost impossible to tell them apart except for the fact that Sally's face was a little fatter than her sister's and twice as cheeky...